THE
PARADISE
CHAPTER

THE PARADISE CHAPTER

DIGITAL
NOMAD
ADVENTURES

BLAKE SALAZAR

SPIRIT HOUSE BOOKS

First published in 2021 by Spirit House Books

ISBN 9798710111482

Designed and set by seagulls.net
Cover designed by Two Associates

To my tribe.
So glad I found you and keep on finding you,
all over the globe.

This entire novel was inspired by my own life as a Digital Nomad (or location-independent entrepreneur, or remote worker, or whatever term you prefer—there's an ongoing, heated debate about this very topic!), and by some of the places I've travelled so far. However, the locations described are not real ones; rather, they are a mishmash of places and islands, both real and imagined. Any places, ideas, people, concepts, gossip, and events are pure and simple creativity, and do not reflect any specific individual, business or location.

All action takes place in a world where Covid-19 does not exist.

"I am homesick for a place I am not sure even exists.
One where my heart is full.
My body loved. And my soul understood."

Melissa Cox

PART I

Welcome to the TribeHut

CHAPTER 1 - ROSE

As she approached the beach bar on her first night in Koh Tanu, Thailand, Rose had no idea that the people she was going to meet would change her life in ways she couldn't yet fathom. The jump to untether herself completely and come out to Thailand had been big on its own, but had she known what was in store, she would have thought it much smaller.

The music in the bar was so loud, Rose had to gesture at the barman to make him understand what she wanted.

Beer in hand, she made her way out of the bamboo-roofed area and toward the sea. She kicked off her flip-flops; the sand was still warm from the blazing heat. She walked closer to the sea, wanting to hear its rush, but the music drowned it out almost completely. Even the salt smell was not as strong as she was used to.

She sipped her drink and looked around for any faces she knew. Before she could spot anyone, a tap on her shoulder made her turn. It was the beefy white Australian guy she had met earlier at the coworking space. Brendan, was it?

"You found it," he said, but she didn't actually hear his voice. She nodded, smiling back.

He tilted his beer toward hers, to clink them.

"To life in a tropical paradise!" He grinned and then knocked back some beer.

She followed suit. "So, how long have you been here?" she shouted into his ear.

"Almost a month, but it's my third time here."

"Wow!"

"Nah, it's not that long. That American woman, over there—" he pointed toward a group of people sprawled on top of a bamboo sofa thing, cushions everywhere "—she's been here nearly four months."

Rose lifted her eyebrows in appreciation.

"Come, I'll introduce you."

She followed him. Brendan stood beside the bamboo sofa and gestured to the people there. She felt a little uneasy. She didn't mind meeting new people—she positively adored that, and it was one of her reasons for travelling—but like this, where she could hardly hear what anyone said? She knew in places like this you always ended up having one-sided conversations. No one heard each other and always answered to what they thought the other person said, until you gave up, bored.

A thin, caramel-skinned older woman lying on the sofa reached out an arm.

"Miriam. Pleasure."

"Rose." They shook hands. Rose noticed the woman's beautiful raven hair.

"Hey. Welcome to Tanu," replied Miriam.

Rose smiled warmly and they clinked their drinks, too.

Brendan was beside her now. The music seemed to go up a notch.

"Most of these guys are digital nomads. Miriam here—" he gestured to try to get her into the conversation "—is a writer of some sort— Ouch!" Miriam had slapped him on the leg, laughing. "Or so she says!" Another playful slap.

"You know what I do. Silly man." She looked to him cheekily, then turned away.

"Serge, lovely old Serge, he is…" Brendan pointed to a forty-something perma-sunburned white guy. "You know what? I don't know what he does. But he's Belgian. Does that help?" He guffawed at his own remark.

"Martin, over there—" Brendan now pointed to a white guy with his back to them "—is a web developer. Don't ask me what that actually entails. I'm a marketing guy, not a nerd. And he's German. Apparently, the rumor is," Brendan said loudly, wanting Martin to hear him, elbowing him on the shoulder with an air of conspiracy, "that he was one of the first guys to understand the potential of his field. He was kind of a big deal in Berlin, back in the day, in his youth. Many, many, MANY years ago. Huh?"

Martin turned around; Rose almost gasped. He was so handsome and cool, with a face she felt she'd seen dozens of times in her dreams. She felt as if time stood almost completely still as she examined the details of that face without really seeing them. It felt like she was trying to look directly at the sun, and it was blinding and stunning her.

Martin nodded and smiled politely. "Whatever Brendan says, it wasn't my fault." He laughed and then turned back to his conversation.

Rose had to make a huge mental effort to actually listen to what Brendan was telling her next. It wasn't easy. "The girl he's talking to is Dahlia. She's French. She has a social media marketing agency."

Rose immediately felt an intense hatred for this woman, an insane jealousy. *She is talking to HIM.* Looking at the features of this Dahlia—her olive complexion, the lustrous dark hair artfully draped over one shoulder, the classic resting French face—Rose couldn't help but compare them one by one with her own features and find herself lacking.

A loud cheer went up from the group, and Rose had to turn to see why. Two women had just joined them. Brendan raced to hug them.

"Oh, my Lord, what is the occasion?" The woman he hugged, a tall, white skinny fortysomething with dirty blond hair, played offended.

"Come on, Brendan. It's not that unusual that Helena and I come out for a drink, is it?" The other woman was a diminutive black woman with very short hair, probably in her twenties.

The Belgian man, Serge, had gotten up. "Must be a leap year!" He laughed. "Shall I get you a drink?"

While they discussed their drinks order, Brendan turned back to Rose. "That's Helena and Laila. Laila is the owner of the TribeHut." He winked.

"Oh, cool. I didn't see her there today," Rose replied. But her eyes were back toward Martin, on Martin's back. His lovely, strong back. She could not look away.

"That's because she keeps a very low profile," Brendan said.

After a long pause, Rose realized Brendan was expecting her to say something, but she had no idea what. "Cool, thank you. It's nice of you to introduce me." She wrenched her gaze back to Brendan.

"Anyway, you'll see everyone at the coworking space, at some point or another," Brendan continued.

Miriam got up and stretched. "So, what do you do?" she shouted in Rose's ear.

"I manage the Etsy stores of various artisans and manufacturers, and I also travel around looking for new products to sell."

"Did you say Etsy?" Miriam asked loudly.

"Yeah." Rose nodded more than spoke.

"Right."

"So, you're—"

Miriam leaned toward Martin, cutting Rose off mid-sentence. "Going to get another drink. Want anything?"

"Nah, I'm cool." Martin shrugged.

As she left toward the bar, Rose was left feeling a little put out. *That was rude.* After a moment of feeling hurt, she decided to believe Miriam hadn't heard her.

"So, how long have you been travelling?" Brendan put his arm around her shoulders and started to steer her away from the music.

"Well, on and off my whole life, almost."

"Indeed."

"Now, solidly, for about six months. I have no plans to stop."

"Me neither." He smiled.

They reached the sea's edge. The music was a little more bearable here. Rose put her feet in the water, grateful. *Wow, the water is so warm.* Then she turned around, throwing a casual glance in Martin's direction, but quickly. She didn't want Brendan or Martin to notice.

"Every night, I come out to the beach. I look out at these stars." Brendan gestured up and she looked, too. The sky was incredibly bright, with thousands of sparkling dots. "And at the fishermen's lights—" now he gestured in front of them at the green twinkly lights dotting the horizon "—I say to myself, 'Wow, Brendan, this is your life!'" He laughed.

"Well, how long have you been travelling, then?" she asked back.

"Three years."

Rose gasped. "Whoa!"

"I do go home about once a year…"

"That's all right, then." She laughed and took another sip of her beer.

He laughed, too. Rose realized her beer was already finished, and Brendan noticed.

"Want to get something else?" he asked her.

"Sure."

"What do you say to a bucket of Sangsom and Coke?" he raised an eyebrow comically.

"What's Sangsom? And why does it come in a bucket?" He laughed a comedy villain laugh. It made her giggle. "Oh, my child. You have so much to learn." He put his arm around her shoulders again. "Shall we?" he inquired.

"Fuck it. Whatever you say, mate."

He started steering them back toward the bar.

Brendan began saying something else but she wasn't listening as she felt her mobile vibrate in her tiny macramé handbag. She fished it out, unlocked it. It was a message from her mum. *Oh God, what now?* Rose thought.

Hi sweetie, I hope Thailand is as fab as you were expecting. Looking forward to hearing your experiences. By the way, I ran into Frances' mum yesterday, she sounded a bit worried about her. Have you any news? Let me know. Love, mum.

Rose stared at it a moment longer, then locked the phone again. They had arrived at the bar; the music levels were unbearable this close. Brendan looked at the barman, then her.

"Sangsom Coke. Bucket." He motioned holding a bucket with his hands.

The barman turned around and shouted "Sangsom Cooooke!" and another barman sprang to life and began making their drink.

CHAPTER 2 - ADRIEN

Adrien was catatonic when the plane bumped down to earth and jolted him awake. His glasses slipped off his face, and he managed to catch them by a temple tip just before they were lost to the narrow space under the seat. His long legs were wedged in an excruciating position that was now shooting pins and needles up and down his calves. It was a miracle that he'd managed to pass out.

He stepped off the plane and the blasting heat surprised him, snatching his breath. The feeling was akin to standing next to a searing-hot open oven. He walked onto the tarmac of the Panat Buri airport and could feel the heat radiating from underneath his feet. It was such that as he looked up, the terminal building shimmered in his gaze, like in those Western movies.

Where the fuck have I taken myself to? Adrien thought, as sweat immediately started trickling between his shoulder blades, chafing between his back and the heavy tech pack he was carrying.

At Arrivals, he navigated a throng of people all advertising hotels, cars, beaches, money changers, SIM cards. He was much taller than most of them, so he could keep his eyes on the prize: the exit. These hustlers were shouting in basic English, like "Hello madam!" or "Beautiful hotel," but he noticed that they addressed him in what he presumed must be Thai. *Oh, no. Here we go.* He had been warned of this. Adrien had never even been to Asia, but others identified him as Asian almost everywhere he went. His parents were originally from Vietnam, but he'd been raised entirely as Canadian.

He didn't speak Vietnamese—he could understand a few expressions—and the closest thing he'd ever experienced of Asia was his mum's delicious home-cooking. But that was it. And now everyone here would presume him to be "Asian." On second thought though, this time he was being considered "one of them" instead of "other." He was intrigued to see how this would pan out. But not now. Now he just needed to get out of this crush.

Once out of the small airport, he was bundled into a crammed minivan packed with other tourists. One of the seats was stacked with a teetering pile of luggage held together by a rope. Of course, Adrien was given the seat right next to that one. He looked up at the luggage stack, worried. But then again it turned out to be a plus, as his jet-lagged body slumped against it and he fell asleep for a few more hours. He didn't even notice when the minivan boarded the ferry.

By the time they arrived on Koh Tanu, it was already night. His first impression of the island was of a dusty, dark road dotted with lights here and there, and that there were crazy scooter drivers. He still had no feeling that he was on an island, by the sea. He got dropped off at a little gate and used the code he'd been given to unlock it. Then he made his way to the bungalow assigned to him, one of about a dozen, strung out along a patchy grass field. A cute welcome package was waiting for him inside: water, a guide to the island, a little message giving him directions to the coworking space, the TribeHut.

Adrien gulped down one whole bottle of water, put the other one in the still-warm fridge, then threw himself on the bed. Sleep took him deeply, and it was only 7:00 p.m.

Adrien was swimming, swimming through a treacle-thick substance, bags, people and debris bumping into him. Then one particularly big piece of debris—he couldn't tell what—bowled into him and overwhelmed him, sending him into the gelatinous mess below. He couldn't breathe…he couldn't— He woke with a start. His body was completely wet from sweating, the bedding drenched. Of course, he had forgotten to turn on the air conditioner and the windows were closed. Damn. It was 1:15 a.m.

With the AC now running, he took a trip to the bathroom. Splashing his face with lukewarm water was a nice relief. He threw himself back onto the bed, hopeful sleep would take him as swiftly as before. No joy. He tossed and turned, then started playing on his phone. Candy Crush was sure to lull him to blessed sleep. But again, no joy. More water, more peeing, more tossing and turning. *This is annoying.*

He got up and peeked out the window. The street was identical to how it looked at 7:00 p.m. Only the very occasional scooter passing by. All was quiet. Then he saw one of those funny contraptions… he thought they were called tak-tak or something like that. It was a scooter with some sort of sidecar turned into a minicart/carriage, with a little roof, used as a cheap taxi. It was pulling in outside the bungalows, carrying two passengers. A woman and a man stumbled out, obviously intoxicated. She was an attractive young woman with long dark hair, and he was tall, older than her. He looked Scandinavian or similar. He paid the driver with some difficulty while the woman was pawing at him, hanging on to him as if she might fall. He turned and kissed her passionately—even from here Adrien could see his tongue glinting—while the driver counted the money. Then they continued their stumbled walk into the resort. They were obviously TribeHutters, or at least one of them was, as this resort was reserved for them.

Adrien went to the bed and sat upright, got his Mac out. He checked the usual news feeds. It was still afternoon for Americans on the West Coast. He read an article about two guys whose app was taking the tech world by storm. Their faces looked idiotic. One of them tried desperately to look hipsterish: a half-formed topknot and a straggly beard made him look like a million other young dudes. The other one, a nondescript, slightly chubby guy, was clearly uncomfortable about having his picture taken and was smiling painfully. *Why are all these "hot-young IT hopes" almost always white?* he thought. *Or am I just annoyed because I can't seem to be able to grow a beard?* He caressed his smooth cheeks.

Adrien scanned the article: the app had launched a month ago and was already selling in the quadruple digits on a weekly basis. Shit! He went to the App Store and downloaded it for a trial. *What do these guys have that's making them so successful?* He spent the next few hours reading more and more about them, their funding and business model, their interviews and reviews. He was wracked by a massive yawn, so he put the Mac aside, got up and stretched. Finally, a reddish glow was coming through on the sky. He checked the time: 5:47a.m. He threw a quick glance around the room. *Should I try to sleep now?* Could he, even? He thought, *Fuck it, jetlag's going to take a while to get rid of.* He opened his luggage.

The road was still eerily quiet. He crossed it toward the side that, at least he believed, led to the beach. A stray dog sleeping next to the ditch perked up at his approach. He looked hopefully up at him, then got up and started following Adrien. It was still basically night, but the sky was lightening more and more every second. The speed of it was stunning. Adrien took a small, paved street lined with tiny resorts, minimarts, scooter rentals, dive shops, massage joints, cafés. All were closed—not a soul in sight. A couple minutes later he finally saw it. The road ended abruptly against a small sand dune, and farther ahead was the beach and the gray sea.

He jumped down the dune and was finally on the beach. He stopped to look left and right. The beach was a gentle crescent shape that stretched a few kilometers long, and he seemed to be roughly in the middle of it. The light-colored sand was bordered by tall, very tall casuarinas, which almost looked like pine trees, so that the various resorts and bars were quite hidden, not visible. Only a few lights still on here and there gave away the existence of something other than the trees. While he looked around, the dog sat down beside him, his tongue lolling out.

The sun was finally coming up behind him, brightening everything. The sky that a minute before looked gray and dull was acquiring depth by the second, a couple of cloud streaks tinged with that red only dawn has. It was warm, but not stiflingly so. The beach was completely empty. Giddy, Adrien removed his shirt and glasses and kicked off his flip-flops. He stepped forward and put his feet in the sea, expecting cool, refreshing water. *My, it's so warm!* He couldn't believe it! *It feels like bathwater…*

Even the air that was coming in from the sea was warmer than the surrounding air. He stopped there, breathing in, again looking all around him, taking in the moment. He looked at the dog still sitting in the sand.

"You don't like the water? It's very nice. You should come in." He turned back around to face the sea and started to wade in. The water was clean, mostly clear, apart from the sand that was being tossed around by the small waves. It was a shade of green that he had never seen, or never noticed. When looked at from a distance, it acquired a metallic sheen, so that the sea all around him appeared cool, very at odds with the warmness of it. He waded deeper and deeper until he threw himself forward and under, the water enveloping him. He stayed under for a few seconds, floating, then came up again. *It feels amazing!* He swam farther out, floating, basking in it. He turned back and the sun was now clearly visible above the trees. It was full day.

He laid back and floated on the water, his ears listening to the underwater sounds while his eyes roamed the sky. He loved doing this; the sensation of weightlessness was priceless and completely relaxing. He let his mind float, too…then he noticed a bird flying high overhead and toward the trees. He stopped floating to get a better look at it. Without his glasses it wasn't ideal. It was flying in wide circles near the shore. *A white-bellied eagle! Beautiful.* Maybe it was trying to hunt some fish? And now another eagle joined it! The two majestic birds were drawing wide but narrowing circles over a specific spot. Adrien thought there might be a school of fish nearby. He smiled at the beauty and randomness of this whole scene. *This is my life now.* His smile got wider and a laughter actually escaped his lips.

Just then, to his left, he saw the first human—a man, his age indiscernible—jogging on the beach. Adrien floated some more, watching the stranger approach. As the man did, the dog got up and started running alongside the jogger. From the other side of the beach now, Adrien could see others on the beach, too. The day was truly underway now, this magical place no longer just his to enjoy. But it was still a paradise.

Just then, he thought… *No one is in the water…what if there is something to be wary of? Like jellyfish…? Or worse…?* That thought sent him swimming back to shore quickly. He got out of the water a little out of breath—he wasn't the fittest guy—then turned around. He was a little taken aback by his own foolishness, at jumping into unknown waters but also losing it so quickly to panic. He sat down on the sand and put his glasses back on.

So this was it: his very own tropical paradise, the place where he would finally crack the software he was working on and make it big. Where he would connect with other digital nomads and entrepreneurs whom he had been hearing so much about. This was finally it.

He got up, grabbed his T-shirt and flip-flops and turned back toward his bungalow. He should get started immediately.

CHAPTER 3 - DAHLIA

Dahlia turned over in her bed, and her head spun vertiginously. She put her hands down beside her as if to steady herself. "Oh, God," she croaked. Very slowly, she turned the other way, toward her bedside cabinet, to reach for her Trash Hero flask. She unscrewed the top and, still very slowly, put the bottle to her lips…but only a few drops reached her mouth. *Shit.*

She fell back onto the bed and groaned. Her head hurt from the sudden movement. She gathered her strength and, with an effort of will, sat up. Her face felt swollen, her mouth dry as sandpaper. She got up and took some tentative steps, her brain all the while complaining and feeling like it was bouncing, squishy, inside her skull. *What is that thing pressing from behind the eyes?* She reached the fridge—*blessed fridge*—and opened it. The chill emanating from it was like a holy hand touching her, and she slumped to her knees to let it hit her fully. She grabbed a bottle of water and drank deeply, water trickling down the sides of her face and to her chest. She stopped for a breath, then gulped down some more. Already she felt more human. *Why do I do this to myself?*

Wiping her mouth with her arm, she put the bottle back, closed the fridge and got up. As she did, she noticed something on the floor: a torn condom wrapper. *Oh*, she thought, *this is interesting. I don't remember this.* For the first time she paid attention to herself and noticed she wasn't wearing anything. *One of those nights, huh?* She smiled.

She looked around for more signs. Another wrapper was nearby in a little pile of rubbish, which she assumed contained the used condoms. "Thank God," she said aloud. She padded back to the bed, then looked around. Where was her phone? She lifted the bedding and the clothes scattered on the floor, but ever so slowly, as her head was raging. She found it under one of her beach towels. *Oh God, my head is such a mess.* She reached for the toiletries bag on the bedside table and, with some effort, fished out a Nurofen pack. She squeezed a caplet out and swallowed it straight. She laid back down on the bed and started scrolling through her phone, giggling. "Let's see who it was." Her Facebook and Instagram feeds were full of pictures from the previous night: random blurry shots of people pulling faces and flashing peace and *shaka* signs to the camera, drinks with limes and flowers perched on the edge of the glass and too many straws stuck through the ice, people hugging and kissing, having the time of their lives. Dahlia turned on her side to get more comfortable and paused the scrolling for a second. *Savor this moment, D. You weren't sure you'd get to live this life, despite what you told everyone else. But you did it.*

She smiled again and resumed scrolling. After a few more flicks of her thumb, she saw a picture of her with a ginger-haired, sunburned guy.

"Is it you?" she wondered aloud, making a face at the same time. "I don't think so." She scrolled some more and stopped at a pic of herself with a cute dark haired guy. "Mm-hmm."

She opened her own photo album for any pics she hadn't uploaded. There were so many, she started deleting ones that made no sense or were just dark blobs. She found the stream of pics in which she was with this cute guy. Dark brown hair, beautiful eyes… *What color are they? Light brown? Dark green? Just gorgeous.* But they were also sad, and his smile was strained. As the series of pictures continued, the two of them were getting closer, pouting for each other, hugging, kissing on the cheek. Then one final picture in which they weren't kissing, but he was looking at her with hungry, if dull, eyes, a sheen of sweat coating his forehead.

"Oh, yes." She grinned. "I think it was you." She bit her lip. She was partly upset that she didn't remember hooking up with this hottie, but that just made it hotter, more random, crazier. She stretched out on the bed; her entire body was sore. She felt sand rubbing between her and the sheets… *Oh, yes, last night's skinny dipping…* She remembered that. Another one of the perks of the tropics: the water was always warm and inviting. The Nurofen was starting to kick in, drowsiness taking over. She stretched again, then rolled into the fetal position, wondering if she was going to run into the mystery cutie at the TribeHut… *What's your name again?* Maybe they could go for a second round when they were less fucked. She didn't usually do that, but it would be a shame to not have any memories of this one. Sleep was dragging her down forcefully now. She let herself slide into it.

CHAPTER 4 - MIRIAM

The hairdresser was trying to be careful not to splash Miriam's face, but at the same time was being quite forceful dyeing poor Miriam's hair. Miriam was lying on a contraption, a strange bed-cum-lounger thing, with her body completely flat and her head dangling into a sink. She looked up. Immediately above Miriam's head, so close that she would need to be careful when it was finally time to stand up again, was one of those spirit houses that Buddhists have. It took her a while to realize what it was, but the trinkets and mock flower garlands hanging from the corners, coupled with the intense aroma of burning incense, told her that's what it was. *Why have I never noticed this before?*

The hairdresser—the only one on this side of the island and therefore the veritable nexus of all local gossip and news—was prattling on to her cousin, who was behind a plastic curtain that divided the shop floor from the kitchen. Miriam preferred it when the cousins talked to each other rather than when the hairdresser, Jie, tried to engage her in conversation. It was stilted at best. Plus, every time Miriam was touched near her ears, her hearing dropped quite significantly, and she couldn't make out what was being said. And trying to read Jie's lips was useless, as she often wore a face mask.

Miriam let herself relax in this position. Jie was scrubbing vigorously, and Miriam knew that, shortly, she would begin the head massage. To be honest, the head massage and washing was the reason she used hairdressers. Most of the time, she could dye her hair herself—yes, it would be messy, long, laborious, and her arms were bound to hurt by the end—but nothing could compare with someone giving your scalp a good seeing to. Nothing. Okay, in fairness, in desperate circumstances when Miriam had to apply the dye herself, she invariably missed one or two locks. She had so much hair, and it was so dark that any little gray patch of regrowth would be very visible, but only after she'd rinsed off and dried it, dammit!

Jie was now getting a bit exasperated in her conversation. "Huh? You don't think men are bad? All men? Huh?" Suddenly, Miriam realized she was being addressed!

Miriam was caught short and wasn't ready for an articulated discussion, so she limited herself to a grunt that could be taken as both approval and mild disagreement. Jie went on.

"Useless. Men do nothing. No work. No cook. No clean. I have baby and work. I do three work!" She started gesticulating around the shop, her sudsy hands flinging bubbles around. "Hairdresser, massage and scooter rent!" Again Miriam grunted, this time with a bit more conviction.

"I say my cousin, 'I don't need man! You have man if you want!'" At this, Jie burst out laughing, and Miriam found herself smiling, too. And there was that head massage. *Oooohhhh*. Miriam was tingling. All her nerve endings were engaged but relaxed. Beautiful. Like a soft buzzing feeling inside her head. Only an orgasm could give you a similar feeling, but it usually didn't last as long, and it wasn't as on demand as a head massage. That got her thinking about— No!

No thinking during a massage, Miriam chided herself. She needed to just chill, relax those tense muscles. Let those shoulders down, exhale and just let those hands do what they needed to.

And just like that, the head massage was over. Miriam was a little bit sad. Another month before she needed to dye her hair again…but then again Jie was always telling her to come in for just a wash and a head massage. She might take her up on that.

With a towel wrapped tightly around her head, Miriam awkwardly got up from the hair washing bed and shuffled back to the swivel chair. Jie massaged her shoulders a little bit more and then started to apply some oil.

"Nice, huh? You tell your friends, yes?" Miriam smiled. Jie was always after new clients, even if she didn't really have the time to fit in the ones she already had, at least in high season.

Jie whipped the towel off and a cascade of black hair tumbled down Miriam's shoulders. She loved her hair, it had always been her pride. She wasn't ready to let it go gray, not yet. Though most of it by now was gray, she thought she still looked natural. She was only forty-six after all. She could get away with it a bit longer. It was a pain in this climate, because she had it up most of the time. The heat and humidity saw to that. But she could not cut it short. Oh, no. *With short hair I look like a particularly unattractive man.* And she was above stupid tricks and makeup to attract men, but still…her long and mostly wild hair exerted an almost magnetic attraction on men. She wasn't going to give that up. Not without a fight at least.

Miriam's hair was still somewhat damp, but she wasn't sure if that was because of the wash or the crazy humidity. She checked her phone's weather app—91 percent humidity. *Fuck.* Was that even possible? The back of her neck was a constant sweat patch. She was keeping her hair down for the moment, as it had just been dyed and washed and she felt like showing it off, but it would soon need to be put up in a bun of some sort or she was going to have rivulets of sweat pouring down her neck.

She walked the ten minutes to the coworking space. The road, paved but full of potholes, was edged by orange-red dirt, a space reserved for pedestrians—such a rare sight here! She had decided to leave her scooter at the coworking space as she wasn't walking as much as she was used to. Plus, in truth, she wasn't that confident on the hellish machine, so she only used it when strictly necessary. But the sun bearing down and the oppressive air were taking their toll. She felt like she needed the umpteenth shower of the day. *Tropical paradise my ass.*

The road was lined with various shops and restaurants, some already open. Some of the staff recognized her and greeted her warmly. There weren't that many people that stayed in a holiday destination for months on end, so she and her fellow long-term digital nomads had become somewhat familiar faces around the island. Which could be a good thing—you often got tables at restaurants more quickly, occasionally something for free, and inside advice. It was also a bad thing—it was hard to mind your own business or to engage in those activities that, for the locals, were considered shameful.

Gone was the anonymity of the big city. In Bangkok, like in Buenos Aires or London, you could bring a different man home every night and no one would notice. Or they might notice but there was an understanding about at least pretending not to. She loved disappearing like that, being able to do crazy last-minute things, to engage with total strangers whom she'd never bump into again, who'd exist only as a piece of her memories.

Here, on Tanu, she was always bumping into people she knew, or they were seeing her even when she didn't see them. It posed certain challenges. She'd made it a rule not to dip her beak in the TribeHut pool, because she knew from experience what a clusterfuck it could become. Gossip, misunderstandings, people sticking their noses where they didn't belong. And so, the guys at the coworking were off-limits to her, with the only exception being if she ever met someone truly worthy, with whom she could establish a connection over time. But that hadn't happened, or at least not yet. In the meantime, any of the men visiting the island for any reason other than working at the TribeHut were fair game. And she had been having her fun. The challenge was keeping it discreet, especially from the people who rented her the bungalow in which she lived. They were a lovely couple and lived right next door—that had been a mistake. They also ran one of the most frequented restaurants of the area, so they were always about, knew everyone and were good at noticing things.

As a result, Miriam had taken to going to her lovers' places instead of hers. She wasn't a huge fan of this, as usually these guys tended to stay in cheap, tatty places that did nothing to enhance the mood. There they would be, entangled under fraying mosquito nets, watched over by lurking spiders in the corners. Occasionally, the bathroom was shared (disgusting!). One memorable time she had hooked up with a guy who was sharing a room with a friend—except he hadn't mentioned it and she hadn't realized it until morning. He'd kept begging her to be quiet—another challenge for her—in his single bed, separated from his friend only by fabric curtains. When she was woken by the sounds of someone else stirring, Miriam got out of there as fast as she could, but not before physically bumping into the friend, who looked her up and down and gave her a wolfish smile. Yet other times, the guy would be sharing a house with family or friends. It was at these times, if it couldn't be arranged for a bit of privacy, that she was forced to take them back to her place. But she had to be careful about that. She instructed them to not talk as they approached the quiet bungalows and to just follow her inside as quickly as possible. She would then play music to obscure any "suspect" sounds. *God, how tiring, and all just for some midrange shag.*

She arrived at the TribeHut, walked through its front garden. Some people were already having lunch on the benches outside. She greeted the ones she knew. Once inside, she retrieved her computer and papers from a locker and set out to find a good spot. Recently it had gotten very busy, and she struggled to find those corner spaces she so loved. There was something unsettling about having people both to the left and right of you, and sometimes in front and behind, tapping away. She felt she never had any privacy like that. Today was a lucky day; someone had just left a side space in the main AC room. She entered the chilled space and took a second to bask in the coolness of the air. She instantly felt better. She said a general hello to the room, hurried to the free spot and plonked her belongings on it, claiming it.

She nodded a greeting to a few more people in the room whom she knew, then went out to the kitchen to get some water and make herself a coffee. There, she ran into Jakob and Greta, a lovely German couple who, like her, had been on the island for a while. They updated her on their diving activities and on the fact that they would soon be leaving Tanu, moving on to Bali.

Miriam was sad. Jakob and Greta had been frequent dinner companions, relied upon to visit the finer dining establishments of the island in search of some novelty or, failing that, cheese— *Oh God, how I miss cheese.* Now she was going to have to find someone else to indulge with.

They talked about Bali, about how nice it was going to be. Miriam was intrigued. Despite having been on Tanu for months, this was her very first time in Asia, she hadn't been anywhere else. And she was loving it so far but hadn't planned on moving around much. It wasn't good for her. She usually ended up eating badly, not exercising and, eventually, feeling down. Staying put in a single good place enabled her to get into a healthy routine. Then again, it was getting to peak season here, more expensive, but after that the flow of people was going to stop, thus reducing the pool of available men; and anyway, at some point her visa was going to expire, as well. Visas—the bane of her existence! She promised Jakob and Greta that she'd think about it and look into Bali. She went back to her desk and finally set up for a long day of getting her head into this text she was editing. Hopefully, she'd have no distractions.

CHAPTER 5 - MARTIN

Bamon was pushing Martin hard today.

After the usual fifteen-minute run and some shadow boxing in the stiflingly hot Muay Thai gym, people got paired off for some technical rounds. Bamon was the guy everyone feared and admired. He'd been a professional fighter, travelling the country for bouts, even going so far as to fight in the World Championships. He was knocked out in the first round, but this still made him the island's most successful fighter. He was now in his fifties and fitter than anybody else Martin had ever seen. His body was seemingly made of rock, and he was so fast you didn't even see when his knee was coming up against your ribcage. It was a blur.

He was such a genial character. He was, according to himself, very gentle with his kicks and punches. When someone reacted in a hurt way, he just laughed it off, putting it down to *farangs*—the Thai word for white people/Westerners—being soft from birth.

Martin was trying to keep up with Bamon's routine. You had to learn the signs for when someone was about to jab, cross, hook or uppercut you, or—a harder trick—when they were about to knee you, elbow you or whip a kick out. In pad training, your partner would exaggerate those signs so that you and he would actually make the same move and you'd hit his pad in the right place. If you misjudged, you could both end up with a painful injury. You did three-minute rounds of this, with your eyes glued to the trainer's limbs and reacting lightning fast to his moves. While you were sweating your guts out to do this, the trainers often were just chatting to each other casually, as if being pummeled was no big deal. Martin thought that, well, it probably wasn't for them. But Bamon, even if he was joking around with the others, managed to keep his focus on you and not let up.

A couple little kids were running around the ramshackle gym, getting in the way of people dodging and ducking punches and lunges. They were wearing mini Muay Thai kits themselves. Martin thought that even a punch from one of them would hurt. *Damn! I'm getting distracted.* Bamon got him on the shoulder, tapping him to show he should have ducked. *I have to watch him closely*, he reminded himself. *Left, right, duck, duck, back, come back with a right knee, left hook and finish with a right hook.*

The electronic bell sounded that the round was over. Martin walked, gasping for air, to where his towel was. Sweat was pouring off him in annoying rivulets, getting into his eyes and lips. Stinging. He wiped it off and took a small swig of water. The side where Bamon kneed him was a bit sore, but he was damned if he was going to let that show. A voice inside him was screaming. *Why the hell are you doing this?! Go back to the swimming pool! What possessed you to do this?! You idiot!* He tried to brush it away, as always.

He went off for another round, this time wearing pads. This exercise put you just in the mindset of reading your opponent without trying to attack yourself. You had to try your best to block his blows one by one. Slipping on Bamon's pads, Martin had a tiny moment of revulsion. They were sweat-soaked and smelled like a slaughterhouse's drain. *Anyway, pay attention now, Martin.* Bamon didn't waste any time. There he came, punching, feinting, ducking back to come on stronger, now going for a one-two, and another, and another. Martin was holding his own.

In a split-second he saw that Bamon was shifting his weight. Martin knew what that meant. He hefted his leg up to the side, knee bent, to block the incoming kneeing. He wasn't as fast as his instructor though, and instead of blocking, their knees collided full frontal. Pain shot through Martin's knee and leg, and he stopped.

Bamon went to pat him, saying, "It's okay, all okay," but Martin wasn't so sure.

"Fuck!" He limped to the edge of the mat and sat down on a stool. One of the gym assistants came over to massage his leg. Martin let him. When he got to the knee, Martin let out a tiny moan but turned it into a grimace, making what he thought of as his strong face. In Muay Thai, when you got hurt, you were supposed to laugh and taunt your opponent. And he, in turn, if he got a point off it, would apologize by bowing to you with his hands joined together. That's exactly what you didn't want to see, because that meant he had bested you.

The guy kept on massaging him and started to apply some Muay cream. Thai kickboxers seemed to think that this magic analgesic cream was a cure for everything, akin to Tiger Balm, which was a Thai panacea. Seriously. It had become a joke between his fellow digital nomads. Every time someone complained of an ailment, anything from headache to constipation, you could be sure that someone was going to pipe up with "Have you tried putting some Tiger Balm on it?" But, to this surprise, the Muay cream now was actually lessening the pain in his knee. He smiled at that, and Bamon mistook it for bravado, so he was pleased.

"Ah, see? *Farang* not so bad. *Farang* strong. *Farang* wanna fight?"

"Huh?" Martin looked up.

"Next month. Big fight. You wanna fight?"

Martin guffawed. Was the trainer being serious? Martin hadn't

even seen a real fight close up. "Maybe, Bamon. Maybe." That
seemed to please him.

At the end of training, Martin had a quick chat with some of the
other guys and girls at the gym. Everyone was exceedingly congratulatory about their own endurance in doing this kind of stuff in
38-degree heat with 80 percent humidity and in the open air, with
some shade. They all seemed very pleased with themselves. Inside,
Martin instead felt he hadn't punished himself enough. He had
slipped, and slipped badly. Last night with Dahlia—*Oh, her French
accent!*—had been a huge mistake. He had come out to the island
to try to get into a good routine of workouts, healthy eating, work
and sobriety. After the excesses of Goa and Bangkok, his Sex Addicts
Anonymous sponsor, Hans, had put his foot down and told Martin
that he wasn't going in the right direction and that, if he wanted
Hans to continue being his sponsor, he had to get his act together.
And he had been doing so well to begin with. He'd had hardly any
drinks and, more importantly, he hadn't had sex for close to six
weeks. And then he had to go and fuck it up. *And fuck it up with a
fellow TribeHutter, no less. Watch now as everything implodes around
me. Hans is going to lose his shit.*

It was the booze. As always, it was the damn fucking booze.
How many times was he going to have to repeat to himself that he
could not just stop at two beers? That if he went out, if he accepted
that first drink, that was invariably where the night would take him?
It sounded like a broken record. He was sick and tired of listening
to it. Actually, no, he was just hearing it and not listening to it
because if he actually listened, he would have stayed away and not
drank. And he would not have ended up shagging Dahlia. Now

he was going to have to see her again at the TribeHut. She didn't seem like the clingy type, but to be honest you never knew. *Had they used protection?* Was he so far gone as to not remember? *Wait...* He remembered opening a pack of condoms...yes, yes, he could remember actually putting one on. *Phew.* Close call. *What the fuck, Martin? Get your shit together.*

He turned to Bamon and asked him if he had a spot in the next training session that was just about to start.

CHAPTER 6 - ROSE

Rose was in the AC room at the TribeHut—a little guilty pleasure for her. She tried to be as environmentally friendly as possible, but the heat in Thailand was much more than she had anticipated. On the first day, she had stayed out on the TribeHut's deck, sitting on a wooden chair at a rickety wooden table. She'd managed to cross her legs in the chair so she was quite comfortable. But she started having trouble with her arms. She was having to type a lot and her forearms were resting on the laptop stand and the laptop itself, and she was sweating. The movement of her arms made her rub the sweat and, eventually, it started itching like crazy. And let's not talk about the bugs…! During the day you'd have jumping spiders and red ants at a minimum—the ants would climb on you with remarkable speed and, at times, bite. Especially the feet. The spiders would also bite, and that was more painful. She was swatting herself on a regular basis against these invisible enemies, and she wasn't the only one.

She noticed that some people were not at all perturbed by the bugs. But only during the day, because once dusk fell, it was an entirely different game. The volume of bugs increased dramatically, and the mosquitoes were out in force. Normally, she wouldn't care. Most mosquito bites would fade after half hour or so, especially if you applied Tiger Balm. She also used a citronella, or lemongrass, natural insect repellent. She loved its smell, and it seemed to be effective. However, it was Dengue fever season, and the mosquitoes that bit at sunset were said to be the most likely to carry the virus. So much so that, as soon as she arrived at the TribeHut, the first thing one of the people told her was to watch out for mosquitoes. Rumors abounded about people having gotten Dengue. A couple of them even had to get medical transport to the mainland because they might need a blood transfusion, which wasn't available on the island. Some who had Dengue said it was just like normal flu with a lot of muscle ache, but a couple others who had had severe symptoms were still not fully recovered. They had lost weight, and the way they discussed the pain they experienced was actually quite frightening.

Rose could not afford to get sick. Literally. If she got sick, all her work would grind to a halt, and as she was really living week to week, she could not drop even a little bit. *Welcome to the freelance life! As if.* Plus, she couldn't pay to go to a clinic. She had no buffer. So, she invested some money in insect repellent and kept herself indoors at dusk.

Which all added up to Rose now working in the AC room. She felt bad for the environment, really. But if she didn't get any work done, she didn't know what she would do... She only had a one-way ticket to Thailand, so she'd have to scrape some money together to...to go where? Her mum's? *No. Never.* She wouldn't hear the end of it. And it would be too much. Hard work, it would wear her out again. She loved her family, but best to keep them at a distance. She guessed that, if she needed, she could return to Spain, to her friends who lived near Oviedo and had taken over an abandoned hamlet. She could regroup there. But Frances could be there, too, and she wasn't sure she could deal with her right now.

But banish these thoughts. If you think negative thoughts, negative things will happen. And she didn't need any of that. *Only positives, please.* She sat upright, took a deep breath and set to work again.

She was okay at concentrating for short bursts of time; however, every time she heard the door open or close, she would look up. She'd been trying to see if she could run into the guy from the other night, the demigod, Martin. So far, she hadn't seen him. She was taking frequent trips to the bathroom, or the kitchen, or to the front area for, ostensibly, a break in the hope of running into him arriving or leaving. But no luck for now.

She shook her head, chiding herself. *Stop thinking about this, Rose. He'll probably be underwhelming when you see him again. And you have other things to concentrate on.* One of those other things was replying to her mother about Frances. She hadn't acknowledged the message, and her mother had sent more messages.

 Hey honey, did you get my last message? Just checking you're OK. Mum.

As if she didn't see the blue double checkmark in WhatsApp? As if she didn't know Rose had read the message?

 Good morning! How is your week going? Frances' mum contacted me again. She's saying you must know where Frances is. Can you get in touch?

Why was this so important to her?

 Darling, I really am sorry to bother you but now you're worrying me. Can you just check in with me and let me know about Frances? Would love to update her mother. 😚

Rose guessed she'd have to reply sooner rather than later. She couldn't believe that at thirty-four, she still had to deal with a clingy mother. Sometimes she thought her mother had the emotional maturity of a seventeen-year-old, that she had remained stuck at the age she'd moved from Australia to the UK, the perpetual teenager. Feeling older and wiser than your mother was an eerie feeling. She did not wish that on anybody.

But the thing was…why was everyone suddenly worried about Frances? Did something specific happen to make them all worry? Rose just didn't have the bandwidth to deal with it right now.

The thing that was more important, at this point in time, was to concentrate on saving enough money to get back on her feet and go on her mindfulness retreat. There she would recharge her batteries—*Oh, how depleted she felt*—and also gain the tools to become a mindfulness coach herself. This would be the next phase of her life. If only she could concentrate and also get paid from her Etsy clients. These artisans and artists she worked for were worse than her when it came to bureaucracy. Invoices would go unpaid for months—and let's not talk about when she didn't even issue them invoices! She hated chasing them down for it, so she was accumulating quite a red balance on her account. She resolved to send some emails to those who had waited the longest to pay her.

A reminder went off on her phone. *YOGA CLASS*, it said, in one hour. Rose had found what she thought was the only free yoga class on the island. She gathered her things and left, casting one last look around for Martin and not finding him, and then she set off on foot down the hot, dusty road toward Palm Yoga. At least now she would clear her mind for a little bit.

The yoga class was okay. The structure, a covered bamboo patio, was nice enough, but the mats were old and worn, even stinky. And the class was oversubscribed. Thankfully, she arrived early and had a spot. A few people had to be turned away. She recognized one or two TribeHutters in the group.

She loved yoga. The way you stretched your body and then, just when you thought you were at your limit, your breathing helped you to go that little bit further, pulling and lengthening everything, reaching for the sky. The instructor, a Swedish man in, she guessed, his thirties, was a little bit too fast for her liking and sometimes slipped Swedish words in here and there. She got the meaning easily enough, but it was a bit annoying.

The heat was quite oppressive. Some clouds were already gathering for what had turned out to be a nightly blackout of the sun—she hadn't yet seen any of Tanu's fabled sunsets. Dull gray clouds rose from the east and made their way west to obscure the silhouette of Koh Mek and Koh Wal.

After class she was extremely sweaty, from both the humid heat and the exertion. She wiped herself with her towel and set off back down the road. Just as she was nearing the path down to her bungalow, she looked up and saw a man approaching. She didn't see who it was but a split-second later she sensed it. It was Martin! He was walking briskly toward her. She looked down, unsure of what to do. Should she meet his eyes when he went past? Should she nod hello, or even stop him for a chat? *Oh, goodness, it had to happen now that I am all sweaty and gross, dust sticking to my slick limbs and hair all over the place!*

She looked up again. He was very near now…her eyes lingered subtly on him. He was wearing some sort of workout outfit and he, too, was incredibly sweaty. He was glugging from a water thermos, a sweatband around his head. He was looking dead straight ahead. Rose took a deep breath as they neared each other, anticipating a look, a nod.

But there was nothing. When his eyes roamed over her there was no pause, no hesitation, no flicker of recognition. He didn't remember her at all.

Rose's stomach dropped about ten feet, and she felt sick, mostly with shame. She hurried her steps and almost ran to her bungalow to hide out for a while.

CHAPTER 7 - MARTIN

Martin was hurting all over. His knee was now swollen and looked red, stinking of Muay cream. It wasn't painful, but it would become so later; he just knew it. He half limped to the chemist, which handily was on the way back to the bungalows. The chemist took one look at the knee and pointed to the Tiger Balm shelf.

"I already got that, thanks. I need an ice pack," said Martin, "and some painkillers, just in case. *Khob khun kap*." He bowed stiffly.

Bag in hand, Martin walked the last couple hundred meters to the TribeHut bungalows. In his room, he placed the icepack in the freezer, then stripped and headed into the shower. He really wanted a cold, chilled shower. He opened one of the two showers, the one not connected to the electric heater. The first gush of water was scalding, almost boiling. He recoiled and put his weight on the wrong leg, pain shooting up. "Ah! Shit!" Now the water was coming out a bit cooler, but to call it cold would be a stretch.

The shower head was only shoulder height for him, so after a few moments of leaning his head down, he grabbed it and held it aloft over himself. After the shower, he dried off and sat on the bed. He wished he could keep that clean feeling for longer than ten minutes, but the heat was relentless and he was reluctant to turn on the AC. If he did, he would just curl up and go back to sleep.

He got dressed and ready, out the door and on his scooter. He loved whizzing around on it. It didn't look very manly. They had given him what the Thais considered a girl's bike—pink decals and flowery patterns—but he didn't mind. It was pretty new and handled well, and he managed to argue for a proper helmet with a big visor, basically an unknown item in those parts.

You still had to be careful though. To begin with, the road wasn't great. There were massive potholes, uneven parts, steps onto and off bridges, gravel, loose items dropped on the road, big ditches either side of the paved strip…all of these could be your undoing in a split-second. On top of that, the locals drove like madmen intent on killing themselves (and others). They wore no helmets and were often three or four to a scooter. But the worst culprits were the guys in the big SUVs and minivans. They felt like the road belonged to them and that two-wheels were just a nuisance. They would overtake by driving all the way in the opposite lane, and it wasn't uncommon to see scooters pushed out of the road by this kind of behavior. Then you had the tuk-tuks, which weren't dangerous, most of the time, but they were slow and caused most other road users to want to overtake, hence some very close calls.

Just recently, two Canadian tourists and a local were killed and others injured when one of the two foreigners and his pillion passenger were driving too fast and swerved into oncoming traffic after an obstacle came up "unexpectedly." As the rider tried to avoid cars, a van hit him full-on, sending him into the path of two other bikes. Carnage.

So yeah, you had to have your wits about you. Every day at the TribeHut Martin would see someone new with fresh bandages all over their legs (and sometimes worse). The resulting scars were known by all and sundry as the "Tanu Tattoo." He would do all he could to avoid getting one.

He zipped around for a bit, taking a longer route than necessary, just so he could feel the breeze cooling him off all over. He went south to a nice café he knew and stopped for a quick espresso. He definitely needed that. When the café owner saw him limping, he joked with him about Muay Thai, throwing some joke punches and kicks. He found that Thai people were either crazy about their national sport—betting at all matches, watching them on TV, following the fighters' training reports—or they knew nothing about it. Much like Germans and football. Love it or hate it, no middle ground.

His own problem was that he just wanted to train in the sport and didn't want anything to do with the rest. He wasn't interested in fighting, just in being fit. But Bamon and his crew were often hassling him about doing a real fight. Fights that featured *farangs* were a big draw, both for locals and tourists, and that meant big money, something which everyone was always after.

But Martin hadn't yet seen a proper fight up close, so he wasn't about to commit to something he didn't know.

Back on the scooter, he zipped back to the TribeHut. As he approached, he saw a long—very long—line of scooters parked alongside it. *Busy day, huh?* It often was on Mondays.

Despite digital nomads constantly telling themselves and others that "The week doesn't mean anything anymore," that, "Every day is a weekend," and so on, a distinct frisson of work ethic made its way across the tribe on a Monday morning. For most, fear and anxiety kicked into gear, entrenched after years of being exposed to so-called normal work, so the little voices in those heads said, *You better get something done this week,* or, *Come on, do this thing and the rest of the week will be plain sailing,* or, *That four-hour week, it can all be accomplished on Monday morning! Then you can relax for the rest of it.*

On Tuesdays the place already felt less frantic. The weekend was positively blissful. As for Martin, he often forgot what day of the week it was, or even the date, so much so that in the past he'd missed planes and overstayed visas completely unwittingly, and let's not even mention deadlines.

He parked quite a way down the road at the first available spot and walked back. Inside, it was quite buzzy already. It was around lunchtime, so there was lots of to-ing and fro-ing with food and Skype calls and coffee breaks. He looked around, trying to find a spot to his liking.

This had become increasingly difficult as the peak season kicked into full swing. He did not like someone directly behind him, or very close on either side of him. The worst would be to be hemmed in on both sides. He particularly loved corner spots. He eyed one now, at the front of the deck. He approached it and noticed a closed Mac on one of the two seats. This meant someone had claimed it and was just off eating or taking a call. What to do?

He looked around again. The place was pretty busy. Most of the other free places where the ones where his legs didn't fit under the table or were very bunched together. With one last look, he decided this corner one was the least bad, and he put his stuff down. He got his Mac and charger out of his bag, connected them, then got his big chunky headphones out and put them on. After booting the Mac, he navigated to his music and put one of his work playlists on. He opened his ongoing software project and just sat there, staring at it, music pumping in his ears.

A Facebook prompt popped up, so of course he went immediately to check what it was. A post on a digital nomad page about accommodation in Bali. Boring.

He switched back to the program and read back what he had been doing the last few days. He opened his Trello board for the notes he had made on what to do. It looked despairingly empty and vague, full of exclamation marks that tried to inject some urgency into the project.

Coffee! He needed another coffee. He got up and went to the kitchen, then made himself a cup of barely drinkable instant. He walked back to his desk and tried again to work. But there was nothing for it.

So, he opened World of Warcraft and started playing. Actually, he started tinkering with his character's equipment first, something he normally never paid any attention to. Once he was satisfied, he entered the game.

The game sucked him in deeply. His fingers whizzed on the keys and mouse, at times frantically. He looked around only once or twice. He would be ashamed if anyone saw what he was doing, but then again part of him didn't give a damn. That's why he loved these corner seats: it was hard for anyone to see his screen. He could play with impunity. The only giveaway was the frantic tapping, but most people were wearing headphones.

His party in WoW entered a pretty hard dungeon. He had never actually completed this one. He was also very close to levelling up, so he kept his eyes on his XP bar. *Maybe this will do it.* He attacked, ducked, blocked—he hadn't dared wearing a microphone headset and talking to his party members, not in a coworking space. Just as they killed the last wave of minions and the big dungeon boss made her appearance, he was distracted by a movement right next to him. He looked to his right briefly then back to the screen, but then did a double take. There she was, Dahlia, from last night, talking to him. *Shit!*

He flicked the screen to go back to the software, but her eyes flitted to it. *Did she see?* Her mouth was moving but he still had his headphones on. He ripped them off as soon as he realized.

"Hey, how's it going?" he said.

"Sorry, I didn't mean to disturb you."

As she said this, she plonked her bag right next to him. And then it dawned on him. She was the one who had claimed the spot beside him. *Oh, crap. Fuck, damn, shit!* What was she going to think now? *Stupid, stupid Martin. Always getting yourself into these shit situations.*

He tried to smile. Then he made to get back to his work, but she went on.

"I was just saying that I'm amazed that we both made it into work today. I don't know about you, but I have a killer hangover." She made a face and sat down.

"Yeah, my head was pretty bad but I got it out of my system at Muay Thai. Flushed all the toxins out."

She made a face as if to say "wow," then took a sip of the coffee she had brought with her.

"I need caffeine to get over it. A lot of it."

"Cool."

Again, he turned back to the laptop, and this time it seemed the awkward conversation was over.

When he snuck back onto WoW, his message feed was full of aggro: he had abandoned the party at a critical moment and the dungeon was lost. People were super pissed. He spent some time sending heartfelt apologies and trying to make plans for a new attempt.

CHAPTER 8 - DAHLIA

Dahlia opened her Mac and tried to focus on what was on the screen, but it was as if she was blind. All of her other senses were just straining to see and hear what Martin, immediately to her left, was doing. Was he going to go back to his game now that she was sitting here? He had looked pretty embarrassed to be caught out. She smiled and tried not to let it show too much.

She brought her focus back to herself, opened her email and skimmed through a couple, but she couldn't concentrate. She thought she shouldn't let too much time go by before she broached the subject with him. She wouldn't want to disturb him, really. And it was better to get this stuff out of the way, truly.

She took another sip of coffee and then turned to her left.

"Martin…?"

"Mm-hmm?" He kept looking at his screen.

"Listen, I just wanted to make sure…" she half whispered, and he turned back around with a slightly frightened look on his face "…you know, I was pretty wasted last night." He nodded. "I just want to be sure we were…safe, you know? Did you use…" and here she mouthed the word *condoms* in an exaggerated way.

After a moment of stunned silence, "Yes! Yes, yes, absolutely." He rushed to assuage her fears. "I would never, without…"

She was relieved. He seemed relieved, too.

"Good. That's a load off my mind. Thanks."

"No worries."

He went back to his laptop, and she turned to hers. For a few moments, tension was thrumming in the air between them, then finally it dissipated as it was clear they were both not going to add anything else. Dahlia was finally able to concentrate on her own stuff.

She had various video calls scheduled for later that day, so she wanted to get more admin done before that. These calls were usually quite draining and required a specific mindset that she found difficult to dip in and out of, so she preferred bunching them all together. It was mostly client meetings in which she either explained what she could do for them, highlighting ways to boost their social media visibility, or what she had already done for them: reports, charts, number crunching, conversion rates. There were some middling figures in. She was going to have to polish those somewhat to make them sound upbeat to the client and get them to invest a little more. But figures for another client had come in that were very encouraging and positive, so she was really looking forward to showing off her and her team's results. She scheduled these good calls toward the end of the day so she would finish on a high.

Dahlia was just finishing up her Pad Thai at her desk when Skype pinged on her screen. It was her brother Jerome.

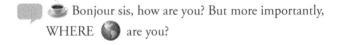

Bonjour sis, how are you? But more importantly, WHERE 🌍 are you?

She had the last mouthful of delicious noodles and put the plate aside before she answered.

I'm in paradise, sweetie. Wanna see?

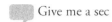 Give me a sec

She grabbed her headphones and phone, locked her computer screen and got up. The deck was a spacious concrete and bamboo-plank structure, open on three sides to allow for maximum ventilation. Tables, chairs, stability balls and higher counters were all around to provide a variety of seating configurations, and the ceiling was dotted with constantly whirring fans. One corner of the space pushed out into a more secluded, quiet area that was full of comfy couches, loungers, bean bags and a table soccer unit. Dahlia walked through this area and into the garden. She put on her headphones and called Jerome. His tired, gorgeous face peeked out of the screen.

"Hey!" she said.

"Hey, shortie, how are you? Show me, show me."

Dahlia laughed and flipped to the rear camera, panning the phone slowly to show her surroundings.

"This is the garden. Say hi to Ganesha." She pointed the phone to the big elephant-head statue that dominated the tropical garden.

"Hello, Ganesha," said Jerome in his sleepy voice. He sat up from wherever he was lying. "Love the outfit." Dahlia giggled. The statue had been dressed with a shiny satin dress and an orange flower garland.

The camera continued panning. "Wow, so green." The garden was a lush tropical setting, fringed with tall palm trees interspersed with banana trees and other flowering plants. The clumps of young bamboo shooting up also provided some shade.

"Yeah, and humid!" Dahlia walked around the area along a sandy path. Here and there, sitting hammocks were strung from the trees in pairs, trios or singles. Some were occupied with people having their own video calls, napping peacefully or reading.

"Those are our Skype workstations." Dahlia pointed to a couple wooden structures called *sala*. Typical of Thai architecture, they were basically little bamboo houses, raised and open on all sides, that you could sit or lie down in, and eat, chill, whatever. They dotted the garden, and some were well hidden. A beautiful butterfly flew in front of Dahlia's face and she gazed at it with a smile. "And over there is the yoga deck." Dahlia pointed off to one end of the garden where a raised wooden platform bordered the grounds.

"Nice! So where is this slice of paradise?" Jerome asked.

"Koh Tanu, Thailand."

"Oh, man. Are you telling me you're near the beach?"

Dahlia laughed. "Yep. It's just over there, behind those palm trees." She pointed to the back of the garden and to a hand-painted sign that read *Beach*. The faint line of the ocean could be seen if one squinted hard enough.

"So, between a bit of work and the next, I take a walk, have a swim, chill out on the beach. Awful, right?"

"Outrageous more like."

She switched the camera back to herself so Jerome could see her.

"And you? Where are you?"

He rubbed his face again, trying to get rid of the sleep in his eyes.

"Come on, what's the time there? Heavy night?"

"Of course." He gave one of his mischievous grins. "I'm actually in Shenzhen. Shithole."

"China? Weren't you Ibiza a couple of weeks ago?"

"Well, I had to—" Jerome got distracted by something offscreen. The image on the phone became all jumbled as he obviously was moving around now. She heard him talk to someone. "Just a minute. Right? What's your problem?!" Jerome could be huffy even at his best.

"Jerome? You there?" Had he forgotten she was on the call? More jumbled images, muffled sounds. Something that sounded suspiciously like a slammed door.

Finally, the image became clear again and Jerome appeared, seemingly sitting on a toilet, in a bathroom.

"Sorry, sis."

"What's happ—"

Someone said something loud where Jerome was, probably outside his door. He reacted violently, slamming his open hand on the door. "I said give me a fucking minute, will you?!" Back to Dahlia. "Dickhead."

"Jerome…" She sighed deeply. "What the hell is going on? Why is it that every time we talk there's some drama going on?"

"Drama?! Don't you start on me, too!" He turned his anger and frustration toward her.

"I'm not starting—"

"Why do you have to be like this, Dahlia? I mean, it's not like you don't have your problems, too. Why do you always have to come down hard on me?"

"Jer, I'm not, I'm just trying to—"

"You're not the Goody Two-shoes you want to appear to be. I know that." At that, Dahlia also got angry.

"Goody Two-shoes? How on earth do you get that? Nice. Really, really nice Jer."

More shouting and banging from behind the door of Jerome's bathroom.

"I am nearly done. Will you give it a fucking rest!" Then to himself, "Fucking Chinese idiot."

Dahlia just looked at him, his head down, sitting on a toilet, God knows where. She felt sorry for him, in amongst the anger.

"Jerome, what can I do?"

He shrugged without looking up. Whoever was behind the door banged on it again.

"I'm coming!" he shouted angrily at the unseen person.

He finally looked back to Dahlia.

"I might need somewhere to stay." Sheepish, but not too contrite.

Dahlia sighed and died inside a little. "Sure, Jerome. Sure."

Not again.

CHAPTER 9 - ADRIEN

Adrien was struggling with the setup of the TribeHut coworking space. First one chair wasn't the right height and couldn't be adjusted, then another was squeaky and tilted. One desk's surface didn't register his mouse signal, and another was an uneven bamboo panel with nails and bumps.

Most of all, he'd been working by himself for so long that being surrounded by dozens of other slumped, concentrated bodies made him feel very peculiar. He was used to listening to music while he worked, which was easily fixed just by using headphones, but he was also used to mumbling to himself, moving about, stretching, farting, sometimes even putting his head down and snoozing for a few minutes. And, of course, he couldn't really do any of these things when he was surrounded on all sides.

This is going to take some getting used to.

Despite the crazy heat, he decided that the full-on approach was best, so he set to work on the open-air patio. This was a large, covered area full of wooden tables and chairs, all facing the tropical garden, interspersed with giant fans that were noisily whirring day and night. He grabbed a couple of cushions from an unused chair to make himself more comfortable, and then set to work trying to wave away this lack of comfort, which niggled at him.

After about an hour, he started to feel some itching on his feet. The TribeHut had a strict no-shoes policy, and you could tell how busy the place was by the mountain of flip-flops (or lack thereof) stacked at the entrance. He bent down to scratch his feet. But the itching became more persistent. Finally, he broke away from work to look at his feet and noticed that they were covered in tiny red bumps.

"What the fuck?"

He scratched more vigorously and looked at them closely. Yep, they were bites. Shit. But bites from what animal? So far he had seen ants and little jumping spiders. Or mosquitoes? No, they didn't look or feel like mosquito bites.

A girl was sitting next to him and noticed his sudden interest in his feet. She removed her big bulky headphones and said, "Hey, you might want to use some of this." And handed him a little bottle. The label was written in Thai, but it had a picture of a mosquito and a snail on it.

Adrien grabbed the bottle offered. "Snail repellent?"

The girl guffawed. "Yeah, I know. But it works with basically everything. Just spray liberally. There's a bunch of bottles over there—" she pointed to a table at the back "—and also some of those burning coils, but personally I don't think they do anything."

"Thanks." He sprayed it gingerly on his bare feet and ankles.

"Oh, and if the itching gets bad, just slather some Tiger Balm on."

"Oh, okay." She put her headphones back on and turned to her laptop.

Adrien sprayed a little more to make sure he had covered every inch of skin; then he put the bottle back on the table next to the girl and nodded in thanks. She nodded back. She was cute, actually, and very nerdy. On realizing this, Adrien flushed bright red and awkwardly stood up. Bathroom? He just needed to get out of there for a moment. He almost ran to the toilet, a ramshackle couple of cubicles with the famous Asian setup of bum gun and a bin for toilet paper (there was even a sign warning of bad repercussions if, God forbid, you forgot to throw the paper in the bin and instead threw it in the toilet!). Outside there was a big drum of water, ready for when, a sign above it informed him helpfully, the water pumps failed. He took a break there and gathered himself again. *Why am I such a complete idiot when dealing with cute girls?* It was like a systems failure every time. Big warning signs, malfunction. Blue screen of death. He had to do something about it. But what? Every time he tried he made such a fool of himself.

He washed his hands in the sink and splashed some water on his face, then went to the kitchen where he made himself a cup of coffee and chatted with some of the people milling about there. It was interesting to hear how long other people had been nomading or where they'd been. A guy told him to join the tribe lunch, the quickest way to make new friends and connections at the Hut.

Adrien walked back to reception, where they had a big white board for the tribe lunch. He saw that it was already full of names. He hovered, hesitating for a moment, then took the marker pen and added his own name. "Great! Is that veggie or nonveggie?" He turned to see who'd spoken to him—a short, smiley blonde at the reception counter.

"Er, meat. Please." She came over and added an "(M)" next to his name.

"No worries. Oh, I'm Laura, by the way." She stretched out her hand. "One of the hosts here."

"Adrien, pleasure." They shook hands, Adrien's hand a bit limp and sweaty.

"So, is this your first tribe lunch, then?" she wondered.

"Yes. It is actually my first day full stop."

"Oh, wow. That's why I haven't seen you before. Well…welcome to the TribeHut." Adrien thanked her and made to walk back to his computer, but she kept talking.

"So, how long are you staying?" He was taken by surprise.

"Er…ehm…actually…I don't know yet."

She started tidying up the reception desk while she talked to him. "That must be so cool. I'd love to just travel… You know… open ended, no plans…no schedule. Just go with the flow!"

"Well, it's not exactly like…"

"So, where are you from? I'm really bad with accents, like all Swiss."

"Oh, you're Swiss? I think I'm the one who has problems with accents. I'm Canadian, from Vancouver."

"You mean you live there? But where are you FROM?" she said while looking at him emphatically.

Adrien pretended not to understand what she meant.

"Like your family, where is it from?"

"Ah, yes. Vietnam, originally. But a very long time ago."

"Ach, Vietnam! I want to go there so bad!" She lit up at the idea. "Pho, fresh rolls, coffee. I just want to tour for the food! But I am not sure which place would be best for a longer stay. Hmm, what do you think?"

"Well…actually I've never been to Vietnam—" Adrien was saved by one of the other Hut hosts, a Thai woman, who interrupted them to ask Laura something. Seeing an opportunity, Adrien slunk back to his computer.

He was startled by a gentle tap on his shoulder. The Thai woman from before—he thought her name was Pat—was trying to get his attention. He removed one headphone. "Tribe lunch is ready." She smiled and pointed toward the front of the building.

"Oh, okay. Thanks." Adrien saved his work and locked his computer. It had been drilled into him to always lock his workstation every time he left it, after years of remote work and the odd occasion of Fraping, where once an idiot had written obscene things on Adrien's FB page, something about his sexual desire for dogs. He was very strict about it. He did it even when just standing up next to his desk talking to someone. Even at home. It just made him feel better.

He walked to the front of the space where there was a kind of garden with some long wooden tables in the middle and steaming bowls of curry and rice spaced out at regular intervals. Half of the seats were already taken. Adrien noticed the mosquito spray girl, but both places next to her were already taken. He picked the next available seat in her vicinity.

The curry, a green, soupy business, was searing hot, which he hadn't expected. But it was also delicious! It contained some small round fruits or vegetables—he wasn't sure what they were—plus carrots, onions, chicken and various leaves. It was so fragrant that the herbs and spices travelled up his nose and made his eyes water a bit. Or maybe it was the chili. He ate some rice to cool his mouth. There were no drinks on the table. Damn, he'd forgotten his cup at this desk. He tried to tough it out, distracting himself by listening to other people's conversations.

There was a big, beefy white guy at the table who was holding court about some programming language over another. Adrien had missed the first bit of the conversation, or speech, as it sounded more like. People around this dude seemed to hang on his every word, to take all he said as God-given verb. Adrien later found out that this guy's name was Ricky Storm, a name he would never, ever forget; he seemed to hold some sort of celebrity status among digital nomads akin to a community guru.

Once he caught up with what Ricky Storm was saying, Adrien thought he was talking bullshit; he didn't agree at all. But he didn't say anything. A good six to eight people were listening, including Bug Spray Girl, and Adrien didn't like confrontations much. He always came out worse in them. So, he continued chomping on his green curry. At which point he was hit by a hiccupping fit. His hiccups were so loud that almost the entire table was taken by surprise and silenced. When the next hiccup hit, they all burst out laughing, while Adrien was desperately trying to hold the whole thing in, including the food he'd just been eating. He felt his face flush, from both the hiccupping and the embarrassment, and at this he started coughing, his eyes streaming. The person sitting next to him gave him a couple firm but not too hard slaps on his back, to try to make sure he wasn't choking.

As everyone tried to get back to conversation or eating, Ricky Storm said, in the silence between one cough and the next, "Man, looks like you can't handle spicy. And I thought you were Asian." A couple people guffawed, while others went quiet. Adrien himself felt hurt and even more embarrassed. Someone handed him a cup of water and he managed to calm his coughing and hiccupping down. Bug Spray Girl shot him an understanding, conspiratorial look but didn't say anything.

As the lunch was breaking up and people started to leave, the man next to Adrien, the one who had slapped him on the back, introduced himself. Serge was a Belgian in his early forties who had a small property empire, which required only a little work here and there, so he was off enjoying the good life. He was very warm and inquisitive. He wanted to make sure Adrien was okay. "And don't worry about that dick. Ricky Storm-in-a-cup is full of himself. Everyone knows that." He winked.

They both got up to clear their plates, and Serge finally inquired about Adrien's own work. After explaining the app he was developing, Adrien mentioned he'd also been deejaying quite a bit recently. At this, Serge's eyes lit up. "You DJ? *Mon dieu*, that's great!" He lit a cigarette and offered one to Adrien, who declined. "Are you going to DJ at the party, then?"

"What party?"

"Come on! What do you mean what party? The TribeHut beach party this Saturday!"

Adrien was still none the wiser, so Serge, between one puff of cherry smoke and the next, elucidated him. There was a cool local beach bar that put on party nights a couple times a week, which drew a lot of people. But most TribeHutters had gotten tired of hearing the same music almost every night, so someone had come up with the idea of throwing their own beach party at the same venue, at which various TribeHutters would deejay.

"So, you going to do it?"

Adrien pictured his DJ sessions, which were usually for himself or a very small group of friends, and he swallowed hard. "DJ? At this party? Well, I don't know—"

"We should talk to Laura. She can give you the details and a slot. You can do maybe like forty minutes. That would be cool, no?" Serge exhaled a last long puff of smoke almost directly in Adrien's face.

"Yeah, sure." Adrien wasn't at all sure, but he thought that this way he could let the matter drop. The two of them started walking back inside toward the work area, and at Reception, Serge almost pulled Adrien to the desk to speak to Laura.

"Laura, we have another DJ for Saturday."

Laura looked up from her computer and beamed at them both. "That's so cool. We cover almost all the globe, we have DJs from Australia, America, Germany, Sweden and now Vietnam!"

"Actually, I'm from—" Adrien got cut off by Serge's enthusiastic whoop.

"It's going to be epic!" Added the Belgian.

CHAPTER 10 - MIRIAM

Miriam's nap was brusquely interrupted by her naked foot being clasped in a grip with claws that dug into her. She sat up with a start and a strangled scream, confused, as the TribeHut's resident cat, Futura, scurried away frightened. Heads turned around to see what the commotion was.

"Damn cat!" She pulled up her foot to inspect it. There was a little bleeding scratch, but not much more.

"Can't even nap in peace," she mumbled. Miriam was lying on a Thai 'sofa,' a bamboo settee with thin, hard cushions. The heat of the day and the hangover had been getting to her, and she functioned much better after a power nap. She was deep into editing an academic paper on the effect of university development in medieval cities, and after a while the words started to blur together on the screen. At those times, even coffee offered only a momentary reprieve. Over many, many years of working by herself at home, Miriam had learned to listen to her body. When she was in danger of hitting the keyboard with her forehead—as had indeed happened once or twice—it was wise to actually give the body what it needed: twenty minutes of blissful sleep. It was like a hard reset, systems powering down and then booting up again. Coffee would be helpful after the nap to give her that boost to start again.

But now that Futura had woken her only a few minutes into her nap, the risk was that she would sleep much longer than a power nap mandated. She knew that if she let it go on for an hour or longer, she would be totally fucked up, waking up as if stuck in a quagmire of molasses that kept trying to pull her under. She had to make a decision. She lay back down, closed her eyes and tried to fall back asleep as quickly as possible. Minimize the interruption and the adrenaline jolt.

An insect of some kind buzzed around her and then alighted on her leg; she waved it away with an arm without opening her eyes or moving too much. Then she turned on her side—the bamboo sofa wasn't the most comfortable place, and she was hot and sweat-wet all down her back.

Then someone's phone trilled—it wasn't on silent and the WhatsApp ping really bore into Miriam's consciousness. She tried to shut it out.

Gradually she became more and more aware of all the little noises around her, particularly the loud insect buzz emanating from the surrounding jungle greenery—a low, tremulous drone that had its own ups and downs and melodies, that could reach a very high pitch and cease at once, and that could get under the skin of even the most mindfully zen of monks.

That's it, I'm not falling asleep now. Frustrated, she got up, bunched her hair into a huge bun yet again and padded to the kitchen. Coffee was now essential. Someone was already using the manual espresso machine in the kitchen, so she had to wait. A tall-ish, dorky Asian guy, probably late twenties, was struggling with unscrewing the machine. "Ouch."

"Is it still too hot?" inquired Miriam.

"Yeah."

"Little trick I know." She approached him, took the espresso machine from his hands and just ran the bottom end under a trickle of running water, turning the implement back and forth to make sure the water cooled it all. "Et voilà." She handed it back to him. He put his hand on it and smiled.

"Cool, thanks."

"No problem. I'm Miriam, by the way." They did a funny hand dance with her proffering her hand to him while his own hands were busy with the coffee maker. They both laughed and shrugged.

"Adrien."

Finally, the espresso machine was clean and Miriam could begin making her own coffee. Adrien walked to the fridge to grab some milk.

"I'm just more used to traditional stove tops or filters. Still getting to grips with this stuff."

"Hey, no excuses needed. I only drink this stuff because it's free and I'm half asleep and busy. Otherwise, I'd go down the road and get a barista-made triple espresso. Granted, it would still be a Thai style triple espresso, but at least it wouldn't be this watery."

Deftly, Miriam prepared the espresso machine with smooth and rapid motions, tamping the fresh grounds. "There's a knack to it." Then she quickly pumped the manual handle, to "express" the coffee into the cup.

Adrien looked on impressed. "Not sure I could replicate your style, I am famously quite clumsy."

"As they say here, never try, never know." She smiled. She washed the espresso maker. "See you later." She walked out with her coffee.

Back at her desk she was reluctant to work, so she faffed about on Facebook and finally checked her phone, as well. *Oh.* She saw the telltale little flame-shaped icon in the top notification tray. Her pace quickened. She opened Tinder to see who had messaged or matched her.

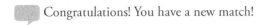 Congratulations! You have a new match!

A little frisson went through her—she was ever the optimist—as she anticipated some sexy, attractive guy matching with her.

She opened his profile to check him out. He was a good-looking Danish man, late thirties, three-day beard (in the photo), and there was very little info in his profile. His nickname was Norse. She was happy they matched, but now she'd have to wait and see if he made contact. Her Tinder was full of people she'd matched with, but there hadn't been any conversation at all. And she wasn't going to make the first move. Experience told her that if a guy didn't make the effort to contact her first, he really wasn't interested, so there wasn't much point in her trying.

Guys usually had to make such little effort anyway. They could at least do this "first move" thing. She hated the anti-feminist undertones of the whole thing; she really did. But she wasn't going to cheat herself of numerous encounters, or get frustrated, just so she could make a point in her head. And on top of that, some of her younger male friends had told her that a standard tactic was to swipe right on every profile and then "skim" through the matches you got. Odious habit.

As these thoughts ran through her head, the screen showed a new notification.

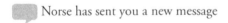 Norse has sent you a new message

Ha! She was delighted. She tapped the message to open it.

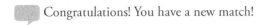 Hello, nice to meet you, beautiful lady. Are you enjoying Tanu?

She harrumphed. All these conversations started the same way. Guiltily she looked at the clock. Now they would begin this polite back and forth to make sure they both knew that they were intelligent, normal and broadly sane people, and that it would be okay for them to engage in casual sex, that she wouldn't feel exploited. But you couldn't come out and just say that. No, you had to go through the motions. She put the phone down without answering and gave herself thirty minutes before replying. She didn't want to come across as desperate.

PART II

Takeover

CHAPTER 11 - MARTIN

Martin was running on the beach, phone strapped to his arm. Skrillex pumped in his ears, almost painful. His bare feet were leaving deep gouges in the wet sand, except where a bigger wave had come in and swept them away. He was concentrating so hard that even when he hit pieces of coral—and that was often—he wouldn't lose his balance or feel too much pain. In the end, his feet would thank him.

He almost couldn't breathe. He pushed a little bit harder. *I can make it to that volleyball net up ahead. Just a little more.* A wave crashed into his feet, threatening to unbalance him, but he managed to ride it out. The rhythm of the song was getting faster, and he tried to keep up with it. A little more. Just a little more.

As the volleyball net swept past him, Martin gradually came to a halt, then doubled over, hands on knees and breathing very, very hard. Gasping. *Who the hell made me decide to run in the middle of the day?!* The sun and heat were atrocious. The sweat dripping off him was like a river.

Getting his breath back, he stood straight again. The beach was mostly empty. The few people about were ensconced under the shade of the casuarinas lining the shore. Only mad people would be out in the sun right now. And he had run out of water, too.

Slowly, still breathing hard, Martin started to make his way up the beach, away from the sea. He walked past Vibe, the beach bar that all TribeHutters frequented like it was church. The Dutch owner, David, a tall white man in his late forties, waved at Martin from the shade of the bar. Martin actually hadn't been to Vibe yet on one of the party nights. The idea didn't appeal. And tonight was the TribeHut takeover—the music would be provided by TribeHut DJs. The idea was fun, but he wasn't sure he should go. The last party night he had been to ended with him shagging Dahlia, and he really didn't want a repeat performance, with her or anyone else. Just then, he had a quick flashback of that terrible feeling he'd experienced, when he'd hit rock bottom and, for the first time in his life, had actually thought of ending things. And a memory of how hard it had been to crawl his way back up from those depths.

No. No. Not again.

He shook the memories off.

He kept walking, crossing the park at the entrance to the beach, past food carts and Thai youths playing football barefoot. At the road, he made a left and walked up to TribeHut, scurrying as quickly as possible across the patio and into the kitchen, where he filled his bottle, drank thirstily and filled it again. Then he made his way to the open-air shower. He rinsed off the sand and salt, peeling off the top he was wearing. His shorts he would change in the bathroom.

Under the running water he could now feel the sun he had taken and the lines it had made on his shoulders. He grabbed his towel, which he'd left there specifically before going for his run, grabbed his water bottle and drank again. Then he walked to the bathroom.

In the mirror, he checked the sunburn. *Shit.* He had a clear vest tan. Not the angry red he'd seen on some newly arrived people, but a clear sunburn mark that would take a while to disappear. He rummaged through his little toiletries bag and got some aloe vera out, then slathered it over his burned shoulders. He winced.

In the toilet stall he finished getting dried and changed; then he stuffed everything in the big gym bag he'd brought and headed back inside to do some work. He was still sweating profusely though, so he decided to head for the AC room instead of the deck. The room itself wasn't that busy, thank Buddha, so he found a decent spot. He couldn't be too picky in this room; you had to get there at seven or eight in the morning to nab the top seats. He plonked his stuff down. This startled the woman sitting beside him, who jumped up.

He mouthed *sorry* to her as he sat down, but she just kept staring at him, a little open-mouthed. Jeez, he hadn't really done anything crazy. He shook his head, then booted up his Mac.

CHAPTER 12 - ROSE

Rose wasn't computing. Her brain had gone into shutdown mode. Almost a whole week of biding her time, stalking the TribeHut for a glimpse of her crush—a week of nothing, or almost nothing, because one day she thought she saw him walking out. She didn't have the presence of mind to find an excuse to go outside, and he was gone.

And now…now…she had been so busy working, head in the game for once, that the "plonk" of the bag next to her had really startled and annoyed her. She had turned to see who it was, who could be so inconsiderate…and there he was: statuesque, rippling with energy and sweat, slicked-back hair. Martin. The man who had been breaking into her dreams. He was even hotter now than she remembered. *How is that possible?*

She had tried so hard to bump into him and now—when by the sheerest luck he'd come into the same room and picked, of all places, the one next to her—her brain, or maybe it was something else, let her down utterly. She had nothing, apart from a tiny, squeaky and faraway voice inside her that shouted *Say something, for God's sake!* And, *Close your mouth at least!* But no, it was no help. She watched in slow motion as he mouthed *sorry* to her, watched her for a response and then, when nothing came from her, as he frowned slightly and turned away, forgetting her entirely.

She continued looking in his direction for a few seconds. When she finally regained control of her face, she brusquely turned back to her laptop, trying to hide what she thought must be a creeping purple blush crawling up her skin. Slowly, even her hearing came back to her, recovered from the whooshing, rushing sound that had enveloped her during this encounter. She again heard the keyboard-clicking sounds, the buzzing of muted mobile phones, the soft chatter of two guys in the corner.

She took a deep breath and willed her concentration to snap back into place. She had two objectives at this specific point in time: to resume her work the way she was going before (*Really well, by the way!*), and to try to find a nonobvious way of engaging Martin in conversation. It was not going to be easy, but at least it was doable. And to cap it all off, she had told her mother she could Skype later that day. *Come on Rose! You can do this!*

Every so often she shot surreptitious glances in Martin's direction, but he seemed entirely wrapped up in his own bubble, headphones and all. She glanced at his screen: lines and lines of thick, dense colored text over black. Damn, she knew nothing about programming, about coding; that was not going to be a conversational hook. Just then her Skype pinged. Mum.

Hey sweetie, I'm up and about. Ready for our call! Xx

Rose huffed and typed back:

Just in the middle of something right now. Text you when free.

OK honey! Xxx

She went back to the accounts she was looking over. Her mild efforts at chasing payments had yielded some results, so some of the oldest invoices had now been paid, but there was still a shocking number of unpaid and old invoices. She steeled herself and then started to write an email to one of her oldest clients, Birdie, who imported jewelry from Western Africa for the European market. Rose loved Birdie, she really did, but the woman was appallingly bad at keeping track of money and her mindset was always that everything was okay and was going to get sorted out sooner or later. It was this "later" that Rose had issues with. The oldest unpaid invoice was over a year old!

She started composing the email in the warmest possible tones, but also tried to be firm. What a balancing act! She hated herself for demanding payment, but she was also annoyed that people didn't pay. She found this side of her business entirely unpleasant.

Skype pinged again.

Sorry hun, are you going to be much longer? I was really hoping to talk to you today because later I am going out.

Rose rolled her eyes.

I'll try not to be too long mum. 10 minutes?

Yes, OK thanks.

Rose tried to get back to the email. She felt she hadn't explained herself enough to Birdie; she was worried the woman was going to take offense. Maybe she should call her instead? Or maybe she should write then call? Or call then write? *Oh, crap.*

She knuckled down again. Getting this email right was imperative. She could use a similar version for other people, too. *Come on Rose, get your best out!*

Just then, someone started talking very near her and she tried tuning it out. But her ears pricked up when she heard Martin answering. Something about tonight. *Tonight what?!* She strained to remain calm, pretend to keep working while eavesdropping on their conversation.

"It should be rad, man. I mean, we have like eight different people DJing. Fred, you know the South African guy? He's, like, a professional DJ, you know? So, yeah, it will be awesome. You should come."

"Yeah, been thinking about it, mate." This was Martin. He was thinking about going. Tonight. To the doo-dah. And she was definitely going. Oh, my God. This could be Rose's chance. *But wait, listen!*

"Nah, seriously, mate. Definite rager. Put your name down for the barbecue, too. Great food."

"I'm really looking forward to that," piped up another guy from the other side of the room.

Just then, Rose's Skype started ringing, out loud. *Damn, not now!* Everyone could hear it because she had forgotten to mute her laptop, so people turned in her direction shooting daggers at her, and there was a brief lull in the conversation as everyone waited for her to put a stop to the ringing.

She quickly muted her laptop and went for her phone, which slipped comically out of her hands and fell down. She clasped her earphones and bent down for the phone, mouthed some apologies and got out of the room, the redness creeping higher and higher on her cheeks, sliding the door closed behind her. She pressed Answer on the phone and plugged one of the earbuds into her ear.

"Mum! Will you just hang on a minute?!"

She cast a glance into the room through the glass door and saw Martin and the other guys continuing to talk, but she couldn't hear anything anymore, so with a sigh she walked away to the outside deck.

She put the phone up now so her mum could see her face.

"Hi, Mum."

"Can you hear me? Rosa, can you see me? I can't see you. Oh, wait—I can now. You can?"

"Yes, Mum, I see you and hear you. Sorry, I was in the middle of something, like I said."

"I know, honey, I just thought if I don't go out now then I'll hit traffic and you know how bad it gets."

"Yes, I know."

"And I really need to talk to you."

Rose had to get out of the way of a Thai guy rolling a big water cylinder through the area into the kitchen, followed by Futura the cat who was jumping around excitedly.

Rose bumped into someone behind her. "Sorry."

"What for, honey?"

"Not you, Mum, I was talking to someone here."

"Oh, okay. So. How's things?"

"Good. Quite good, actually."

"That's great news. How long are you staying there?"

"I don't know, Mum." Rose was getting annoyed. What was the urgency of this small talk? Every time they spoke, their decade-old arguments lurked under the surface and made every interaction tense and almost rude. It was like they were communicating on another level that didn't include whatever it was they were actually saying in the moment.

"Anyway, yes, I wanted to ask you about Frances."

Rose had been braced for some family drama or another lecture about her directionless life. *But Frances?*

"What about Frances?"

"So, as I mentioned, the other day I ran into her mum. She was asking me if you'd said anything about her. To be honest, I forgot all about it. Except that yesterday she called me. I didn't even know she had my new number."

"Right." Rose continued to see if she could understand anything of the conversation still going on in the AC room, but at this distance it was like watching a film with the sound off.

"In any case, she wanted me to ask you if you'd heard from her."

"From Frances' mother?" Rose's attention was back on the call.

"No, sweetie. From Frances!"

"Oh." Rose started to walk into the garden. "No, I actually haven't heard from her in a bit. We…kind of…I guess we're taking a break?" She didn't know what else to call it. It made it sound as if the two of them were a couple. In a sense, they were. Joined at the hip since their teens, they had been mistaken for a lesbian couple more than a handful of times. Which could come in handy when one wanted to dissuade a particularly annoying guy, or spare someone's feelings. But other times it could be downright unfortunate, when the guy you fancied had not even considered you because he thought you were a married lesbian. Anyway, she and Frances… Over the last couple years their lives had taken on different and, at times, clashing orbits. To the point that in recent months their interactions had been…difficult, to say the least. The last time they'd talked—*when was it? A month ago? Six weeks?* It scared Rose that she couldn't actually remember—they had "agreed to disagree," and after a long, harsh silence, they'd just said their goodbyes.

Rose approached an empty sitting hammock and levered herself into it.

"Oh, you didn't mention anything about that," her mother piped up.

"Well, Mum, I don't need to tell you everything, do I?" The rhetorical question escaped Rose's lips before she could stop herself, and her petulant tone annoyed even herself.

"Well, but—"

"What else did Alison say?" Rose cut her short. The hammock was swinging her pleasurably.

"She said that they had lost track of where Frances was. She had told them she was going to stay in Oviedo, you know? But then some of your friends from there reached out to her because she never made it."

"She's probably met some of her 'mates' and ended up tagging along. I wouldn't worry too much."

"So, you don't know where she is?"

"No. I mean, she had been talking about India a lot. That seems to be on her mind. With these people she's been hanging out with, many of them go to India often."

"Oh, India. Where? Such a big country."

"No idea, Mum. They have a community out there. Like I said, we've not been talking much recently, and this is one of the issues. These people around her…" The screen fuzzed a little and her mum's face was stuck in a particularly unflattering pose.

"Mum?"

"I'm sorry, honey, the line went bad there. What did you say? What people?" Her face started moving again halfway through the sentence.

Rose tried to explain in the most succinct way possible and without giving too many details to her mother, as she tended to be a worrier. She didn't want to add that kind of fuel.

The reality was that both Rose and Frances had been on a quest for something deeper for a while. And to begin with, they had followed the same path and shared many of these experiences together. Oviedo had been a haven for both of them. The conscious community there was warm and welcoming, and they would spend days and days talking about all aspects of spirituality, mindfulness and life while getting on with the daily chores of gardening, cooking, etc. But one time when Rose wasn't around—she had gone back to the UK for a wedding—a new couple had arrived in the community and brought with them news of another community that was growing and thriving in India. Rose thought it might be Varanasi but she wasn't sure. At the time, it was all Frances could talk about, she seemed to have a complete crush for this couple, spending all her time with them and learning about this community. When Rose returned, the couple had already left, and Frances was distraught. Frances continued keeping in touch with them, and they connected her with more and more people passing through who were from the Indian community.

Frances tried to get Rose interested, as well. She told her all about the community and its female guru, Sahana Maa, and shared a book by her that the couple had left behind. Frances seemed to think that this guru, this community and its "new" philosophy and approach were the answer to what she had been searching for. Rose tried her best but wasn't that convinced. She was interested, sure, but not overwhelmed. And this is where their divisions began.

Rose pulled herself back to the present, took a deep breath.

"Okay, darling, so you'll ask around?" Her mother concluded.

"Yes, I will. I wouldn't worry too much. But tell Alison to keep contacting other people she might know. I am no longer the best person to know Frances' movements."

"Thank you, Rosa, darling."

Rose felt defeated. "Oh, Mum, it's Rose. It's been Rose for twenty years. Yeah?"

"Sorry, sorry, darling you're right, I—"

"How's Dad? Tell me what's been going on with you guys."

Rose closed Skype. She took a big breath, closed her eyes and did one of her exercises to center herself and be mindful. It was very useful. She tuned out all surrounding noises and focused on her breathing, in and out. The gentle swaying of the hammock really helped. It was only a few seconds, but it really did something. When she opened her eyes again, she felt ready to tackle things. She walked into the kitchen and made herself a herbal tea from the special stash she had brought—a Tibetan mountain tea.

As she walked back to the AC room holding her tea, she remembered the conversation that had been going on there and hurried, but not only was all quiet in there, Martin was also gone! All his stuff was gone! She couldn't believe it. *I am out of the room for a few minutes and I missed a crucial opportunity. Fuck.*

She sat down and attempted to have a quick think about the best people to contact about Frances. She shot off a few messages, kind of generic; she didn't want to alarm anyone, nor give the impression that the two of them were not talking anymore. Then she tried to resume work.

After another hour or so, her concentration was shot to pieces. She packed up her stuff to go home. As she made to get out, the guy Martin had been talking to called out, "Hey, you're going this evening?"

She turned around, halfway through the door.

"To the party?"

He nodded. She glanced around, sensing a chance. "Who else is going?"

"Everyone is!" He stretched out his arms to encompass the room. Various people's heads popped up to nod and yay their assent.

"Right. Cool. Then I guess I'll see you later." She smiled, hoping he meant Martin, too. As she left, she swished the sliding door shut with a little flourish.

CHAPTER 13 - ADRIEN

For the past three days Adrien hadn't managed to make any progress in developing his app at all. Even with his paid work, he had managed to put most things off by claiming illness—it was easy for people to believe the nightmare food poisoning scenario when you had just arrived in Thailand—and gotten away with a couple boring Skype calls and some Slack channel chats to help out other colleagues.

Since he had been roped into deejaying for the party, it was all he could think about. At first, he managed to obsess mostly over the playlist—*Which tunes will the others play? Which mood am I going to have to fit in? How hot is it going to be during my time slot? Are people actually going to dance? On the sand?*—but as time went on he began fixating on the fear that he was going to turn this into a disaster, that he was going to become the TribeHut's laughingstock. He felt like he was strapped on rails and the train was fast approaching.

In his room, AC blasting full tilt, for the millionth time he went through his playlist, song by song, transition by transition, mood by mood, justifying to himself—and to a putative judging panel—each choice, each skip and jump.

Back home, even though he had been practicing and having fun deejaying for himself for years, he had only ever deejayed publicly a handful of times. And even then, only at the urging of friends. Mostly it had gone okay—apart from a couple stumbles that he hoped no one noticed but that he of course could never forget. He'd had short, quick sets in the middle of shambolic warehouse parties and the like, while a large part of the audience was either off their heads or busy shouting into each other's ears. He had been surprised that he had been able to go through with it, but that sense of cold doom, of a heavy sickness at the bottom of his stomach, had never left him. Every single time he thought about or remembered one of his sessions, there was that dull ache, lurking, waiting for him to fuck up again and rear its head and scream into his face, *I told you so!* The sense that, behind the decks, he felt like an impostor could not be overstated.

And now he was going to be found out. The whole TribeHut was going to see him make a fool of himself, laugh at him and deride him forevermore as the guy who ruined their party. He could not let it happen. How could he let himself be roped into something like this on the very first day he arrived here, to begin a new life? A life that was going to be full of joy, free of stress, in which he would blossom and be who he had always meant to be? He had to get out of it.

But then, he realized that, backing out now would also be termi-nally embarrassing. The running order had been set and people had their slots. If he told them now, two hours before the start, that he wasn't going to make it, there was going to have to be some last-min-ute scrambling and some upset and stressed people. No, he couldn't do that. Despite all his fears and anxieties, the way Adrien had been raised was with an overarching—and at times overwhelming—sense of responsibility. He couldn't let people down. He would feel like crap, but letting them down would make him feel even crappier. So, he steeled himself and went over the playlist once again.

CHAPTER 14 - JEROME

The ferry from Nakorn Thara to Koh Tanu was a veritable Petri dish of touristy Thailand. Inside, where the air-conditioning was so strong that 90 percent of people would come down with a cold by the end of the three-hour trip, the rows of seats were occupied by Thai people—who would not be outside in the sun even if their life depended on it—families with children of varying ages, the more elderly Western tourists and the occasional slumped party person. It was packed to the gills so there was no space to stretch out. The backpackers who had come straight from partying somewhere like Phuket, Samui or a similar place were mostly holding on to their backpacks and using them as pillows, mouths agape, dead to the world.

Outside, all around the edges of the interior cabins, Western tourists and travelers thronged the sides, front and back of the ferry. They sprawled over mounds of luggage, basking in the ferocious winter sun but cooled off by the breeze and spray created by the ferry itself. Some of them were excitedly taking photos or making new friends, while others were sleeping right there, out in the full sun, skin reddening second by second. Jerome thought some of them were going to regret this choice bitterly later that day.

He was sitting outside but had found a small corner of shade directly under the viewing gallery of the pilot. Best spot. Cool and refreshed by the breeze but inhaling the sea goodness. God knows he needed it. Shenzhen had wrecked his lungs, skin and eyes and now he needed to restore them. He breathed in deeply. The smell of the sea here was not as strong as it was in the Med, but it still reminded him of holidays with his maternal grandparents. The few sporadic good memories of his childhood. Every time he smelled the sea, he could not help but smile and be in a good mood.

But he was also bone-tired. He had been on the road for three days. Having had to leave that loser Li Chen in the middle of the night after that awful, final fight, he had waited for a few hours at the bus terminal, where he finally caught a bus to Hong Kong. He was pretty broke so had to travel in the cheapest possible way, which meant crappy, slow, crowded buses full of people eating unmentionable snack food. Once in Hong Kong, Dahlia had to scramble to get him a decent flight out to Thailand, which meant spending eleven hours waiting. Waiting in an airport, tired and with no money was not fun, plus the guards at Hong Kong airport didn't like it if it looked like you were homeless or trying to get some sleep. Which was completely at odds with the fact that everywhere else in the whole of China you could sleep virtually undisturbed (and it was often encouraged). Park benches, under desks in offices, coffee shops, street corners, cars, subway cars, buses, trains, doorways and gyms were all perfectly normal places to sleep, but not the airport, where you were more likely to spend hours and hours waiting.

Spending the last of his Renminbi to buy a Western-style coffee––which turned out to taste burnt, bitter––had allowed him to sit on the metal chairs linked to the café and doze off. He woke up just in time to make his flight. Dahlia would never forgive him if he missed it.

Now, on the ferry, he felt like sleeping. The rhythmic bobbing up and down of the boat, the low drone of the engines, it all conspired to lull him to sleep. He leaned his head onto the bulkhead next to him, his only bag clutched tight against his chest.

The ferry jolted up, free-falling back down for a split-second. Jerome came to with a lurch, an empty feeling in his stomach. People laughed and oooh-ed at the jump, which was a bit like hitting an air pocket when flying. He hated being awoken rudely and tried to capture that blissful sleep again, but no luck.

He looked around, and now the island was visible just ahead: a high, steep ridge covered in greenery jutted up out of the calm green sea. It didn't look that big or inhabited. Then he looked down and saw that at the foot of the ridge, the land was pretty flat and occupied by a bustling if ramshackle town with lots of houses on stilts covering the entire visible shore. Numerous boats and ferries were coming and going around the island, used as taxi boats, he presumed, but some looked like pleasure boats, too.

The ferry hit a wave from a passing boat and, with the jolt, Jerome's body slammed into his neighbor.

"Sorry! Sorry, mate," he said.

"No worries, mate."

Only now Jerome noticed him—a young, beautiful blond man, sun-kissed and, of course, with an Australian accent. Jerome smiled at him, and the boy smiled back.

"They do this every day. You'd think they'd get better at piloting these things, wouldn't you?" the Aussie ventured.

"Oh, I don't know. It's my first ever time in Thailand."

OZ Boy looked at him with some surprise.

"Oh, really? Well…you'll see. They are very organized, in their own way, but there's just some basic things that never change here."

As if on cue, the ferry lurched again into the down wave from a speedboat. "Like this." They both chuckled.

Jerome tried to see if this boy was on his own or with someone. He hadn't heard him talk to anyone during the trip, but then again, he hadn't been paying much attention. As the young man's head was turned toward shore, Jerome took his time to check him out properly. He had a very toned body, skin smoothed by sea, sand and God knows what else. A strip of his belly was peeking out between his ripped shorts and T-shirt, which rode up his stomach as he turned. His stomach was deliciously tanned and firm. Jerome started imagining putting his hand on it, rubbing it and then moving down to unbutton those ripped shorts—

"So, where are you staying on the island?"

Jerome had to snap his eyes back up to the face pretty sharpish. "Err…to be honest, I have no idea."

"What? Where are you booked?"

"Well…the thing is…" Should he mention his sister? This might make him sound like a guy who needed babysitting. But then again, if he had no clue, maybe that made him sound like an idiot, which wasn't much better.

"Thing is, I'm coming to visit my sister, so she's arranged it all."

"Ah, okay. Cool."

"And you?"

"I live in White Sand Beach. In the north of the island. I work for a diving company here."

"Oh, right. That's great. Diving, huh?"

"Yes, it's just rad. I get to dive every day and get paid for it. Living the dream, man."

The ferry was now approaching the docking pier.

"Wow, that's like, awesome. So, if I wanted to learn to dive…?"

The blond boy reached down to grab his backpack.

"Ah, yeah, sure. I can hook you up." He turned the front of the pack toward Jerome, showing a logo embroidered on it. "Diving Paradise, that's us."

The ferry had docked, and everyone started to get up in a frenzy to get off the boat, jostling for position in front of the gangplank that was being secured. In the squeeze, Jerome and the blond boy got separated by other passengers muscling in.

The Aussie turned around, his head above a crowd of Thais, and said to Jerome, loudly, "Look us up." He made the *shaka* gesture, then turned around and was swept up the gangplank by the swell of people.

Jerome was about to shout back, "I will," but he realized the guy was too far away already. He had to concentrate on not getting knocked down by the herd of people eager to be off. He held onto his bag even tighter. He was finally at the gangplank himself. It was flanked by two Thai guys who were straddling the gap between the ferry and the dock, as if it was the most natural thing in the world and as if they couldn't just fall into the gap and get smushed by the ferry. They were holding people's elbows as they stepped up the metal gangplank, and helping them with their bags.

One of them grabbed Jerome's arm in a viselike grip. Jerome took two steps and the guy let go, handing him off to yet another man who was waiting at the end of the gangplank on the dock. This last guy eased Jerome onto land and waved him on hastily.

Stumbling a little, Jerome made his way through the thronging crowd. *Why do people who get off something—a boat, an escalator, a lift—tend to just stop dead in front of it? Don't they realize there are other people behind them trying to do the same?* It drove him nuts. As he elbowed his way out of the crush, the heat started to bear down. Without the sea breeze the sun was really, really strong.

The crowd was funneled into a snaking line bordered by metal barriers. At the head, a couple of smiling locals collected what the signs called a "cleaning tax," to keep the island clean. Dahlia had warned him of this but he still didn't have small currency; all his Baht were large denomination. The man collecting the tax must have gone through this kind of thing hundreds of times a day, and he shouted at Jerome but made no move to take the money or look for change. After a bit of a kerfuffle with some foreigners who also did not have small change, they got together and paid as one, foregoing the bit of change due. *Anything to get out of this crush!*

Finally, Jerome could look around at the madhouse of the ferry terminal. Touts were shouting and trying to get people's attention, shuttling groups of bumbling Asian tourists, haggling for the price of hotels or transfers, selling food, water, souvenirs and diving trips. The tourists, for their own part, were mostly bewildered and trying to make sense of their surroundings amongst the chaos.

Jerome remembered the rest of what Dahlia had said. Get out of the ferry terminal and past the gauntlet of tuk-tuk drivers—she'd be waiting out there. This was easier said than done. The crowd was funneled through other metal barriers where these touts were lined up either side, gesticulating, grabbing and trying to get a fare as people walked past. Jerome felt himself getting worked up by this pushiness and started to push back rudely. His Moroccan side came out in these situations, and he was not afraid to stand his ground.

After a final elbowing session, he was out. He could breathe a little easier. He watched as tuk-tuks and *songthaews* left, laden with people and luggage, and kept his eyes ahead. And there she was. His gorgeous sister, leaning on a pole, in the only spot of shade in the street, staring intently into her phone.

He was already smiling when she must have sensed his approach and looked up. Her face went from frowning to a huge smile, and she ran out into the sun to hug him. "Jerome!"

He hugged her fiercely while still holding his bag. Her long black hair smelled different than he remembered; he buried his nose in it.

"Missed you, chicken shit."

"Missed you, too, gnome." Despite being older, she had always been much shorter than him; actually, she was the shortest in the family, hence the nickname. His was because he'd always hid behind her at scary moments.

The hug ended and they looked at each other appraisingly. Dahlia was very tanned, a deep caramel, and her normally jet-black hair had taken on a few lighter highlights. Their North African heritage seemed to like Thailand. "Looking well, sis."

She looked up at him and he detected a worried look in her eyes. "And you look like shit."

He guffawed. She turned and put her keys in a parked scooter. "Let's go. There's a big party tonight and I want to get some rest beforehand."

"You must really be getting old. A disco nap?"

She slapped him on the arm, laughing. She moved the scooter out of parking and flipped the passenger footrests open. He straddled it, bag looped over his shoulders and on his back.

"You sure you know how to dominate this thing?"

She put her sunglasses on and smiled. "Watch me." She twisted the accelerator and off they went.

Zooming through Tanu on the scooter was fun but, especially at first, decidedly scary. Somehow Jerome did not have much faith in his sister's riding skills, so he held on for dear life and gave little squeaks every time another moving object was in their field of view, afraid they were going to hit it. His fear brought back memories of their bike rides as children. They both loved it but had gotten into some scary situations. One time, in the mountains, Dahlia was ahead on a downhill tarmac road, and Jerome was well behind. Apparently, she told him later, she was worried about him as it had started to rain and so she kept on turning around to check that he was indeed following. One of those times though, as she was zipping down the incline, instead of just turning her head she turned her whole upper body, including the handlebars. Jerome watched from a distance as the bike flipped forward, launching Dahlia ahead and down onto the road surface. When he got there, her face was badly scraped, bleeding, and a huge lump was swelling on her forehead. She still had to bike all the way home, there was no other way, and her head took ages to heal.

But actually, he had to give it to her, Dahlia's scooter driving was pretty good. Not crazy fast, but smooth and experienced, and safe. She constantly kept a look behind her and only overtook when it was obviously safe to do so—meaning when they were stuck behind slow-moving tuk-tuks and the road was otherwise clear. The large SUVs had to be avoided at all costs—they wouldn't think twice about running a scooter off the side of the road in their speeding and overtaking frenzy. After all, they were the kings of these roads.

As they drove away from the ferry terminal, the road stretched out before them, mostly straight and flanked by endless rows of shops, restaurants, bars and massage places. On the left side, behind a row of businesses, the jungle-covered ridge rose up sharply into a dominating peak.

Dogs, cats, chickens and goats crossed the street randomly, and this was probably one of the things you had to be most careful about. That, and potholes. They almost hit a couple that looked like craters! They did hit one or two that were not as big, thank goodness, but they still jolted the whole scooter and made Jerome hold on tighter.

The road became more winding and less busy; they went uphill, then downhill. The steep jungle walls receded in the distance. In between businesses there were patches of jungle, often full of rubbish just piled there. A random skinny cow was tethered near a corner, munching lazily on the grass on the verge.

It was so hot that Jerome's back, where his bag was resting on it, was now completely drenched, while his arms and front were cooled by the breeze. He really wanted a shower, badly. He almost forgot when he had last had one.

A row of nondescript bungalows bordered one side of the road, and Dahlia said that the sea and beach where on the opposite side. But you could not see the sea from there. They parked the scooter at the front and walked back to one of the identical bungalows. Jerome realized it was Dahlia's by her colorful clothes draped outside on the chairs and hammock on the little veranda. They kicked off their shoes and went in. Inside it, the chilly AC hit Jerome like a welcome bucket of water. He took his bag off, followed by his wet T-shirt.

"God, it feels like I just came out of a sauna."

Dahlia picked up a towel from her bed and threw it at him.

"Shower is nice and cool."

The room was quite chaotic: clothing everywhere, a desk occupied by a laptop, a notepad, cables and a small speaker. The bathroom was even worse, like a smelly explosion in a cosmetics store. Bottles, jars, tubes and the like abounded, some open, some empty; there were remnants of make-up remover, an overflowing rubbish bin.

"Oh, and here, when you use the toilet, you need to put the toilet paper in the bin." She pointed to it. "Don't flush it. I'm serious."

"I was just in China, sis, not France! Duh."

Jerome finished undressing then took a long cold shower. When he turned the water off, he heard that his sister had turned on music, something quite relaxed. He came out still drying off.

"So, what's the plan? Where am I staying?"

"Well…oh, by the way…it is dry season at the moment, so you might want to go easy on the water usage. We periodically run out so…"

"Great." Jerome rolled his eyes and opened his bag to find some clean underwear.

"The thing is…it is also high season and places aren't cheap. So, for now, you'll have to stay with me," Dahlia said a little sheepishly.

Jerome whipped around in shock.

"Here? The two of us?!" He looked around, trying to wrap his head around the two of them sharing such a small, chaotic space.

"But…how? Where would I put my things? Where would I sleep?"

"I cleared you some closet space." Dahlia opened the wardrobe to show him. "And we'll share the double bed. It's not so bad."

"But…but…I thought you said this was a cheap paradise!"

"Well, it is…if you work!" Jerome sat down heavily on the bed. Dahlia's demeanor changed suddenly.

"Jerome, you can't expect me to be able to support you fully. There are other costs too…do you have any money? Any income?"

Jerome's head hung down, and he held it between his hands. "Not really."

"Then there's no choice. No other option. Staying with me means you can live here very cheaply."

"I guess."

"And that can give you the time to get back on your feet, figure out what to do and so on."

Jerome took a deep breath, still not looking at his sister. Then he got up and went back to his bag, trying to find some clothes.

"You know, I could even teach you a bit of my work and you could start earning some money pretty quickly."

"What? And spend my days chained to a laptop? No, thanks."

This remark seemed to hurt Dahlia deeply. She got up, turned up the speaker volume, then went straight to the bathroom without another word.

Jerome couldn't seem to find anything in his small bag. Damn.

CHAPTER 15 - MIRIAM

Miriam awoke and stretched out farther on her Tunisian wrap. The sand underneath was hot but not unpleasantly so; it almost felt like a hot towel placed on your back at a spa. She pulled her headphones off of her ears and turned to her left. Jakob and Greta were not there, but their double towel and bag, not far from her, were still there. She came up on her elbows and looked out to the sea; she squinted against the sun, but she couldn't see them.

She got up and put her phone and headphones away in her bag. She moved a few paces away and started doing some stretching exercises, which she had missed that morning in the rush to get out when the German couple had asked her last-minute whether she wanted to come east for a beach day. She got into child pose and then up on her hands, stretching her whole back.

As she stretched, she thought back to the last couple days. That Tinder match, Norse, had turned out to be a man called Niels. That first night, after group dinner, Miriam had made her excuses, saying she had work to do, and made her way to Sunset Beach by scooter. It was around midnight. Niels said he'd wait for her on the beach, in front of the resort he was staying at, so that he had Wi-Fi reception. She knew the resort well. It wasn't that far from Vibe, or even the TribeHut, and she was worried someone would see her. But the beach was deserted. It was also a black moon night, so even the few people who were around would be impossible to see until you came right upon them, and even then it would be difficult to know who they were.

As she made her way across the sand to the resort, a fleeting worry hit her that this would be a great way for someone to rob or assault her in some way. She firmly pushed the thought aside and strode toward the resort. She finally saw a shape taking form from the shadows. He was tall and wearing a white linen shirt. He waved hello and she waved back. When she got close, they both said hi and kissed each other on one cheek. He was even better looking than in his profile pics, and a lot taller than her.

Both slightly embarrassed, they started to walk down the beach side by side, making that excruciating small talk that seemed to be a prerequisite of all hookups.

Niels was from a town in Denmark that Miriam couldn't even pronounce. He was an engineer on holiday with his extended family, which was boring for him as all his siblings were paired up and had children. They had tried to house him with his teenage nephew, and he had sternly refused, so he got a room of his own. (Miriam did a little happy somersault inside herself at the mention of this.) He and his family were just making the most of island life. Niels was intrigued by Miriam's lifestyle (most people who weren't digital nomads were) and asked her a lot of questions.

As they walked, they saw a moving light coming up ahead. It resolved into a group of three people holding a mobile phone as a torch, looking for something in the sand. As the light moved around, the shadows of hermit crabs and bigger crabs scuttled about trying to hide and get out of the way. Miriam and Niels tried to ask if they needed help, but they could not understand each other's languages, so they soon moved on.

Miriam was walking closer to the shore when a big silent wave unexpectedly washed up and reached up to their thighs. She jumped up and almost grabbed onto Niels to escape the water. She was wearing long loose Thai pants and they had gotten completely soaked. They laughed and moved up away from the sea a little.

They approached another resort, which was set back from the beach and dark, looking abandoned, and Niels proposed they sit down on some plastic deckchairs that were still out. They sat and talked. So far, no flirting or innuendo had been exchanged. They discussed their respective jobs, what it was like to live in Denmark (Niels), and in the UK, US and Spain (Miriam), especially living away from one's hometown. Miriam usually steered clear of these topics. She didn't want to give too much information away, but that night she felt very talkative and he was a good listener. She told him how she grew up in the Valley in Los Angeles, helping out at her parents' bodega, of how they encouraged her to study to improve herself—until it became clear she was into academic study and not professional work. Grabbing the chance of a lifetime to go on a scholarship to Madrid, she had never looked back and never really moved back to the US. Her parents had long ago given up on her doing even remotely what they had wished for her. She told him how she ended up in London, which had been her dream, and how she became trapped in an abusive relationship with an older man (she didn't go into much detail here, she didn't want the whole conversation to take a negative turn). She described how she got out of it and how she eventually had to move out of London for her own sanity, and how this led to her now itinerant lifestyle. She felt like she had talked for hours but she realized that summing up most of her life to date had only taken twenty minutes or so. Niels had listened attentively and asked a couple questions here and there, particularly when his grasp of some English words faltered.

When she realized she'd been talking a bit too much, she got up with the excuse of drying her pants: they were still sopping wet from the wave and sticking to her legs. Niels got up, too and must have gotten closer as she looked down, because when she looked up again, they were face-to-face and only a couple inches apart. She had been wondering where the night was going, so she was a little taken aback at this change of gear. This close, his body radiated heat. She felt a sudden electric charge between them. He leaned in closer and kissed her, putting his arm around her back and pulling her to him.

She forgot all about her wet Thai pants and gave herself to the kiss. It soon became an all-body thing, their hands and arms travelling up and down their bodies, mouths coming up for air every so often. Niels sat back down and pulled her on top of him, so that she straddled him. He looked up at her.

"You're so beautiful. Sexy."

She smiled and then bent down to kiss him. Her mass of hair fell between them though, and they laughed again. She pulled her hair up with one hand then went in for the kiss again. It was really sexy kissing like this, in the pitch-black of the beach, hearing the waves crash nearby, and this hot, sexy man running his hands up and down her body, her breasts.

After a good while, when things could only progress to sand in uncomfortable places, Miriam had the presence of mind to whisper, "What about your room?" He was delighted and half dragged her there, both of them giggling.

The room was nondescript Asian chic, comfortable and quite big. He was incredibly strong and had a lot of stamina, which was unexpected and fabulous. They used all available surfaces for the next few hours. She slunk back to her accommodation at about 6:00 a.m., tired and glowing.

For the next couple days, Niels kept in touch in an amusing, flirty and kinky way, sending her WhatsApp messages and pictures.

He was quite busy with his family in the daytime but was trying to free himself up for another night with her. Strangely though, he showed a different, sterner side. He was very specific about what he wanted to do with her and had made anal sex a prerequisite for their next hookup. Miriam didn't know what to make of that; usually her contrarian self would bristle at what she saw as an order and she would reject it outright. But their time together had been fun, and he aroused her, so she thought, *Why not? Go with the flow.* So that night, after the beach party, they were going to meet up again, back in his hotel, and let loose. When she had agreed to the anal sex, she had given him quite specific instructions as to the lube needed. She smiled inwardly at the thought of him running around to the island's chemists, looking for a scent-free, water-based lube, as she had requested.

"Hey, did you have a nice nap?"

Greta's voice snapped Miriam back to the present.

"Oh, hi. Well…I'm not sure. I must have dozed off but I didn't even realize! I obviously needed it."

"We went up the other end of the beach and started talking to a really funny fisherman. He showed us his catch of the day." Jakob beamed.

"Wow, cool. Is he cooking it for us?" Miriam's thoughts always strayed to food and eating.

"Unfortunately not. But he told us of a place on the way back home that is great for fresh fish." Jakob added with a smile.

"Fabulous."

Greta grabbed her water bottle and drank. Miriam untied her hair an asked, "You guys fancy a dip? I'm drenched and need to cool off."

"Sure." Greta joined her.

"I've got a couple of emails I need to reply to. I'll join you in a bit," said Jakob.

The two women walked out toward the shore and smiled about Jakob always putting work first.

Hat Bang was probably Miriam's favorite beach on Tanu. It was far to the east, kind of near the famed party area, and it was a smallish crescent of almost white beach, nestled between two steep cliffs with a jungle stream at the back. Development had been quite low-key and recent, so the beach was mostly empty and relaxed. At low tide, some rocks made swimming a little hazardous, but at high tide you wouldn't even know they were there. The turquoise crystal water beckoned lustily.

Greta dived in quickly, her long blonde hair floating up for a second on the surface. Miriam followed suit and stayed underwater for a few seconds, enjoying the relatively refreshing water and the underwater sounds of the sea. When she surfaced, Greta was doing some aqua aerobic exercises already.

"Shall we?" she asked. Miriam laughed and joined in. It was a weird sensation sweating in water that was almost as warm as your sweat.

"So, are you going to this beach party tonight, then, Miriam?"

"Well, you know it's not my scene, really, but I'll probably check it out. Just to hang out, really."

"I hope the music is better than usual. I really can't take any more deep house. Sometimes I wake in the night and I feel my body and brain thrumming to that deep house beat. Not cool."

Miriam laughed. "Yes, I know what you mean. But I thought you liked it?"

"Not really. Jakob is a fan. I go for him. But tonight, it should be something else entirely."

"Let's hope so." They continued exercising. "By the way, remind me again, what day do you guys leave?"

"On Wednesday," Greta replied sadly.

"Bummer. I wish you weren't leaving."

"Me either."

"Let me know what you want to do for your last—"

"AAAHH!!" Greta's scream startled Miriam mid-sentence.

"What?!" Images of sharks and various sea monsters popped into Miriam's head.

"Aw, aw, awww!!" Greta was thrashing in the water, turning this way and that.

"What is it?!" Miriam looked around in the water, anxious and a bit frantic.

"Shit, I think a jellyfish got me!" With tears in her eyes, Greta started swimming back to shore.

"Really? I haven't seen any today. Bastards."

Miriam followed her, head high above the water on the lookout for the jelly devils.

Greta's moans were quite distressing, but she seemed to be okay moving around. As they approached shore, Miriam spotted something in the water.

"There! I see one." A transparent jellyfish with purple veins was just bobbing on the surface. It was the size of a clementine.

Greta was now on her feet.

"Can you look?"

Miriam approached her.

"Where does it hurt?"

Jakob, seeing the two of them lingering, got up and started coming closer.

"On my back. Here." Greta tried pointing with her hand to a place near her shoulder blade.

And indeed, there was a large red area, swelling up by the second.

"Yep, definitely looks like a sting. How bad is it?"

"Have you ever had a hot poker shoved in your back? Like that."

Jakob had reached them and saw the welt on Greta's back.

"Oh, honey? What is it?"

"We think it was a jellyfish," Miriam suggested.

As Jakob inspected the swelling, Miriam looked out again into the water, and now she spotted another jellyfish. And another. And another. *Jesus.*

"I think we can safely say no more swimming today."

"Miriam, do you have anything for this kind of thing?"

"No, sorry. So far, I've been lucky. But we can drive to a chemist and get something. Or if it's bad we should go to the clinic."

Greta started walking back to the towels.

"It's painful but not overwhelming. Let's see how it goes."

Jakob went up and grabbed her water bottle, handing it to her. Greta drank deeply.

"Thanks." She then asked him to splash some cool water on the sting.

"Can I take a picture of it?" Jakob asked enthusiastically. "I never thought that's what it would look like." He was right: it was just raised skin, like a large mosquito bite without the bite. And red.

Greta smiled and nodded. "Sure. I also want to see what it looks like. But let ME Instagram it?" She laughed weakly.

Jakob grabbed his iPhone and snapped away. "Someone told me that apparently a good method for the pain is to pee on it?"

Greta and Miriam both looked daggers at Jakob.

"What?! They say the ammonia in the pee acts as a disinfectant, or something."

"Have you ever heard the term *urban legend*, Jakob?" was Miriam's sarcastic response.

"Well, apparently there is some truth in this thing…" Greta piped up, visibly less pained. "But no way is anyone peeing on me."

CHAPTER 16 - ROSE

Rose was getting ready for the party at Vibe. The night promised to be a long one involving lots of alcohol, and she wanted to look her best.

She had showered at length and marveled at how she looked in the mirror. She was more tanned than she'd ever been in her life, and it suited her! Gone was the wishfully named "English rose" complexion, replaced by a light caramel glow, especially on her cheekbones. Her blue eyes seemed brighter than ever, and her hair, eyebrows and eyelashes had lightened considerably. More freckles dotted her face. She loved it. She decided to wear a new dress she had brought with her—it was long but the hem was irregular, very flowy, with a stylized floral pattern. It emphasized her cleavage and collar bone in a way that she found very flattering, which in turn gave her more confidence than normal. She topped the look off with a necklace she had bought from a Congolese artisan years before—stone and coconut shell, very apt. On her feet, only flip-flops. She had learned that, at beach parties, people would just flip them off as soon as they arrived and then put them back on when it was time to leave; that is, if they found them.

She had arranged to go to the party with Laura, the host, who was staying at the TribeHut bungalows, which were on the way from Rose's own bungalow to the beach party. They met outside; Laura was waiting in the shade for Rose. Her Swiss complexion hadn't reacted as well as Rose's to the Thai sun and it was blotchy and red.

Laura, too, was dressed fancier than usual, a marker of the big deal this event represented for the TribeHut community.

They started looking around the road in the late afternoon sun for a tuk-tuk. The plan was to get to Vibe just before sunset, when the first DJ set would begin, and they could watch sunset while downing some glorious cocktails. The road was dusty, on top of the heat, so Rose's confidence started to trickle down with the sweat making its way down her back. Laura gave a scream when she flagged down an available tuk-tuk. After the usual haggling over the price, the two of them climbed on awkwardly—you always had to be careful where you sat on one of those contraptions, as it could affect the ride significantly. The driver sped off and they let themselves be cooled by the air.

They were both dying to gossip preparty, which they had to do at quite a loud level over the constant put-putting of the tuk-tuk. Laura updated Rose on who was going to DJ, who had cancelled last-minute and who was gearing up for a rager. Rose kept her ears sharp for Martin's name but it never came up, which she took as a good sign. Laura had her eye on an Irish guy who had been flirting with her for days, she hoped tonight something would happen.

There were already loads of scooters parked by Vibe, next to the sculpture-cum-border made of beer bottles filled with sand and stuck fast, headfirst, into the ground. The music could be heard from the little dust road that led to the bar, except that, for once, it wasn't a heavy bass thrumming in the inner ear. Rose and Laura looked at each other excitedly. The air was thick with smoke from the barbecue that was roaring beside the bar. The whole place was just a perfect beach bar. There was a bamboo/driftwood counter staffed by funky-looking Thai rastas, mostly shirtless and tattooed; various *salas* and loungers dotting the beach in front, toward the sea, bedecked with comfy cushions and candles; gorgeous young party goers eager to live their Thai coworking experience to the max.

The DJ booth was manned, at the moment, by a diminutive Asian woman whom Rose had noticed at TribeHut. Her hair was shaved on one side and the slightly longer side had the tips changing to a bright green. The DJ was so engrossed in what she was doing that she didn't notice the guy trying to hand her a drink from outside the booth. The music was a good chillout mix and, as such, no one was dancing. Most people were milling around the bar or stretched out on the loungers waiting for sunset. Rose and Laura were beckoned by a group where there were a few spaces left.

"Hey, girls! Glad you made it for sunset," said someone in the already tipsy crowd.

"What you want?" one of the bartenders was already at Rose's elbow, startling her. Laura already knew what she fancied.

"A berry bomb, please!"

"Okay. You?"

Rose hadn't even seen the menu, but Laura was enthusiastic.

"We're getting a 70 percent discount tonight. Just order the same. If you don't like it, you can order something else and I'll drink yours."

"Okay, then, another berry bomb."

"Okay. Two berry bomb." The bartender shuffled away in the sand.

"Isn't Wendy doing great?" Wendy, Rose assumed, was the DJ. She nodded enthusiastically. She was ready to chill out, but it was still so hot. And mosquitoes were around. Thankfully, she had sprayed.

"How does the barbecue work?" she asked Laura. "I ordered the vegetarian option."

"When it's ready, they tell us, and we just go there to take food."

A guy Rose didn't know came to talk to Laura, so Rose turned back to the sea, to admire the sun. Surreptitiously, she kept on scanning the crowd, as if looking for the barman or another friend, to see if she could spot Martin. But no luck so far.

It was a glorious sunset. The sky near them was clear but in the distance, high, thin clouds were scattered about, creating a bright orange glow overhead, interspersed by visible light rays that were hitting the ocean in a gorgeous, painting-like way. Rose wished she had a good camera and photographic skills to capture the moment. The bottom of the sun was almost touching the ocean. She knew it would be very fast: in only a few minutes, the entire, glowing ember of the sun would be sunk behind the sea line, leaving a red trail overhead. Just then, as if on cue, a small boat with a single fisherman came into view, silhouetted by the sun. Some people wowed, most rushed to get their iPhones out to capture that travel guide snap. The guy was moving ever so slowly, almost lingering in the sightline of the sun.

"Here. Sixty baht each." The tattooed barman had just deposited on their table two bright purple frozen concoctions, topped by frangipani flowers. Rose felt smug that she'd worked out that in Thai these flowers were called *Lilawadee*. After paying, Laura, eyes wide, grabbed her drink and clinked it to Rose's before Rose had even taken hers. She turned around to continue talking and, Rose now saw, one of the people she was talking to was Thomas, that Irish guy Laura had been talking about. With a smile, Rose turned back to the sunset.

She delicately picked the frangipani out of the glass—someone had told her they sprayed them with all sorts of toxic substances, so it was important not to mix them with food or drinks—and took a sip. The frozen blast, aptly named, hit her forehead and made her scrunch her eyes. She put the frangipani flower behind her ear and thought she might look like one of Gauguin's Tahitian women. Just then, someone elbowed her in the back. Determined not to be distracted away from the sunset, she seated herself more firmly on the raised platform and looked out again. The sun was halfway down.

People started cheering the sun and the sunset, pictures continued being taken. The DJ, sensing the mood, played a very atmospheric piece. Another limb in her back made Rose squirm and wriggle back, hoping she was returning some discomfort to whoever it was that was jostling in beside her.

Finally, the last of the sun was dipping behind view and the music reached a beautiful and suspenseful pause... In the final instant of silence you could hear a pin drop, as all eyes were westward. A few moments later, the music started again, groovy and beautiful, and a huge cheer went up from the crowd. A guy broke off from the group, running out to the shore. He stripped his T-shirt off, screamed, "This is my life!" at the top of his lungs and then jumped into the sea, followed by the laughter of most other people.

But Rose froze: the laughter she heard next to her pricked her ears. *It can't be. Can it?* She turned to speak to Laura, but in reality she wanted to check who her rude new neighbor was. As her eyes found Martin, the berry blast she was downing threatened to go down the wrong way. But she held on and spoke.

"Laura" came out like a strangled cat crying. Rose swallowed and tried again. "Laura."

Laura turned, and so did Martin, who was talking to someone else. Rose's inner voice was screaming to her *Be cool! Whatever you do, be cool, woman!* So, she raised her glass to her Swiss friend.

"Great choice." And she winked.

Laura beamed back and raised her own glass.

"What is that? Looks like a fruit shake." It was him. He had actually addressed her. As her neurons raced to compute this momentous event, her hand made the wise decision to shove the straw back in her mouth, to buy some time.

He was looking at her, then at the drink, then at her again, focusing on her mouth, pursed like that holding the straw. She felt as if a furnace had been lit under her and the heat was covering her, toe to head. More than that, in that gaze it was as if he'd already undressed her and explored every little secret fold and crevice of her body, and had found that he adored each one of them.

Rose kept sucking on the cocktail until a message registered that her mouth was full. Finally, she tried to swallow, but started coughing a little.

"My, looks like you love it. Can I try it?" he asked.

Rose nodded and offered him the glass. *An actual exchange of saliva might be occurring!* He put his hand around hers to steady the drink, then took a swig from the straw. It was her turn now to glaze over as she watched his mouth grasp the straw and purse. It was happening like the slow motion in a film, all sound had been drowned out and she was only aware of the heat of his hand pressing against hers.

In reality, it was only a split-second. Martin swallowed the drink and paused for a second, tasting it.

"It's actually not as sweet as I expected. Mmm." He smacked his lips a little. "And it's refreshing, too. I'll go for it."

As his arm pushed the drink back toward Rose, he added: "You want another?"

Again, as if on autopilot, she had the presence of mind to nod. At this, Martin raised his arm and, as if by magic, another tattooed helper appeared at his side. "Two of those." He pointed at her drink.

Rose stealthily brought the straw back to her mouth and drank, thinking that just a few seconds ago it had been in his godlike mouth. When he smiled, he was even more gorgeous than when he was serious. His smile was a little crooked on one side, which gave him that imperfect perfection she always sought in the jewelry pieces she bought. She tried to see if she could taste him on the straw.

"Martin. Hi." He held out his hand and she took it.

The little voice inside her was screaming *Don't say that you already met! Just go with it!* So, she stopped herself just short of saying something and changed it to "Rose. Pleasure." And they started talking.

CHAPTER 17 - MIRIAM

Miriam was riding on her own scooter following Jakob and Greta's. She licked her lips, still slightly salty from the sea. Her damp hair was whipping behind her from under the helmet. They had just gone through one of her favorite island spots: a long, straight and slightly up-and-down section of road that was bordered by jungle on both sides. On one side you could just about see the glint of the sea beyond. It was a stretch where you often found monkeys, monitor lizards or elephants crossing or roaming. It was so much fun!

Jakob was an experienced rider and was going faster than Miriam was used to. But since he was in front and even with a passenger, she felt safe enough to keep up. Greta's sarong was flapping wildly behind her.

They rode past a turnoff that led to a charming jungle café (or mosquito café, as Miriam liked to think of it) and a row of bungalows. The green of the jungle, the smell of frangipani and the sun in front of her just made Miriam smile, inwardly and outwardly. She could get used to this life.

They rounded a downhill corner and, in the blink of an eye, Jakob's rear wheel was sliding sideways, before the whole scooter skidded down. Miriam only had time to tap her brakes—thankfully she wasn't going that fast—but her scooter seemed to dip down under her and away, then slid sideways on some loose gravel. Almost as if in slow motion, she realized she was about to hit the ground. When her leg and arm scraped the asphalt, her teeth clacked together a few times, but in an instant, she somehow managed to get off the scooter while it continued sliding down. She screamed out in shock, as if the shout would stop the accident from happening, rewind time. The whole thing felt like being thrown in the spin cycle of a high-powered washing machine.

She found herself sitting up on the road, and before her she saw her own scooter stopped a few meters down, and Jakob and Greta both off their scooter, which had crashed into another scooter ahead. By this last scooter, two more people were sitting or slumped.

"Fuck! What happened?!" she screamed to the people at the bottom of the road. She quickly got up and then looked down. Her left leg was a red and brown mess of skin, blood and grit. She didn't feel pain or anything. It looked like someone had painted special effects all down her calf.

After a brief dizzy spell, she started walking toward her friends, adrenaline pumping in her veins. Her beach bag and its contents were scattered about. Jakob's scooter was still revving. The chaos around her echoed the ongoing tumbling inside her head. As she walked down, she heard a car come around the bend. She whipped around, senses alert, and the car broke suddenly in front of the accident.

"Stay there so other cars see you!" she shouted to the big SUV that had stopped behind her, her brain trying to kick into gear and be aware of all dangers.

She turned back toward her friends, who were finally moving and trying to get up, when she heard the SUV move off, overtake them and speed away.

"Wanker!" she shouted after it.

The two people next to the crashed scooter were, at first glance and at a guess, two Japanese boys; they were panicked, shouting at each other. Miriam arrived at her friends' scooter and turned off the ignition, so it stopped revving.

"Guys, are you okay? What happened?"

Greta was moaning in pain and Jakob was dazed. Miriam knelt down next to Greta, and pain shot up her leg. "Aaaagh!" No, she could not actually kneel. Awkwardly, she squatted near her friend. Greta's helmet had come off. She had bloody grazes on her face and all over her body.

"Don't move, sweetie."

She turned back to the Japanese panickers, who did not seem to be injured.

"Do you speak English?" she asked.

They just looked at her.

"English?" she said again.

One of them nodded vigorously. The other just stared at her dumbly.

"Call the clinic. Phone. Ambulance. Okay?"

They started jabbering in Japanese to each other.

Miriam turned to Greta. "It's okay, Greta, we'll take care of this." She looked now at Jakob. "Hey, man, how are you? Talk to me. Jakob." He remained quiet. "Talk to me."

She shuffled over to him. "Hey, hey." He looked really dazed, his eyes unfocused.

He needed medical attention. Heck, they both did. She turned back to the Japanese.

"Ambulance?" One of them was on the phone but did not seem to be making himself understood.

She held out her arm and hand. He put the phone in it.

"Hello?"

"Sawasdee-kaa," said the woman at the other end.

"We need an ambulance. We've had a scooter crash. My friends are hurt."

"You need ambulance?"

"Yes."

"Where is the accident?"

Miriam thought how to explain it. She looked up and there was a restaurant up ahead. She'd been there before. It was called Aroy. "We're near Aroy restaurant, before Pon beach."

"Pon beach? Too far for us, *kaa*. You must call East Tanu Doctors. They send ambulance, *kaa*."

"What? Can't you send them? Please."

"Call East Tanu Doctors. You have number?"

"No, I don't have the bloody number!" Miriam shouted, almost crying. "I'm sorry. We just need help."

At this point, a couple of Thai people from the restaurant approached. One of them was on the phone.

Miriam looked up. The Thais attempted to speak with the Japanese, but to say that what passed was lost in translation was an understatement. The Thai guy with the phone came closer to her.

"Can you call East Tanu Doctors?" Miriam asked him.

He pointed to the phone he was holding.

"East Tanu. Ambulance." He nodded.

Miriam put the Japanese guy's phone down and turned back to her friends. Greta was sitting up.

"Jakob… ach, Jakob… *Wie geht es dir?*"

Jakob was holding his head, his hands going for the helmet clasp.

"No, no, Jakob. Wait." Miriam stopped his hands. "Not that it makes a huge difference, but wait. The ambulance will be here soon. Try not to move."

A car and scooter had stopped in the meantime. Thai conversation was flowing all around them. Two guys started to try to lift Greta; Miriam thought they wanted to put her in the SUV flatbed. "No! No, wait. Ambulance coming. Ambulance!"

Greta was confused, looking around at these people. "They're just trying to help us, sweetie, but it'll be okay soon."

Finally, she could hear the sound of the siren approaching.

The ride in the ambulance was probably more eventful than the crash itself, but at least the orderlies were nice and capable. The clinic had been warned of their arrival. They took Jakob first as he was dazed and unresponsive. They fitted him with one of those neck braces, Greta, too, but she complained that her scrapes were being rubbed by it. No one took much notice of Miriam as she was up and about. She had to push to ride in the ambulance herself. And, well…it was really just a white truck with space for a bed inside…

The clinic was quiet, clean, small. A few people milled in the waiting area, but Jakob and Greta were seen immediately. Miriam was asked to wait. She sat down and then she thought she needed to drink. She got up and went to the water dispenser. She drank one, two, three cups of water, then sat back down.

A young couple were there, sitting in front of her. She thought they might be Swedish by the way the spoke. They had a small baby with them, less than one year old. None of them had any visible injuries. Miriam found herself curious about what had brought them in. Her body finally started to release the tension that had accumulated. She leaned back and, as she almost dozed off, a wave of cold overcame her, causing her to start shivering, harder and harder. She looked around, identifying where the AC vent was, and moved away from it.

But it wasn't the cold making her shiver. She realized it must be the shock. She went up to Reception to ask for hot tea, but as she tried to talk to the receptionist, she felt really light-headed and stumbled slightly, shaking. The girl got a bit frightened, came around and helped Miriam to a seat, then she went off. Soon, one of the nurses was out there, talking to her, bringing her into the clinic proper.

CHAPTER 18 - ADRIEN

Adrien was sitting on a lounger in Vibe. The party was getting into full swing, but he seemed to be in his own world. The constant sweating that was the faithful companion of life in Southeast Asia had been replaced by cold, clammy sweats and minor bursts of panic.

Earlier, he had tried to say to Laura that, if the sets were over-running, he could just easily drop out, no problem (wasn't he such a good team player?). She actually went out of her way to ensure he would get his slot, much to his dismay and nervous stomach. Serge kept supplying Adrien with frozen cocktails, to stop the sweating (and accidentally increasing the cold sweats) and to take the edge off the nervousness.

"You'll be great, mate. Don't worry."

Just the words all panicked people loved to hear.

Adrien dutifully sucked on the straws and willed the alcohol to do its work, to no avail. He was so spaced out all he could hear was the music's beat, drowning out all the little reminders he had kept on repeating as a mantra in his mind.

Laura came over. The other DJ was almost finished, so Adrien should go and get himself set up. He stayed sitting. She thought he hadn't understood her, so she leaned in closer and repeated herself in his ear, pointing to the DJ booth for good measure. He nodded but still didn't get up. Laura looked at Serge enquiringly, and he motioned to her to give Adrien a minute. Adrien was trying to get up, really, he was pushing up with all his strength, but it was as if someone had glued his bum to the bamboo lounger.

Finally, Serge whispered in his ear, "Hey, shall I help you get set?"

Adrien turned his head to face the Belgian man beside him and nodded. Serge looped his arm through Adrien's and then, on the count of three, got up, half dragging him, too. Somehow Adrien was up. Serge grabbed the bag that contained the stuff Adrien needed to DJ, and they walked toward the booth. As Adrien grew steadier, Serge removed his arm but continued walking beside him.

Everything in Adrien's mind was screaming at him, *Turn back—turn away now and never attempt anything like this again!* What a fool he had been for even thinking he could do this. So arrogant. How stupid of him. Now everyone would see what a loser geek he was.

The DJ booth was looming now. The Swedish DJ that was finishing his set looked up and nodded in a friendly manner. Adrien's lead legs managed to go up the two steps into the booth. Serge handed him the bag and placed his drink in a visible but out of the way place. He gave Adrien the thumbs-up, but Adrien was too transfixed by the equipment to return it. Serge walked away shaking his head and smiling a little.

The DJ deck was actually much less technical and complicated than others Adrien had encountered. He had also had a dry run on it a couple days before, so really, none of this should flummox him. He tried to take a few deep breaths. Took another swig of his cocktail. He could feel the Swedish DJ's eyes fixed on him, as he wasn't moving, wasn't getting ready.

Adrien tried to make himself think. What would he need first? Shit, what was in the bag again? Oh, yes, the playlist on his iPod.

He went for the bag and struggled with the zipper, which slipped in his clammy hands. He tried once, twice. He dried his hands on his shorts and took another breath. This time the zipper opened. He fished his iPod out; this was his deejaying iPod, containing his most prized playlists.

Somehow, working around the other guy, Adrien managed to get the iPod plugged in and cued to the right point in the playlist from which he wanted to start. The other DJ slipped one headphone off his ear and spoke in Adrien's ear.

"You ready after this track?"

Adrien froze. Was he ready? *Fuck.* He needed to check and double-check. Without saying anything back, he started flicking through the iPod to make sure, again and again, that the track was the right one. He checked the cable, unplugged it and plugged it back in at both ends, sending a crackling noise to the main speakers and causing a few heads to turn. He checked the other set of headphones. His shorts were not too wet when the tried to wipe his hands on them.

The track was ending and the Swedish DJ, with one more look at Adrien, looped another track on, to give him more time. Adrien was hyperventilating.

"Before the end of this track, cut in with yours. Cool?"

Adrien managed to nod.

"Just check the beat. Okay?"

Another nod.

The Swedish man stood aside to make room for Adrien. Now with headphones on, he used the equalizer to sync up the tracks. His vision was blurry, he couldn't understand if the equalizer was on or not. Finally, he seemed to be okay. He looked up at the Swede and they kind of nodded to each other. As one lowered the volume on his track, the other raised it on his. Except that…Adrien's song played for two seconds then looped back! Disaster.

The beat was missed and the people dancing turned around in disappointment. Adrien's face flushed lobster red as he looked down to his iPod and tried to restart the track. He faffed about a couple of seconds. Someone shouted out, "Play the tune!" followed by laughter; Adrien stumbled once more, then the track went on. People resumed dancing and he heaved a sigh of relief.

"It's okay, man, it happens," said the Swede with a manly pat on Adrien's soaked back. Adrien seemed to be sweating more now than before. He hadn't thought that was possible.

CHAPTER 19 - DAHLIA

Dahlia and Jerome crashed the party when it was already in full swing. They'd been out for some food, where Jerome proceeded to swig beer after beer (Chang, Singha, Leo, he wanted to try them all), delighted by the fact that they cost so little he could afford to buy them himself.

Various TribeHutters they encountered were already well sozzled and ruby-cheeked. The tunes were awesome, and there was a good crowd dancing. The siblings each grabbed a cocktail at the bar, then turned to each other, clinked their glasses and downed a sip.

"Okay. Have fun, sis. See you later."

"You, too. You have the key to the room, right?"

Jerome patted the back of his shorts.

"Check."

"Cool. Don't do anything I wouldn't do…" After a brief, silent look, both of them burst out laughing, then walked off in separate directions.

Dahlia shuffled to the sand dancefloor, kicked her flip-flops into the pile gathering by one of the bamboo posts and joined the other dancers. She knew most people here from TribeHut, but there were also some faces she didn't recognize. Maybe they were newcomers, or people who had joined the private party by just walking up the beach. She noticed Martin leaning on a bamboo lounger, deeply engrossed in conversation with a couple people. One of them was a woman she'd seen at the Hut. Dahlia smiled a little. She wanted to

see what he would get out of this party. Would he go off with someone else? Would he make a beeline for her? She continued to dance,
hoping he'd look in her direction.

Laura, the host, came over all buzzy and hyper. She gave Dahlia
the biggest, tightest hug.

"You made it!" Laura's breath in Dahlia's face was hot and a
bit heavy.

"Yeah!"

They clinked glasses and downed their drinks.

"Selfie time!" said Laura, who extended her phone up above
them, hugging Dahlia to herself, her glass shoved in Dahlia's face.
Both of them pursed their lips and then the flash went, blinding
them. Laura walked off without showing Dahlia the result.

Dahlia saw Jerome already talking to people. He was good like
that. He had no hang-ups, was outspoken, and at least at first, could
relate to virtually anyone. He was a social chameleon. She guessed
they both were, having had to learn from a young age to navigate
wildly different worlds, classes and environments, and to subtly
judge their own place within them.

A track she loved came on, she whooped and looked over at the
DJ. It was that tall, gangly Asian kid she'd seen around the Tribe-
Hut. She was a bit surprised that he would play such an ace tune,
but she went with it and danced away. The couple of disco lights
fitted under the bamboo roof strobed here and there, but she loved
looking up and seeing the sky and the myriad stars while dancing,
enveloped in music and the pleasant buzz of alcohol. Tonight, the
stars were really putting on a show: clusters of brighter light gave
way to shades of dark blue in arcing sweeps. This far south, familiar
constellations were sideways and got crowded out by so many others
twinkling brightly.

Just as Dahlia was losing herself in the sky, the music ended abruptly. She stopped dancing and looked at the booth. The Asian guy was desperately thumbing a drive or something, while another man next to him attempted to help. She laughed. So professional! Very loud crackles and pops came on the speaker system. Then a loud, painful noise. People covered their ears and moaned, but it soon stopped. From the corner of her eye, Dahlia saw the owner of Vibe, in all the glory of his full-body tattoos, rush over. She knew the tattoos were full body—she'd had him stark naked and all to herself some weeks back. The man basically yanked the Asian guy off the deck, pressed a couple things and the music came back on. But it was a different tune.

Most people were so high or drunk that they forgot about this in a few seconds, but the Asian guy was slouching away, his head hanging in shame. Dahlia reached him and put her cocktail in his hand.

"Just drink the pain away," she said.

"Err…what?"

"You know…who fucking cares what happened? People are already dancing again. If you feel bad, you need to do something about it."

She nodded to the drink, then walked back to the bar and she ordered two more cocktails. She looked over and he was just standing there, holding the drink in his hand and watching her dumbfounded. As soon as she had the drinks, she walked back to him.

"You still haven't finished that one? Come on!"

She took a big slurp of her drink and watched encouragingly as he slurped his, which was nearly finished anyway. She handed him the other drink she was carrying.

"Good?" she asked.

"Mm-hmm."

"Better?"

"I'm probably already drunk. That's why I messed that change up," he said.

She kept sipping her drink and watching him. He was actually quite cute, in a dorky, pigeon-chested kind of way.

"I've been drinking since five p.m."

"And you'll be drinking till five a.m. now. I'm Dahlia."

She looped her arm with his elbow and started to direct him away from the bar, toward the sandy beach and crashing waves.

CHAPTER 20 - MARTIN

Martin downed another gulp of delicious, sweet iciness. If anyone had told him at sixteen that he would so enjoy cocktails at thirty-eight, he'd have thought them mad. Beer was all he was after then, for many years. And other mood stimulants, sure. But cocktails? They were for girls.

And now here he was, trying cocktail after cocktail from the funnily spelled menu (Google Translate seemed to fail within the Thai borders), and going back to the top once he reached the bottom. Out of the corner of his eye he saw Dahlia walking arm in arm with a tall dude. They both seemed into their drink already. *Good on her!* He was relieved she was not angling for him tonight.

Rose, the English girl he had been talking to, lost and then found again, was also on her umpteenth drink, and it showed. Her cheeks were mad red, her eyes half-closed but twinkly, her laugh shrill and triggered by just about anything. Her hand was on his thigh.

He sensed the deliciousness of this moment; all his senses opened up to embrace it, to lose himself in it. He could see the rest of the night unfolding before him: a few more drinks and getting cozier with Rose, maybe a couple clumsy dances, where they would get closer and closer. Then he'd say he was too hot and wanted to get some sea air. He'd walk her away from the music, people, noise, lights; they would sit on the sand making some more small talk, until he could finally catch just the right moment to lean in for a kiss. She would act a little shy, coy, but she'd totally be into it, judging by how flirty she was being right then. They would fumble around in the sand until it would become clear it was time to move the party indoors. They would go back to his, or hers… *Better hers…* Did he have condoms with him? *Yes.* Despite telling himself that he wouldn't have random drunken sex again, he was never unprepared.

Damn. There was that rational voice again. *What the hell are you doing, Martin? Here we are, yet again. As Thai people might say, "Same same, but not different." Drunk? Check. Horny? Hell, check. Willing, hot, random woman? Double check. Result? Bad hangover the next day accompanied by a tasty side of regret, self-loathing and self-doubt. What the actual fuck?*

He straightened up and took a full, deep breath. Did he really want to rinse and repeat this scene he had lived out dozens and dozens of times, with the full knowledge of how it would make him feel? Of how it would set him back, yet again? Some cobwebs seemed to finally clear from his mind. He put his drink down.

"You want another?" slurred Rose, noticing his empty hand.

"No, I'm okay. Thanks."

She smiled at him before taking another gulp.

"Shall we—"

He stood up. *It's now or never.* He interrupted her with a mumbled apology. "Actually, I think I'm going to go."

She didn't seem to have taken it in.

Laura came over, but she was so drunk she didn't recognize either of them. She was babbling something about a bonfire, a secret beach. Rose seemed interested, so Martin took this as his cue. He started making his way down the beach.

As he got farther from the bar, he took in bigger gulps of air. It was warm but it helped.

"Wait!" the urgent call made him turn around. Rose was staggering forward, hampered by the sand. "You're leaving?" she asked in a slightly pleading, incredulous and slurred tone.

What could he possibly answer to that? *Yes, of course I am leaving, isn't it obvious? No, I am just going for a piss behind the trees, duh. Sorry, I needed to stretch my legs...* Before his brain could formulate an apt response, with a final stumbly step, Rose reached him and sort of slumped into him, her mouth aiming for his.

She almost got it, hitting his cheek instead, but undeterred, her lips moved toward his, seeking. He managed to hold her head firmly away from him a little, her breath tasting of all those colorful cocktails and none. Her eyes were still closed.

"I think we've had way too much, Rose," he managed to mumble. She opened her eyes, but he could see she was too far gone to take in anything that was going on.

"What? I don't—"

"You get home safe, okay? Find Laura or someone. You hear me?" He nudged her back toward the party; she nodded and started walking away, unsteady. He watched her go for a few seconds, to make sure she was okay, then he set off in the opposite direction.

A few seconds later, he turned around to give her one last look, but before he could see, he tripped over something in the sand and fell, followed by a yelp.

"Damn!" He sat up only to see a dark mound resolve into two people, intertwined, limbs everywhere.

"Watch where you're going!" a voice hissed. It was Dahlia, tangled up with that guy from before.

Martin wasn't sure she'd seen that it was him, so he turned quickly, hoping for the best. He scrambled up and, once he was away, threw back a garbled "Sorry!" Last thing he needed was for her to think he had been stalking her!

He scurried away, hoping for no more surprises.

"What a night," he mumbled under his breath. As he trudged up the beach, pitch-black now, a shooting star streaked across the sky right in front of him. It was so bright and long it took seconds to draw its arc in the darkness. It took Martin's breath away; he stopped.

Frantically, he tried to come up with a wish. A comet like that deserved a commensurate wish. He couldn't miss this opportunity—he was a bit superstitious like that—but nothing. His mind was blank and a bit woozy. Now that he looked at it, the sky was incredible. He'd never seen anything like it. Even in the dark areas, you could see distant clusters of stars. The depth and brilliance of this view was…well, he didn't know what it was. It left him speechless. And just then, another huge shooting star appeared out from the right of his vision, streaking through the heavens westward. His eyes followed, and in that second, his mind came up with the wish he had been struggling to find.

"May I continue to improve the balance in my life. May I continue to want to meet nice people, to be healthy, to have hope, to see things like these," he half whispered into the warm night breeze. As he finished sending out his wish, the comet winked out near the horizon.

A moment of total stillness ensued. The air rustled his hair and clothes. The soft murmur of the sea churned ahead. All was quiet.

Martin couldn't believe he'd turned down Rose. A woman he fancied, dangling from his lips—he had been in that situation countless times. And every time, he had made the most of it. But now, his recent resolve had finally kicked in. No more random one-offs. He needed to rein in his excesses, and for the first time, it seemed like he was succeeding. *Yes!* A feeling of contentment was spreading in his chest, to the point that he smiled, alone in the dark.

Finally, he turned around and set off to find the path he knew was between the trees, to join the road and head back to his bungalow. He felt light and happy—the cocktails surely helped.

Once he was walking through the small woods, it was much darker than on the beach. He took his phone out for the light but realized the battery had died. He cursed. He hurried his steps and kept his eyes on the dark path.

Suddenly, from his left, a growl emerged from the gloom. It startled him. He looked without stopping. Another growl, now a bark. He saw a dog, hackles raised, barking toward the trees. What the fuck was the dog doing? Nothing good, for sure. He had slowed down to look, and now he could see what the dog was growling at—a cobra, its head raised defensively, trying to face off with the canine. "Fuck!"

Just then, the dog sprang toward the snake, and the two became ensnared. Martin turned back to the road, this time running for his life.

CHAPTER 21 - JEROME

Thailand was a lark. It was blissfully warm in winter, though humid, and everything you desired was at your fingertips.

In China, too, you could get everything you wanted, if you knew the right people, but it always required a lot of wheeling and dealing, a lot of sucking up (sometimes literally) and a lot of knowing when and how to butter up people. But the weather trumped everything. Jerome asked himself why it had taken him so long to make his way to these paradise locations. Now that he was here, he was hearing all about Bali, the Philippines, Borneo and other gorgeous locations. He started making a list in his mind.

The party was okay. Mostly, people were interested to know what you did, and Jerome was pitifully dry on that score. So, he started making stuff up, just for the fun of it. To one guy he said he was involved in developing a new invisible fabric (it did exist!); to another, a girl, he said he was assistant to an unspecified mogul/CEO that let him work remotely but meant he had to be available 24/7; and to yet another he said he was an artist, funding his travels through his art sales and shows.

Funnily, all those things could potentially be true, if he ever applied himself.

As the evening wore on though, and people drank more, everyone stopped wanting to network and just started having some real fun. Discussions were random and funny, started and interrupted without anyone blinking an eye. People were going to and from the bar, the dancefloor, the seating and the sea in a constant motion and changeover.

He noticed Dahlia going off with a dorky guy, and now alone, not knowing anyone, Jerome was finally in his element: the bullshit element. He could spread his wings and do whatever (be whoever and do whomever) he wanted. As per usual, he managed to get people to buy him drinks repeatedly without seeming to take advantage. When he went to the bar for a round of drinks, he charmed the girl waiting next to him so much that she bought the drinks on his behalf. Sorted!

The fauna was interesting. He had always thought that all these geeks would be half-formed, pasty indoor weaklings. Yet just at this party he could see a fit, tanned and tall Dutchman (all the more appealing for his geeky specs); an incredibly built and tattooed Australian who turned out to be a star coder (too bad his girlfriend was glued to his side, or Jerome would have enjoyed flirting with him); and various not-so-bad-looking guys of various ages, including a clutch of twentysomething babies who were really to Jerome's liking but who wouldn't usually provide the perks that older men did. *Or maybe if they're young Silicon Valley moguls in the making, they could? No, better to bet safely.*

Reflexively, he checked his phone, though he had only just put a Thai SIM card in, so no one had his number. Li Chen surely would not contact him anymore and his existing contacts had kind of dried up. He put the phone away again and made a mental note to look into Tinder and Grinder… Who knew what he could find there.

Later, he found himself in a round discussion, mostly guys, being led by a man who, hilariously, introduced himself as Ricky Storm—*a fake name if there ever was one*—and felt he was the alpha male, way superior to the mutts surrounding him. Consequently, he was spewing wisdom regarding some Asian destination or other. The way he made it sound, the place hadn't even existed before he went there, but—and there was the rub—it was now so touristy and trendy that it was completely over. Basically, you would need a time machine to be as cool as this dude. Jerome smirked and wasn't afraid to hide it. He knew a bullshitter when he saw one. Kindred spirits. A description of this guy floated up in Jerome's mind. Yes. *King of the #humblebrag.*

Ricky Storm noticed the smirk and proceeded to ignore Jerome for the rest of the conversation, trying to cut him out of the group. It was funny, because Jerome wasn't saying anything and was just buffeted by the group, going along to see where the bullshit would lead.

Then, suddenly, a girl grabbed Ricky across the chest with a playful grasp and urgently whispered something in his ear. He looked at her. "Really? You game?"

She smiled back in a wide grin.

Ricky turned to the group with a wicked look. After a dramatic pause, he put his drink down and declared, "It's skinny-dipping time!"

Hollers and whistles rose up from the group and the people around. The girl grabbed Ricky by the hand, and he made a show of being led by her in front of everyone. As they walked farther down the beach, the girl slowly unlaced her top, letting it fall to the sand, and Ricky followed suit, revealing a muscly, if doughy upper body. Jerome walked just behind them with the group.

More and more people were being ensnared by the gravitational pull of the scene, surrounding the couple. The girl finally dropped her shorts, ran into the water and then, barely a visible shape now, pulled off her bikini bottoms and threw them back on the beach, whooping in delight. Ricky didn't waste a moment pulling off his own shorts and running stark naked into the waves and into the arms of the girl.

To more shouts and squeals of excitement, others were following suit, dropping clothing where they stood and launching themselves into the warm, welcoming water. Jerome enjoyed the show of so many men undressing unselfconsciously. He also noticed, to one side, a group of TribeHutters looking on with disdain. He guessed these were either people who hadn't drank enough or who were too prudish for a moonlight swim.

When he clocked the Dutch dude starting to undress, Jerome also put his drink down and joined in, running alongside the hottie and whooping. The sea was warm soup. There were now so many people they kept bumping into each other.

A girl squealed about something touching her leg. Jerome used the opportunity to "accidentally on purpose" graze men's buttocks and dicks with the back of his hand. No one was going to find him out! He smiled deliciously, unseen in the dark. Once he got near the Dutch guy, Darius, he thought he was called, and strategically floated his hand in the water at crotch height, the cock he felt seemed huge. He was getting a hard-on, but Darius whipped around startled, floated slightly away from the group.

Jerome, bobbing on the surface, the water maybe just over a couple meters deep, bumped his back into someone. He turned and was confronted by the sight of Ricky Storm swapping saliva big-time with the girl who first went into the water. So much pashing that they were struggling to stay afloat. She was using him as some sort of rock and he valiantly floated for them both.

Ugh. Jerome turned back and swam away.

As everyone was slowly getting back to shore and gathering their things, Jerome heard someone ask, "Where's my phone?" in a panicked voice.

A couple people started to search through their own clothing. "And my money. It's gone!"

"Shit!" cried another. "My iPhone!"

Jerome rushed to his stuff. He could not afford to lose anything, not even a single Thai baht, and definitely not his phone. At first he couldn't find his clothes. A rising wave of panic was engulfing him, thudding in his ears. He rummaged in the dark, aware that it was hard to tell one color from another. He looked for distinguishing features, his nakedness all but forgotten. Other cries around him, people realizing their things had been taken. Finally, under someone's shoes, he found his clothes. He stuck his hand in the back pocket of his shorts and, to his relief, felt the familiar bulge of the phone. To be on the safe side, he pulled it out alongside his very little money and room key. He exhaled audibly. "Thank fuck."

He got dressed and watched as other people were dealing with their items being stolen. Someone said it must have been someone in cahoots with the bar, others said it was a gang of Thais scouring the beaches for stupid *farangs* who left their things unattended. Yet others couldn't fathom how this could have happened while some of their own friends hadn't joined the skinny-dipping and were therefore right there on the beach when it happened. Disbelief and suspicions arose, and voices got raised.

Ricky Storm was one of the few spared, but his girl's phone was gone, and she was desperate, almost hysterical. He tried to calm her down but his superior manner—"We'll just order you a new phone tomorrow"—just made things worse. She and her friends stormed off in a huff, despite his shrill attempts to get her to stay.

Ricky's disappointed face showed how he had thought this was going to turn into a hot and steamy all-night thing. He was left with nothing apart from, probably, a hard-on. Under his breath, Jerome thought he heard Ricky mutter, "Bitch."

Jerome walked away; he had been spared and didn't want to get involved in the drama. He debated whether to have another drink or to go home. He looked around—no Dahlia. He hoped she was having a better time and better luck. *To hell with it*. He had cheated bad luck. That deserved another drink.

At the bar, he fell in talking with more people. All anyone could discuss was the theft, which he found incredibly boring, so he gulped down his drink and decided to call it a night. As he started making his way to the back of the bar and the road, he passed the toilets and decided to go in for a quick wee.

There were only two stalls, the doors a flimsy jumble of artsy driftwood. Just as he closed the door on his stall, he thought he heard a moan from the one next door. He smiled. At least someone was having fun! He peed, flushed and got out of the stall.

He washed his hands and was transfixed by his own reflection in the small mirror. He could already see the beginnings of a tan on his cheeks. He looked so much hotter when tanned! He adjusted his hair this way and that, when he heard another moan and a thud from the cubicle.

What the— thought Jerome. Another strangled moan. Curiosity won over and Jerome approached the door which, he now saw, wasn't locked. He pushed it slightly to reveal Ricky Storm, sitting on the toilet wanking himself furiously.

Ricky Storm looked up and blinked, a look of befuddlement painted on his face, and slowed down. Jerome smiled and came closer.

"Oh, don't stop now, big boy." Before Ricky could say or do anything, Jerome started helping him out.

PART III
Aftermath

CHAPTER 22 - MIRIAM

Sleeping while trying not to move was harder than Miriam had thought.

Her whole left leg, from about halfway down her thigh to almost the tip of her foot, was tightly bandaged. The outside was very tender, so she could not sleep on the left side, her favorite. Some pus or other humor had been seeping through the bandages and stained them darker, all down the leg. Mostly it was just really bad scraping, but in two places they had to put stitches on skin flaps. She would have to take really good care of these, and then have the stitches out.

Her arm was also a bit scraped (in the confusion of the accident, she hadn't even noticed) and had been bandaged; thankfully it was on the same side, so her right side was almost untouched. She had lain down carefully on the squeaky bed, "ouch-ing" and "ow-ing" at every little movement, her skin pulling against the stitches and the bandages. The problem was that her entire body was sore—this was a familiar feeling from when she was involved in a bad car crash in her teens. In the moment of a vehicle accident, your body doesn't know what's going on or where the damage is coming from, so it contracts throughout to try to protect the vital organs. The result is a god-awful full body soreness, a deep ache that knows no rest or comfortable place. She counted herself lucky that her head had not hit anything, even with her crappy toy helmet.

As she fell asleep and relaxed, her body wanted to get in a familiar and comfortable place, so she tried to turn to the left side (major no, no, no!) then to place her left arm over her face (excruciating, ow, ow, ow!), waking her up every few minutes. As a result, as dawn broke, she was shattered and sleep-deprived on top of being in pain.

With a superhuman effort, or what felt like one, she stretched her left arm to the bedside table and reached for her water bottle. Unfortunately, only a few drops came out of it. She must have drunk it in the night. She put it down and now reached for her cell phone.

Various people had messaged, wondering where she was, asking when she was going to get to the party, and as the time wore on, more worried messages appeared. *Oh, shit. I forgot.*

Are you OK?

Things here are mental! Come join the cray-cray!

The fuck are you Miriam?? Don't leave me here with these whipper snappers!

Come to think of it, where are Greta and Jakob? Worried. Pls text.

There seemed to be a bunch of Tinder messages and matches, too, but in her state she just swiped left on the notifications to make them disappear. She doubted she would get up to much fun for a little while.

But most importantly, there were several messages from Niels. Oh, shit! In the mess of the accident, she had completely forgotten they had arranged to meet last night! *Fuck!*

She scrolled to his messages; to begin with he was flirty and asking for specifics. What time and where they were going to meet. Then he became a bit put out. Said if he didn't hear from her by 10:00 p.m. he was going to make other plans. Finally, he had sent one last message, this one quite late, in the early hours of the morning.

Well, if you didn't want to meet up again, you could have had the courage to say so and not wasted my time. Have a nice life.

Damn. She hated accidents. In a split-second, her beautiful mood, her joyful openness to life, had come crashing down painfully. She began typing a reply to Niels, to explain what had happened, but then she noticed that there was a text on Messenger from Greta! Shit!

Hey Miriam, how are you? Where are you? I woke up, they don't tell me where you are. Jakob is next to me but they are talking about sending him to the mainland. Not sure about what is wrong with him.

It was from a couple hours earlier. Miriam typed back:

Sorry honey, they sent me home (not injured enough 🙁), I'm coming over shortly. We'll sort this out.

She had to take a moment to gather her resolve before she hauled herself up; her entire body screamed in protest. She stayed sitting for a few moments, dizzy with the pain.

"Jesus." Her clothes were scattered around, some of them bloody. She couldn't deal with that now. Slowly she got up and walked to the bathroom. She felt positively ancient. *This must be what being eighty is like. Thank God that's still a few years off.*

In the bathroom she splashed her face, or more accurately, slowly patted wet hands to her face. She looked a fright in the mirror. Again, she couldn't deal with that right now.

Back in the room, she stood and thought about what she could wear. Something that would not rub her wounds.

In the wardrobe she pulled out a maxi dress, long but with no pressure points on her wounds. She slid it on with some discomfort—pulling her arm up into the shoulder straps was not exactly easy. She would go without a bra; the idea of having to fiddle around with one of those gave her a feeling of dread, so she left it. Her middle-aged boobs would be free today, and fuck anyone who minded that.

Miriam started looking around for her helmet and scooter keys, chiding herself for always misplacing them. Then a "d'oh" moment snapped into place—her scooter was wrecked on the side of the road, duh. She made sure she had money in her tiny fabric purse, left the room, locked the door and shuffled off.

It was damn hot outside already, despite it being only 7:00 a.m. It never got cool here, not even in the middle of the night. It only ever got more or less humid, and that altered your perception of temperature.

She reached the main road and looked around. She needed to get a tuk-tuk to the clinic, and usually at this time they were hard to come by. She might need to walk to the nearest 7-Eleven. *Fuck, I really could do without this.*

She looked up and down the dusty road—empty. She turned left and started walking toward the 7-Eleven. The sun was on her right thankfully, keeping the wounds in shade. She would get the clinic to look at them and dress them again.

Walking was not too bad if she kept her pace slow and steady. She thought she might need to reply to some of those worried texts from last night, so she pulled out her phone and tried to text. But the effort of walking carefully to avoid pain and trying to text proved too much: she stumbled and almost fell. She decided to leave the texting till later (maybe on the tuk-tuk? That is, if she could find one).

Finally, she rounded the curve and the shop was in sight. She spotted the familiar shape of the spring roll cart parked in the front entrance. Delicious vegetarian spring rolls for only ten baht each! Her stomach growled. Maybe she should buy a few. She couldn't see any tuk-tuks yet.

She wobbled on, laboring. She hated not being able to get around easily. And she missed her scooter. But at that thought, she got a flashback of the crash, so she tried to coax her mind away from the topic.

Finally, she was almost there. Behind the spring roll cart was the blessed view of an idle tuk-tuk, the driver asleep on the passenger seat. Her heart skipped and she almost broke into a lopsided run.

"Sawasdee-kaa," she said to the spring roll lady, who knew her well. The lady—or actually, she was probably more of a girl—smiled at her warmly. Then her eyes went to the bandages.

"Oh? What happen?"

"Motorbike accident." Miriam mimed holding the handlebar with her hands.

"Ooohh. Bad, sorry. You okay?"

"Yes, thanks, I'm okay. Just a few cuts."

She lifted a bit of her maxi dress to show the other bandages.

"Can I have four vegetarian spring rolls?"

The lady swiftly picked four steaming hot rolls and put them in a paper bag for Miriam, who already had the forty baht ready in coins.

"Kob-khun-kaa," Miriam murmured as she gave a tiny bow. She turned to the tuk-tuk and, louder, addressed the slumbering driver.

"Sawasdee-kaa!"

Nothing.

"Sawasdee-kaa!!" Nothing.

The spring roll lady behind her giggled, then said something in Thai that Miriam couldn't catch.

The man startled awake.

A brief conversation ensued between him and the cart lady, in which she seemed to tease him mercilessly.

Finally, he clocked the fact that there may be a paying fare waiting and looked at Miriam. After a brief negotiation, she climbed on and he turned on the scooter engine.

As he pushed off, she told him, "Slow, soft." Making a calming gesture with her hand and showing him the bandages. He nodded, but then ripped the accelerator all the same.

CHAPTER 23 - ROSE

The skin on her face felt very tight, so Rose, half-asleep—and totally and blissfully oblivious as to where she was—brought up one arm to wipe her face. In doing so, she got a face-full of sand. She came to, sitting up, spluttering, batting the sand away from her face as if it was a poisonous powder.

When she finally could open her eyes without fear of blinding herself for the next few hours, she looked around. Sunset Beach was still mostly empty, but a few tiny people in the distance signaled the day was underway. The sun was hot and bright behind her shoulders. Her whole body felt sheathed in salt. She grimaced when she felt her eye make-up was smudged and caked with sand.

Vibe was only a short distance away from her, the front of it littered with the party's remains: glasses and bottles, stray flip-flops, towels, party lights, a firepit. Thankfully, she was the only human relic in sight.

After the little she could remember of the Martin debacle—better not to dwell on trying to remember the precise details; she remembered the gist, the rejection, and pushed the thought firmly aside—she had slumped down before she could get back to the bar. Eventually she'd puked in a corner, managed to get some water from the bar, but the party atmosphere was then extremely grating, so she walked away a bit, to sit alone in the dark and ponder.

It had been going so well! She was still half-sober when the conversation with Martin was in full flow. There had been other people, too, but with a flush of pride she remembered how his attention hadn't really wavered from her, how he had seen her, for the first time, how he had kept her engaged in the group conversation, making it look like they were together, how he had sought the telltale physical contact that was a prelude to something more happening. She remembered others sensed this, too, slowly dropping away and leaving the two of them to their own private, and at times wordless, conversation.

The drinks had flowed, from him and from her. She could still taste the whole fruit rainbow on her tongue, with an aftertaste of sick. She hadn't worried about how much she was spending, how shit she was going to feel today or anything else. She was matching him drink for drink, joke for joke; she would ride this night all the way, wherever it was going to lead.

Except that it had led here, to an empty beach at whatever time in the morning it was. It had led to sand permeating her clothing and her hair, to sitting alone once again and contemplating life. *Why does this always happen to me?* She was aware she had a habit of falling head over heels for guys she barely knew. Take Andrew, for example. When they met, in Oviedo, she remembered telling Frances that she had literally felt that telltale lightning strike that people went on about, that bolt from above. She had become a lovesick puppy, following him around in ways that, in hindsight, were extremely embarrassing. Frances had tried to get her to see reason, but where Andrew was concerned, Rose was wearing rose-tinted glasses. She hadn't wanted to see that, sadly, heartbreakingly, he did not return her feelings. Or at least not in the way that she wanted him to. And the same thing had happened again since with other men. And now, here she was again!

Oh, how desperately she wanted to talk to Frances. But to the Frances of before, the Frances of crazy nights like these, who would stay up with her smoking joints and dissecting the night's events, analyzing all that had happened and what it could mean, where it would go next. The Frances who would not judge.

Rose wanted her friend to hug her and tell her that it was Martin's loss, that she hadn't done anything wrong, that he was an idiot, that she deserved better, that she was amazing and beautiful and a goddess, and that the right guy would come along, "Just you wait."

She didn't want the Frances of the last few months, with whom every conversation ended in argument, who rejected all discussions of relationships as useless, who banged on about Rose having to open her eyes and her heart to the infinite love of God (or whatever she called him or her or it then).

If only she could have her friend back, but not the person she had become. If Frances ever got back in touch with her, the real Frances, everything would be okay. But if it was the new Frances that got in touch, better not to have her back at all.

At this thought, Rose started crying. She had never really admitted it to herself—that the way her friend had become in the last few months was something Rose hated. It was like Frances was possessed by an entirely different person, and Rose didn't want that person. She didn't love her. She didn't even like her. It felt like she was mourning Frances' death, but she hadn't actually died.

Everything was different now. Her old life was gone. Who knew where Frances was, what she was doing, how she was feeling? Rose didn't know, had no clue. The hole this left in her heart was a carefully shielded wound. Even in her own mind she hardly ever went there. She had to keep her sanity, and focusing on something she couldn't do anything about was sure to send her spinning into her own depression. She couldn't do it; she must not. She had to be sane and look after herself.

But, damn, was it hard to do that all alone. She had always felt that Frances would be right there next to her, throughout life's ups and downs, whatever happened, all the way to old age. Oh, how they would laugh about all their hang-ups and stresses, all their romantic adventures and crazy escapades! They would be full of stories.

But now the pages that continued their stories had been ripped away and blown into the wind. All that remained was a cut off beginning and scraps of paper that Rose felt she had to fill in by herself.

She had to snap out of this. It was no good dwelling on something she had absolutely no power over. Years of meditation, therapy and mindfulness had taught her that much.

She got up, stretched, swept some sand off herself. She was going to be a bit sunburned. She didn't know how long the sun had been up for, but she could feel it on her skin.

She set off to find her flip-flops in the aftermath of the party. She tried to locate which platform she had sat down on originally, the one Martin happened to sit on, too. A little flashback of their conversation came over her then, his hand briefly touching her arm. She smiled. Immediately after she felt sad, and angry. She had never been very good at handling rejection—that's why she had never been the confrontational type.

She took a deep breath and started rummaging in the sand by the foot of the platform. The bar was deserted and quiet. She didn't know what time anyone would come in to start cleaning up and getting ready for lunch, but she sure didn't want to be here when they did.

Nothing, no flip-flops on that side. She worked her way around the platform; she found a single Havaianas thong, adrift in the sand. God knows where its mate had ended up. She started on a different area, using her feet to move mounds of sand around and dig for hidden shoe treasure. Nothing. Then, next to one of the big teak poles that held up the bar roof, she felt something under the sand. She started using her hands to dig, finally unearthing a pair of Fipper flip-flops. Her heart sank. They were much bigger than her feet.

She had to accept her own flip-flops were gone. She got up, cast one last look around then put on these other flip-flops and started to walk down the dirt road back to the main road. It was going to be a long walk home.

CHAPTER 24 - MARTIN

Martin felt elated. For the first time ever, he had been able to pull back from the brink. To have drinks and not get shit-faced, to not take anything other than alcohol, and most importantly, when an opportunity for sex was staring him right in the face, he had decided to walk away. Not only that! When the girl in question had followed him and literally thrown herself into his arms, he was able to actually say no, to hold her at arm's length and go on his way.

He had gone home, showered and tried to sleep, but he was buzzing from this new development so he decided to text his SAA sponsor, Hans. He hadn't been in contact with Hans as much as he'd have liked (or should have) since getting to the island, because there wasn't much to report, but he knew that his sponsor would accept anything that Martin had to say.

He was very enthusiastic in his text, and he wasn't really asking for help or a question; he just wanted to share the good news. He didn't get an immediate reply but that wasn't unusual, what with the time difference (Hans was in Germany) and Hans' weird work hours (he was a nurse). Feeling accomplished, Martin fell into a deep sleep, the likes of which he hadn't experienced in months.

He awoke at a decent time, around 11:00 a.m., feeling somewhat refreshed and only a little hungover. He had a long shower and was thinking about what to do with the rest of his day. Should he get a massage? Go to one of the more remote beaches? Go for some more Muay Thai? Try to do some real work? His synapses were firing on all cylinders.

He got out and started toweling himself dry. It was only then that he checked his phone and saw Hans' reply.

Hey Martin, are you still awake? We should talk.

That was a few hours ago. Of course, Martin had been asleep by then.

OK, I guess you're not awake. Hit me up when you are awake, whatever the time is. I'd like us to talk. It's been too long.

Martin deftly typed back, swiping the message using only his right thumb.

Just woke up now man, let me know if you're around.

Martin went back into the bathroom to put his towel up to dry. He worked some gel into his hair and by the time he turned around to get dressed, Hans had already replied:

I'm up. Skype?

Martin was pleasantly surprised. And no time like the present. He opened Skype on his phone, plugged in his earbuds and called Hans.

"Hey man, how are you?" Martin said.

The video stream coagulated into the image of a dark bedroom, a face staring out of the gloom.

"I'm good. Good. Hang on…"

After some rustling, Hans turned a bedside lamp on, so Martin could see his puffy, bearded face quite well.

"Hey, won't your girlfriend mind?"

"No. She's visiting her parents this weekend," Hans replied as he rubbed his sleepy eyes.

"Cool. Hey, thanks for your time."

"No problem. Always. You know that."

A moment of silence.

"So," Hans broke in, "tell me about tonight. Or last night, whatever." The time difference always confused him.

"Yeah. So…I'm psyched. You know…my trouble has always been the slippery slope. If I start, I can't stop, and one thing leads to another, blah blah blah. And in fact, just last week it was exactly like that."

"Last week?" Hans asked.

"Oh, yeah…" Martin realized he hadn't mentioned the Dahlia slipup to Hans. "There was this girl from the same coworking space I use," he said.

"Okay. What happened with her?"

"The usual, you know? Drinks on the beach with everyone else. Alcohol getting me randy, she's cute, obviously available and just kind of all over me. It was such a small step to take."

"It always is, isn't it? And the step back always feels so much bigger."

"Yeah. Yeah, brother. So true."

"So, you hooked up with this girl…"

"Yes. Textbook. I left before dawn, etcetera, etcetera."

"Safe?"

"Yes, thankfully I was… We were safe," Martin said.

"Good. Well, I mean…not good. The rest…ach, you know what I mean."

Martin did know, and they were silent for a while.

Hans repositioned himself; he had been sliding down his pillow.

"Will you be okay with work, Hans?"

"Yes, yes, I'm on lates at the moment."

Martin nodded. He turned round for a swig of water.

"So, last night?"

"Yes. So, I meet this girl randomly, Rose. She was sitting next to me at a get-together."

"Wait, wait. Why did you decide to go? That's one of your flash points. Party. Alcohol, etcetera."

"I know! I know. I just…I haven't been able to master that fully, yet. Working on it."

"It works if you work it."

They both chuckled at this.

Martin described all that had happened, the woozy cocktail drinking, the flirting, the joyous mood, and then the realization that this was the moment in which he could decide, in which he could pull back. Instead of following the rut carved by hundreds of encounters that were so similar they blurred in his memory, he had decided to skip out of the rut and start carving a new one. Why this time, he had no idea. But maybe all his work was finally paying off.

When he had finished, he took another sip of water and waited for Hans, subconsciously expecting a pat on the back. But Hans was quiet.

Martin cleared his throat, signaling he had stopped talking and it wasn't just a lag in the Skype connection.

"Okay" was all that Hans said.

"Okay," Martin repeated in a more upbeat tone. He felt Hans had given his seal of approval. "So, how are you, man?"

Hans shook his head. "Wait, Martin, let's finish this first, shall we?"

Martin was taken aback. "Finish? Okay."

"I have to say, I am very glad you had this moment of recognition, a moment that you were able to act upon. This is big, I don't deny that."

Martin nodded along enthusiastically.

"But I'm worried you're being too congratulatory of yourself... too smug, when first of all you allowed yourself to get really drunk, again. And let's not mention the fact that you had a relapse a week ago and it didn't occur to you to talk to me about it. Leaving all of that aside..."

Martin tried to open his mouth and say something, but the lag meant Hans would not hear him until mid-sentence, and once Hans was mid-sentence, nothing could stop him.

"...There is this poor girl, with whom you've flirted all night, for whom you've bought drinks, on whom you've focused your considerable powers of attention... She throws herself at you, makes herself vulnerable and, rightly for you, you reject her. But you haven't spared even a thought for her. How must she be feeling right now?"

Silence. Martin closed his still open mouth.

Hans was right. Not once had he thought how this must have been from Rose's point of view. He was a shithead. An utter and complete shithead.

"The pain we cause others, Martin. That is the greatest price we pay. If we were the only ones to suffer, it would be an easy—okay, well, an eas*ier*—burden to carry. But we are not."

Martin hung his head. "Two fucking steps back," he said.

"No, no!" Hans sat up, his face looming closer to camera. "Martin, please, don't let your negativity bring you down once again. Yes, you fucked up, but there is hope here. You made some real progress. Bit by bit, day by day, mate. You know that."

Martin nodded.

"So, what should I do, now? With the girl…"

"There's only one thing, really…"

Martin looked up into Hans' bleary eyes.

"You have to apologize to her…be good to her…explain…"

CHAPTER 25 - JEROME

Jerome had woken around dawn. He was extremely uncomfortable. You couldn't really call it a bed, the thing he was sleeping on.

After the Ricky Storm encounter—in which the pin-up of the digital nomad movement had left with his legs shaking while zipping up his pants, looking around to make sure no one had noticed the two of them in the bathroom stall together—Jerome was in a silly, crazy mood. He had walked away from Vibe and its dying party and made his way to the main road. Dahlia had gone home with that lanky dude, so he knew he had time to kill. It was not going to be a sleepover, he knew that much, but she needed time to have fun, so he decided to explore.

He'd walked in the same direction as various scooters and tuk-tuks. One of them stopped and started trying to get him to pay a fare of a hundred Thai baht to wherever he wanted to go. Jerome had some fun trying to explain to the man that, a) he had nowhere to go, and b) he had no money to get there. The guy laughed unbelievingly and kept trying. Jerome explained that he was looking for a party. Fun, anywhere.

The man said, "Party, aah?" with a knowing smirk, and made a gesture like he was smoking a spliff and exhaling happily.

Jerome laughed. "Yeah, party!"

"One hundred baht." The man held his hand out.

"Oh, man, I really have no money." He turned out his shorts' pockets to show him no cash.

"You have money. One hundred baht."

"No, no, seriously. No money. Nothing!" Jerome was getting a bit annoyed.

The Thai man laughed once more, then revved his tuk-tuk and started moving away. Jerome waved at him dismissively, then the man turned back once more.

"Eighty baht?"

"No! Jesus, no." Jerome made a gesture for the man to keep going. Then he was alone again. He kept walking in the night heat until, rising high in the distance, he saw the 7-Eleven symbol, lit up and beckoning him.

The little forecourt of the 7-Eleven was a microcosm of its own. There was a stall selling spring rolls (the lady behind it asleep astride her scooter-cum-stall), and another one selling fried chicken, doing brisk trade with various legless white people. Two or three tuk-tuks were idling around, touting for fare from every living being in sight, even people who arrived driving their own scooters. They sounded like broken records. Two dogs were play-fighting among all this, running around under wheels and legs, weaving around the stacked crates of water bottles and toilet paper rolls left in piles outside the store like an obstacle course.

People in various states of drunkenness walked in and out of the 7-Eleven clutching bags or super hot toasties in cardboard pockets.

Despite having no money, Jerome decided to take a look inside. As soon as the sliding door parted, the cool breath of the polar AC welcomed him like a long-lost son. He stood there on the threshold for a few seconds, until someone elbowed him out of the way.

The light was excruciatingly bright, searing into his retinas with an explosion of colorful packaging everywhere he looked.

It was a small shop, three or four aisles cramped together to offer the most disparate selection of goods this equally disparate group of customers might need.

One aisle was, he guessed, the toiletries one. It included some necessity goods, such as snail-based creams for skin whitening (!); various styles of fake, long nails; face masks and things that looked like medication bottles but that turned out to be things you sniff (against bad odors, he guessed), all jammed next to the more usual toothpastes and toothbrushes.

The bread aisle was similarly amusing. Single slices wrapped in bright cellophane, miniloaves and even chocolate flavored bread. All sweet, Dahlia had told him. Locals loved sweet flavors, so they stuck sugar into everything.

The next aisle along was a wild selection of crisps, chips, prawn crackers and "cuttlefish puffs" with a little cartoon squid cheerfully dancing along the packaging. Jerome was very tempted to try all these; he had a thing about sampling weird snacks wherever he went. They even had the normal Lays crisps but in flavors he'd never seen before, and damn if he wanted to know what they tasted like!

The final aisle was the fridge aisle. Drinks upon drinks stacked floor to ceiling, from alcohol, to water, to the original Red Bull and the new one, to milk in all its million guises.

The effects of the various drinks and puffs of smoke Jerome had had throughout the night were finally wearing off. He checked the time: 4:15 a.m. Still too early to go back. He stepped outside the 7-Eleven, and that's when he literally bumped into his next party. Three young Thai guys—one of whom probably was the opposite of a ladyboy, a woman passing as a man—were joking and pushing each other as they walked inside. In the process, one of them slammed bodily into Jerome. Smiled excuses followed; the guys were obviously high on something and extremely giggly, and they drew Jerome into their little bubble. He had nothing else to do.

They bought drinks and walked back outside, giving Jerome one of their drinks. They, of course, kept talking to each other in Thai and interspersing some English words here and there, so Jerome was trying to understand the conversation but without success. They were just happy to have him with them, so they kept on hugging and patting him cheerfully. The group started walking down the road, the same direction Jerome had walked from. In stilted English, one of the guys started to make some conversation with him. His name was Tong. He was a student on a break, and he and his friends had just sat a big exam three days prior, so they had come to Tanu to let loose after months of pressure. And they had been really letting loose. In fact, it seemed they hadn't really slept at all since they'd arrived because at first they couldn't even find their accommodation.

They turned off a tiny dirt road that seemed to lead down to the beach but instead became a warren of tiny dirt roads branching out into hostels, guesthouses and even resorts. Finally, it appeared that they found the right house—one of the few traditional Thai constructions left around, a house on stilts, basically. Before they walked in, Jerome took a good look around, worried he had kind of lost his way and wouldn't know how to get back to the main road.

As usual, all shoes had to be taken off before entering. Once inside, Jerome was sure these guys hadn't actually slept at all. There were only their small unpacked backpacks, a few warm bottles of water and various surfaces that Jerome suspected were the beds. But no bedding or similar things anywhere.

The guys continued cracking open the drinks they'd bought, then sat down and started rolling joints. Who was Jerome to say no to that? They put on some music that he assumed was Thai (but could have been anything, really), and he let himself be swept up and over by the fuzzy warmth now spreading inside him. Bliss.

At some point they must have moved onto these beds, because that's where Jerome now found himself. His back was killing him. Sleeping on a dead hard surface really wasn't his thing. He preferred plush pillows and gorgeous mattresses, Egyptian cotton sheets. He squirmed to realign his back and noticed that both he and the guy lying next to him were naked from the waist down. And now it came to him, he remembered the fun fumbling around once they were all completely stoned. The guy was also cute, but it wasn't Tong. He hadn't caught this guy's name.

The whole thing had been fun and interesting, but he was dead tired and needed a proper sleep and a shower. He got up, trying not to make too much noise; although, his joints did crack loudly a couple times. Jerome put his shorts back on, still sandy from the earlier skinny-dip, then took a last look around. On the floor, where they had been sitting and smoking, there were a few small bags of weed. He knelt and quietly grabbed one, then put it in his pocket. They weren't going to miss it.

He let himself out as quietly as he could. Finally, dawn was breaking so he could see around, and the little dirt road didn't seem so scary and different as it had only a few hours before. He set off in what he thought was the direction of the main road, and home.

CHAPTER 26 - MIRIAM

The clinic at this hour was thankfully calmer than it had been the previous day and evening. No one with nonemergency problems would come in at 7:00 a.m.

Miriam found Greta in the same room she had left her last night; she was dozing. Miriam hated to wake her but wanted to ask about Jakob.

She looked her friend over. They had disinfected and cleaned the various cuts and grazes that dotted her face and body. One of her arms was plastered—she had actually broken it in the fall. But the plaster was a temporary one as the arm was also wounded, so they had to keep airing the wound and dressing it.

Thankfully, the neck collar was off. Greta hadn't sustained any spinal or head injuries. Miriam placed her hand lightly on her friend's arm, away from any injured spots, and called her name softly.

Greta's head jerked up a little, and she was awake.

"Miriam," Greta said.

Miriam smiled.

"Hey…how are you feeling?"

Greta was clearly in pain but said, "I'm okay. How are you?" At this she looked Miriam up and down.

Miriam took a step back and showed her all her bandages. "I have to get them changed already."

"Yes, I can see that. Are they painful?" Greta asked.

"Mostly it just pulls, you know? And I didn't get much sleep last night. But it's okay."

Greta tried to reach for some water that was on a little bedside tray. Miriam stepped in to help. Both were moving painfully slowly. A little laugh escaped Miriam's lips.

"Look at us. Like two infirm biddies!"

Greta frowned. "What is bides?" she asked, mispronouncing the word slowly.

"Biddies." Miriam smiled. "The Brits love this word. Silly old women." She smiled again with a bitter edge.

"So, tell me about Jakob."

Her friend's face darkened at that.

"He is like two rooms away, there." With some effort, Greta turned to her right side, pointing somewhere behind her.

"How is he doing? What have they told you?"

Greta sat up a little and made an effort to concentrate. "They said he had...wait...contusion?" She tapped her phone to turn it on.

"Did you make some notes? That's good."

Greta scrolled down her note. "Yes. Mild contusion." She looked up at Miriam. "But they say he may have some bleeding in his brain." She touched her temple. "So they need to do more tests and monitor. And maybe surgery. That's why they say he needs to go to a main hospital. A clinic is not enough."

"Oh, God. I'm so sorry." Miriam rubbed Greta's arm where she could, trying to comfort her. "How is he doing? Is he conscious?"

"I have not seen him in a while, but he was very strange. Like half-asleep, confused, you know?"

"Okay. And what's the deal with your insurance?"

"Okay. This is good. I was able to speak to Jakob's mother a few hours ago. I gave her the details and she is calling the insurance, so that should all be sorted. No one here asked me any more about it, so I think it's okay."

"Yes, that's good. How did she react to the news?"

"Well…you can imagine…she was telling me she wants to get on a plane to come help." Greta fidgeted with her phone, looking down. "But I know they don't have much money, and plus what is she going to do right now? Better that we get him to the hospital and see what the situation is, no? And we don't know which hospital anyway."

"I think you're right."

Miriam refilled Greta's glass and poured one for herself.

"Have you contacted your insurance?" Greta asked.

"Not yet. But if I remember correctly, what I paid is probably very close to my excess, so it may not make much sense to claim. When are they saying they want to move him?"

At this, Greta was a little teary. "Today." She shot a look back to where Jakob should be. "But they said they cannot take me with him. He has to go alone." She looked up into Miriam's eyes, a plea written clearly across her frown.

"Jesus. Why?"

"I don't know." Now the tears came. "I don't know."

"Hey, hey…" Miriam tried to hug Greta, but it was difficult with the plastered arm and various bandages, not to mention Miriam's own pain and discomfort. "It's going to be okay. Let me go and talk to them, see what's what. We'll straighten all this out and you'll both be well again in no time." She pulled away a little so she could look Greta straight in the eyes. "You hear me? No time." Greta nodded. "And here we thought the most interesting thing happening this week was that jellyfish sting, huh?" Miriam smiled at Greta, who half cried, half laughed.

Miriam went over to Jakob's room. It was darker than the one Greta was in but not hugely different. She had half expected to find Jakob in a high-tech bed surrounded by beeping machinery, like in TV shows, but she should have known better. There wasn't anything scary or different. Jakob was asleep (or unconscious), a bandage on one side of his head where, she assumed, he had injured himself. One of his hands was completely wrapped in a bandage and the rest of his body was covered by the clinic blanket. The room was positively freezing, the AC turned up as high as it would go.

She approached the bed, put her hand on Jakob's unbandaged hand.

"Hey, friend. How are you doing?" she said softly and a little unsteady, unsure of whether he could hear her. He didn't really respond. She kept her hand on his, then leaned closer.

"I saw Greta. She's fine. Don't you worry about her. Just some cuts and grazes—she's totally fine. I'll look after her. And you," she added for good measure.

"Everything will be all right, Jakob. Everything is fine. We're all here looking after you."

She remembered reading something about the brain hearing and absorbing what was being said even when the person was unconscious, so she was trying to send her friend some positive messages.

She felt a bit stupid and wracked her brain for more things to tell him but drew a total blank. Just then a nurse entered the room and said hello to Miriam with that little smile and bow of the head that Thais seemed to do a lot.

Miriam reciprocated the bow, then watched as the nurse checked Jakob's drip and bandage. She took out a little flashlight and gently tried to rouse him.

"Excuse me," the nurse said to Jakob in a soft but firm manner.

She moved his head slightly, then shone the flashlight first in one eye then the other. He groaned, trying to keep his eyelids shut, but his effort was feeble.

"What are you checking for?" Miriam asked, genuinely curious.

The nurse smiled at her. "We just check his pupils are normal."

"And are they?"

"Yes, everything is okay," the nurse said.

Jakob seemed to have just gone back to sleep instantaneously.

"Okay, thanks." The nurse scribbled a note on Jakob's chart. Just before she left the room, Miriam came to and stopped her.

"Excuse me. Can I speak to the doctor, please? The doctor that's looking after my friend?"

"Sure. Come with me to reception. *Kaa.*" The nurse bobbed her head again swiftly and left, expecting Miriam to follow.

They walked through the various corridors and stairs that made up the clinic, so that Miriam was lost—the nurse needed to drop something off in another room—until they arrived once again at Reception. The nurse directed Miriam to an empty side room.

"Please wait here," the nurse said, pointing to one of the chairs.

Miriam levered herself down to the chair and waited.

After a few moments, she took out her mobile and started scrolling through the other messages. Their other friends didn't know yet about the accident, so she decided to create a Facebook messenger group, including the TribeHutter's owner, Laila, to update them on the situation.

She kept it brief, stressing that she and Greta were okay, that Jakob being moved was only a precaution, and apologizing for having disappeared.

About one minute after sending it, she already got the first reply, a shocked "Oh, no!" from Laura. Miriam could see the moving dots icon below, meaning someone, maybe still Laura, was typing a new message. Just then the doctor walked in and said hello, so Miriam quickly shut off the screen and put her phone in her bag.

She made to get up and greet the doctor, but the surprisingly young woman motioned for Miriam to stay seated. "No, please, sit. I know you were injured, too."

Only now Miriam noticed that the doctor was carrying two steaming glasses of green tea, which she placed on the small table in the middle of the room.

"Did you have any questions?" With that, the doctor sat down across from Miriam.

"Yes, yes I do."

"Please." The woman motioned to the tea. Automatically Miriam reached for the glass but she only held it in her hands, without drinking.

The doctor took her drink, took a first sip and then cupped it, warming her hands.

"So, about my friend Jakob,"

The doctor smiled, encouraging.

"Can you tell me more about his condition?"

"Your friend sustained a brain contusion. This is likely just a bruise on his brain, which explains his drowsiness and mild unresponsiveness."

"Okay, but how serious is it?"

"Most bruises of this type are eventually reabsorbed and everything goes back to normal. In his case we have to check that there isn't any active bleeding going on. It could be very small so we need specialist machines to check. And we also must check if he has any more...damage than the bruise. For that also we need other machines we don't have here."

"So, where are you going to take him?"

"We think Amput hospital is the best option. It is not too far, and it is a very good hospital."

"And the insurance are on board?"

The doctor was puzzled.

"What do you mean?"

"The insurance are happy with you moving him there?"

"Yes, yes of course." The doctor seemed a little put out by this question and took another sip of her tea, which reminded Miriam that she was holding her own glass. She brought it to her lips but only wet them. She detested tea of all kinds, but she'd found that trying to explain why she was refusing something so integral to many cultures required more effort than she was happy to provide on a regular basis.

"Okay. And Greta?"

"She is well, considering. You are both very lucky."

"Yes." In the following silence, Miriam started replaying the accident in her mind.

"Nothing to worry about, she just needs to take care of the wounds. Like you."

"On that note, I need my dressings changed already." Miriam lifted the side of her maxi dress to show the leg bandages, already very stained.

"Oh, yes. Yes, definitely. I'll tell the nurse."

"But about Greta…can she not go with Jakob? They are together, and she wants to accompany him."

"In the ambulance? No, it's not possible."

"Why not?"

"You have seen our ambulance. It is very small and there is no room for two patients. Only one patient."

"Can you not arrange for a bigger one?"

"Bigger? There are no other ambulances on Tanu. Ours are some of the best."

"But...I don't know. Could she not go in the front seat, for example?"

"No, front seat is for the nurse that travels with the patient. So, you see, it isn't possible. And I don't think your friend would like to travel many hours now, with her injuries."

"How long will he be in Amput for?"

"We cannot say at this time. It depends what the tests find."

The doctor sipped the tea again.

"Can Greta not go in a normal car, following the ambulance?"

"Of course she can, but who's going to pay? The insurance covers only his medical transport. She is okay. It isn't necessary for her to be moved to another hospital."

Miriam waited. So as usual it was down to money. Stupid insurance, and stupid rules. It made her so angry.

"She's really upset at the idea of him going away by himself in this state!"

The doctor did not respond.

Miriam thought of all the times she had been told that in Thailand, if you look, you will find whatever it is you want. If you can pay. She took a deep breath.

"Could you, as a doctor, say she also needed to be transferred?" A beat, while Miriam's hands went to her purse, opening it. "That would be really helpful. If there was anything I could do...to help you do that—"

The doctor stood up. "Your aggressiveness is not welcome, miss."

Miriam was left open-mouthed. "But...I..."

"I told you what the situation is. You're not even a relative of the patient. Now excuse me…"

She turned around and left with a brisk step.

Dammit, trust Miriam to bungle trying to offer some money to lubricate an unfavorable situation! She'd heard stories of all types, from people falsifying medical records, police reports, rental agreements…and she couldn't even get this little thing done for Greta!

There was nothing for it. She would have to enlist the help of their friends. After all, out here in this untethered environment, they were each other's family, each other's safety net. She would see to it.

CHAPTER 27 - ADRIEN

Adrien woke to one of the worst hangovers he'd ever had. It was so bad he felt he couldn't even open his eyes. His mouth was a sticky version of the Sahara Desert, but the thumping headache won over the desire to get up and find water.

He snuggled slightly to get more comfortable, and that was when his eyes jolted open, and his head whipped up. He felt another body right next to him.

This sudden movement sent splinters into his brain, making him groan painfully. He held his head in his hand.

The body next to him started squirming, and memories now flashed in his mind: deejaying, fucking up, Dahlia, drinking, shots, the beach, Dahlia, smoking joints, walking down the beach, Dahlia pulling him close, kissing him and falling onto the sand.

"Oww!" This time he lay back and waited for the wave of nausea to pass. Slowly, he opened his eyes to get his bearings. Was he in his bungalow or hers? He looked around: the room was familiar, but something was off. Then he remembered—she was also staying at the same bungalows, and her room was a mirror image of his. How confusing for a sluggish brain.

His body was also sore, sandy and tired, but his head was really something. He was never, never going to drink and smoke again. Not ever.

Fuck! What time is it? He lifted his arm, slowly, until his wrist was above his eyes. His Apple Watch showed 8:19 a.m. Not too bad, thankfully. He put his arm over his eyes to get a breather...

And woke up with a start, again! Now the watch said 10:47 a.m. How was that possible? He started swearing, but it came out as unintelligible mumbling due to his extremely dry mouth. At the noise, Dahlia stirred, turned around and looked at him through half-closed eyes.

"You're still here?" she asked.

Adrien wasn't sure if it was a complaint or a surprised statement. Either way, it did not make him feel good.

He grunted assent, got up and started to rummage around the room for his clothes. He was still drunk and dizzy, and fell down with a thud.

"What the fuck, man. Can't you let me sleep?"

Okay, definitely a complaint, then.

"I...I just need some water," he said.

"Mm-hmm, in the fridge." Dahlia snuggled deeper under the covers and hid her face.

When Adrien finally opened the front door, his way was almost blocked by a big mass hanging directly outside.

"What the fuck...?" He saw that someone was curled up in the hammock, sleeping soundly. It took him a very long moment to remember that Dahlia had mentioned her brother arriving and staying with her. Adrien presumed this must be him, or otherwise it didn't make much sense. He shrugged and left.

Back in his own bungalow, Adrien drank more water, had a quick shower and fully intended to do some work, but his body had other ideas. Still wrapped in his towel, he lay down on the bed and could seemingly move no more. Sleep took him again.

Adrien was woken by the hungry growl in his belly. It shocked him to see it was dark outside. What time was it? The hunger turned into sickness when he thought about the whole day having been lost to…to what? Being hungover? Recovering? He berated himself for it. Another day gone when he could have been improving his app.

But then again…last night had been epic, truly. His DJ debut outside of Vancouver—even if he did mess it up toward the end—then hanging out with TribeHutters for once, chilling…and then, Dahlia…

He shook his head to try to focus again. He needed to chalk this up to experience, to life…but his sense of inadequacy was gnawing at him. He was already thirty, positively ancient compared to most of these innovative tech kids who were making a killing, or at least their name, in apps and start-ups.

He had come up with a good idea; he knew it. But he was making slow progress on it. The idea had just come to him one night when he realized he was struggling to keep up with new music releases, and that he was discovering tracks he should have discovered years before: an app that seamlessly curated your own personal playlist. Not based on user feedback on songs, but on an algorithm that analyzed your tastes in music (including YouTube videos and similar), how much you played a track or how often you skipped it, and other parameters. It could also learn from your moods depending on time of day or what you were doing, provided you gave it permission to "snoop" anonymously on most of your digital life.

He was at the make-or-break stage. He was trying to get his first fully functional prototype ready so he could crowd-fund the full development, but he was struggling with various aspects of the prototype. He had to hurry, or there was bound to be a similar product coming out any moment now. In this field, timing was everything. If he continued procrastinating, he would be very, very sorry.

The thing was...he didn't want to give up but was terrified of involving others in the project for various reasons: lack of trust; lack of self-confidence (as his inner gremlin liked to remind him every day—scratch that, every hour!); a very concrete fear that someone would fuck him over and steal the project, or even worse, that they would turn it into something different (as *Silicon Valley* had shown remarkably well for a comedy show). But probably, he reasoned, his main fear was down to his inability to communicate well what was in his head. It had always been so, and he didn't know what to do about it. Why hadn't anyone invented real telepathy yet?

He got up to look out the window, and as he did so, he remembered what he had seen on his first night here. It was only now that he realized it was Dahlia... It was late; she was coming back with a man. They were drunk, all over each other, kissing, stumbling inside... he guessed then that it was a normal thing for her, coming back home with a different guy from time to time. This hit him like a punch in the gut. But why should it? There was no sense in harboring any romantic feelings here, as she had made abundantly clear that she wasn't into that. Still...part of him had thought she had picked him specially, for his unique, quirky traits, and not just as a warm available body.

"Enough, Adrien! Out of your head!" he spat out loud, angry. He looked at the time: 10:40 p.m. *Shit. I am going to have trouble finding a decent meal at this time.* He grabbed his Kindle, money and scooter keys, and left. *Let's just end this day on a high note,* he thought, *let's get some filling late-night food and then I'll get up early tomorrow and crack on.*

CHAPTER 28 - ROSE

Rose was swaying gently on a hammock. Her head was too tender for anything more strenuous. She was wearing massive sunglasses, hiding her hangover eyes, and an open book was resting on her stomach.

She had been drifting in and out of sleep the whole day, but coming out here alone, to the north of the island where the beaches were less frequented, had been a great idea. She wasn't in the mood to see or talk to anyone. And this area of the island had a great spiritual vibe she loved.

A fresh coconut, now empty, was on the small driftwood table next to the hammock. She loved how you could make a day of it by simply ordering such a cheap and delicious thing and then use the facilities all day. This made her think of all the cocktails she had bought the previous night, and of how her bank balance was going to look later, but with effort she brushed that aside. *Can't do anything about that now.*

Rose leaned back and looked over to the sea, her feet framing the picture beautifully. As if by a miracle, a slight breeze was also stirring, and the hammock had been set up under a screen so she was in the shade. *It doesn't get more perfect than this.*

She picked up her book again. It was *Shantaram*. She had struggled to get into it. In truth, she wasn't a great reader but she tried her best. All her friends had been raving about it, so she had decided to give it a go. She started reading again but couldn't find her place, so she went back, one page, then two…had she read this part or had she left the book open at the wrong page? She ended up having to backtrack quite a bit to a place she could remember reading.

Just as she was finally back into the story, someone called out her name in surprise.

"Rose! I didn't know you were here!"

Oh, goody. Rose lowered her book in the slowest possible way, giving her face the time to prepare a decent smile.

"Oh, Laura. Hi," she said. Only now Rose remembered the two of them had made tentative plans to hang out today, to dissect the previous night's events. *Shit.* Rose hadn't even checked her phone at all. "Sorry, it was a last-minute thing. I am soooo hungover!" Rose said by way of apology.

"That's okay, I'm hungover, as well." Laura turned to two women next to her, and only now Rose clocked them. "Do you guys know each other? Rose, this is Dahlia and Liz. Girls, this is Rose."

Liz was a diminutive American girl, super smiley with red hair. And Dahlia…she already knew who Dahlia was, and now that Rose saw her in daylight, showing off her olive complexion and sexy, petite body in a bikini, her stomach clenched with jealousy, envy and shame. She flashed back to last night, to Martin. She thought Dahlia had had him all to herself, while Rose wasn't good enough for him. *Stop it. Get a hold of yourself.*

The three women all nodded and smiled.

"Yes. I mean, we haven't met officially, I don't think, but I've seen you at the Hut, right?" said Dahlia.

"Yes, sure. Nice to meet you." *So not nice. Did you have to crash my bliss?*

"Nice to meet you, too," said Liz.

Laura plonked her beach bag into the hammock next to Rose. "Sweet spot you got here!"

Inside, Rose groaned. Her bliss was gone. Laura was oblivious to having crashed it, but Dahlia seemed to sense something.

"You sure you don't want to be nearer the water, Laura?"

"Ach, with this sunburn?" Laura took her top off and Rose gasped. The silhouette of a dress was clearly imprinted on Laura's skin in a pattern of bright red and white stripes and swoops. Liz was quite shocked by it.

"Oh God, Laura…what did you do?"

"Well…what didn't I? Of course, forgetting sunscreen is the mistake number one, *ja*. And walking around in the sun also is not good."

"No kidding." This was Dahlia.

"Ah, well, it's done now. I just need to be careful."

When Laura turned, Rose could see a specific spot, high up on her shoulder, where the skin had peeled back and was so burned it was almost raw flesh. She winced inwardly. "Yes, Laura, please. You must be. Maybe even wear a T-shirt if you go swimming."

Laura turned her head to try to see where Rose was pointing.

"Is it that bad?"

Rose got up off the hammock. Her first step was a bit woozy, and she had to take a moment. She approached Laura to inspect the burn. It had a straight shape and it followed what Rose thought had been the dress strap. It appeared like a long wound, almost a whiplash. It was wet and oozing something, the innermost section of it an angry and live red.

"Did you put anything on this?"

"No…why?"

"Hang on a sec."

Rose went back to her bag—it was a huge beach bag as she never could travel light. She rummaged inside it for a while, pulling out various things like her sunglasses case, another book, a couple pots that were not what she was looking for… Finally, she found it! *I feel a little bit like Mary Poppins!*

She opened the little pot and dipped her finger into it.

"This will burn at first but then it will be very soothing."

Laura looked a little panicked. "What is it?"

"It's a great little cream for this kind of thing. Mostly aloe, but a couple other goodies in there. It should help a lot," Rose said as she applied the cream.

Laura winced a little. "Okay. Thank you."

"But, really, Laura. No sun for a while. You risk serious damage."

Dahlia and Liz exchanged a funny look at Rose's mothering tone. She noticed and smiled.

"I'm sorry. It's just that my mum is Australian. Sun protection was drilled into us from an early age. Nothing I can do about it."

"It's cool, actually. In Europe, when I was growing up, no one cared. In fact—" Dahlia just remembered "—they used tanning oil! Oh, my God! It was like basted turkeys everywhere!" They all laughed.

"And do you remember those, like, little panel folds? You opened them and they were mirrored on the inside, and you held them to your face to get a massive dose of sun on your face and neck?" asked Liz.

"Yes! Yes!" Dahlia was in hysterics.

"Jeez, those sound like they would have been outlawed in Australia!" said Rose as she put her little pot back in her bag.

"Fuck, those things were insane!" Dahlia reminisced. "I am glad I didn't get into all of that. I was lucky I didn't need it—" she gestured to her naturally warmer skin tone "—but that didn't stop my friends from being envious about it. Actually…" She started laughing again at a memory. "I had these two friends. We were what, twelve? Thirteen? They were both quite pale. One was Polish, the other French, and you know what? I really envied their pale, freckly faces! Dammit. But they loved my 'tan' and so they wanted to use bronzer or whatever." All three women were listening to Dahlia while getting more sunscreen on, drinking water or settling into the hammocks. "The problem was their mothers forbade them from wearing any makeup. So every morning, on the way to school, these two idiots would ask me to stand guard while they hid behind dumpsters to apply bronzer! Hilarious!" She continued laughing. "But wait… the best thing was that they only applied it to the face—" she used her fingers to contour her temples and jaw "—but not to the neck or hands!" She was almost crying with laughter here. "They looked ridiculous! And they thought that everyone believed they were tanned from going skiing! Jesus!"

Amongst the laughter, Laura sat up and made a move to get their attention. "Oh, by the way, have you heard about the accident?" she asked conspiratorially.

"What accident?" asked Liz, but Dahlia was already replying. "The German couple, right? What are their names?"

Rose tried to keep up as the girls pooled all the information they had about a scooter crash that had happened the day before.

The afternoon wore on in a really pleasant way. Rose had thought she would be bummed out, having her chill day gate-crashed by these women, but they turned out to be a lot of fun and they got her out of her funk. They swam; they napped; they talked; they walked along the beach. At one point they even had a short game of beach volleyball with some locals, though it was a bit too much for a recovery day.

As sunset approached, they were back in their hammocks, shooting the breeze with fresh juices in their hands—it had been decreed, unanimously, an alcohol-free day. Talk, inevitably, turned to the previous night's party. All the girls were eager to hear from Laura about her conquest. As per her designs, she had pulled the Irish guy she'd had her eye on. His name was Thomas, and she was gushing.

The girls hooted and trilled, and grilled Laura for all the juicy details down to penis size and type, techniques employed, number of orgasms, and minutes of sleep achieved. At first Laura turned bright red (almost matching her sunburn), but she clearly relished being the center of attention on this and really enjoyed telling them all about it. Of course, at the end of it, after a suitable pause, Liz leaned forward and asked, "Are you guys going to see each other again?"

Laura played coy and laughed. "Well…he has been texting already!" She held her phone toward them as proof. The girls let out an *oooh* sound unanimously.

"Well done, Laura!!" Dahlia congratulated her.

"Yeah, good job. Sounds like it was fun," echoed Liz.

Rose was feeling a little vulnerable, but still, she was happy her friend had scored, and with the guy she'd had her eye on, to boot! "Sounds amazing, Laura. I hope you do go out with him again." She winked. "Keep us posted."

"What about you girls?" Liz asked Rose and Dahlia with a conspiratorial air.

"Nah, nothing interesting for me," Rose rushed to blurt out. "How about you, Liz?"

Dahlia interrupted Liz's reply. "But wait, Rose, didn't I see you deep in conversation with a guy?" Rose's blood froze.

"Yes! I remember distinctly, before the raging drunkenness, that you were talking to someone...who was it?" Laura had to put her foot in it, as always. *No subtlety, that woman.*

"Oh, really, Rose? Who? You don't want to say?" Liz laughed.

"I think...I may be wrong but...wasn't it that German guy? What's his name? You know which one I mean, the tall one..." Dahlia teased.

"Martin! Yes, I got it! It was Martin!" Laura called out as if she had won a quiz show. Rose groaned inwardly.

"Ah, yes. Sure, I talked to him a bit." She took a sip of her juice. "But he's not really my type. He's soooo full of himself," she exaggerated the sentiment for comedic effect. "He could only really talk at me, if you know what I mean." *Please, please, stop asking me about him.*

"Oh, yes, I hate guys like that," concurred Liz, while Laura, sucking on her straw, just made a sound in agreement.

But Rose could see that Dahlia was watching her intently, not saying anything. Afraid that her emotions were going to show, Rose picked up her phone and got up. "I'm going to get some sunset snaps." She walked off toward the shore.

Why did they have to notice? She was trying to just forget about the whole thing, at least for today.

She zigzagged her way to the water, distracted by various shells and shapes in the sand. At least now it was possible to walk on the beach without burning the soles of your feet! As she got closer, more and more shells of all shapes and sizes appeared. Little translucent crabs scurried sideways away from her. A lone hermit crab was dragging itself away from the water, making slow progress. She watched it for a few seconds, noting the telltale claw print it left behind and seeing it repeated all over the beach.

Finally, she was at the water, her feet in. The sound of the sea was so soothing, especially when uninterrupted by human noise. There were no loud beach bars here, no boom boxes, no gaggles of loud teenagers. Just her and the sea, and a few birds flitting around.

The sun was still a ways off from setting, but already the sky was turning a light pink. A huge cloud formation to the right looked like a floating castle fortress, lit up from below. She breathed in the salt air.

She unlocked her phone with her fingerprint and went to tap the camera icon, but of course straight off she noticed the piled-up messages—Messenger, WhatsApp, Line and various messaging service icons—blinking at the top for her attention. Her finger hovered over the phone. She had avoided this all day, but now the spell was broken. Her mind was back on what had happened. And she had been having a good day, after all, so maybe she could deal with the world. She swiped down to get a look at all the unread messages.

She scanned the various headers. Most were unrelated messages, either from people back home or group conversations, but one thing drew her attention. On Facebook Messenger she had a request from someone who was not a contact. She tapped it.

The sharp intake of breath took her by surprise—the contact request was from Martin! *What the fuck?! Whatthefuck, whatthefuck, whatthefuckkkk?!?!?*

Without even thinking, she accepted the message request and opened the text.

 Hey Rose, hope your hangover is not as bad as mine. I wanted to apologize, and explain, about what happened last night. I understand if you tell me to fuck off, but I'd like a chance to tell you face to face. Please let me know if we can find some time today or in the next couple of days to do that. Thanks, Martin.

She re-read the message a couple times because her brain just wasn't computing it.

Apologize? Explain? She felt some kind of cold rage rising up inside her, mixed with shame. *Yeah, I'll definitely tell him to fuck off—who does he think he is?*

She shut off the phone again and tried to concentrate on the beautiful sunset in front of her.

CHAPTER 29 - DAHLIA

This beach day was turning out to be quite fun; although, Dahlia had very little patience for Laura and her astounding lack of subtleness. She could only take the woman in small doses. Laura was one of those people who never could read the signs when someone wanted to be alone, or just be quiet for a moment. She was the quintessential bull in a china shop. But today she was on okay form, and there were two other people acting as buffer, so it wasn't too bad.

Dahlia's hangover was finally receding, thanks to the plentiful hydration of juices and the electrolytes she had taken earlier that morning. And of course, lounging on a hammock at the beach really helped.

The irritation she had felt at Adrien's clumsiness had started her morning off on the wrong foot. Why couldn't he understand that she needed her sleep, alone? She wondered if she may have been too rude to him, but then again, she wasn't worried about it.

Rose, the woman she had seen being chatted up by Martin, was already at the beach when they arrived. Dahlia had been fully prepared not to like her. Dahlia had this instinctive competitive edge with other women, which usually only disappeared when they were clearly after different things/in different leagues, like with Laura. Rose though…she was obviously pretty, but somehow…not aware of it. Which by rights should have enraged Dahlia even more. But as soon as they started talking, she found Rose to be quite pleasant and fun. The afternoon was gliding on peacefully.

But of course, Laura had to show off about last night's conquest, as if Dahlia hadn't already had the whole story twice earlier on while they waited for Liz. So, she joined in with the conversation and made all the right noises when their friend was repeating the whole thing again, this time in technicolor, to impress the others. So now the Irish guy was a total stud, the whole thing was very romantic.

Dahlia's attention, though, was focused on Rose. She felt—no— she knew something had happened with Martin, and she wanted to ferret out what it was. Dahlia didn't know why she wanted to, maybe a little out of masochism, a little out of curiosity, and a lot out of competition. She wanted to see how she compared. And in addition, she had gotten the distinct feeling that Martin was one of those beautiful and damned souls, those guys whose behavior was just begging for someone (usually a woman) to "save" them. Dahlia found that very funny. Her father had played the very same card all his life, with her mother and others, so she was able to see right through it. But she was curious as to what effect this would have on Rose. For Dahlia, Martin was just another notch on her bedpost, albeit a gorgeous one, but Rose had an air about her of a little nurse, of Florence Nightingale, so she might fall for the whole act.

As Laura finally got to the end of her story, Liz inquired about Dahlia's and Rose's evenings in terms of romantic (or sexual) success. Rose dismissed it out of hand and asked Liz about hers. But Dahlia wasn't satisfied, so she threw out a little tease, something she was very good at, to get the others asking Rose again and get the truth out of her. None of them knew that Dahlia had hooked up with Martin some time ago, so she felt she could pretend some genuine curiosity about Rose's interaction with him.

She thought that it would not be hard to get Rose to open up and admit to sleeping with Martin (or whatever it was they'd done), but she was able to dodge the question by dissing Martin's behavior and gaining the other girls' sympathy. The conversation moved on, but Dahlia kept her eyes on Rose.

Rose must have sensed this, because soon she came up with an excuse to walk away and drop out of the whole thing. Laura and Liz twittered on about various gossip from the party, the various funny moments (they mentioned Adrien's deejaying fuckup but didn't clock that Dahlia had helped him after it), the music, the food and, of course, who had tried it on with whom, or snogged or fucked or whatever. The main piece of gossip was about Ricky Storm and some random girl having sex (apparently) in the ocean right in front of Vibe. Liz had been swimming in the same group and she swore she was sure they had been at it in the water. Ew! The girls concurred it was disgusting, but they were very curious as to the logistics of it.

Dahlia kept quiet about her and Adrien's night. She didn't at all mind people knowing, about this or any other partners, but she didn't broadcast her sex life. It had landed her in hot water before and she wasn't keen to repeat the experience. She was open about it if asked but would not go out of her way to share the information, especially with casual acquaintances.

Dahlia kept throwing glances toward Rose, who was now pacing back and forth along the shore, looking like she was having a phone conversation. Dahlia went back to the boring discussion that was now basically Liz and Laura comparing drunken sex stories. *That's never good to listen to!* She grabbed her phone and lay down in her hammock, isolating herself from the chat. She scrolled her Facebook, Twitter and Instagram feeds. She checked that Laura and Liz could not see her screen, then navigated to the TribeHut's internal membership and looked Adrien up. She read his profile and looked at his picture. *Truly, the picture doesn't do him justice! That cute nerdiness doesn't translate into pixels.* She wondered if he was thinking about her and about what happened. From what transpired between them, he was quite inexperienced, and goofy. He had been a little bit bewildered by her sexual assertiveness—she found that quite adorable. Usually, guys were very careful to sell themselves as sex gods, very experienced and completely detached from the proceedings. Adrien instead had been disarming. He couldn't hide his clumsiness, and at times, sheer terror. There was no mask, no pretense. Similarly, he could not hide his pleasure, his surprise and joy at it and at her willing body. It was almost childlike. This also worried her, because someone like that could very easily and quickly get attached, and that wasn't what she wanted. That was why she had been very clear with him and got him out of her place at first light.

She looked at Rose again, who was now sitting down by the shore. Dahlia decided to go and talk to her. The other two were still deep in conversation and they almost didn't notice Dahlia getting up and joining Rose.

Sunset was happening all around. From the initial pink, the light was now a bright yellow gold. Streaky clouds bordered the sky, looking like road markings pointing the way for the fishing boats that were setting out for their night trips. Rose was beautifully framed in this paradise view, her silhouette standing alone at the shore. Dahlia snapped a picture, then came and sat next to her.

Checking that Rose wasn't on a call, Dahlia turned and said, "Hi."

Rose turned and smiled at her.

"Gorgeous, isn't it?" said Dahlia turning back to face the sunset, the sun off to their left. Rose just made a sound that meant she agreed.

"You look great," Dahlia said, handing Rose the phone with the picture she had just taken.

"Wow." Rose was genuinely pleased. She handed the phone back to Dahlia, who put it back in her waterproof case.

"I'll send it to you."

Dahlia got up again and brushed the sand off her bum. "Actually, it's the perfect moment for a swim!" She almost ran into the water, joyous. She went in until it was almost impossible to run, and then she dived in. The water was warm, welcoming. She surfaced again and opened her eyes, the water running in them and stinging, but she kept them open without rubbing them, a habit she had learned from years of swimming training. She was facing the sun, and looking at this spectacle from the water line was even more glorious. There was NOTHING in front of her, no sign of humans, just the sun touching the horizon and shimmering.

Dahlia heard a splash, and in a couple of seconds Rose's head bobbed up next to hers.

"Swim further out?" Rose said. Dahlia nodded and the two of them started gliding forward, eyes still firmly on that setting sun.

Once they got far enough that they couldn't touch the bottom, they stopped and just floated there. The silence was just right, the whooshing of the ocean and the call of birds their only distraction. The light kept changing second by second, like God was playing with Photoshop.

When the sun was almost all in the water, Rose finally spoke. "Have you heard the thing about the green ray?"

"What thing?"

"They say that the last ray shining out of the setting sun, just before it is gone, is a single green ray."

"Really?" Dahlia was skeptical. "Have you ever seen it?"

"No. My friend who is into astronomy told me about it. Something to do with the refraction of light through the atmosphere."

The sun was plunging fast.

"Let's see if we can see it."

The two women watched intently. Rose put a hand in front of her face, shielding some of the sun's light. "Apparently this way you can see it better. Or with a camera."

And then it was done. The sun had set fully.

Dahlia turned to Rose, who was still intent on the scene, and splashed some water straight in her face.

"Hey!" Rose's head twisted away while Dahlia laughed like an idiot.

"Sorry, couldn't help it!"

Rose rubbed her eyes then, with a grin, splashed Dahlia right back.

A massive splash fight ensued, with the two of them laughing hysterically. The other two must have heard because soon both Laura and Liz were in the water, joining in.

CHAPTER 30 - MARTIN

Martin was at his favorite spot to relax and contemplate: a wooden hut built on a sheer cliff plunging into the sea, facing the setting sun. The perfect spot for a cooling drink after a long, hot day.

Of course, after the previous day, he was off the booze, so he had to content himself with a watermelon shake (no sugar), and a plate of spring rolls. The waiters knew him well, so they brought him little snacks, too. After the call with Hans, Martin had spent more time in his room, meditating, relaxing. Then he had a punishing midday Muay Thai session—he probably lost ten liters of sweat—followed by an afternoon dip in the sea below the bar he was now sitting at. On the side of the hut, there was a very rickety wooden stair that led down to a tiny beach nestled among the rocks. He had been alone on it and relished the quiet.

All the while, throughout the day, he had been rehearsing in his head what he'd decided he needed to tell Rose. He had gone over it again and again, changing, removing and adding things, rehearsing when and how he would do it. Would it be in person or via a message? Would he let her ask questions, speak, or would he just blurt it all out and leave? Would he ask to talk to her, or try to get her to one side at one of the many group outings? He had no idea. All he knew was that, for his own sanity, and out of respect to her, he had to do it. He typed a message to Rose but then thought better of it and stopped.

Hans had been crystal clear: this was a bad relapse, in terms of Martin's behavior. Now that he was on the right road, he needed to own up when he messed up. So, an apology and explanation to Rose were essential. He went back to the message. He deleted some of it, retyped it. Then deleted what he had just written. *The simpler the better*, he thought. He wrote just a few words and, before he could change his mind, hit Send.

Now, the issue of how he was going to apologize to and continue being around Rose was going to be tricky.

Sometimes the direct approach worked well; other times it created more problems. Also, he was a long-term resident of the Hut and so was she. They were going to be around each other for a while. Wait…he could also choose to leave…couldn't he? It hadn't occurred to him that he could just up sticks and go. But…but… he would still have to talk to her… Sure. *Otherwise Hans is going to have my hide for breakfast.* But he could do it and then go, so he wouldn't have to face her after that… Mm-hmm, this merited some more thinking.

The bar owner interrupted this train of thought, telling Martin he had just gotten a delivery of freshly caught lobster, if he wanted one. Martin was known for exactly this kind of extravagant ordering, to impress others or simply to go through the motions of "living the life." *Lobster is the kind of thing you order when money is no object, right?*

But today he had to decline politely. He thanked the man and nibbled on a spring roll while sunset put on its daily show.

"Hey," the female voice behind him made him turn around a little too quickly, his gut clenching, worried it may be Rose.

Miriam had just walked into the shack, all sweaty and looking a bit stressed. "Hey." He said back with relief.

Before he could invite her over or say anything, she gingerly approached the counter and half threw her bag onto it, then perched herself on the stool next to his ever so carefully.

"Please tell me that is alcohol," Miriam said as she shot a look at his innocent watermelon shake, which looked like a cocktail. "On second thought, it might be better if it wasn't."

With a flourish, she fished some tablets out of her bag and put them on the dark, polished counter. "I'm on these, so no alcohol for the moment."

Several bits of information finally coalesced into a full picture in Martin's mind: the way she walked, his eyes travelled to Miriam's bandaged arm and leg, and he understood. "Of course. The accident…I heard. How are you?" He sat up and leaned closer to her.

"Well, I've been better," she said a little dismissively. "But, to tell the truth, it could have been a lot worse. And it was worse, for poor Jakob."

"Oh, that's right. Was it both of them?" Martin recalled his impression of Jakob and Greta as a boring-looking, probably frigid couple. He remembered how he had thought he could show Greta a much better time. He pushed the thought out of his mind with an almost physical heave.

"Yes, so unlucky. Greta managed to get off mostly okay, though she did break her arm. But Jakob has a concussion. They will be driving him to the mainland for more tests."

"Shit. That sounds awful." For a moment, Martin froze, remembering the accident, all those years ago, shivering inside. Then he reviewed every single close call he'd had on his scooter, all those times he wasn't wearing a helmet, or was pissed or high when riding…and he thanked his lucky stars. He promised himself to never do that again. *But you swear the exact same thing EVERY SINGLE TIME there is a bad accident on the island.*

"So awful. I'm trying to get people to help with the transport. They only require Jakob to go to Amput, but Greta is not happy about him going alone. So, we have to pay for a separate car for her."

"Right. How much is it?"

"It's ten thousand baht."

"What?!"

"Yes, well, it's a few hours and it would be a private car. We can't send her in a minivan packed to the gills with a bunch of backpackers, can we?"

"No, of course not…" Martin tried to recover his composure. "But three hundred euros…that's basically the cost of a flight home."

"Don't I know it. But if we all pitch in, it won't be much." She shot Martin a sidelong glance.

One of the servers came, and Miriam ordered a drink as well, and some food. Then she got her phone out and scrolled through messages.

Martin resumed drinking his juice and nibbling his food. He pushed the plate toward her, telling her to help herself. Miriam thanked him and took a piece of spring roll.

"I wasn't saying about the money for you to donate, but you know…if you could…"

Martin started mumbling something, but Miriam continued.

"We're already at seven thousand, so we're not far off, but we need to act quickly. I would just pay it all myself if I had it right now. But I—"

"No, no, it's not that, Miriam. I do want to help. Problem is I just paid my scooter rent, so I only have a little on me and can't withdraw—"

They continued interrupting each other for a few seconds. It looked like a poor British comedy of manners. After a short pause, they both burst out laughing.

"It's okay, really. Whatever you can give…it'll be appreciated."

Martin smiled, but inside, he was worried. His fame preceded him and, to be fair, he had boasted for years about making lots of money and doing it easily. Now that he had fallen on harder times, he found it very difficult to admit to it.

"Sure, sure. Here," he said, opening his wallet, "I can do five hundred baht right now."

"Thanks." Miriam took the money and started making a note on her phone.

"And let me know how things go later, I may be able to do more." *Why are you saying this, stupid man? Shut up!* He could have just gotten away with the five hundred, but now looking at Miriam's lit smile, he knew she'd take him up on it. Idiot. His tongue had always worked faster than his brain.

CHAPTER 31 - MIRIAM

Miriam needed to collect her thoughts and try to scrape together the last bits of money needed to send Greta to Amput. Due to her own injuries, she could not swim or sunbathe, so she decided to go to the only place where she knew she could relax—the cliff hut. Even just getting there was an undertaking. She had had to get another scooter—there was no way to get around the island easily without one—but she was still badly shaken by the accident. When she got it from her trusted renter, she wobbled along at first, trying to get a feel for the different bike. She was so stiff her entire neck and shoulders ached with the tension. She kept looking back to her blind spot and driving very slowly, lest something bad happened again. After a few minutes, she achieved a modicum of peace of mind—no, just a lower state of agitation—and made her way west. Of course, wherever she went, she was bound to run into someone she knew. It turned out to be Martin, which was okay. She had pegged him as someone who knew to mind his own business when called for, and who knew when to interact and have fun.

She had sat down next to him and only later it dawned on her that he may have wanted some peace and quiet himself. But by then it was too late, and they were already in full flow.

He let her recount the whole scooter accident, which she realized she hadn't really processed. She let him see how scared and shocked she'd been, even when she was taking charge of the situation, having realized Greta and Jakob were seriously hurt. It felt good to get it out. Martin didn't say much; he nodded and murmured at all the right places, asking the occasional clarifying question. He told her how he, too, had been in a pretty bad car crash when he was in his teens, and about the effects that had had on him—the flashbacks, the cold sweats and stomach clenches when he thought something was going to crash into him. To this day, he had never driven a car nor gotten his license. She thought he was shaken, remembering how he felt, but at the end he seemed to be glad he was here now, able to drive a scooter and get around.

"I suppose that's why I have never really left Berlin. You don't need a car!" He laughed.

"Yeah, I feel the same about scooters. I'll be glad when I don't need to drive another one."

"Well, you're in the wrong place for that," he mused.

Miriam, unfortunately for her, agreed. Koh Tanu was perfect in almost every sense, but the scooter thing… She had tried walking, cycling and tuk-tuking, but they simply did not give you the freedom, the flexibility, to explore the island as you'd want. Not to mention it would make it really hard, logistically speaking, to have any hookups.

Her food arrived and she attacked it with relish. She hadn't really had a proper meal in the last couple days. Penang curry with chicken, and steamed rice was one of her favorite dishes. She first ate one of the cucumber slices that accompanied every single Thai meal. The freshness and sharpness of it cleansed her palate, readying it for the blossoming of herbal flavors the curry would bring. And the chili heat. She had asked for *pet pet*, very spicy, but she knew that, as a *farang*, the Thais would still not make it as hot as they would have it themselves. Which, on balance, was probably okay. She had grown up eating super hot food. Habaneros were the order of the day in her Mexican household, but Asian chilies were fired by a different kind of heat, not to mention that spending twenty years in Europe had reduced her heat tolerance by a significant margin.

Martin was telling her about his Muay Thai training, which she found intensely boring, but he seemed very into it. She was glad she had been able to wheedle some money out of him. He could be so stingy! And apparently, he wasn't doing badly, so she really couldn't understand what all the fuss was about. She was living month to month most of the time, so these kinds of unexpected big expenses, like helping a friend with medical costs, were really a problem. She'd already had to pay around $250 for her own treatment. Sure, her insurance would reimburse most of that, but her premium would go up, and in any case, she'd had to fork it out immediately, so she was unable to pay for Greta's car.

Her phone pinged. She got a message from Laura, saying she was in for three hundred baht—she was after all working as a host on a work experience basis—and her Irish friend (no idea who that was) was in for another two hundred. That was an extra five hundred baht. With Martin's five hundred, all they now needed was two thousand baht. She had about three hours to scrape it together.

Eating good food was having a great effect on Miriam. For the first time since the accident, she felt a little more relaxed and able to concentrate. She looked out onto the sea. Koh Mek, the island of clouds, was to the far right, and there was only a small, isolated islet right in front, but it was still so far that she could not make out its features. She had been told there was great diving to be had there. She would have to take people's word for it. There was no way in hell she would ever dive. She was a very basic swimmer and was actually quite fearful of the ocean and its unseen dangers. Greta's jellyfish sting the other day had been the perfect case in point. She would not swim where she could not touch the bottom, so all snorkeling trips had been out of the question for her.

"Hey, can I run something by you?" Martin's voice reminded her she was not alone.

"Sure," she mumbled through a mouthful of curry.

"I…well…" All of a sudden, Martin seemed very unsure of himself. This different side to him caught her completely off guard. He shot a glance at her and, out of kindness, Miriam turned her eyes back to her food, and forked a new mouthful.

"I'm not sure how I can put this. I just…I guess I am after a female point of view?" he said, the tone of his voice doubtful.

"Okay. Shoot."

"So…let's see if I can put this in a way that makes sense…"

His hands kept playing with the cutlery, plate and glass in front of him, endlessly rearranging them, squaring them against each other, wiping droplets of condensation off the wood. He took a breath and now turned to look at her.

"Let's say you meet a guy at a social event, you like him, he appears to like you. You drink, you talk, you flirt. Crazy flirt. All night long. He does not move on to other people, and neither do you."

"Okay. I don't know this guy?"

"No. You've just met him."

"Go on." Another mouthful of curry went in.

"It is obvious to both of you where the night is going."

"It is?" Miriam looked at Martin with a puzzled expression, and after a second she broke into a grin and laughed. "Just kidding. Sure, we know where this is going."

Martin pulled his face into a semblance of a smile.

"So, at some point, the guy—who until that moment seemed into you and all that—gets up and, with an excuse, walks away."

"He just goes, doesn't tell me to follow?"

"No. He just goes."

"Mm-hmm. Ooookay."

Martin looked at Miriam as if waiting for her to continue, but she just shrugged.

"How would that make you feel?"

"Honestly?" Miriam took a swig. "Royally pissed off. There's nothing I hate more than a pussy-tease."

Martin almost spat out his own drink. "A what?" he managed through laughter and wiping his mouth.

Miriam enjoyed watching his reaction. "A pussy-tease. You know, the female version of a prick-tease." She stuck her tongue out at him briefly.

"Wow…well…I didn't know women also felt that way…"

"Another lie peddled by the hated patriarchy, my dear. Anyone who tells you women don't enjoy sex as much as men, he has no idea what he's talking about. Or he's lying."

Martin' eyebrows shot up.

"Granted, women and men probably don't enjoy sex in the same way. However, the intensity, desire, enjoyment and longing for it…I would argue they are similar. We just sublimate them in different ways."

Martin seemed to digest this a bit. She watched intently, almost seeing the cogs turning in his brain.

"I guess…I guess I'd never thought of it this way."

Miriam's phone pinged. Laila had agreed to contribute some money. Miriam's heart was instantly lighter. She scrolled through the message and… She wanted to contribute two thousand baht! That was fabulous! They now had the money to help Greta!

Miriam started putting her things in her bag. "Another time you'll tell me what other ways you'd thought about it. It'll be fun to find out. Deal?"

Martin smiled. "Deal."

"I have to shoot off. I managed to get the money, so I have to collect it and go pay the driver. AND…I have to do it all while driving super slow." She left some money on the counter; it would cover her meal. "Enjoy the rest of your evening, my dear," and she rushed off to her new scooter.

CHAPTER 32 - ADRIEN

Sleep had eluded Adrien. He had ended up at 7-Eleven, gorging on hot toasties, which seemed to be the budget traveler's food of choice. The amount of plastic they came in was bewildering. There was a clear plastic tray in which the toasty sat, then it was wrapped in a plastic bag. After you paid, one of the cashiers deftly opened the bag and put the toastie on their industrial-grade toaster. As soon as it was hot (under a minute, Adrien calculated), using tongs they would slide the atomic-hot item into a cardboard sleeve, and then that went into a small plastic bag. This would be repeated for every toastie even if you bought ten (some people did). And immediately outside the 7-Eleven you would scarf this marvel of modern food processing and chuck all its attendant packaging in the bin. Jesus.

He grabbed some chocolate soy milk for good measure, a one-liter carton, and went back home. He tried to read himself to sleep, but somehow it would not come. Maybe he had slept too much during the day, despite the hangover. Reading usually did the trick, but he kept tossing and turning. Ideas, to-do lists and similar things were flying through his mind. He looked at his watch again. It was 1:00 a.m. and he was wide-awake. He got up, got dressed again, grabbed his laptop and left.

As he approached the TribeHut at that hour, the whole thing looked spooky. There were no scooters parked outside, which meant he would be on his own. The front entrance was dark, but he felt things scuttling about (the cat, or roaches or other critters—who knew?), and that made him nervous. He turned on the light of his iPhone and used it as a torch. It seemed to him that there was movement around the edges of the light. He hurried to the door. It was locked with a keypad. Damn, what was the code? In order to look it up he had to use the phone, which meant casting the light down.

He scrolled through messages to find the welcome email from the TribeHut. Welcome… Food… AC… Meeting rooms… Quiet room… *Yeah, yeah, where is the door code?* Updated code of conduct… Community Slack channel… Yes! There it was! He punched it in and the door beeped loudly—no good.

"What the…?"

Adrien looked at the email again, read the code, he tried it again. *BEEP*. No joy.

"Fuck."

This time, when he looked down, his gaze focused on the floor around his feet, illuminated by the phone light. He saw for the first time that the whole area was covered in slimy slugs and snails. They were all around his feet! A wave of disgust engulfed him. He quickly looked at the damned code again, then punched it in slowly, one by one, looking at the phone at every step. He didn't dare lift his feet for fear of stepping over a snail. The crunching sound they made was just… *No, don't think about it!*

He pressed Enter for the third time and the door gave a more benevolent *beep-beep* sound and clicked open.

"Thank fuck!"

He shoved the door open, took one very long step so as not to tread on any dark steps where snails may lurk, and he was in. He pushed the door closed and waited till the automated mechanism locked it again. He breathed a sigh of relief.

He went to the side and turned the light on. He could not understand why, if it was a twenty-four-hour place, there wasn't a single light left on.

He turned right into the room that he used most days. It smelled bad in there. But then again, the door had been left closed and the AC off. He turned the light on, then the AC and also the fan for good measure. It felt a little gloomy to be here, in this now bright box, against the pitch-black outside.

Adrien picked his favorite spot, which was facing the door, and made himself comfortable.

Strangely, contrary to what he would do every day (opening Facebook and Slack, faffing about on various news sites, reading blogs and the like), all he did was open his work and set to it, all within minutes of sitting down. He didn't even need his headphones and music on.

The peace and quiet was total.

After a while, he became acutely aware of the sound of his own typing and clicking. He smiled.

He got up and walked to the kitchen, all the while stepping lightly as the whole way there was dark. In the kitchen he refilled his water canteen and stood there drinking. The kitchen was an outdoor one, so he listened for a while to the sounds of the surrounding jungle. He could not make anything out other than the now familiar birdlike call of the small geckos. Everything else was unknown and, in his mind, could belong to anything from a tiny insect to a monstrous monitor lizard. Of course, the worst stuff you never heard. Like snakes...

At the thought of that, he ran back to the safety of the AC room and resumed his work.

He was awakened suddenly by a sharp, hot pain in his leg. *Fuck!*

His hand automatically went down to his calf to swat away whatever it was, and he felt something furry and winged. He recoiled quickly. He hadn't even realized he had fallen asleep at the desk!

He looked down and saw a slow-moving insect near his foot. He pushed back on the wheeled chair to get away from it. His leg was painfully hot and sore. He looked at where the pain was, and a lump could be seen clearly puffing up, red. He could see the pinhead prick at the center.

He looked again at the agonizing insect. It was some kind of wasp or hornet or something. It was now writhing on the floor, but he wasn't sure why. Had he hit it that hard? Or…he remembered reading somewhere that if they stung, these creatures would die. Yes! *Take that, you fucking pain monster!*

He got up, trying to walk the pain off. Then he thought maybe he should try to get the stinger out of his leg. He sat back down, grabbed his phone. First of all, he took a picture of the wasp on the floor, then of the sting itself. Finally, he turned on the torch and examined it carefully. Slowly, he approached with his pinched fingers, but the stinger was too short and fine for them to grab. Finally, he went in using only the tips of his fingers, nails out, and managed to grab it. Pulling it out was painful, but he hoped he was avoiding at least some of the poison this way.

He wrapped the stinger in some tissues, thankfully there were always little boxes of toilet-paper-like tissues dotted around the space. This was what Thai people use instead of napkins. He balled it, then dabbed his wound, which was seeping a tiny bit. Finally, he threw the ball in the trash.

He checked the time and it was 3:00 a.m. He clearly needed real sleep, so he packed his things up. The wasp had finally stopped moving. As he walked out of the door, a sudden movement froze him in place.

"What the—" It was another wasp! Adrien ducked and dodged. But now, in the dim light of the lobby, he could see more than one insect flying around. Shit! There was probably a nest somewhere in the wood of the building. Then, ping, he felt something small bump into his chest, looked down and saw another wasp, a little dizzy, buzz around him. The more he looked around, the more wasps he could see literally coming out of the woodwork. Another one flew right into him: that was his cue to leg it back to the bungalow. He would notify the staff the next day, but he imagined they would find the wasps themselves, come morning.

In the quiet of his room, Adrien showered and got himself ready to sleep. He was mulling over all the recent events. He felt simultaneously that he had made huge strides in his personal life, but also that he had started on completely the wrong foot and didn't have much to show for his arrival in Thailand. He had hoped to start with a bang, and he hadn't succeeded. He sat down and did some meditation and focusing exercises that he had learned long ago. He tried to picture in his mind the goal he wanted to achieve in the long term, and how it was made up of small, infinitesimal incremental steps. And he then concluded by keeping the next tiny step firmly at the forefront of his mind.

He finally lay down and drifted off to sleep, his heart heavy with anticipation and excitement.

When a super loud rooster crow jolted him awake at 6:30 a.m. though, all he could think of was that he needed more sleep, and his leg was throbbing.

PART IV

Island Life

CHAPTER 33 - JEROME

Jerome felt like he had been let in on a big, huge secret. Since arriving on the island he had been surrounded by all sorts of people, of all ages and nationalities (though mainly "first world" ones, or hybrid), and a smattering of different sexual orientations and races, doing a huge variety of digital jobs, almost completely untethered to "normal" office hours, dress codes and rules. Almost. Because some of them still had to pretend, to clients or bosses, that they were somewhere else—somewhere not so exotic, beautiful or warm—or that they were at home or in the same time zone as them. Some people, he had found out, hadn't even told their companies that they weren't home/in their usual place, so had to keep European or US office hours. Other than that, these people were utterly, intoxicatingly, bewilderingly free. He had only experienced something similar when hanging out with the independently wealthy. These digital nomads could certainly not be called wealthy—there were even some who, by most standards, would be considered quite poor—but they seemed to possess that same "why not?" attitude that many rich people had.

If a woman wanted to become a life coach and ditch the normal day job she had? *Why not?* If a guy wanted to become a fitness influencer and travel the globe for Instagram-worthy shots? *Why not?* If people wanted to step away from work and grab a coffee on a beach a twenty-minute ride away, then spend time talking about random, interesting stuff? *Then why the hell not?*

Every day while working with Dahlia at the TribeHut, Jerome had this little personal challenge of saying yes to at least one random request, and that is how he found himself getting to know the island, various digital nomads and also some locals. Work could be put aside at the drop of a hat—much to Dahlia's chagrin and veiled daggers she would shoot at him—and so he did exactly that, getting onto the scooter and following someone who knew a secret beach, café, bar, sunset spot, monkey-grazing area, fishing location or whatnot.

This is how he became notorious quite quickly around the island. This…and going out to the bars every night. Dahlia always marveled at his ability to survive with very little sleep, but he had never really needed it and could fall asleep whenever, wherever.

Only now that he was being asked to use his skills in different ways, and to concentrate on learning and applying new things, had he started to notice how he could focus on something for only twenty or thirty minutes at a time, really. After that the words started to meander across the screen and blur his vision, until he had to stop. He did not like this at all and had no intention of checking to see if slowing down on the partying, drinking, and so on would have a positive effect. *No sir!*

He had always thought he had to make the most of whatever situation he found himself in, and this was no different. The only difference was that here, these temptations, these opportunities, were on a repeating loop, with the constant arrival of new people. For him, the only factor that could influence his response was money—he was still desperately strapped for cash and Dahlia only threw him some scraps—which he hated, although as always he was very adept at spending very little and at getting other people to pay for him. Not maliciously, of course, just through his charms and their wanting to spend more time with him.

A couple times he'd had words with Dahlia about it. He couldn't understand why she was always worried about work, working long hours and having a go at him for not working hard enough, and she said she didn't understand how he could not be worried about where he was going, how he was going to live, and so on and so forth. Their sharing a room was also starting to take its toll, as it was hard to take a break from each other, so Jerome attempted as much as possible to spend nights and time away from the TribeHut bungalows. He'd had various hookups and had even gone looking for the Aussie boy from the ferry, the divemaster—who had turned out to be depressingly and firmly heterosexual. Jerome had recently started to see one boy in particular, a Thai barman, who seemed completely besotted with him. As Thaim shared a little house with an understanding friend, Jerome could actually spend the night there whenever he wanted, and this gave him and Dahlia some breathing room.

He and Thaim had met one night when he had followed some TribeHutters. After a nice dinner (he still needed to eat) and some beachside beers, Serge, a long-term resident of the Hut, had mentioned that that night there was going to be a big local party at a jungle venue, somewhere that tourists never went to.

Jerome's ears, and those of the people all around, pricked up at this. Everyone was always after exclusive, unique, nontouristy experiences that would make their trips more authentic, less curated. And so, without asking many questions, they had all gotten onto their scooters and driven about half an hour through the jungle and island, up and down roads, whizzing by little wooden shacks and stray dogs (one of the scooters almost crashed while trying to avoid a dog that had been sleeping bang in the middle of the road!), until they arrived at a clearing in the jungle in front of a large, low building.

Jerome could hear no music and was wondering if Serge had gotten his wires crossed. But the clearing was clearly a car park and it was almost full of scooters and pickup trucks. They walked up to the door, and only then did Jerome see a couple of bouncers emerging from the gloom. The men flashed their torches at them but as soon as they realized they were a group of *farangs*, they waved them in without further ado. As the big door swung open, a wall of sound hit them. They stepped into the darkness and around a corner and found themselves in a huge space, more akin to a concert hall than a club. It was all painted black, with a stage all along one side where a band was busy rocking out and whipping up the audience. Jerome tried to guess what tune they were playing; it was familiar to him, but he couldn't place it. He tried to listen to the lyrics but no luck.

All around them, the floor was full almost to bursting with young Thai people, some sitting on stools along long tables, some standing and dancing by the stage, most of them smoking and drinking out of the ubiquitous plastic buckets loaded with handfuls of straws. The temperature was positively chilling in there, with huge AC units every few paces and tons of fans whirling from all corners. The audience was suitably dressed up with closed shoes and long-sleeved tops, something so incongruous with island life that Jerome was hit by a very weird feeling of having been transported somewhere entirely different than a tropical island. He and the other Hutters were dressed in their regulation uniform of vests, shorts and flip-flops, and therefore were woefully underdressed compared to the vast majority of punters.

Just as Jerome was getting his bearings, Serge tugged at his arm and pointed to the stage. One of the singers on stage—there seemed to be two—was pointing at them, their group, and speaking in Thai. No clue about what he was saying, but now the eyes of the entire venue were upon them. He could not see any faces that were not Thai. The Hutters giggled uncomfortably and then a waitress, tottering on vertiginous heels and wearing skimpy hotpants, came to usher them to a table right by the stage, which was hastily cleared for them by shoving some locals onto another table.

They struggled to order; the lighting was poor so they could hardly see the menu, which they later realized was quite expensive for the island, and someone wondered aloud whether they had been given the tourist menu. The music was also so loud that everything had to be done with hand gestures. Almost everyone around Jerome lit up a cigarette. This seemed to be something that Westerners loved—smoking had become such a pariah activity in the West, and here in Thailand you could smoke almost anywhere. And at such dirt-cheap prices, even many nonsmokers took the chance to enjoy this novel situation. From the tables around them, many people were watching them intently, smiling, laughing. The song being played ended and people went a bit crazy clapping and cheering. When the next song started, Jerome recognized it immediately: it was "Zombie" by the Cranberries. Except…except these weren't the right words! What the hell was going on? Then the penny finally dropped: they were singing in Thai! Jerome laughed to himself and started to sing along with the tune, but in English.

A few hours later, well sozzled on beer and occasional sips of Sang-som and Coke from strangers' buckets, Jerome was dancing by the stage, mock head-banging, when Thaim approached him and put a drink in his hand. Jerome smiled and danced with him, until, at the end of the night, they drove (shakily, slowly, dangerously) back to Thaim's place. And that was it. Now the other TribeHutters mocked him gently about being a househusband, about getting serious about getting a Thai visa through marriage, about no more fucking around with other boys on nights out. Of course, none of this actually was remotely close to the truth, but Jerome went along for the giggles and did his own thing anyway. Thaim was not possessive. He was young and had already had one serious boyfriend he had introduced to his parents, so dating Jerome openly was not a big deal. He was actually interested in who Jerome liked and why, so Jerome was half expecting, at some point soon, that Thaim would broach the subject of a threesome. Or that he would simply initiate one.

Talking with Serge, who was also gay, Jerome had realized how unusual his relationship with Thaim was. Usually, the foreign half of the couple was the one with money and status, and the Thai half was considered "fortunate" to be chosen; there was an implied power imbalance and transaction going on in most Thai-foreigner relationships, but in their case it was actually reversed. Jerome was the low-earning, unreliable fuckup who liked others to take care of him, and Thaim was the well-adjusted, decent earner and spoiler of the two. It worked like a charm. Now the only thing that Jerome had to improve was his situation with Dahlia and work. He felt he had talent for this online marketing malarkey, but no patience whatsoever, and so he wavered on a daily basis on whether to stick with it or try something else. But Dahlia wouldn't let him quit. He was going to have to find a solution.

CHAPTER 34 - MIRIAM

Island life had its own kind of rhythm.

Mondays were usually beach BBQ's at Tom's, an expat place on the east coast of the island—he often had line-caught fresh fish and delicious side dishes, plus discounted beer and wine, making it a nice, low-key evening.

On Tuesdays, Miriam often went to the north side of Tanu, where there was a kind of open air spa—a sweat tent, an open fire, massage areas, meditation and flotation pools. She would get a nice scrub and massage followed by chilling out with similar, like-minded people; sometimes they even played live music and she sang along.

Wednesdays was usually a Tribe day, there would be a community event of some sort, like lunch or dinner, or drinks by the beach, a karaoke night, a networking event, a movie night—it was nice because it was the kind of night that, if she was overworked or just had had enough social interaction, she could easily do on autopilot.

On Thursdays, expats and long-term residents met at the island's oldest bar, Porn—yeah, the name had made her guffaw at the start, but in Thailand it was a legit name—a wooden construction on stilts over the water, near the ferry port. The place itself wasn't anything special, but Porn's warm welcome and friendliness was a balm for these travelling souls, and plus you could bet on running into friends there, so it would be super chill and devoid of the dreaded travelling-small-talk tunnel she sometimes got stuck in at Tribe events. And Porn's delicious cocktails surely helped.

Friday was usually a party night; most people would want to let their hair down after the working week, so the Tribe chose a place on rotation depending on what DJ was playing, and who was in the mood for what. At least once a month the chosen place would be Vibe, handy for Miriam because she lived just nearby, but also a kind of obvious spot where you were bound to be surrounded by lots of people you knew.

On Saturdays, Miriam would usually tag along on small group outings: a beach trip, a ride around the island, a jungle or hill trek, a cooking class, a batik class, a meditation workshop high in the jungle, a botanical walk, a quad-bike ride around the island, a zip-line adventure… Really, there was so much to do on the island that she never got bored.

But Sunday…Sunday was her absolute favorite, and she didn't follow anyone else's plans. She would sleep in (bliss!), then go for a super long Yin yoga session—oh, how she needed that stretching!—followed by a relaxed brunch, which sometimes turned into a board game session with Greta and Jakob. Or, they would drive inland to the secret jungle café for brownies and spliffs. Finally, around 4:00 p.m., Miriam would go wherever the Trash Hero clean-up event was happening. The island was big and had lots of beaches, plus the sea currents changed at different times of the year, and so there was always a patch of beach that needed cleaning up, as it had become choked by garbage, mostly plastic. The Trash Hero people provided sacks, gloves and even tongs for picking up various bits of rubbish, and usually a nice group of people turned up to help out. It made Miriam feel good to do this, to have a visible effect on her environment and to feel like she was, in small measure, giving something back to this place she loved so much.

Sometimes it was gross, truly. Debris would get lodged under the shallow roots of beachside trees, and digging them out took all her willpower. Not to mention the fact that at any moment, a spider or other beastie could crawl out from wherever she was rummaging. She did not do well with spiders. And the gamut of items washed up by the sea was truly staggering: from your usual bottles and cans to shoes of all types, fishing equipment, polystyrene containers, lighters, fireworks (or remnants of), toys, scooter tires and thousands and thousands of bits of plastic. It made her sad to see what humans (herself included) were doing to the planet, and this small contribution at least helped her feel less doom and gloom about it all. Often there would also be whole families joining in, both foreign and locals, and the whole thing became a bit of a party. A sweaty, hard-working party, to be sure, but it was fun.

As every other Sunday, she advertised the clean-up event on the Tribe community channels. Sometimes no one would join her, but usually someone would. This time Adrien had said he'd join her and the two of them met for an iced coffee just before. She had been enjoying getting to know Adrien. Their fields of expertise were so far apart that they never ended up having a boring work conversation; instead, they usually talked big ideas and worldly stuff. Plus, they shared this second generation, almost third culture kid identity, albeit in very different ways, and it was refreshing to be able to discuss these things with someone similar. The vast majority of travelers she had met were white and Western, and so there weren't many chances of having these kinds of open conversations around shared experiences.

Adrien was complaining, with a smile on his face, about constantly being mistaken for Thai here.

"Every time I walk into a place, off they go, rattling off in Thai, without waiting for me." He laughed. "I try to walk in already speaking in English, but it's no use. Even after a few tries, they still can't believe I don't speak Thai. The height though, that freaks them out even more!" He was tall indeed; even Miriam felt tall in Southeast Asia, and she was of mid to low height. She had never been considered tall in her life until she came here.

"With me it's weird. They can tell I am a foreigner, but they are really not sure what to make of me, with my skin," she mused. "Sometimes they treat me full-on *farang*, especially if I'm with other tourists. Other times they eye me up suspiciously and kind of freeze."

She had seen very few black, brown or Latin foreigners here, so she was a bit of a novelty. And in Asia they seemed to be obsessed with lightening their skin, women especially. They would never sunbathe, which she loved, and they constantly applied sunscreen and white make-up. Meanwhile, in the West, people were paying to go to tanning salons and applied dark foundation. What a mindfuck.

"And when I say I am American, their eyes go as wide as saucers! They don't believe me. Then I add, my parents are from Mexico, and they go all, 'Aaaaaah,' and their mental world order is restored." She chuckled.

"Hey, by the way, is it time to go?" Adrien looked at his phone.

"What's the time?"

"Just gone four."

"Shit. Let's make a move."

They had tried to stay together during the clean-up. You had to carry three different bags in your hand, as garbage had to be sorted according to the way it could be recycled. General plastic in one bag, nonrecyclables in another bag, polystyrene in a third bag. Glass, which they found a little of, could be dropped off in a big bucket by the staging post. Apparently, it was quite complicated to recycle glass on the island, and so sometimes buying a plastic bottle was better than glass, because it could be recycled. Insane.

Adrien worked beside her and often asked Miriam "Is this one recyclable or not?" when picking up a hard-to-define item of rubbish. She helped him along. Today the sky was crystal clear and the sun was beating down on them, so Miriam tried to work from every little bit of shade she could find. She was dripping with sweat.

She heard a big roar behind her, coming from the water. She stopped and turned to watch. A huge speedboat was coming in, probably to drop people off who had been on a snorkeling trip. The water was that clear green she had come to love dearly, even where the engines churned up the sand, turning the sea a strange color like English tea. Adrien had also stopped to look at the newcomers. "Wouldn't mind a dip myself. It's so hot, right?" She motioned toward the sea. His reply was an unintelligible grunt.

Just as she turned back to resume garbage picking, out of the corner of her eye she saw a sudden movement. She turned back just as Adrien was collapsing to the sand. "Adrien!" She rushed to him.

He was sprawled down, sand all over, but was already coming to. "What…?" he was mumbling.

"Hey, darling. I think you fainted. You okay?" She lifted his head up a little. "Let me get you some water." She opened her bag and got her canteen out.

Just then, a couple of the other volunteers, alerted by her shout, arrived to help.

"Hey, what's going on? Is he okay?" asked one.

"I think it's just the heat," said Miriam as she gave Adrien the canteen. He drank greedily.

She put a hand on his head. "You're very hot." She took the canteen back and splashed some water on his head and neck. "This will cool you. Let's move you to the shade." She looked up to the guys who had rushed to help. One of them bent down and helped her get Adrien up. They walked a few steps to a rock that was in the shade of a casuarina tree and set him down there. "Thanks guys,"

One of the other volunteers came back with a fresh and cold bottle of water and some electrolytes. "Here,"

"Cheers." Miriam opened it, mixed in the electrolytes and handed it to Adrien.

"Ade…you gave me a fright." He drank from this fresh bottle. "You went down like a sack of potatoes!"

He guffawed.

"Should have stayed more in the shade!" She wagged her finger at him. "Seriously though, are you okay?"

He nodded emphatically, drank again.

Miriam resumed her work while Adrien recouped in the shade. This fainting thing in the heat happened so often that she wasn't surprised anymore. Thankfully, it tended to happen on the sand where the risk of injury was minimal.

When they packed up for the day, they had collected something like over thirty bags full of garbage, most going to recycling. They took the obligatory group photo and then people started to be on their way.

"Do you feel like a swim now?" she asked Adrien. "I feel so dirty and sweaty I just want everything off."

They had a lovely swim while waiting for the sun to set. The beach was almost completely empty; it was magical. They floated there, faces toward the sun on the far left of the bay, and basked.

"How can I go back to normal life after this?" he asked her all of a sudden.

She laughed. "Who says this isn't normal life?"

"Aw, come on. None of us can stay here, like this, forever. How do I…keep this feeling?"

"Well, if you find out, be sure to let me know. I've been wanting to know for a while."

Miriam went home to get ready; that night she had been invited to see a big Muay Thai fight. She was good friends with a local Thai family whose head, Bamon, was the chief trainer at a local gym. One of his guys was fighting and it would be impolite to refuse. She had been to a couple fights. She enjoyed the spectacle, but in her mind all the fights blurred into one. She was more into it for the social aspect. Plus, before the fight Bamon's wife was cooking for all of them, and this was the bit she was looking forward to the most.

CHAPTER 35 - MARTIN

The trucks had been going up and down the road and around the island. Their sides were plastered with colorful posters bearing the faces of angry, determined people looking straight to camera, gloved fists up. The speakers, pointing in all directions, blasted the prerecorded message about the upcoming fight in both Thai and English, accompanied by the traditional *sarama* music, hypnotic and exotic to Martin's ears. The ear-splitting English voice was a cartoonish boom promising a "BIIIIIG FIGHT" a "REAL FIGHT, NOT SHOW"—famously, there were places where fights had been staged, especially with *farangs*—and "ENTERTAINMENT FOR ALL THE FAMILY," which Martin thought was a bit rich, if he was honest. But they had their effect: everyone was asking everyone else if they'd be going to the fight. Bamon had explained that this was the first big fight of the season and, in true Thai fashion, tradition dictated that if this first big one went well, then the season would also go well.

Their gym was fielding three fighters that day. One was a *farang* woman from Bulgaria who had had fights in Europe and was making her Thai debut; one was a young Thai guy, a rising star upon whom many hopes rode; and finally there was Nuay, one of the gym's trainers, who was headlining the night.

Martin had been working hard with Nuay as well—lots of sparring—and he knew how tough and dedicated he was to his chosen profession. The night promised to be electrifying. Martin had promoted it with his fellow TribeHutters, trying to buy tickets in advance from Bamon and Nuay so that they would get a cut of the action. Martin had been shocked to learn how little these guys made by training, and also fighting. Only the winning headline fighter took home something a little more decent, and so a percentage of ticket sales was really a big help for the whole team.

Martin had not yet seen a live fight—the trainers had made him watch countless YouTube videos in the hope of convincing him to fight himself—and so he was looking forward to it. After a group dinner nearby, they all walked the last couple hundred meters toward the "stadium," a glorified hut, really. It had a corrugated iron sheet roof supported by beams on four corners and a weathered ring in the middle, surrounded by crude stands made from rough-hewn timber planks; the steps were so high that most people had to crawl up using their hands, too. You could tell it was a big night by the sheer number of cars and bikes parked outside and the dozens of waiting tuk-tuks. Anyone showing up without a prepaid ticket was almost grabbed by the various trainers and hagglers to claim them as their own, in order to pocket the commission.

Martin and the group filed in, one by one, handing in their tickets and receiving in exchange a huge stamp on their arms—a blue logo that, in seconds, thanks to the stifling heat, humidity and sweating, turned into an indiscernible blue blob that would take days to fade away. As there were a lot of people already there, the group broke up, trying to find good viewing seats. The top of the stands had a gap on the back, just under the roof, so it stood to reason they would be the freshest seats. Martin spied a couple free places up there and made his way up. After he sat down, followed by Serge and Brendan, he scanned the crowd and noticed so many faces he knew. Miriam was there, in a low seat behind the trainers' bench. He found this surprising—he never would have made her for a Muay Thai enthusiast. And then he saw her: Rose. She was almost across the ring from him, on the opposite stand. She had grabbed her long hair in one hand and was holding it up, fanning her neck. How cute. She was deep in conversation with someone…was it…? No! Dahlia? Fuck. That was all he needed.

He wrenched his attention away and asked Serge and Brendan whether they wanted a drink. They were both into it, so Martin climbed back down the high steps and made his way to the small bar in the corner and bought three ice-cold Chang beers. Chang was called by various nicknames in Thailand, and it meant elephant, but mostly it was considered a woman's drink as it was the lightest of the lagers available, akin to water. But Martin could attest that you still got a stonking hangover if you drank enough Chang…

He got back to his seat and the three men clinked beers. The stadium was a cacophony of noises and lights. On top of the ring, a blinking stroboscopic light was on, almost blinding them for no reason as its effect was invisible to anyone outside its radius. Loud club music was blaring from the speakers. A rush of movement to the left made everyone turn their heads in that direction. Now Martin could see the first two fighters approach, their oiled bodies wrapped in colorful, fringed capes, their heads adorned with a thing that looked like a cross between an upside-down tennis racket without strings, and a coiled cobra. It was very odd. When they reached the ring, the announcer said a few things in hyperbolic Thai and then another man, an Aussie, Martin thought, announced that everyone would now stand in tribute to the King. A lot of the *farangs* were puzzled at this, but Martin was expecting it. It was the same if you went to the cinema or any public performance. A song or film would be played, with images of the King; the soundtrack was, he thought, the Thai national anthem, but in truth he had no idea. The whole thing was just a demonstration of the love and respect that Thai people had for their beloved King.

Everyone stood, the Thais mostly with heads bowed, for the two or three minutes it took to play the song. Looking around discreetly, Martin saw some people who were not respecting the moment, especially a group of guys that looked like they were trying to soothe their hideous sunburns with gallons of beer. Thai people, Martin had found, positively shirked confrontation, so no one said anything at their continued loud talking, banter, and shoving. But the eyes told a different story, and many locals were eyeing these tourists in a passive aggressive manner. Near them, another group of *farangs* was visibly embarrassed. One of them, an older European guy, attempted to motion the rowdy group to calm down, but the louts just burst out laughing and tried to stifle it.

At the end of the song, Thai people performed the *wai*, the Thai thank-you or greeting gesture. The *farangs* clapped enthusiastically and finally they were good to go. The first fighters climbed up into the ring and, to Martin's dismay, they looked like very young children. They were deceptively skinny; he knew they would probably already have developed granitelike limbs with training, but nevertheless they appeared scared and out of their depth, their big dark eyes looking around nervously.

Brendan giggled at this. "Is this playtime or what? Here, Martin, let's make a bet. I think the little belter in the blue pants is going to kick the shit out the red pants. What say you?"

Serge looked at Brendan aghast, his mouth hanging open about to say something.

"You're on." Martin smiled.

"How much you good for, my man?" Brendan made to put his hand in his pocket, but Serge stopped him with his hand.

"Guys… What the fuck?! Betting is illegal in Thailand! Stop it!" He looked around nervously to make sure no one had noticed.

Brendan laughed uproariously. "Oh, Serge. You're so naive, my man! What do you think all of those guys over there are doing? Huh?" He pointed to the other side of the ring, which was occupied mostly by locals, where a few guys slightly more smartly dressed than the others paced up and down, occasionally pulling out a little notebook and quickly pocketing it again.

Serge looked over; he seemed really nervous.

"Betting is the whole point of the thing!" added Brendan.

"Come on, I'm sure it's not the whole thing," wondered Martin.

At Brendan's utterly "ya think?!" face, Martin burst out laughing.

"All right, all right, maybe they are betting," conceded Serge, "but we are *farangs*. If we get caught, they will give us a lot of shit! You know that."

Martin looked around once more. It was true that only Thai people seemed to be talking to the bookies. No foreigners. "Maybe Serge has got a point."

"What? What a pussy!" Brendan shrugged.

"Why don't we just keep it to a low bet and between us? Who's to know?"

Serge tried to say something, but Martin continued, "No one can tell. If later one of us buys the other a beer, who's to say? Come on!"

Brendan let out a huge smile. "Right on!" He fist-bumped Martin.

Before Serge could protest, a hush fell on the stadium and the hypnotic *sarama* music started. The two boys, now without their superhero capes but still wearing those funny headdresses, started a kind of fight-dance around the ring, bowing to the four corners, tracing the rope with a gloved hand, moving anti-clockwise around the ring. Everyone watched enraptured. Martin had never seen this on YouTube, as the trainers just showed him the fights and not the filler.

The first boy to complete the circuit then moved toward the center of the ring and started making some moves that partly resembled Muay Thai, and partly were a bouncy kind of dance. The other one joined him in the center. They twirled their arms, went down on one knee and rocked back and forth while stretching the back leg in and out. The whole thing reminded Martin of a graceful snake emerging out of its basket at the behest of its charmer. Despite the fact that it was quite a delicate, sedate dance, Martin could see that it was meant to show off the fighters' prowess and preparedness.

The music died down and everyone clapped. Each boy went to his respective corner where their coaches removed the headdress, put a mouthguard in and gave them a final sip of water. Finally, the coaches both whispered something in the boys' ears, then the boys bowed respectfully and went back into the middle of the ring. The referee (or umpire?) had a quick word with the boys, wiped each set of gloves with a rag and then flicked his hand up and down. Then the bell went. The crowd cheered.

The boys, who until that moment hadn't even looked, now stared intently at each other, in between their gloves. They were such tiny boys, Martin reasoned, that the gloves looked humongous at the end of their stick thin arms.

One boy flicked his leg up and over, in a feint. The other made to block, then went in with a light punch. They were tasting each other, Bamon had explained to Martin. It apparently was bad form to go in all guns blazing; respect dictated that the first few seconds of round one should be a kind of polite "hello, how you doing" dance, with fists bumping lightly, and measures being taken.

Despite spending a lot of time in Asia over the years, Serge had explained that he had never been into Muay Thai, had never seen a fight, even on video, and was only coming along because they were all going. It was a social event for him, but he abhorred the whole violence aspect of it. Back in Belgium, his father had been boxing mad and had made Serge take classes. The memory of other boys pummeling him with punches while the instructor shouted at Serge to defend himself still haunted him after all these years. And now, as Red Pants Boy finally threw a knee that had some force in it, Martin heard a squeal from his right. He turned and saw Serge shrinking back, his hands over his face, shielding his eyes. "Oh, mon Dieu! I cannot watch this. It is too much."

"Come on, this is fun! Look at them, with their skinny arms," piped up Brendan, who was fully into it and hunched forward in anticipation. "This is awesome!"

Martin tried to focus again on the fight, but through the writhing mass of the grappling boys he saw Rose, who was sporting a similar pose to Serge: hands across her mouth, eyes wide but unable to look away, leaning back in muted shock. Dahlia, beside her, was engrossed in conversation with someone on her other side, completely oblivious to both the fight itself and Rose's discomfort. With every punch, kick or elbow, the noise from the crowd surged a little, and Rose flinched as if hit herself. But still she watched.

"Woah!" Brendan slapped Martin across the chest in his enthusiasm for a kick that Blue Pants Boy had just delivered to the side of the ribcage of the other boy. "Get ready to buy me that beer, dear Martin!" He laughed wholeheartedly.

Just then, the red pants boy executed a super fast block and knee to the chest of his opponent, knocking him back and making him stagger. The crowd held its breath, and in that gap, the scrawny red pants fighter whirled around with a round kick, sending the blue panted boy crashing to the dirty mat. The stadium erupted, everyone standing up excitedly.

"I think you mean, get ready to buy me a beer…" Martin smirked as Brendan watched dumbfounded.

"Get up, come on, get up!" Serge screamed and then stood up, watching intently.

One side of the crowd, by the red corner, was cheering and rejoicing, waving at the referee to count the knockout. The blue side was shouting uncontrollably at the blue boy, urging him to get up. Thankfully, Martin noted, he hadn't been knocked unconscious, and so he was trying to scramble to his feet while the referee made sure the other boy was well away. Funnily, the red pant boy was himself shocked at what he had done, and so was looking at his family and trainers to make sure it was all really happening. They were waving their arms up at him, in a victory gesture, but he just continued looking at them in his boxing stance, gloves up.

The referee reluctantly started the count—it was quite unusual for a children's fight to go to knockout, and so early in a match—and this provided the spur needed by Blue Pants Boy. He shot up, then became a little unsteady, but just then the bell rang for the end of the round, so he was reprieved. As the music started back up in earnest, complete with strobe lights, the boys both shuffled to the respective corners, where a square aluminum tray was pulled up from God knows where, and a little stool was placed in the center. A couple trainers on each side got into the ring. One grabbed the red pant boy under the armpits and lifted him up, stretching his whole back.

Once he was sitting down, a bucket full of ice water was basically chucked over him, while the trainer rubbed the boy's thin arms and legs. Martin observed that each one of the boy's thighs was thinner, much thinner, than his own forearm. As the trainer rubbed his muscles he also spoke to the boy, probably giving him advice and encouragement. The boy nodded while keeping his eyes focused on something in the distance. People started to sit back down in the stands. It was clear the match was not over yet.

The bell rang again, the boys got wiped down with a rag and all the various implements were removed from the ring. The boys approached one another, and the referee made that little chopping-block motion with his hand to signal the fight could resume. Again, it seemed they were just tasting and testing each other, like at the start.

"Come on, come on!" Brendan cheered.

Serge seemed to relax a little more since there had been no bloodshed or serious injury, for now. People were clapping, talking, and the flow of people going to and from the bar, halted by the shock knockdown, had resumed.

The fight went on in this slow, timid fashion for the whole round. Neither boy seemed to be able to land anything more than a half-hearted knee. In the next round though, Blue Pant Boy came back all guns blazing as soon as the referee gave the start signal.

He landed a quick punch to make room and then used a kick to push Red Pants back. It wasn't a hard kick, but a tactical one. Once the boy was at the desired distance, the blue pant kid started to pummel him with all he had. The crowd roared and Brendan hoisted his beer in the air, splashing everyone around, screaming, "Kill him, for God's sake, kill him!"

Even Serge was up on his feet, screaming something unintelligible, and Martin felt the crowd surge around them.

The red pant kid continued blocking with his arms over his head. It seemed like it would never end and then, the moment the blue boy slowed down a notch, the red boy's right arm came out with a textbook hook, catching the unguarded boy's head square on the temple. Blue Pants hit the mat among a huge roar. "Fuck!" groaned Brendan. This time the referee did not hesitate and started the count. The blue boy was down, rolling a little, but made no move to get up. His opponent walked back to his corner, catching his breath. The count went on… Four, five… The crowd was shouting, they wanted the boy to get up, but Martin thought the fight had gone out of him.

"Ten!" shouted the referee, the bell rang, and he made a match-over gesture with his hands. While half the crowd cheered and half the crowd slumped, Red Pants Boy rushed to his opponent, knelt and bowed, gloved hands joined, to apologize for having hurt him. Then the referee grabbed his hand and hoisted it up high. He was the winner.

CHAPTER 36 - ROSE

Rose wasn't sure why she had agreed to come to this god-awful thing. Dahlia had managed to get some free tickets—Rose would never have paid for violent entertainment—and had convinced her it would be a fun, thrilling event. She wasn't wrong about the thrilling part, but the fun was nowhere to be found. The whole place stank of something she couldn't quite place, something surely to do with sweat, and fear, and various oils and creams. The seats were super uncomfortable; her cute skirt had snagged several times on the roughly hewn surface of the planks that served as seats, to the point that she was worried she had ruined it.

The people-watching, at least, was interesting. The two of them had come in quite early. Dahlia had gotten the time wrong—or maybe it was something to do with being allowed in for free?—and so had picked seats that later filled with mostly Thai people. On the other three sides of them was the entire *farang* spectacle. She surmised that this kind of event served as just another bit of entertainment for holidaymakers, akin to a fire show or a traditional dance show, or just a night sitting at a beach bar. The vast majority of them were brightly sunburned, clutching a beer and generally coupled. She felt really out of place.

The conversation with Dahlia was interesting and fun. She filled Rose in on all the gossip, who fancied who, who was sleeping with who, who had a spat, who was just a wannabe digital nomad, who had a job that wasn't really a job but was scamming other people. Rose didn't have much to add but was happy to listen.

Things had been improving for her. The initial Martin setback was starting to recede from memory and she no longer unconsciously flinched when she heard his voice, saw him or when his name was mentioned. The atmosphere at the TribeHut was also super helpful. Everyone there—well, almost everyone—was very focused and put in good amounts of work, and this rubbed off on her. She had been getting up early every morning, either doing yoga in her room or managing to go to those few free classes, and then straight to the TribeHut for a productive day. Things were ticking along nicely, and she had managed to get payment for some of the oldest outstanding invoices she still had. She had also made contact with some local jewelry manufacturers on the island who didn't yet have an online presence, and they had wanted her to help them set it up. Of course, she was thrilled, but she was also worried as she was a tourist in Thailand and didn't want to incur any legal trouble. She had been clear from the start that she could not take on local work, so she was in a dilemma.

While talking with Dahlia, who was continuously complaining about her feckless brother Jerome, Rose was struck by a serendipitous idea—she could teach a local person how to set up Etsy for these local businesses, and then that person would have the skill to keep doing it and earn money. She would do it for free; in exchange she would only have a good feeling and lots of good karma. Yes, this was a great idea. She was so enthused by it that she almost ran out of the stadium to start working on it there and then.

And that's when she saw Martin walk into the stadium. For a moment her stomach dropped. Of course, she should have expected him to come. She watched him strut in, flanked by his posse of overgrown children, particularly Brendan. They were such bros. She was pleased that she was on this side with Dahlia. She pushed Martin out of her mind and resumed paying attention to her surroundings.

She was surprised by the fact that, for Thais, this fight really was a family event. Entire families were here together, huddled on the smaller, lower benches below her. She saw a number of babies, cradled to sleep or crying, and quite a few toddlers and older children running around. The loud music drowned any noise the kids were making so it seemed to work.

When the fighting started, she truly could not conceive of the fact that she was seeing two children pummel each other. They must have been no older than ten years old, skinny, frightened little things, and yet the whole stadium was screaming and cheering them on, egging them on to hurt one another. It was too much for her. She watched from between her fingers. Dahlia seemed to be oblivious, checking her phone in between watching the fight. But Rose thought she could feel every punch, every kick, every elbow and knee hitting those bony bodies, and flinched at every one of them. And yet...while in her head, a little voice was shouting to get out of there, to not be a witness to this child abuse, she was glued to her seat and her eyes were glued to these boys. She did not have it in her.

When one of the boys was finally declared the victor, she sagged back onto the bench closing her eyes, head in her hands, and seemed to breathe again for the first time in ages.

"Dahlia. This is insane," she said while still looking at the ring. But the music had started back up, super loud, while the children were being ushered off the ring, so Dahlia didn't hear her. She was still looking at her phone. Rose reached out and grabbed her arm. "Dahlia. What the fuck?"

Dahlia gave her a puzzled look.

"This is insane." She held out her arms to take in the scene.

Dahlia laughed. "It is, isn't it? I love it." Dahlia chugged back some of her beer, but the bottle was empty. "Do you want a drink?" she asked Rose as she made to get up.

"Let me go and get us one. I need to stretch my legs," Rose said.

Dahlia nodded and went back to her phone.

Rose left their seats and slowly made her way around the ring, jostling with other people coming and going. She realized that the atmosphere would have been a fun one if only she could get over what was happening in the ring. She felt she owed Dahlia a drink, for scoring them the free seats, but she decided that after this she was going to leave. It really wasn't her thing.

CHAPTER 37 - MARTIN

The tension in the stadium had been ratcheting up with each fight and each beer they drank. At this point the standings were that Martin had bet on two winning matches and Brendan on three. Serge had finally caved in and joined in the betting fun a little later, but he had only picked losers so far. The Belgian was returning to their seats with a fresh batch of Changs, the bottles glistening with perspiration and threatening to slip out of his fingers.

"Gotta take a leak," said Brendan. He put his beer on the plank and went down to the toilets.

After a few moments of silence, Serge, now again at Martin's side, piped up sheepishly, "I can't believe I'm enjoying this, Martin. I really can't." Martin turned to look at him.

"Was it that bad? With your dad, I mean."

"Well, yes, I think. I was very young and I think at that age things seem so huge and, you know, overwhelming." Serge sipped his beer. "And it's weird. The sounds, the smells here kind of take me back there, but it doesn't actually feel terrifying anymore, or however it felt."

Martin brought his own bottle toward Serge's, and they clinked.

"Still, it doesn't justify grown men enjoy watching kids kick the shit out of each other," said Serge with a laugh. Martin already had beer in his mouth and had to struggle not to let it out with a laugh.

They were at the penultimate fight; the stakes were much higher and so was the talent. The two guys coming into the ring now were perfect specimens of honed muscle and graceful speed, and still

Martin did a double take when seeing them up close and realizing how short these guys were. Most of them would barely reach his shoulder. Dahlia and Rose seemed to be completely enraptured by checking out the fighters' bodies. He felt a stab of envy. Could he get his body in shape to that level?

The atmosphere in the stadium was even more fevered than before. He had gotten used to the chaos—or was that the beer?—and now just reveled in it. It was full to bursting, the bar was doing brisk trade and so were the bookies, or so it seemed at least.

The starting bell caught him by surprise. Where did the whole initial music and ceremony go? He must have missed it. These guys were not dicking around. That getting-to-know-you moment lasted maybe two or three seconds, and then they were straight into serious fighting mode, with kicks and punches landing here and there, the smacking noise cutting through the busy stadium and the roar of the crowd.

He could feel the energy from up here; it felt like watching two tigers lurking and pouncing on each other. One fighter, in red pants, managed to slip in close to the other using an up elbow, and then hit him with a one-two and then a hook. The referee stepped closer, in case he had to separate them. However, the Blue Fighter took the hits and managed to push his rival off him and away. The referee took a step back.

Just then, in the blink of an eye, the Blue Fighter lashed out with a front kick, hitting the other guy in the gut and making him stagger back, and then, with a grace and a speed that took Martin's breath away, the Blue Fighter stepped out a little and launched a high kick, so fast that his leg was a blur.

He caught the Red Fighter square on the side of the head and down he went. The whole stadium shot up, screaming and in awe.

It was a master move and only a few seconds into the encounter. The roar from the crowd was deafening, drowning out the referee's counting. The Red Fighter was out cold.

Martin looked up into the opposite stands. Everyone was up but he could see Rose was still sitting down, hand over mouth and watching in shock. The crowd now was also chanting the count-down. The referee got closer to the downed fighter, shook him, but nothing. He motioned to the red corner and they rushed into the ring to help their fighter. Before the count was even up, the referee took the Blue Fighter's hand and lifted it high over their heads. A huge cheer went up from the crowd while on the ring a few people busied themselves around the fallen man. The Blue Fighter did a quick round of the ring, bowing and thanking each side in turn, and then knelt and bowed next to his opponent.

"Wow, man! That was so fast!" shouted Brendan in Martin's ear. "We didn't even have time to pick a side!" The background music started again, and many people started to go down for a toilet break or for one more drink. There was one more fight to go. Martin looked over to the other side and Rose was still sitting there, hand over mouth. He looked again at the ring and now many people were around the fighter, who still didn't seem to be moving. He noticed that a small stretcher was being brought onto the ring.

When Rose noticed this, she seemed to come out of her stupor, shake her head and reach for Dahlia beside her. She said something quick and then got up and made to leave, almost running.

Martin instinctively stepped off the stands and walked toward the exit, struggling to catch up with Rose. When he caught up with her, he grabbed her arm but then acted as if he was just bumping into her.

"Hey, leaving already? There's one more fight."

As she turned to face him, he at last saw that she had tears coming out of her eyes. She gave him a puzzled look, shook her arm out of his hand, turned back and left. There was nothing he felt he could say.

The bar had run out of Chang, so Martin had had to switch to the more expensive Leo beer. Serge and Brendan were amped up for the last fight, because the headline fighter, Nuay, was from Martin's own gym and he had been talking about it a lot. He had seen Nuay train and had trained with him, too, so he felt he had a personal stake in this fight. Above all, he didn't want Nuay to get hurt and maybe end up like the guy in the previous fight. Since they were all for Nuay to win, Brendan played devil's advocate and switched the bet to which round the fight would end. The ones who picked the wrong rounds would get the drinks for the one who chose well, and since there were five rounds and Serge was losing already, the Belgian would only get one pick and Martin and Brendan would get two each. Serge grumbled but went along with it.

The fighters approached to the sound of "The Eye of the Tiger" as if they were in a *Rocky* movie, their retinues now bigger and swaggering behind their respective fighters, egging the audience on. A lot of the *farangs* were miming or singing along to the song chorus, throwing pretend punches. Out of the corner of his eye, Martin saw the bookies doing feverish business. This was going to be a great fight.

In Nuay's retinue, Bamon, the head trainer, walked slowly, looking around the audience and nodding formally to people he knew. Martin had spotted a few of the gym regulars, including the British owner, all around the space. When Bamon saw Martin, he locked eyes with him, nodded and pointed to Martin to come follow him.

"Is that your trainer?" Brendan asked Martin above the noise.

"Yeah," Martin continued looking at Bamon, now reprising his walk behind Nuay and arriving at the red corner.

"I guess he wants you to see the action up close, huh?" Brendan slapped Martin on his back. Martin was so sweaty, his shirt so stuck to his skin, that the slap had a wet sound to it. Serge egged him on, and Martin made his way down through the throng.

The fighters began the ceremonial dance.

Martin approached the red corner, Bamon turned around and, with a look, showed him where to sit: a bench right behind him. Bamon motioned for the people sitting there to shift, which they did promptly. Martin took his seat and Bamon turned around to face him. Martin bowed in thanks and almost bumped heads with Bamon as the Thai man bent over to talk in Martin's ear.

"You look. You look good," Bamon said while using two fingers to point to his own eyes and then to the ring. "Look Nuay. Learn. Fight good." He repeated the gesture a couple of times and stared at Martin until he said he understood. Bamon turned away and walked onto the ring for some last-minute advice to Nuay as the dance was coming to a close.

Being so close, Martin had to crane his neck to take in the whole ring. Bamon approached Nuay, whispering in his ear. Nuay was looking dead ahead, almost in a trancelike state. Another trainer was rubbing Nuay's body to keep him warm and oiled; he glistened like a Christmas turkey. The referee came to check all was well. Bamon removed the headgear from Nuay, slipped the mouthguard in his protégé's mouth and stepped out of the ring, nimble as a cat.

When the bell rang, the entire stadium at once stood up with a roar. Every single person in the building was shouting, gesturing, getting completely worked up. A girl to Martin's left screamed a piercing banshee cry. He turned to her to check she wasn't being harmed. But no, she was just excited. The fighters seemed oblivious to anything other than the space within the ring, in their own world. When they started sparring, they were so fast that Martin found it hard to tell what was actually happening.

They were pretty evenly matched, and also experienced—he thought Nuay had done a few dozen professional fights, at the very least—and so neither of them was going full-on in this first round. A wise fighter knew to keep his stamina for the five rounds. Martin remembered being in the ring himself, and being pummeled by Nuay, thinking, *the round will soon be over*, but three minutes can feel like a lifetime in those situations. The first round ended without anyone claiming a clear superiority.

Back in their respective corners, the fighters got massaged, doused with ice water and a few more wise words in their ear. Bamon massaged Nuay's belly downward, where he had received a couple knee hits. Nuay was like a doll, having all these things done to him, having completely surrendered his body to these other people for the two-minute break.

As the bell rang for round two, a new, deafening noise joined the fray. It sounded like an airplane propeller, like a huge fan had just been turned on above them. It took Martin a moment to realize that a sudden shower of rain was drumming on the corrugated iron roof. Its noise rose to such a level that nothing else in the stadium could be heard, and Martin had the curious sensation that he was watching a silent video.

He turned to look at Brendan and Serge, who were completely engrossed in the fight. In this round, Nuay's opponent got him with a good kick, so he really needed to up his game in order to win.

During the next break, Bamon was quite fierce with Nuay. He kept on repeating something to him, and Martin noticed Bamon make an elbow gesture. Martin recalled Bamon telling him that in his youth, when Bamon was a top fighter, his signature killing move was his left elbow, by which he had won many fights. This now seemed to be is go-to for any situation, but Nuay's style was quite different from Bamon's, so Martin wasn't sure how it would pan out. Bamon almost slapped the younger man to get him to understand.

Back in the fight, both of the fighters seemed to have renewed vigor, God knew where from. The action seemed to become even more fast-paced than before. Their bodies were now even more slick, the sweat pouring off them. Every time they clinched, they were struggling to keep a hold of each other. With every hit, half the crowd roared a big "Oh," depending on which side they supported, and the whole thing became almost a singing contest with a crazy crescendo.

Martin felt they were close to the end of the third round when a flurry of knees, punches and kicks resolved into Nuay sliding forward with his left foot and bringing his left elbow across and around, to slam into his opponent's head dead-on. The guy spun counterclockwise, a spray of sweat and Tiger Balm escaping in an arc, and fell down on his front, his head bouncing on the mat.

Without even waiting for the referee, Nuay's team launched themselves onto the ring and Bamon grabbed him by the legs, hoisting him up in victory. Most of the stadium cheered while the other guy's supporters simply up and left as quickly as they could, any interest now disappeared. Martin hadn't realized, but he was also on his feet and cheering, almost climbing on top of the ring.

The celebration party for Nuay's victory had been going on for a while at a Thai-owned beach bar. All the gym trainers and fighters and most of its customers were out in force, drinking, smoking joints and God knows what else. Martin was still with Serge and Brendan. Brendan had ended up winning their bet and had requested his friends get him a Sangsom bucket, which he proceeded to drink quite quickly, to Serge's astonished glare.

This was some time ago, and now they were all well on their way to a stonking hangover. Martin went to the bar and bought a round of drinks to bring to the trainers. He knew Bamon loved Singha so he made sure to get that. He approached the trainers and passed the drinks around. They all smiled at him and cheered, "*Chok-dee!*" clinking bottles, bowing, drinking.

As Martin made to move, Bamon pulled at his vest and told him to sit next to him.

"You like fight?" Bamon said, pointing to Nuay, who was still in his fighting gear and had an ecstatic grin on his face but was almost asleep.

"Yeah, it was great. Nuay fought very, very well."

"Yes." Bamon nodded. "Fight next month?" he asked, pointing his finger to Martin.

"He's fighting again next month?" He nodded his head toward Nuay. "Sure, I'll be there."

"You," Bamon stressed, while pointing to Martin. "You, fight next month, okay?" Bamon smiled and Martin smiled, too. Was the man joking?

Bamon clapped him on the shoulder and then said something to the group in Thai, and everybody erupted in happiness and came to slap Martin on the back, to high-five him and shake his hand. The fighters were delirious. *What did I get myself in for?*

CHAPTER 38 - DAHLIA

Dahlia had not felt this settled in a very long time, if ever. She had spent the previous three years moving from one place to the next, often at the last minute and on a whim, without too much planning. She was exhausted by that but hadn't really thought about an alternative.

When she had arrived at the TribeHut, on the advice of a Russian girl she had met in Malaysia, she was planning to stay maximum a month. But the people she met, the productive environment and the ease of life had all conspired to keep here there longer. And now she had Jerome there, too, who seemed settled into his love affair with Thaim. She was still struggling to get him to work enough, but that had also eased into a decent rhythm. Additionally, the constant flow of people in and out of the Tribe ensured both a ready supply of hot guys and interesting networking opportunities.

She had had to fly to Cambodia for a few days, to get a new visa, but she was back and ready to spend a few more months here, where life tasted sweet. She had even started taking Thai language lessons! It gave her such a thrill when she could say a few things or order food in Thai, and people really appreciated it, though her French accent made everything a bit harder.

Slowly, she had been training Jerome in some of her work. Giving someone a foundation in marketing starting from scratch was not as simple as she had expected, especially since Jerome was the laziest student. What enraged her was that he was superbright.

She knew that he could master, and did master, anything that he put his mind to. But he just wasn't interested. While she was going through things with him, he would start to play with his clothes, her hair, or anything that was on hand. She would hide their phones for the duration of their lectures—they would achieve nothing otherwise—but he hadn't finished reading any of the books she had assigned him. He still lacked a basic grasp of the most fundamental marketing concepts, but he had been interested in picking up the Facebook-related topics she had to share.

She had set him daily tasks and, to begin with, used him as a kind of VA, or virtual assistant, to answer her emails, schedule calls and seminars, look over reports, all in order to give him a bird's-eye view of the business. Still, she felt it was an uphill struggle. As it stood, he still wasn't earning much money, and he'd been with her for a month already. She was going to have to address this.

Another new and unexpected thing was Dahlia's blossoming friendship with Rose. They had taken to each other seamlessly and in a really nice way. Dahlia did not feel threatened or in competition with Rose, maybe because they had both had a run-in with Martin, and also because Rose did not seem to be interested in any of the other guys, despite Dahlia's pushiness. They went out together a lot and had fun. But they also worked a lot, often sitting together in the TribeHut or taking meals at the same time. She had never really had a close female friend, and at times she didn't know how to handle it.

For example, when Rose had found out that Dahlia and Adrien had been seeing each other quite regularly, Rose was super thrilled by it and had wanted to know all the details. She'd bombarded Dahlia with questions and demanded to know what Dahlia "wanted out of it," and what "Adrien's intentions were," and "blah, blah, blah."

At this, Dahlia had shut down; she felt attacked by this kind of questioning. It had taken a while to calm down and realize that Rose was only curious and had no ulterior motives.

And so it was that they ended up talking about the Adrien thing, and the Martin thing. Dahlia really couldn't relate to the whole incident between Martin and Rose. If it had happened to her—unlikely, because she was the type of woman who got what she wanted—she would have shrugged it off and moved on, thinking that it was his loss. But Rose brooded over this, again and again, even if she wouldn't say so outright. Dahlia had caught her watching Martin and studiously avoiding him. Not rudely or openly, just very carefully. Rose kept saying she wasn't interested in Martin, but Dahlia thought otherwise. Additionally, Dahlia felt that Rose was hurt by the idea that she and Martin had actually slept together—though Dahlia could hardly remember it—but this also bolstered Rose's conviction to stay away from him, as if he were now sort of tainted by having slept with someone else, or someone she knew.

And on the Adrien front...Dahlia had to tell Rose various times to stop asking her about it. She didn't want to define it, and she thought Adrien felt the same. The first time Rose saw Dahlia go off with a different guy, the next morning she was peppering Dahlia with new questions. Was it all over with Adrien? Did she like this guy more than Adrien? What did she say to the guy about Adrien? And to Adrien himself?

"Sometimes you're so...traditional, Rose," Dahlia would say. "A bit boring. No?"

Rose was very embarrassed by this kind of comment; she would blush, and stammer, and try to talk through an excuse, and explain what she "meant to say."

It made Dahlia smile. She tried over time to loosen Rose up, but there was a fundamental difference in how they saw love, sex, men and all that stuff. For Dahlia, she had long known that she could only ever rely on herself, so she wasn't looking for anyone to lean on, never mind a soulmate! On the contrary, she thought relationships only ever brought trouble, of many different kinds, and she was determined not to waste her time on them. Sex, for her, was a wonderful aspect of life that she was curious about, and the crazier the better. For Rose, instead, her entire being was reaching toward this ideal of the missing half to become complete, which Dahlia found way too romanticized. And so, Rose hadn't had much experience with casual flings. Serial monogamist to the core. Dahlia was working hard to try to change that, or at least to give Rose a flavor of what she was missing out on, before she eventually found this elusive soulmate.

After Rose left during the Muay Thai fight, Dahlia messaged Adrien to see what he was up to. He texted back saying he was at home resting, as he had had a fainting spell. *What?!* She asked for more information, but he didn't reply, so she went back to the bungalows and went to Adrien's. His door was unlocked, and he was lying on the bed, reading off his Kindle.

"Why didn't you reply?"

He looked up and shrugged. His phone was untouched on the other side of the bed.

"You got me worried. What's this about fainting?"

Adrien sheepishly told her about the beach cleanup. After she made sure he was really okay, she made plans go get them some takeout food and chill while watching a movie. He was looking at her as if she were an alien.

"What?" she demanded.

"Nothing, nothing." He shook his head. "It's just funny to see you in this…nurse mode." He chuckled and went to get his laptop to choose a film.

She shoved him in the shoulder. "Well, don't get used to it!"

CHAPTER 39 - ADRIEN

Adrien had to make some decisions. His original plan was to stay on the island for two months and then move on to Chiang Mai, where the developer and bootstrapping scene was supposed to be huge. And after that, Bali, to continue working and to finally learn to surf. But life on Tanu was so…nice. He hadn't expected it to be like this. He'd never been a beach person but being here made him feel good. The pace of life, the constant sound and smell of the sea, the walks on the beach.

He had been making full use of the beach and the great weather, and he had even started to get some exercise in, swimming and occasionally visiting a gym for some sort of bootcamp classes. Every time he Skyped with friends or family back home, they all remarked how healthy he looked. And he felt it!

He had been getting on with work quite well; the atmosphere at the TribeHut was weirdly productive. You could see everyone crunching away, even on the weekend or late at night. He had made some progress on his own app, but not as much as he should have by now. But he started to think he could get to a point where he could do a live demo for the TribeHutters and get some feedback. To finally open himself and this app up to the wider world. It was scary, but electrifying, too.

Of course, much of both his enjoyment of the island and not having made so much progress on the app could be laid at Dahlia's feet. Those lovely, beautiful feet. It had required a seismic shift in his mind to try to be cool with everything, to take things one day at a time and go with the flow. It really went against all his instincts.

From the first time they'd slept together, he had wanted to cuddle, to take her out on a date and hold her hand, to plan things together, to sleep—actually sleep, not have sex—together. But Dahlia resisted each and every one of these attempts. He would have to do things her way or not at all.

He took some time to think about it. He had never before found himself in a similar situation. Granted, he didn't have a massive curriculum when it came to relationships, but he still didn't have any examples of people like him who had embarked on something similar. Or maybe they had, and he just didn't know it.

The no monogamy thing, weirdly, seemed to be the easiest for him to get over. Not because it meant that, if he wanted to, he could also sleep with other people—he wasn't that interested, at least for now. No. He just had never been the jealous type. He thought it was because he had seen how suffocating ownership could be and had decided long ago that he wanted no part of it. And knowing that it was something that Dahlia could derive pleasure from only made it more appealing somehow.

He was a little more worried about his insecurities, the idea that if (when) Dahlia slept with someone else, she would be comparing their sexual prowess with his. This bothered him. *But then,* he reasoned, *she probably already did that when we first slept together, so what's the difference?*

What bothered him more, though, was these rules about being in public. Rationally, Dahlia made a lot of sense. It was no one else's business what they had between them.

She mentioned situations in which people were in open relationships and friends or acquaintances had gone to tell their partner about them cheating on them and stuff like that. All unnecessary. And it was also true that they were in a very small, very gossipy and circumscribed community, so it would be better to keep things under wraps and just do their own thing.

He understood all of this, but he still couldn't help but want to be affectionate with her, if the moment called for it. If they happened to be at a bar with other people they knew, why should that stop him? *What would be so bad about me holding her hand or giving her a kiss?* And so, he went back to the rational arguments and gave himself the reason why.

Not that Dahlia was happy about him calling whatever they had a relationship. She positively hated the word. She was happy to talk about everything related to it, just not to use the dreaded word. No labels. Another small price to pay.

And as for the sleeping-over thing, at least on that, eventually he had won her over. At first, she would kick him out or, if they were at his, she'd leave his bungalow as soon as the sex was over and done with. But he worked on her… He started to suggest they may want to go another round in a little while, and so they slowly started spending more time in bed without actually fucking. She learned to fall asleep in the same bed and, eventually, to stay asleep and not freak out when she found him next to her on awakening. He was very happy about this. He loved those moments, after or in-between sex, when they would cuddle and have sometimes deep, sometimes meaningless conversations, whispered into the fine hair of the nape of her neck or in his ear, which would always tickle. When you didn't know if the words you heard were yours, hers or coming from a half dream, when every little movement would mutate into a nuzzling motion or breathing in her delicious scent.

One day he had gone out to do a beach clean-up with Miriam; she had been badgering him about it. And to be fair, he did want to get more involved in doing things that were good for, you know, the world, and not just Adrien Dao. But, in a classic Adrien move, he had gotten too hot and ended up fainting on the beach. He was so embarrassed!

Everyone had stopped what they were doing and had come to rescue him. He tried to tell them it was okay, it had happened before, it wasn't a big deal, but no. They made a big fuss. So finally, to get away from it all, he asked to be taken home to rest.

To his delighted shock, Dahlia fussed over him to make sure he was okay, and even suggested they spend the night together eating and watching a film, in a totally boyfriend-girlfriend kind of way. He couldn't believe it. Had he known this would have such an effect on her, he would have made her more aware of his weaknesses earlier!

As they lay in his bed watching *Jumanji*—her choice!—the conversation landed on where they were going next, geographically speaking. Dahlia was not much of a planner, but Bali had been on her radar, too. At the mention of Bali, his ears perked up and he mentioned he had also been wanting to go there.

"But Ubud, if anything. As long as it's not Canggu!" she said authoritatively.

"Is Ubud inland?" Adrien bit his tongue.

"Yeah. Why? The sea in Bali, in the more developed part, is not as nice as in Thailand."

"Nothing." He didn't dare say he had been specifically looking at Canggu, because of the surf schools and nomading scene. He also wanted to just say, "Maybe we can go together?" but was terrified she would take it as a step further into a relationship and so he held his tongue. He just wanted to enjoy the cuddling a bit more.

PART V

Songkhran

CHAPTER 40 - MARTIN

To begin with, Martin had waited eagerly for Rose's reply to his message. He kept checking his phone compulsively. He saw that the message had been delivered and read. But still no reply. He told himself she was thinking about how to answer, that she was upset at his behavior so was punishing him by making him wait for her answer.

He did say, in his text, that it was okay for her to tell him to fuck off, but in reality, he hadn't really contemplated that eventuality. And in any case, her silence did not amount to her telling him to fuck off. Or did it? The whole thing niggled at him like a badly healed mosquito bite.

When he next saw Rose at the TribeHut after the Vibe incident, he kind of waited for her to say something—"Oh, geez, I forgot to reply to you! Duh!"—slapping her forehead and such, but she just looked through him and continued to work. He was hurt.

After that, it had become a game of studiously avoiding each other, so that no one else really noticed that they were doing it, though the two of them were super aware of it. She was never rude to him, but somehow she managed to never acknowledge him or interact with him, just letting his presence slide over her without any resistance.

It had been bothering him to the point of making plans to leave the island, but Hans was a steadfast presence in this, telling him that, first of all, if she didn't want to hear him out, that was her choice and he should respect it, and secondly, one of Martin's big problems was that he thought running away from problems was, actually, a solution. He had been doing it all his life—passport, money, bags and heart all packed and ready to go at a moment's notice. But, Hans said, this just left unresolved issues that still needed to be dealt with, and just added new ones to Martin's plate, as a new location invariably brought with it new connections, people, problems.

Every day Martin would look through Kayak and check flights to other destinations that had been floating around in his mind: Bali, Chiang Mai, Vietnam, the Philippines, Korea, Taiwan. But he never booked.

On this late morning, he found himself still in his room, no Muay Thai today as it was Songkhran, the most awaited day of the year in the whole of Thailand. It was, basically, as far as he understood it, kind of like Thai New Year. All businesses stopped, people went to visit their families, pay their respects, eat lots of food (strange how it seemed that holidays like these were the same all over the world!) but, most uniquely, the day itself would be marked by an all-day, island-wide, no-holds-barred water fight.

Martin had heard stories of this epic water fight. It struck him as odd that, in a place that often ran out of water, they would have an entire holiday dedicated to wasting a lot of it. But then again, the rainy season was approaching, so maybe it didn't make that much of a difference.

Friends of Martin's who had been in Chiang Mai during this time reported that you could not leave the house for days without getting completely drenched; in Bangkok, he'd heard of entire city blocks brought to a standstill by street parties for a whole week. Here on this island, he had been told that, because it sustained itself entirely on tourism, the celebrations had, by universal agreement, been shortened to a single day. The TribeHut itself would be closed, most travel halted, and only a handful of restaurants and cafés would be open—and even those would be a fulcrum of Songkhran activity.

The TribeHut staff had repeatedly told members that, today, they should not, under any circumstances, bring any of their electronics out of their rooms. Laptops should stay home, closed and dry. Phones could be brought along but at your own peril. In fact, in the days leading up to the celebrations, the sale of waterproof dry bags (normally used by divers) went through the roof, alongside water guns and toys. Martin himself had bought a badass, pump-action water shotgun. It was bright pink and green and waited for him by the door.

He toyed with the idea of doing a little work—it was, after all, a working day in Europe—but his heart wasn't in it. He went to the bathroom and proceeded to apply sunscreen to his entire body. The "vest tan" had finally faded and he wasn't going to make the same mistake again. He applied SPF 50 to his shoulders and face, SPF 30 to the rest of his body. His skin never dealt well with the sun.

After he got dressed, he grabbed his dry bag, put his phone, sunglasses case and money in it, and left. His trusty scooter was waiting outside, in the sun. When he sat on the black fake leather seat, he could swear the searing heat stripped some of the skin off his inner thighs.

The surrounding area was quiet—no people, no vehicles, which in itself was very odd. He roared up the road.

Immediately after the turn, he got his first taste of Songkhran. On the side of the road, in front of a little restaurant, a group of people were huddled around a huge plastic vat. Music was blasting from a massive speaker nearby. As they saw him approach, the people got all excited and started aiming for him with their plastic guns and buckets. He noticed that they were all, without exception, sopping wet. He managed to swerve his scooter wide and avoid most of their jets, and they screamed some well-meaning curses at him as he zoomed off.

He was now nearing the area where he knew most people would be, concentrated around a cluster of long-standing expat bars and restaurants. The road here narrowed so he knew it would be difficult to avoid the drenching, but he would try, just for the sake of it. He could park the scooter farther up the road and then join in the fun.

As he approached, he was taken aback by the sheer number of people, and by the picture of happy chaos that formed in front of him. The road was flooded, the red earth staining the tarmac for a few dozen meters; there were so many people that traffic had crawled to a standstill as the occupants of scooters, pick-up trucks and bikes gracefully accepted showers of water and gun jets, then moved on. Various songs were blasting from several different places, melding into an indistinguishable jumble; off to the sides and in the courtyards in front of restaurants, hundreds and hundreds of people were busy filling their buckets and pistols from water tanks, and even a water truck that was parked on the side.

In a split-second he saw a few people he recognized and tried to give them a wide berth with his scooter, but traffic was backing up in front of him. He tried to maneuver around a pick-up truck, its bed full of giggling Thai teenagers shooting back at the crowd, so that he could have a clear shot at getting out of this chokepoint, when *bam*—icy coldness hit him in a blast, from the side of his head (and in his ear), down to his body, under clothes and to his foot. In the surprise and shock, he gasped audibly and stopped his scooter dead. He turned toward where the water had come from.

CHAPTER 41 - ROSE

Rose watched as Martin turned around, his face a mask of pure shock and hatred. His eyes scanned the crowd around him and, in a flash, zeroed in on the now empty bucket she was holding, then travelled up her arms to her face.

She held her breath, open-mouthed, waiting to see how he'd react. He seemed puzzled and, strangely, a little bit hurt that it had been Rose to drench him.

Speechless, dripping with water, he stared at her for a few moments. Then she burst out laughing and shook him out of it. Other TribeHutters nearby also joined in with the laughter. Martin snapped out of it. With a determined move, he pushed the scooter to the side of the road, put the stand on, dismounted and then ran to one of the massive water tanks nearby. He grabbed an empty container there, filled it in haste and then ran back toward Rose, who had been watching him all along. When she realized what he was about to do, she bolted through the crowd, weaving in and out, trying to lose him. She was breathless from laughing and running. She could hear him shouting, "I'll get you!"

She almost bodily slammed into Brendan, then dodged Darren and used Ingrid as a human shield, moving her to get in between her and the pursuing Martin. But he wouldn't give up. Her breath was more and more labored, because all along she kept laughing hysterically, a child playing her favorite game of tag.

Finally, she spied another water tank to the left. She made a sudden turn toward it and dived, sticking her bucket back in, refilling it. But just as the bucket was full, she was splashed hard from behind, her upper back taking the full force. "Ha!" Martin shouted, triumphant.

Rose didn't react for a second and then, with a whirl, she brought the bucket up in an arc and physically hit him with it, sending the water all over him and in his face. He spluttered.

Just as they stood there, catching their breath and spluttering, Laura, Brendan, Dahlia and some of the other TribeHutters joined them around the tank and a huge, personal water fight ensued. There was no mercy, no quarter. Everyone had to be totally drenched, and special celebrations were reserved for when you could get ahold of ice water. You'd sneak up behind someone and then slowly pour the icy cold water down their back, watching as the person screamed or shivered as a result. People were in fits of laughter the whole time.

An older Thai woman, Rose never got her name, somehow got fixated on Rose and the two of them played a game of cat and mouse the whole day. Just when Rose thought she was safe and that the woman had gone, there she was again, spraying Rose in the eyes with a gun or giving her a little icy gift. And Rose then returned the favor. And so it went for most of the day. Rose never saw the woman again after Songkhran.

Martin seemed to have fully joined in. She kept on seeing him here and there, locked in a chase with someone or other, being drenched or drenching, shooting at the cars that were slowing down in the middle of the road, generally having a good time. The two of them bumped into each other quite a few times, and every time they tried tricks and feints, just to outdo each other.

Time seemed to stand still. The sun was still high in the sky, until suddenly it wasn't, and Rose realized it must be getting on for sunset. She had been at this for around six hours!

All of a sudden, she felt exhausted. She walked away from the road a few steps and found a vacant chair. She ordered a Coke from a passing waiter and drank it greedily. She'd only had breakfast that morning—no wonder she was hungry and tired.

A few other TribeHutters seemed to gather around her. Most had tired faces but sported big grins; this day was so much fun, no one could hide how much they were enjoying it.

Jie, the owner of the only local hairdressing salon, came around. She was wet but still very composed. "Rose, you had your blessing?"

Blessing, what blessing?

Jie was put out but she tried to explain: Songkhran was a day of renewal, transformation, change. In the morning, she had gone to the temple to make some offerings and to wash the Buddha's statue, together with her family. They then washed each other, purifying themselves and washing away all their sins and bad luck, to begin the new year as clean and as pure as possible.

Everyone gathered around to listen to her, and she explained more of the Songkhran traditions of paying respect to your elders, visiting with your family, and receiving a blessing for the year ahead. She demonstrated the latter by taking out a small metal container from her bag and opening it. It was full of white powder, chalk, that she daubed on Rose's forehead and cheeks. She said a brief sentence in Thai (or so Rose assumed) and bowed to her. Rose bowed back joining her hands together as she had learned to do in Thailand. She loved this gesture and had been using it a lot.

Jie embraced her and Rose wished her a happy and prosperous New Year. Jie beamed, then moved on to the person next to

Rose to perform the blessing on them. Rose noticed that Dahlia had to really hold in a smirk and, a few steps to the side, Rose spied Martin. When he clocked what was happening, he turned around and walked away.

After a few minutes, Jie walked away amongst the thanks and bows of the entire group. Laura was sprawled on one of the chairs but piped up, "Where should we go to next? I think things here are wrapping up."

Rose could see it was true: as the sun was coming down, fewer people remained on the sides of the road and fewer vehicles were coming by. And in any case, everywhere she looked, she could only see people who were wet from their head to their toes, so she did not think there was any dry person around that needed splashing.

"Rasta Bar, anyone?" asked Brendan. Rose knew Rasta Bar was his favorite place. There was a small treehouse built on the edge of the forest, and it was the perfect sunset spot, although on this island there were many such places! No one had any other suggestion, so the group made a move, and everyone went to get their scooters to ride down to the beach. Rose hitched a ride with Brendan.

CHAPTER 42 - DAHLIA

Being completely soaking wet was not one of Dahlia's favorite feelings, so she was quite happy when the party moved to the beach. On arrival, she stripped off her dripping vest top and skirt. She had wisely been wearing her bikini underneath, so in just a few seconds she put her clothes on the back of a bamboo chair to dry, and she was running down to the shore and into the water. Many people followed suit.

Truth be told, she had left joining the Songkhran festivities till late, and she had gotten bored of it after ten minutes. She could not understand where the fun was in splashing someone who was already completely soaked. She truly tried to understand and go along with it, but it really escaped her. Ever since she had been small, she had never enjoyed forced fun. Why plan for Carnival when you could dress up any day? Why wait for Christmas—when she hardly got any presents—when you could try to wheedle a present out of relatives and grown-ups at any time of the year if you were crafty enough? She was a much more go-with-the-flow kind of person, and today, her flow did not match the Songkhran vibe.

So, she had spent her time pretending to take part in the water fight but had really just checked people out. People-watching was one of her favorite activities, especially trying to work out who liked whom, who had been with whom, who hated whom and so on and so forth. It was a game she liked to play, and Jerome was the perfect partner in this.

Having him stay over had not been as bad as she had feared. Most nights he was out late or did not come back at all, and it was super fun having someone in whom she could confide all the gossip from her day. He was as gossipy, watchful and catty as she was, and they had a grand old time dissecting all the various interactions of TribeHutters and other island characters. They also started giving most people nicknames, which was a huge source of fun. They just had to be careful about not using a nickname in front of the person it referred to, as had happened on a couple occasions. They were able to fudge it and put it down to language barriers, but there had been close calls. Among her favorite nicks they had "Famous in Asia" (he looked like a boy-band relic in his late thirties); "Two-time Tony" (self-explanatory, really); "Sado-Sandy" (she had revealed she was into bondage, and Jerome just blurted it out in front of the group—Dahlia thought some others were now using it too); and "Grandpa Joe" (his name was not Joe at all, but he just looked like one of those guys who liked much younger women).

The sea was, as always, warm and inviting. Today the waves were stronger than normal. The sea around the island was usually quite calm, not suited for things such as surfing or kite surfing. Maybe the tide was coming in? The waves churned the water and lifted the light gray sand off the ocean floor, murking the green waters and making it impossible to spot any potential dangers. Dahlia did not care.

As she floated in the water, her face toward the setting sun, more TribeHutters arrived to join her. Brendan—who was clearly smitten with her and whom she had "parked" on the side, keeping him for a lonely night—half walked, half swam toward her, holding two highball glasses aloft that contained yellow-red drinks.

"Tequila sunrise, for sunset!" He beamed.

She smiled and took one of the drinks. Awkwardly floating on the waves, she drank from the straw. It was strong! As she turned to thank Brendan, she felt something bump into her leg.

"What was that?!" She whipped round, alarmed.

"What?" said Rose, who had also just come in for a swim.

"Hopefully nothing." Dahlia calmed down. She clinked her glass to Brendan's. "Thank you."

"My pleasure." Brendan took a sip.

"Ouch!" Rose screamed.

Everyone turned their heads toward her.

"What was it?" Dahlia inquired eagerly.

At the same time Martin, who was also floating nearby, asked "Are you okay?" and swam closer to Rose.

Dahlia groaned inwardly. If only these two would stop tiptoeing around each other! After the night of the TribeHut Takeover, as she had grown closer to Rose, she had seen her give Martin the cold shoulder, and relished in that. But today things seemed different. *Have they been seeing each other in secret?* Why was he being so solicitous toward Rose? It was fishy. But she could not believe that, had anything happened, Rose wouldn't have told her already.

"I am okay. I don't know…something…touched me."

Brendan sniggered.

"I felt something, too, earlier," Dahlia said.

"Probably someone bumped into you," someone else said. Dahlia remembered Jerome and his penis touch game in the water. She looked at Brendan suspiciously.

"No… It was…soft?" Rose said with doubt in her voice, and Dahlia guffawed.

"You do know they have deadly box jellyfish here in Thailand, right?" Brendan interjected with a knowing and smug tone, laughing at the girls.

"What the fuck?!" A couple people were stunned by this information and made their excuses to get back to shore. Brendan was laughing his ass off. He seemed to revel in annoying or scaring people.

"Brendan, why do you always have to spoil the party?" This was Martin.

"Come on, man! If you come to Thailand and you don't know that they have box jellyfish, you deserve to be stung by them! And anyway, if it had been a box jelly, they'd all be dead by now, so…"

"Okay, okay, it wasn't a damn box jellyfish, of course. But still… I did feel something…blobby." Dahlia said.

Rose laughed at that. "Yeah, blobby. Exactly."

"Well, I don't care, I'm enjoying my sunset chill." Brendan took another slurp off his Tequila sunrise.

"Oh!" someone else in the group piped up. "Yeah. Definitely felt something."

A new girl Dahlia didn't know, she thought she was Irish, suddenly squeaked. She let off a high-pitched scream and kind of shivered all over. Immediately she started swimming back in horror, screaming, "No! No! No way!"

"Mary! Hey, Mary! It's okay!" Brendan called after her.

Everyone was on edge now. No one was talking. Every few seconds someone would go, "Yeah" or "Here" or even "Yikes!" as they all felt things bumping into them. Dahlia turned toward the beach and saw a couple of the people who had swam back standing on the shore, waving at them. She waved back.

"Ah!" Rose squealed. "Sorry guys, I got another one. I'm out."

"But are you stung?" Martin asked.

Rose seemed to think for a moment. She probably was running her hands over her body, where she had felt it. "No…at least I don't think so. But it's freaking me out."

Rose started to swim back and, like an obedient puppy dog, Martin followed her.

Eventually, only Dahlia and Brendan remained, drinks in hand, having fun to the last.

CHAPTER 43 - JEROME

Jerome's Thai almost-boyfriend, Thaim, had insisted Jerome join him and his family in their Songkhran rituals. Jerome was naturally averse to all this kind of stuff. He and Dahlia had had such a dysfunctional upbringing that any mention of family events, traditions or the like brought back some awful memories and a sick feeling in his stomach.

Icy Christmas meals spent with their evil paternal grandparents—as opposed to their loving maternal grandparents—where they had to dress up formally and sit ramrod straight in the carved, antique, high-back chairs in the farming estate's smokey dining hall, a room opened only a couple of times a year for such an occasion. All while white-gloved old servants served a meal based around the game shot by their grandfather—sometimes with pellets still inside—and the vegetables grown under their grandmother's supervision. All of this almost in silence.

Of course, their absent mother could not be mentioned, lest it upset the elders and cause an argument, and watching their father take his parents' criticism without replying but simmering with an unspent rage, seared itself in the youngsters' memories.

At that time, they never discussed those feelings, they only did that when they were older and could process them. What they did talk about at the time, though, was having to witness their cousins—their white, well-bred, legitimate cousins—open present after expensive present to the delighted "umms" and "aahs" of the adults, while Dahlia and Jerome had a couple of pitiful token gifts set aside. Louis, their uncle's first born—the one who would "carry the family name forward," in their grandfather's own words—unwrapped a brand-new PlayStation (the siblings had never seen one before), shiny rollerblades and, on one memorable occasion, their grandfather's Rolex, which he had inherited from his own father.

Dahlia and Jerome were forced to watch this and express their admiration, their envy even, while at the same time unwrapping a scarf, a box of socks or even the dreaded money salami, a row of coins stacked in a pile and then wrapped in foil. It amounted to very little money but this way it looked like it was much more valuable. And to top it all off, they had to be thankful for these pitiful gifts, the difference for which was usually put down to Santa Claus being absent-minded, Jerome not having done well enough in school and general misbehavior. Dahlia started arguing about how Santa could have given Grandfather's Rolex as a gift—it wasn't logistically possible—and their father had to intervene and shush her, causing a further freezing in the atmosphere.

So, no wonder family occasions were not something Jerome jumped at. Even now, although rationally he had processed what had happened to them as emotional abuse, his gut still could not reconcile this, and thus pulled him away from any such eventuality.

This morning he had texted Thaim to say that he was not feeling so well, but Thaim was already outside their bungalows, eagerly waiting on his scooter. Jerome thought at least he would get some free food out of this. Thaim had bought presents for the both of them to offer his family, so they set off for the twenty-five-minute drive to the inland location of Thaim's parents' house. Tanu was truly paradise on earth. As they weaved in and out of little villages and huts, dogs and children perked up their ears, the children waving as they sped by. A monkey crossed the road in front of them, almost daring them to run it over. Jerome screamed at Thaim, slapping his back because he thought the monkey was going to get hit, and Thaim laughed. Farther on, Thaim slowed down to show Jerome something on the side of the road—a huge monitor lizard was leisurely walking beside the road, in the shade. They kept their pace slow to match it for a bit, but the engine noise must have annoyed it because it turned its head toward them, flicked its tongue angrily and then turned the other way into the jungle. Thaim sped off.

When they arrived at the traditional Thai house, a concrete and wooden construction raised off the ground, Thaim's family greeted them very warmly. It was a peculiarity of Thai culture that no one questioned who Jerome was and why he was there, he was simply accepted as a guest of Songkhran and welcomed with open arms. Also, to them he was *farang* and this gave him a raised status, which wasn't something he was used to.

Shortly after they arrived, the whole family went to the local temple to pray and make offerings. Again, Thaim had thought of everything and had arranged a basket of food offerings for the temple on behalf of Jerome. Thaim explained that normally they would have gone to the temple first thing in the morning, which his parents had actually done, but they had waited for Thaim and Jerome to get there so they could all go as a family.

The temple affair was surprisingly brief, though during the prayer proper Jerome was zoning out over the droning chanting of the monks. He was kept from falling asleep only due to his discomfort at being cross-legged for long. He watched and bowed, hands joined, when everyone else did the same, another thing taught to him by endless church services with his grandparents—both his good and evil grandparents were very religious.

He had refused to learn the prayers, the words, the customs. Both he and Dahlia had learned enough to fool their grandmother, who would hit them with a large wooden spoon if they failed to pray to her satisfaction, kneeling by their beds at bedtime. They learned that if you said out loud the first and last word of a verse but mumbled in the middle, no one would actually notice.

"Our father…mumble mumble…heaven…" or Jerome's favorite: "Holy Mary…mumble mumble…us sinners…" He once overheard his grandparents mention his mother and describe her as a sinner. As a grown-up he realized how Old Testament this conversation must have been, and so, in his heart, he squarely aligned himself with the sinners, almost in a genetic way. What was so bad about sin anyway? It sounded like all fun things were sins, and almost all sins were fun things. Come to think of it, this view hadn't really changed over the years. And so now, as then, he kept a watchful eye around him while seemingly having his eyes closed or lowered, and he mimicked what everyone else was doing. Not that anyone here would criticize him if he didn't do it right—they weren't expecting him to know—but still, it felt like the safer course of action.

The prayer ended with a blessing from the monks. Each person's forehead was smeared first with oil, then with chalk. Jerome almost slithered away at this point, but everyone was smiling at him and he felt himself carried away in the moment.

Back at the house, the feast could finally begin. Thaim's parents and family had obviously been working overtime to cook the myriad dishes now laid out for all to enjoy. Thaim presented the family with his and Jerome's gifts (some electronic gadgets, a new phone and other bits), and everyone was hugging everyone else. People kept talking to him in Thai and he just smiled and nodded. Plates of food were being placed in his hands and so it was that he tried everything.

Some things he could truly say he'd not bother to try again—he suspected offal in some dishes and the texture of that really put him off—but others…oh, my! So much taste, so much heat, punchiness, saltiness and umami in every mouthful! His favorite, he thought, was this dish of deep fried…anchovies? At least that's what they looked like. Tiny, crispy and crunchy fish packed full of chili heat. His forehead started springing sweat droplets, always a good sign.

Interestingly, there was no alcohol at this feast, only water, Thai tea and coffee—both full of sugar and with condensed milk—plus juices. When the fruit dishes were brought out, Jerome, stomach already full to bursting, groaned, then launched himself at some dragon fruit slices.

CHAPTER 44 - ADRIEN

Adrien had elected to spend the day in his room, working. Finally, the work bug had bitten him. He had had a stern talk with himself and set some hard targets for his work. He had so far managed to more or less hit them, which filled him with nervous energy.

To add to that, Dahlia continued with her totally unexpected booty calls. She continued to say that she didn't want anyone to know what was going on, and so she'd sneak into his room in the dead of night, or vice versa, but in truth, he thought everyone knew.

So, all in all, he was feeling good about himself, even working on a holiday. Just as he was congratulating himself for being so focused, his eyes went to his phone, lying on the desk next to his laptop. He had of course muted it, but the notification icon still blinked. He had been able to ignore it for most of the day, but he was getting quite tired now, so his determination wavered. He picked it up.

His eyes jumped to the TribeHut's group chat, which had been quiet for most of the day. He imagined that had something to do with people having to have their phones sealed away for the famed water fights, but it was now lighting up with messages and photos.

Someone posted a gorgeous sunset picture with a sizeable group of Hutters with their backs to the sea. Most appeared both still drenched and quite sozzled. Adrien's FOMO started to kick in. He checked his Apple watch. *I have been at this for nine hours now.* He thought this was good going on a supposedly holy day, so in a split-second he saved his work, shut the laptop and got ready to go out.

When he arrived at Rasta Bar, sunset was well and truly over. Night here descended so quickly, he hadn't gotten used to that yet. But the whole area was buzzing with people coming and going so it did not feel late. He identified TribeHutters by the fact that they were the largest group there; he approached and started exchanging greetings with people and hearing their Songkhran stories. Everyone wanted to know where he was, where he had been and why he wasn't drenched, like they were. He lamely replied he had work to do, and the most popular response was a real-life version of sadface, with an accompanying "awwww" sound. This suited him fine; he didn't want to go into specifics. He looked around, hoping to see Dahlia, but didn't. He ordered a beer from the bar and walked back out onto the sand. Even on a day such as this, the beach was hardly crowded. He loved this.

Now that he looked closely, he could see a couple people right by the water, frantically waving their arms and shouting something toward the sea where, he now saw, two people were swimming, holding glasses aloft.

He walked closer. The people on the shore were Laura and another guy he didn't know.

"Hey, Laura. What's going on?"

She turned to look at him, her face looking quite harassed and angry.

"I'm trying to tell them to come back. The bar owner told me that the fishermen saw a box jellyfish today."

"A box jellyfish?"

"Come on guys!" the other guy shouted to sea.

"Yes, you know? Very dangerous, very poisonous. Bad, bad. But these people are like, playing mute, you know? How do you say?"

"Playing dumb?"

"Yes! Argh!"

Adrien turned to look at the people swimming and was not surprised to notice that one of them was Dahlia, her long black hair slicked back. "Oh, fuck. Why are they still out there?"

"God knows! Look, no one else is in the water!" Laura said, spreading her arms and looking around. "And I'm not risking my life going out there!"

The other guy there threw one last loud scream, then turned on his heels and started walking back to the bar. But Dahlia and the other person out there, Brendan he thought it was, finally had turned toward them, toward shore.

"Come back!" Laura screamed, hands cupped around her mouth. Adrien gestured broadly with his arm to return to shore.

He saw that Dahlia frowned and looked at him, recognizing him. Was this going to make her stay out longer, stubbornly, or return? He genuinely didn't know.

But to his relief, the both of them started swimming back. Laura let out a huge sigh.

"You do know that it isn't your responsibility, right, Laura?" he quizzed her.

"Yes, of course I know but still… If it was me in the water, I'd want to know!"

As they approached shore, Brendan was the first to talk.

"What's going on guys? Can a man not enjoy a good cocktail in the waves?" He took a sip from an almost empty cocktail glass.

"Well, yes Brendan, sure. But apparently, they have spotted some box jellyfish in the area, so they are saying people shouldn't swim." Laura said.

"For real?" He looked around.

"Yes, no joke. No one is in the water, see?" Laura gestured

all around.

"I thought you guys were joking with us," said a crestfallen Brendan.

Dahlia didn't say anything. She slurped the last of the cocktail and handed the glass to Brendan. "Thanks."

"Why didn't they put flags out?" Brendan complained.

Come to think of it, Adrien hadn't seen any flags on any of these beaches, and no lifeguards.

Laura started to walk back to the bar and Adrien was about to turn around, too, when Brendan added, "Well, I guess the only thing left to do is get smashed and do a mushroom shake. What do you say?" He looked expectantly at both Dahlia and Adrien, while Laura let out a noise that sounded, to Adrien's ears, like the equivalent of "I can't take this shit anymore" and walked off.

Dahlia smiled her delicious, wicked smile Adrien had come to know so well. Brendan smiled back, then turned to him, eyes glinting. All Adrien could do was shrug.

CHAPTER 45 - MIRIAM

By the time Miriam reached Rasta Bar, people had been there far too long, and it showed. Conversations were incoherent, looping and repetitive, but that's what you got with all-day drinking.

Brendan, leading a small group of people, approached her conspiratorially and tried—and failed—to whisper, "We're going to get mushroom shakes, you in?"

Miriam threw a glance at the group behind Brendan. It was quite mixed. There were some younger people she didn't know, but Martin, Rose, Adrien and others she knew were there. "I could be. Where are you getting them from?"

It turned out Brendan was good friends with the head barman of the Jungle Bar, who apparently was in charge of growing and harvesting the mushrooms for these famous shakes. Brendan swore by them. They were not too heavy, kicked in quickly, left no comedown, and most importantly, nothing dodgy was added to them. The group started walking toward the Jungle Bar, which was up the beach. During the walk, people were giddily recounting Songkhran stories, which Miriam listened to with a smile on her face. She had heard so much of this Songhkran tradition, and it sounded like a lot of fun…if you were in the right mood. And the truth was…she wasn't. So today she had taken a personal day at the beach, reading all day. Her scabs had finally healed enough that she could swim in the sea again, and she wasn't going to waste the opportunity. She regularly needed these days to herself. Being surrounded by a loving and enthusiastic community at all times was all well and good, but she had long ago worked out that she recharged her batteries by spending time alone. She knew that if she had gone to the Songkhran celebrations, it would have taken a lot of energy for her, and she wasn't prepared for that. Plus, she planned to visit Chiang Mai, and this festival came into its own there, so she didn't mind missing out now.

When they arrived at Jungle Bar, it seemed a bit dead to Miriam, but the barman, Chart, soon turned the music up on seeing their group, and by sheer number they made the place feel buzzing.

Brendan turned around and counted how many of them there were. A couple people interrupted him, saying they'd share a single shake, so some time was lost in getting the right number. Finally, Brendan turned to Chart and ordered something like twelve mushroom shakes. Chart's face was a picture. He smiled and said, "Only for you, Brendan!" and went to the back to prepare the shakes.

PART VI

Long Goodbyes

CHAPTER 46 - ROSE

The days had been growing steadily longer, if only by a few minutes overall, so she didn't have to rush for sunset every day. The rain had finally come, with a vengeance, on the evening of Songkhran, while they were all off their faces and swimming in the sea. It had been a sobering moment, and she loved experiencing the awesome power of nature in all its glory. Her hair had stood on end at each powerful thunder bolt, closer and closer, until all they could hear was the roar of the rain. It was a beautiful, if uncomfortable, end to the long and momentous day.

Sloshing home soaked through muddy rivers that were once roads, with flip-flops being sucked in by the quagmire and having to be retrieved by hand, had not been fun. About halfway home, Rose had started really feeling the cold and damp. It was almost dawn, and she had been on the go for sixteen hours straight, running, jumping, drinking, swimming and of course blitzing out on mushrooms. She had hardly had any food, and now her body was ringing a lot of alarm bells.

Once the group made it to the main road, which now resembled more a lake than anything else, she prayed to the goddesses to send a tuk-tuk her way. She didn't care how much it was going to cost. She would gladly pay the price. But there was nothing moving on the road, no lights, no one waiting at the corners of the alleys down to the big resorts. Dejected and tired, they all started making their way south. At some point she realized that Dahlia was not with them. Where had she got to? But she looked around and couldn't see Adrien either, so they must have gone off together.

Most of the people in the group were staying at the TribeHut bungalows, but Rose was staying in a jungle bungalow. It was a little farther away, up a dirt road which, on a good day, was bumpy as hell and today was guaranteed to be a sludgy mess. She steeled herself for the walk ahead and continued trudging in the rain.

"I kind of wish I hadn't left my scooter behind," said Martin, a couple steps ahead and to the right of her.

"I hear your pain. And I would have gladly gotten a lift. But then again…would you trust yourself to drive in this state, and in this weather?" Rose asked.

"I know. But I really hate this— Ach!" His flip-flop had, yet again, been sucked down by mud, and he had put his foot down in the warm sludge. Rose smiled; at least it was funny when it was happening to someone else.

Martin bent down to retrieve the stray shoe.

"You're lucky. Think of poor Laura. She couldn't even find her thongs anymore."

Martin put his sandal back on and continued trudging.

"I guess so…" He looked down and she did the same. Their legs and feet were entirely covered in mud. "Not that it makes much difference."

They both started chuckling.

The roads were so empty that the group, maybe around twenty people, had become a straggly mass of smaller units. Normally you'd have to walk in single file to avoid being hit by speeding scooters, tuk-tuks or massive SUVs, but since there was no traffic whatsoever, people had ended up walking almost in the middle of the road, where it was relatively drier and less muddy. So it was that Martin and Rose found themselves alone, a few meters of darkness separating them from people both in front and behind. Somehow, Rose felt that Martin was watching her closely, but she was so tired and cold, she didn't care why.

"Rose… Are you still angry with me?" he said finally.

She stopped walking. *What on earth—?*

He stopped, too, and looked at her.

"It's okay if you are, I just…wanted to know where we stand. I tried so many times to talk to you, to apologize…"

She held up a hand. "Martin…why are you asking me that now? I just want to get home. I want to get cleaned up and crawl into bed. Oh God, I want that so much!"

She started walking again, and after a second, he followed suit. And despite the tiredness, and the fixed thought of just getting home throbbing in her mind like a flashing neon sign on top of a massive building, looming over her, she realized she had started to analyze whether she actually was angry with Martin. And the annoying thing was that…she wasn't sure.

"I don't know," she said in the silence. They continued walking and Martin nodded slightly. "I mean…I definitely was angry at you. You behaved abominably—"

"I know—" He tried to object but cut himself off.

"You know…you hurt me. And granted, it probably wasn't all you. I've got my own issues, sure. But then you just wanted to talk and talk and wanted to apologize and…you know, I didn't want to dwell on it. I just needed space. Not everything is always about you, you know."

At this she felt that he wanted to interject, but she lightly held up her hand to stall him. "It is something that I am working on. I needed to get control back of how I felt and…yeah…that's what made me angry, that even the apology had to be on your terms."

They had stopped walking and were facing each other now. Martin closed his mouth, obviously changing his mind about saying what he was going to say, the rain making rivulets over his cheeks and chin.

After a few seconds of silence, he hung his head and said, "I can understand that." He looked up at her again. "I apologize, Rose…"

She smiled and shook her head. *He had done it again.* She started walking again. "Come on, let's go." The TribeHut bungalows were just ahead now, in a few minutes they'd be there.

From behind them, Laura piped up, "Home sweet home!" and threw her arms wide. People seemed then to pick up their pace to get home more quickly.

Rose lagged behind, dreading having to continue on alone. Once she drew level with the gate, most people had hastily retreated inside. Martin stopped, still standing in the rain.

"Why don't you come inside, wait for the rain to stop at least?"

Rose hesitated. She looked at the sky. It was still dark, but she could see that there was no break in the clouds. It was amazing to think that only an hour earlier they were looking up at a clear sky full of stars.

The road was still dark and empty, the rivers of rainwater growing larger by the minute. She estimated it would take her another fifteen minutes at least to walk home. Her heart sank. She turned to Martin, trying to read his expression. He had really been confusing her with his wildly mixed messages over these last few weeks. Was he genuinely just offering her shelter? Was he after anything more, or was this something else she couldn't even fathom? Most of all, could she trust herself to get into a situation like this and not fall into her usual patterns once more?

Martin kept looking at her. "Come on, let's get out of this rain. I'm going to grow mold any moment now."

Rose was too tired to continue mulling over her doubts. She started walking toward the gate.

CHAPTER 47 - MARTIN

The gate to the TribeHut bungalows had been turned into a scene from *Apocalypse Now*. A thick sludge of red mud spread across the entire width, dotted with puddles. Footprints tracked a path through, and Martin tried to follow them. In Asia, you never knew how deep the puddles went. Or what could be hiding in them.

He turned to Rose and beckoned her over. They walked in.

Martin was replaying their conversation in his head. He wasn't sure he knew where they stood or what she understood. He just hoped he hadn't put himself in a situation he would regret, again. He had really just offered her a place to dry off, nothing more. *Oh, really?* Said the little voice inside him. *You can't think of anything else that may happen in your room?* He tried to shut it off. *Yes, I just made her a friendly offer to come out of the rain. I would have wanted the same, if the roles were reversed.*

For the last few steps, he seemed to go faster and faster. Suddenly, he could not stand the wetness a second longer. At the foot of the steps up to his bungalow he pulled off his flip-flops—they made a weird sucking sound from how much mud he had on his feet—and walked up carefully, slipping once or twice. On the veranda he stood still for a moment, wiped his eyes and face with his hands, flicked water off his fingertips and heaved a sigh of relief.

"Man, it feels good being out of the rain." He looked at Rose. She was doing much the same.

As Martin made to open the door, he remembered the state his room was in and pulled the door toward him, turning to face her.

"I just want to apologize in advance for the state of my room…"

"Oh, Martin, why would I care?" Rose said as she pushed past him into the room. "I just want to get dry—" She stopped talking when she saw the chaos. Piles of clothes everywhere, randomly discarded exercise equipment, bottles of water at various states of fullness. "Well, yeah…" She turned to him, a little embarrassed (*For me?*). "I'm just going to use the toilet, if that's okay?"

"Sure," said Martin, then remembered that the bathroom was even worse than the room. "Actually, just give me a sec!" He lunged in front of her before she could reach the door. Rose fell back and just stood there while Martin went into the bathroom and tried to make it look less like a grimy crime scene. There was only one little shelf in the bathroom, and he piled all his products there. He rinsed the sink to remove his beard hair and toothpaste stains, then grabbed a fresh roll of toilet paper and placed it in the holder, replacing the empty one.

He came out the door and motioned for Rose to go in. She had remained rooted to the spot, but her eyes were scanning the room.

After she went into the bathroom, Martin frantically went around the room picking his clothes up and flinging them inside the wardrobe. The rubbish and random items he gathered up into a corner of the room. He picked up the light blanket of his bed, bunched up on one side, shook it out and spread it almost evenly across the bed. He cast a glance and the room looked nearly normal again. Just in time, as he heard the sound of the bum gun, followed by the flush.

He opened the back patio door, took off his drenched T-shirt and wrung the water out of it, then spread it over a chair to dry.

He walked back in and slid the glass door closed just as Rose was coming out of the bathroom.

"Everything okay?" he asked.

She nodded a yes and he saw her eyes noticing he was bare-chested.

"I wrung it out and put it outside. Want to do the same?"

"I guess…" Rose said as she looked down at herself and at the puddles of water she had left in her wake. She walked to the glass door and opened it. She stepped outside, picked up the sides of her vest and threw a glance in his direction. He turned away, pretending to be busy with something.

She made a disgusted sound while she peeled off her vest, then wrung it out and put it next to his own T-shirt. She was now only wearing a bra. A kind of lacy, almost see-through bra. He tried hard not to look at it. Somehow, during their midnight swim, he had not registered this. Or had she been swimming topless? His memory was murky.

"My shorts are also super soaked." She looked at him question-ingly. They both chuckled, then he motioned for her to wait and went to the bathroom, picked up a towel and walked back, handing it to her. She pulled her shorts off in much the same way as the vest, but then wrapped the towel around her. She wrung the shorts out, and then her hair, and finally walked back inside, closing the door. She stood by one side of the bed, he on the other, and they looked at each other.

He looked past her, through the window. "It's still raining heavily. Might be a while before it eases up. Sit." He motioned to the bed.

She sat down on the edge of it, and he sat more comfortably on his side. After a moment of hesitation, he grabbed the remote control and turned on the TV. She seemed to relax and sat back on the pillows, the towel tightly wrapped around her.

Martin came to with a start. He must have nodded off. He looked up and saw that another episode of *Law & Order* was starting on the TV. It must have been its weird, sudden jingle that shook him awake. He turned to his right and saw that Rose's face was turned slightly away from him, so he couldn't tell whether she was sleeping or not.

He had no idea how much time had passed. It was still dark outside; of that he was sure. The rain was still pounding, and he vaguely remembered that when he had turned the TV on, the *Law & Order* episode seemed to be halfway in, so all in all it could have been only a few minutes ago that he had fallen asleep.

The new episode started, and Martin was amused anew at the out-of-sync sound that all Thai TV channels seemed to have, at least on this island. The sound came first and then you watched to see the images try to catch up. At times this could be hilarious. Otherwise, it was just mildly annoying.

Rose must have sensed his chuckle because she turned toward him. "I thought you were fast asleep," she said.

"Yeah, sorry, must have dozed off."

"No need to apologize. It is late."

"Yeah, but still." He shrugged.

"Though you should apologize for snoring…" she shot back, sheepishly.

"What?!" He was aghast. "No way! There is no way that I was snoring."

"Yes, yes you were. Swear to God. Like a chainsaw." And she started doing an impression of his snoring.

Martin started to protest again but stopped and looked at her. Was she being serious or was she joking? No one had ever complained about him snoring. If he truly had been, it was mortifying.

"For real?" he asked, a pleading note in his voice.

"Uh-uh," Rose said in a serious tone. Then *bam*! A pillow hit him square in the face. Rose cackled maniacally and pulled the pillow back, ready to strike again. "You should have seen your face!" she continued laughing heartily. "Oh, man!"

He felt a mixture of relief and annoyance. *Oh, really? I'll show you.* He dug behind him, whipped his own pillow out, lifted it high and brought it down on her head, scoring a hit while she still laughed.

"What the hell?! Ow!" she complained as she lifted her head up again. With her face still in a grimace, she brought her pillow round from the side and whacked him in the shoulder. "Back atcha!" They went on like that for a while.

Except that the pillows weren't particularly pillow-y or feather-y, and soon they had either hit the other's eye, or been elbowed painfully, and so found themselves breathing hard but kind of trying to stop the fight.

He watched Rose carefully, especially her hands, in case she brought the pillow up in a flash. He wasn't sure if she was truly done or was tricking him again.

Between laughing and play-fighting, Rose was trying to catch her breath. She held up her hand to try to get a break.

"You had enough?"

She nodded back.

"You're not just saying it?" he asked.

"No, really. I'm done." As a seeming show of goodwill, she threw the pillow away from her and showed her bare hands, as if being held at gunpoint.

Martin took a deep breath, then slowly put his own pillow back against the wall and sat back, leaning on it.

Rose blew air from her cheeks; she scooched down the bed a bit and then turned to her pillow. In a flash, Martin was sitting up and had grabbed his pillow again.

"No, no! Wait! I was just getting comfortable!" she said with a scared-sounding laugh. "Look." She fluffed the pillow and then lay down on her side, facing him, burrowing a bit and making the pillow conform to her head and neck. "See?"

"Mmmkay." He continued looking at her with mock suspicion as he copied her action of lying down on his side, facing her, and finding the most comfortable position.

They had lain down in such a way that their noses were only a few centimeters apart. Martin felt his breath slow down, but not too much. He was hyperaware of her, her breath, her presence. The shape of her body intertwined with the towel and the bedding. He tried very hard to not be aware of all of this. He closed his eyes and breathed more deeply. When he opened them again, she was still looking into his eyes.

"Martin…" she murmured.

"Hmm?" was all he could muster, trying to not breathe in her scent. This close, she smelled of fresh vanilla and something else he couldn't quite place.

"I'm not angry with you anymore." She smiled.

CHAPTER 48 - MIRIAM

Miriam woke up exceedingly late, which was unusual for her. She hadn't set the alarm clock and now she could see, behind the curtains, that the sun was full, high and strong. Wasn't it raining last night? She felt her hair and, yes, it was still damp from the night or morning before. She stretched her body fully, working out various aches and pains. She turned on her side, reaching her arm out over the empty side of the bed. She huffed.

Wouldn't it have been nice to wake up next to an attractive man? The only option the night before had been Brendan, who had tried it on with her, and with every other female there (she knew), repeatedly, winkingly, jokingly, but seriously, nonetheless. He really was not her type, and she had tried many times—not just last night—to explain to him that sex for her was not enjoyable with just anyone. There had to be a measure of attraction, complicity, chemistry, otherwise it was just a mechanical act. But this fact did not penetrate his thick skull, and so he persisted in badgering all his female friends for some intimate times whenever other prospects had dried up.

She thought back to last night. It had gone better than she expected. She truly was surrounded by a bunch of mostly lovely people. The whole thing felt seamless and just blissful. Even the rain, when it came, added to their mood. Now she felt the dampness all over her body and wasn't so happy about it, but still…it had been good. No, it had been great.

And just as well. Her time on the island was fast coming to an end. Her visa was running out, and she didn't think she should push it by returning immediately to Thailand. It was time to move on, which she found hard. Koh Tanu had truly come to feel like home, like nowhere else had in the past few years. But she had to go. Question was, where? Just the idea of having to deal with this made her tired. She turned and buried her head under the pillow.

These were those moments where she wished she wasn't alone in dealing with this. That she had someone to make the decision with, to share the load of researching and planning. But it was just wishful thinking. She had to make some plans; there was no way around it. She had heard from Jakob and Greta. They had returned to Germany so that Jakob could recover fully. They were staying with his parents, which Greta did not seem to mind. They'd decided to take some time to stay in Germany and reconnect. They'd be out travelling again, likely to Bali, but not immediately. Greta was keen to link up with Miriam again, but she knew it wouldn't be anytime soon, so that left a gap.

Or maybe…? She could go home, too. Visit her parents. She hadn't been back to Cali in… *Hang on, how many years is it?* She couldn't even remember. She knew it had been at Christmas time, but for the life of her she could not remember what year it was. Had it been that long? The thought scared her.

Her parents were getting old. They didn't complain too much about it, but she read between the lines when they wrote to her or occasionally when they spoke over Skype. Her dad in particular had been struggling. Both her brothers were now working full time in the bodega so that her dad could take more time off, and her mum could look after him, though she also helped look after Miriam's five nephews and nieces.

Overall, her parents had built a good life for themselves and their family. They had come to the US from Mexico with almost nothing and worked very hard, eventually buying the bodega when Miriam had been only a few years old. She still thought back with a mix of fondness, boredom and anger on all the years she had spent working there, helping out. Every weekend, every holiday, every summer vacation and spare moment was spent helping relieve their parents' burden, as they had no employees. In the first few years, when the children were all very young, it meant that her father practically lived in the bodega, and they wouldn't see him for days and days. It was a competitive business and you had to be open seven days a week and long hours if you wanted to make it. Which her parents did.

One of her father's cousins came over from Texas to work at the bodega and ended up living with them for two or three years, so Miriam and her brothers were stacked three to a tiny room for all that time. It had not been fun. She was the eldest and only girl, which meant Robi and Juan always ganged up on her and eventually got the better of her. She could not wait to get out of there, get out of that room, that house, that bodega, that neighborhood, that city and, yes, even that country.

Her parents had fought so hard to immigrate to the US, to blend in and become true Americans. They thought it shameful for her to even think about wanting to leave the country. No amount of discussion could make her parents understand that all she wanted to do was exploit the advantage they had worked so hard to give her—a US passport. Travelling as a Mexican was not really an option, not for someone like her, with little money and no connections. But with an American passport, she could go anywhere; opportunities would be open to her that her parents hadn't even dreamed of.

However, at some point she had realized that they would never get it, and so she kept these dreams to herself, put her head down and threw herself into academic study, which seemed the most direct and—for her—the easiest route out. When she won that scholarship to Spain, instead of skipping home happy and cracking open the champagne, she had sat on the news for days, thinking of ways to spin it, waiting for the right moment to tell them so she would not break their hearts.

Her parents had wanted her to study business or medicine, which in their eyes were the only two disciplines that university existed for. She hated both of those—medicine because she didn't have the aptitude for it, or the iron will she knew she would need to make it as a doctor, and business because... *Oh, please.* What was she going to do with a business degree?

What she wanted, really wanted, was to study English, history, literature, but to her parents these were almost dirty words. Eventually she was able to settle for English with business studies, to appease them, but term by term she secretly whittled down the business bit off her degree, and when she got the scholarship, she was on track to be an English major. The scholarship had been to study a Masters in English and Spanish Comparative Literature at Madrid's Complutense, and there was no getting away from the fact that there was nothing business-y about it.

Miriam, in what became a trademark style, decided to tell her parents everything in one go, one thing after the other, starting with the most painful piece of information and not stopping, so that by the end, her parents were completely desensitized to the fact that she was moving abroad. In the whirlwind of revelations, she tried to have the family cheer for her for achieving her major and for having beaten hundreds of other applicants to a full-ride scholarship. But no. All they could concentrate on was that she wasn't graduating in business and oh, Lord what was going to become of her?

Well, what had become of her was a fiercely independent, intelligent and unconventional woman—unfortunately, all things her parents considered flaws and not virtues. And that was what made being close to them difficult, if not impossible.

The unspoken disapproval they felt was clearly written on their faces and in every interaction they had with her. But it wasn't angry disapproval; it was tinged with sadness. Sadness for her that she hadn't—in their view—made a success of her life, and sadness for them because they could not see where they had gone wrong, and they did not have a daughter close to them in their final years, as would be expected. So, yeah, going home would mean having to deal with ALL of that afresh.

Her brothers, despite being younger and having grown up in modern-day Los Angeles, held the same views as her parents when it came to her, and they treated her with suppressed disapproval. This she could not accept. It was one thing for her parents to see her this way; they were from another place, another culture, another time. But her brothers? She knew that outside the home they were modern American guys, they even travelled abroad, for fuck's sake! But Miriam should have done what her parents had wanted; after all, hadn't Juan and Robi done so? And Miriam should be at home being a dutiful daughter to her elderly parents. But her parents were elderly and in need of help only when Miriam was being discussed, as her brothers had no qualms about using their mum as an unpaid child-minder five days a week.

She was really torn. Despite all this heavy baggage, she loved her parents very much…maybe she just didn't like them enough. She was aware that time was not infinite, and one day it would be too late to spend quality time with them. Maybe she could keep the visit to a manageable short time? It would be expensive, but maybe it would provide enough fuel for her to keep going for a while after that, and also offer a bit of respite from them always asking her to come home. Although, she found it really funny that whenever she was home, all her relatives could ask her was "When are you coming back again?" She wanted to scream back "I am here now! Enjoy this moment!" But she never did.

She finally got up to face the day, and the planning she needed to do.

CHAPTER 49 - DAHLIA

Dahlia shot up from her bed in the throes of a vomit heave. She rushed into her bathroom and made it to the toilet bowl just in time. A splash of dark-colored slop made its way from her mouth to the water at the bottom of the bowl. She took a breath in—she had always hated vomiting for that split-second when you thought you were going to choke on it—but then another wave hit her, from deep down, and more of the disgusting stuff came out of her. She closed her eyes lest the sight of it made her even more prone to vomit.

When it subsided, she sat back and wiped her mouth with toilet paper. She got up and washed her face in the sink. *Damn mushroom shake.* It always seemed to have this effect on her, even when the shrooms were good. Other people did not seem to have this problem, and that's why she went easy on the fun drink.

She crawled back to bed and wrapped herself in the blanket. Today would be a wasted day. Thank God Jerome was not around. It wasn't fun sharing a small place when you were sick. It was interesting that the sickness only came onto her in the morning, after she had come home from the night's revels.

When the rain had started, she and Adrien had ended up huddling near Brendan and Laura, who were still blissfully unaware of the rest of the world and going at it by the bar. Everyone was still high, and she couldn't remember exactly how—or maybe she didn't really want to remember—she and Adrien had been pulled into Brendan and Laura's orbit, until the four of them decided to walk to Brendan's luxury beach cabana and continue the party there. Thankfully, the cabana was nearby. The rain was heavy but walking on the beach made you feel you were at one with nature.

Even in her high, Dahlia was clear about what was going to happen at Brendan's place, but she thought that Adrien did not have an inkling. She was curious at how he'd react. She had seen him watch with interest as she and Laura had kissed, but he had made no move to join them or encourage them in any way.

Brendan's abode was quite luxurious. It was right on the beach, with full height glass sliding doors. It had a wide deck with a hot tub—Brendan even attempted to suggest they all got into it, but it was clear it was made for two and the whole thing would turn into a human Tetris game—and a beautiful bedroom overlooking the sea. It was cool inside; the walls were polished concrete and the whole thing was quite minimalist. Brendan had made it his own by strewing his clothing on almost all available surfaces.

Once inside, they dried off and Brendan staggered to the fridge where he got some drinks out. He handed them out randomly. They were at that stage of the night were people would drink anything that was in their hands.

They sat down at the foot of the bed, on an assortment of cushions, bean bags, and Thai-style recliners. As soon as they were more or less horizontal, Laura launched herself onto Brendan with renewed vigor. Dahlia turned to Adrien and started kissing him passionately. At some point she was aware that Brendan must have put on some music in the room.

They snogged and drank; time seemed to have no meaning. Laura interrupted them by placing a hand on Dahlia's arm. She looked at Adrien pointedly, then leaned in and kissed Dahlia full on the mouth. Dahlia closed her eyes and after some time she felt another hand, another face close by. It was Brendan. Now she was kissing him while Laura kissed her neck and touched her boobs.

Dahlia had turned then, to see what Adrien was doing. He was frozen, beer bottle halfway to his mouth, his gaze locked on the scene before him. Laura must have sensed Dahlia's attention shift and she turned to Adrien. She gently took the beer from his hand, took a swig and put it down out of the way. Then she not so gently grabbed the front of Adrien's T-shirt and pulled him toward her, snogging him fiercely. At this point, Dahlia's face was turned back by Brendan's hand, and the whole thing became a tangle of limbs and bodies.

After a few hours, tired and a bit sore, Dahlia had woken up much more sober. The others were slumbering around her, naked, entangled. She gently lifted somebody's arm off her and slid out, got dressed and left, all quiet as a mouse. No one stirred.

She needed to be alone. She had never liked post-sex moments. It was unlike her to have fallen asleep like this. Blame the mushrooms. The rain had almost stopped, so getting back to the bungalows was not too hard. Dawn was breaking and she snuck into the bungalow without encountering another soul. She showered, dried and went to bed, only to be awoken not much later by the dreaded shroom vomit.

Despite the upset tummy, she was relishing the memory of the previous night. A foursome was something new to her—she had had threesomes before—and she was quite intrigued at how well Adrien had fit in. After that initial shock, when it finally must have dawned on him what was about to happen, he enthusiastically joined in kissing both Laura and Dahlia. He hesitated a couple of times when he saw Brendan kissing, or later, fucking, Dahlia, which if she was being perfectly honest warmed her heart. But it hadn't stopped him from enjoying himself with both girls and, if memory served, even with Brendan at some point when they were so entangled it was difficult to know what belonged to whom.

It was one of those nights that could only happen in an unplanned, organic way—though she knew Brendan was always angling for such an occasion. Yet the chance of it actually happening even for him was definitely in the single digits or less, and the mushrooms definitely were integral to that. If anything embarrassing happened, one could always ascribe it to the drugs. She was quite pleased with herself that she had notched another interesting experience. Laura had been quite a revelation—though Dahlia didn't like her all that much when she was sober and straight—and even Brendan was kind of perfect for this kind of scenario.

A knock on the door pulled her out of her reverie. It was still really early. Was Jerome back? Dahlia got up, holding the blanket around her.

"Jerome?" she asked in a low, curious voice when she got to the door.

"No, it's Adrien. Can you let me in?"

Dahlia opened the door and Adrien almost ran in. He turned around, anger etched across his face. "What the fuck, Dahlia? You just left? No message, no waking me up. Shit!"

Dahlia was dumbfounded. "I—"

"Do you know how embarrassing it was, waking up with those two and you nowhere to be seen? They started going at it again!" Adrien was working himself up. "As if I wasn't even there!"

At this, she gagged again, the heat rising in her throat. She ran to the bathroom and puked again.

Afterward, Dahlia went to sit on the bed. Adrien had been silent the whole time.

"I'm sorry, Ade. You know what I'm like."

Adrien gave a sigh. "No, Dahlia. I am starting to think I really don't know what you are like. I thought..." At this he hesitated. He looked at her, maybe waiting for her to say something. But Dahlia just waited. *What did he mean? What did he think?*

In the awkward silence that ensued, Dahlia made herself more comfortable on the bed. Then, after a while said, "Do you mind continuing this later? I'm not feeling great and I need to sleep a bit. I have a lot of work to do later."

"And I don't? Dahlia, it's already, like, seven. Might as well be up already."

"Seven? Shit." *No! That's so late already.* She had taken Songkhran off—there was no point in trying to work on a day like that—but all her clients expected her caught up today with all the work from yesterday and on point for today. Her stomach tightened another knot.

Adrien was still standing in the middle of the room, moving back and forth, a nervous energy coursing through him.

"What do you want me to do?" she said, tired and exasperated. He took a long look at her and seemed to soften.

"Hey. I know. We had a big day yesterday. We're both tired. And probably hungry. I don't know about you, but yesterday I didn't have any proper food. What do you say, shall we go out for a nice breakfast? Then we can get to work with some more energy. Huh?"

The idea of food was both enticing—she also hadn't had a proper meal in God knows how long—and sickening, due to the ongoing mushroom disruption.

"I don't know if I can keep anything down," she said, rubbing her stomach.

"Well, let's try. You definitely need to try and keep your energy up. Let's get you some electrolytes, too."

The only place open at that time of the day was a perennial favorite with TribeHutters. The ubiquitous, aptly named Sofa, a large patio deck with many, many sofas, armchairs and tables throughout. Fans were already whirring, giving the impression of a spring breeze. It was one of the few places that was open all year, run by a local family. They greeted Dahlia and Adrien warmly and told them to sit wherever they wanted.

Only a couple other tables were occupied; it was nice that things were finally quieting down for the start of low season. Dahlia was sad that she would have to leave soon and made a mental note to return to this island during the off season, so as to enjoy more of the quiet and to stay away from crowds and too much partying. The rain, which had continued for a few hours, had finally cleared the air and cooled the temperature down. All the waiters commented on that. They were stoked the rain had finally come. Dahlia, for the first time, realized that these people worked on their feet all day in the open air. No such luxury as air con for them. Suddenly her privilege seemed like a heavy stone on her chest.

They ordered their breakfast, coffee and juice, and waited. Adrien was still fidgety. She decided to address things.

"Adrien, listen…"

He looked up.

"I'm sorry I left without saying anything. I just…I don't know what it is. I just can't do that shit, you know?"

He seemed to just take it in, absorb it. Then he shook his head and started again.

"And what shit is that, Dahlia? Please, be specific, because with you I don't know anymore. Is it the sleeping shit, the sex shit, the romance shit? Huh?!"

CHAPTER 50 - ADRIEN

Adrien was livid. What did she mean? Since they had met, since the very first time they had slept together, Dahlia had been sending him mixed messages. One minute she was waving under his nose the fact that she was interested in sleeping with other people—if not the fact that indeed she was sleeping with other people. The next she was all over him, staying the night in his room, even while telling him she didn't do cuddles and overnights. The next she was ignoring him. Then she would sit next to him at work every day, invite him for lunch and walks on the beach, where she would take his hand and be romantic, only to pull her hand away if they saw anyone they knew. What the hell was she playing at? He was so turned around, he felt almost seasick.

And now, she had orchestrated that foursome, with Laura and... and with Brendan. Flashbacks of the night intruded in Adrien's mind. Brendan kissing Dahlia. Laura kissing Dahlia. Brendan's hand reaching forward to touch Dahlia as he took her from behind— *No! Don't think about that now.*

Dahlia was still looking at him without saying anything.

"What is it that you can't do? One minute it's one thing, but the next you're doing exactly that thing. So, forgive me if I—" The waitress had just arrived, bringing their drinks. Adrien ate his words and waited, nervous, for the waitress to place the drinks on the table in an irritatingly slow way.

They both thanked the waitress and waited till she was out of earshot. Then both spoke at the same time.

"Forgive me if I—"

"I'm not sure where—"

They both stopped speaking at exactly the same second. At another time it would have been a cute, sweet moment. Adrien reached out for his cappuccino and took a sip. Caffeine surely would help with this headache that was building up. Unfortunately, it was so hot it seared his lips and mouth. He was so tense he held his reaction.

Dahlia took her mango smoothie and put the stainless-steel straw in her mouth. It was glistening. Her mouth was so cute when she drank with a straw. *Dammit.*

Adrien took a deep breath. He should start over.

"Have I ever asked you to stay the night?"

She looked at him questioningly.

"Have I ever taken your hand in public, or kissed you when others were around?"

She shook her head.

"Have I ever made plans for our future or made any demands of you? Any demands?"

Dahlia looked down and replied in a half whisper, "No."

"Glad we established that," Adrien said, in a tone that came out a little more peeved than he would have liked. He grabbed his cup and drank more scalding coffee.

"Well, you don't have to be a dick about it." Dahlia half slammed her mango smoothie down. The waitress was back, this time carrying plates with their breakfast.

They started eating in weighted silence. Adrien noticed how crunchy the sound was when Dahlia bit into her avocado toast. He was still so annoyed with her. All this time, she had just presumed he wanted more from her, specifically that he wanted from her exactly what she wasn't prepared to give. He felt like she did not give him enough credit. Adrien had no idea what he wanted. Or maybe he did have a tiny bit of an idea, but definitely not so much as to start making demands on her. He had just thrown himself into this wild ride, into this new lifestyle, and was just clinging on for dear life to see where it was going to take him. The effort required for trying to make her understand this seemed to be beyond him at this moment.

"Dahlia…I don't want anything…more, anything, how can I say, specific? I don't have a list and go 'Oh, yes, she must be like this or we must do this, etcetera, etcetera.'" He looked into her eyes to make sure she was listening.

"All I want is what we're already having, already experiencing. Okay? That said…I was pissed this morning because after something like last night—you know, kind of a big deal for me—it seemed to me that you didn't spare a single thought for how it would be when we woke up, and that's just lack of respect, on a basic human level, you see? I don't mean like, 'My girlfriend should have waited for me,'" he said in his best mock crybaby tone, "I just mean, shit. I'm in a dude's place I hardly know, we just had random group sex—" At her alarmed look, Adrien lowered his voice "—and the only person here I actually know has decided to ditch me. And when I pull you up on it, you go all, 'I can't do this shit,' on me."

He stopped talking and resumed eating. He hated it when food went cold. Admittedly, in Thailand the food didn't actually get cold, just lukewarm, but still he hated it. Lukewarm eggs? Ugh.

Dahlia had continued to watch him all the while, and now she observed as he ate.

After breakfast, which continued more or less in silence, they lugged their kits to the coworking space. It was dead quiet, not even the staff were in yet.

Without conferring, they made their way to the open-air area and picked two seats that were not strictly side by side but were near each other. They started unpacking their things. Adrien went to the wall and pulled the cord to activate the fan, then stood there for a moment to receive the blessed air from it.

Just as he turned back to the desk, Dahlia was standing there, facing him, words blurting out of her as if held in for a long time.

"You're right, okay? You are right, I know that. And…and… What do you want me to do about it? I don't know what to do about it! I don't like it, there, I said it. I don't like it…but I don't know what the alternative is." She looked up at him sheepishly. "I really am sorry."

He rushed to her and grabbed her in a full-body hug. And for the first time, he felt Dahlia letting herself feel the hug and participate completely. The hug went on for a long time; they held each other tight, the only sounds around them the birdsong from the jungle trees.

He buried his face in her hair, the smell of it was heady. "Well… for starters, don't abandon me again in the middle of group sex, okay?"

She laughed.

"We can agree on that, can't we?"

"Sure."

He leaned back to look at her. They both smiled like idiots.

Just then, a sound nearby startled them, and they both turned. One of the cleaning staff was just walking out with all her cleaning gear; she bowed her head briefly to them. They bowed back but remained together. The cleaning lady moved away to begin her work.

"Are you feeling any better?" Adrien asked Dahlia.

"A little. Breakfast helped."

"So…" He took a big breath. "What do you have on today?"

"A lot of catching up." Dahlia now moved toward her laptop. "But also, it is time I figure out my next steps. My visa is running out, I can't put it off anymore."

"Yeah, same here."

She turned and looked at him. "I know you said Chiang Mai, for you."

"Yes, potentially. But I still need to pop out of Thailand first. And you? Do you have any ideas?"

"Either back to Malaysia—that's an easy option—or continue on to Cambodia, Laos, or Vietnam."

"I thought you wanted to go to Bali?"

"Yeah, that's a good option for sure. Lots of TribeHutters have been there or are going there."

"It's really high on my list. I could go there before Chiang Mai." He said with a hint in his voice.

Dahlia raised her eyebrows and her mouth became a perfect O.

"No pressure, of course. But…at least we could share the research. It would help us both."

"That's a great idea." She looked around to check if they were still alone, then she ducked in and kissed him on the lips. "You do accommodation and I'll take coworking, then we compare notes. Deal?"

CHAPTER 51 - JEROME

Jerome was in a bind. He hadn't come to Thailand to fall in love. He had come to lick his wounds, get himself back on his feet and then continue on his path. Not that he had known what his path actually was, but he had felt he was on it, nonetheless.

And he had not planned or even fantasized about falling in love. At least that is what he thought that he felt. He had never been in love before—to be brutally honest he didn't really believe in love as a real-life thing. He had been loved, for sure, by men here and there… then again, had it been love? Maybe they thought they were in love, and they verbalized it, but who was to know the reality of it? Can one truly be in love without being loved back? And is it the same kind of love? He had never asked himself any of this, but now there he was, in love with Thaim. What was he going to do?

Thaim loved him; of this he was pretty certain. Not only because Thaim told him so, often, but also because Jerome could see it in a lot of little everyday gestures. How he checked repeatedly that Jerome was okay—was the fan too high or too low? Was the food okay? Was he having fun? How Thaim had wanted to introduce him to his family, to make it official. How he talked openly and without fear of a future together, of plans. And he thought Thaim was sure Jerome felt the same about him. There was a solid, earthy certainty about the relationship coming off Thaim, and this gave Jerome a feeling that he had never experienced before: contentedness.

It was such a novel feeling that he examined it often. He pried it open; he analyzed it; he questioned it, prodded it and vivisected it to see what it truly was. The reality was that, deep down, it frightened him. This idea of being settled down with someone at twenty-seven... He had never even given it a single thought. Was this what he wanted? What he needed? Should he just go with the flow and see where it led? Or should he go back to what he did best?

Because being with Thaim long-term meant staying in Thailand and getting a job and...well, that's probably not what Jerome had in mind.

And so, unsure of what he wanted, he started getting back on apps and websites for sugar daddies/sugar babies and began chatting to various prospects. He told himself that there was no harm in chatting to them, and that this way at least he kept a door open for himself.

But of course, he did not disclose this to Thaim. He went along when Thaim talked about the future, letting himself get caught up in it and even offer his own views, as if he were telling the plot of a film. "And then we'll get a dog. And we could buy a piece of land and build our own home!" This last thing particularly excited Thaim. It kind of felt like another game, albeit a good one.

The work with Dahlia was getting better. There were now some things he could do alone and to what she referred to as "satisfactory level," such as some SEO optimization things and the like. A little bit of money was trickling in, and Dahlia was positive that he could do more. But his heart wasn't in it.

He had to make a decision as to what he was going to do. He could potentially stay in Thailand indefinitely, with Thaim, to see how things would go, but there was the issue of visa—what a palaver that was!

Or he could travel with Dahlia. She had mentioned Vietnam or somewhere similar. He could kind of tag along and continue working with her.

But then again, he could continue working with her from wherever, if he wanted to, and so he could really go anywhere he pleased… He tended to be a hit with Chinese guys, because of what they called his "exotic" looks, and most of the sugar daddies that contacted him were Chinese. He could go back there and live a good life. Unless the sugar daddy turned out to be a psycho like the last guy.

Oh, what was he going to do? The thought accompanied him all day, and time was running out.

PART VII

Laa Gorn

CHAPTER 52 - MARTIN

Martin's training had kicked up a notch. Now there were only a few days left to his fight, and he felt the time to joke around had come and gone. His new regime expected him to wake up at 6:00 a.m., have a protein shake, then go for a 5K run. This was followed by a two-hour session in the Muay Thai gym—warm-up, skipping rope, ab work, sparring and a few technical rounds with Bamon, perfecting techniques he had only ever seen and not tried out.

By 10:00 a.m., he was shattered. He would shower then go for a big breakfast, try to do some work, often would succumb to a nap, but then he'd have to be up for another forty-five-minute training at 4:00 p.m. This one was more speed rounds, circuits and core work.

Oh, and no alcohol whatsoever. Which, if he was honest, was probably a good thing overall.

His body had been getting more and more toned, more sculpted. Still not the body of a model or anything, but he liked the results; it felt good. And that was regardless of the various little injuries he had acquired: a few grazes and scratches, plenty of bruises, a mushed toe, and just a general soreness in his whole body. Part of the regime was to get a full-body massage every day, which he usually got in the evening before bed. He was so tired he was out and asleep by 10:00 p.m. His social life had taken a dive but, again, not a bad thing.

Rose had left the island two days after Songkhran. They had ended up staying up all that night, talking. He had finally plucked up the courage to tell her about his sex addiction, how he was struggling with it. And he had implied that that was behind the events of the Vibe party. She had seemed to understand, asked him a bunch of questions, her eyes widening when he hinted at his past sexual excesses. But she hadn't pried. And for that he was grateful. It was only a small step to start feeling boastful about it again, and he was trying really hard to not go down that road.

She had also opened up a little. About her insecurities, her feeling that she was always going after unavailable guys but couldn't help it—they both chuckled at that—and she also mentioned briefly her friend Frances. But she said she wasn't ready to talk about that, not yet. In the late morning, he'd retrieved his scooter and driven them to one of his favorite cafés for breakfast, where they ran into other TribeHutters, and spent a few hours eating, drinking coffee, and laughing about the previous night's shenanigans.

The night before Rose left, after dinner, as a group of them walked along the beach chasing hermit crabs, she'd smiled and said, "You know, I am glad I finally let you apologize. It feels good to be friends." *Friends.* He'd smiled and nodded.

Rose was only going to Singapore or somewhere like that for a few days to bounce her visa and get back into Thailand for a few more weeks. It was all planned out, but after that night they had grown really close, and to have her be away suddenly had left him a bit confused. Bereft, even. But that meant he threw himself into training with gusto. And Rose would be back exactly on his fight day, so he would see her at the stadium and she would see him in all his glory—or not—in the ring. It was an exciting and scary prospect. And it powered him to train harder.

He had been talking to Hans every few days and had been good at keeping his SAA sponsor up to date with all goings-on. When he had told Hans about the night he spent with Rose, with the two of them half-naked in bed, it took a lot of convincing for Hans to believe that nothing had happened between them, not even a kiss. But eventually, seeing Martin's open face, Hans agreed that this was a positive big step. Although he sounded a warning about Martin continuing to put himself in dangerous situations, overall he said he felt that Martin was coming along great.

"So, you see, you don't have to run away from uncomfortable things," Hans told him one late night on a video call. "Even the uncomfortable bit isn't as bad as you imagine it will be. And it passes quickly, no?"

Martin agreed.

But what he didn't tell Hans—and almost didn't admit to himself, because he was afraid of what it meant—was that Rose had been on his mind a lot. A lot. On that night, he had felt the impulse to reach out and kiss her, hold her, clear as a bell. And with a clarity of mind he had never possessed up to that point, he had seen exactly how it would go had he caved to those impulses. She would kiss him back at first, because the moment was just perfect. He knew that from how she looked at him and how relaxed she seemed. He could practically smell it. But then she would get ahold of herself. The past hurt of their interaction and all the baggage that came with it and with him would surge up, and she would be upset that he had kissed her, showing her that he had learned nothing. And then she would leave and never speak to him again.

And so, he hadn't moved. He had looked at her, willing his mind to learn, and to show it. He had savored the pain it cost him not to follow those impulses and tried to turn it into a positive.

Now that they were friends, they were texting constantly.

WTF does everyone love *The Crown*? Makes me cry to see all the suppressed emotion 😭

You're a Brit, you should know! I think you guys are suckers for doomed monarchs 🤮

I'll have you know I am half Aussie so monarchy is something that rankles... 🤣 What are you watching?

I was halfway through Mad Men, but Bamon has me watching Muay Thai videos constantly. If I fail as a fighter I think I can carve out a new career as commentator 🥊 Plus my YouTube algorithm is now fucked forever

OMG, omw to airport and our ferry is carrying an elephant! 🐘

WTF?

Poor thing is all tied up and left in the sun! 😡 I've half a mind to unchain it and let it rampage free!!!!

Err, maybe wait till you're OFF the ferry?! You know, just sayin' 🙄

Man, I need to revive my original life plan: open a sanctuary for all these abused creatures. Frances and I were so going to do it.

What happened to that dream?

I guess it just disappeared… kinda like Frances herself.

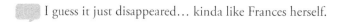 …

And so, she flew out of the country. She had made him promise to train hard and be safe, and said she was looking forward to seeing his fight, but he clearly saw that she was worried about him. Her reaction to the other Muay Thai fight had stayed with him, and he was determined to not be hurt in the fight—actually, he was determined to win.

CHAPTER 53 - MIRIAM

Miriam's bags were finally packed. It was amazing how much crap she had accumulated, yet again, in these few months. She had spent a couple days rehousing anything that could be rehoused— kettle, rice cooker, bowls, beach mats, plastic jugs, yoga mat, salt and pepper grinders and assorted excess groceries— and bringing anything else to local charities, like unwanted clothing, books and towels. She was a lot lighter by the end, since she had to fit it all in the big trolley and little trolley that she had arrived with. But my, how she hated packing!

Her pickup for the ferry was early the next morning. She decided to spend her last afternoon alone on the beach. She didn't tell anyone where she was going to be. She wanted to have one last swim and savor one last sunset all alone. She drove down to one of her favorite beaches, not too far from home, and sat down to take it all in. Ever since she was a child, every time she left a place she had this sort of little ritual she had to do: go to her favorite place or a significant place, alone, in quietness, and recite a kind of thank-you mantra. *Thank you, powdery white beach. Thank you, hermit crabs and corals. Thank you, warm, green waves. Thank you, palm trees. Thank you, monkeys. Thank you, fish...* And then at the end she would say goodbye to all of that, a kind of *I see you* pushed out into the universe as a positive energy force. It helped her to be less sad about leaving and more hopeful about returning one day.

She had her last blissful swim as the sun went down into the water. The beach was so quiet; there was almost no one there. Afterward, she dried off and then drove to a regular beach restaurant where she had told people to come and see her off.

When she arrived, a few minutes later than she'd said she would be, she was gob-smacked to see a huge group of people already there, all waiting for her! Joy and Mark, her landlords, with a couple of the staff from their restaurant, Laila and her girlfriend, Bamon with almost the entire family, Jie with her two daughters and her new puppy dog—which everyone was cooing over and playing with—and of course a huge number of TribeHutters, even some she had only met briefly and recently. Everyone had turned out to say goodbye.

When they saw her approach, a huge cheer went up, along with cries of, "There she is!" and the like, and she stopped, for a moment overwhelmed by the feeling of knowing they were all there for her. She wasn't crying. No. Only some water was gathering in her eyes and threatening to spill out.

Serge ran up to her and hugged her. "Thank God you're here, honey. I'm starving!" he joked as he pulled her in toward the rest of the group, and they swallowed her up.

The evening was beautiful. They sat along the seafront, with the last color of the sunset disappearing from the sky. Food, drinks and conversation had flowed all night. People playfully fought to sit next to Miriam for a few minutes, to say their goodbyes or just shoot the breeze as normal.

Most of the conversation was a repeat of "Where are you going next?" or "What time is your pick-up?" or, better yet, "When are you coming back?" She answered amiably to all, even though she thought she sounded like a recorded announcement.

Martin put a hand on her shoulder and leaned in. "Mate, I am sorry, but I have got to get going. Fight is in two days and I need my beauty sleep."

She stood up to hug him. "Of course. I understand. I'm bummed I won't get to see it. Make sure someone does a live video of it, okay? I'll try to watch!"

"Sure thing." He hugged her again. "Oh, and Rose also says goodbye. She said she's sorry to have missed you."

"Thanks, give her my love when you see her."

They looked at each other, smiling.

"It's been grand, hasn't it?" she offered.

"More than." And they both laughed.

"See you around, then?"

"You bet." She smiled and Martin walked off. As she turned, she noticed that Bamon was watching him go with a smile on his face, so she walked toward the Thai trainer and sat down next to him.

"How do you think he will do?"

He chuckled at her question. "No one ever knows, really. But he has a good mind for it."

Miriam threw one last look at Martin's receding form among the palm trees.

"If he can let his mind lead him, he can do it." The Thai man added.

People left in dribs and drabs, and every time, Miriam got up, hugged them and exchanged a few final words. It was kind of like being at your own birthday party, where you had to stay till the very last guest remained. At the end she was left with Serge, Dahlia and Adrien and a couple of the restaurant staff who knew her well. They were at the end of their shift and had sat down to enjoy a drink and a chat. The sound of the sea, the breeze coming from it, was like a soothing balm and gave rhythm to their conversations. The restaurant dogs—a fixture of every Thai establishment—lolled about contentedly now that the place was quiet. The conversation had, thankfully, moved on from Miriam's leaving and they had ended up talking politics. They sparred playfully and poked each other's ideas and statements, as they had done many times over the past few months. She was going to miss this.

Adrien and Dahlia seemed loved up, but in a strange way. She had sensed before that there was something going on between them, but she hadn't wanted to stick her nose in out of respect. She knew how important it was that one's business remained one's own. But tonight, they were openly affectionate with each other, even if not at the level of an established couple. It was nice to see.

When the two of them made a move to leave, Miriam knew it was time to wrap things up. After saying goodbye to them and to the restaurant staff, she and Serge went for a short walk on the beach. It was very dark now, no moon, and the breeze ensured that there was not a single cloud in the sky, so the firmament shone brightly above them. She drank it all in, the smell, the sensation, the feeling of the cool coral sand on her feet. They didn't speak much.

After a while they turned back. The tide was rising, and if they weren't careful, it was going to cut them off from the restaurant. Just before they walked up the steps dug out of rock that led back to the restaurant, Miriam turned and took one last long look.

"How does one ever get used to not being here, Serge? To not seeing this every day?"

He laughed, puffing out the smoke of his cigarette. "Fuck if I know! I haven't tried it yet."

CHAPTER 54 - JEROME

One evening, Thaim and Jerome went to dinner at a supper club, a secret location on the island that was revealed to you only after booking—and paying—where you would experience an eclectic meal by a local chef. They drove inland for quite a while, then started going up one of the central mountains of the island and had to look out for a hidden turn in the road. The overgrown path—you really could not call it a road—ended at a beautiful wooden house on stilts that overlooked one of Tanu's famed crescent beaches. The house had been decked in tasteful tealights and shell pendants, along with small water features with floating lily pads. A delicate incense fragrance was burning in the air nearby. Jerome was curious what the view would be like in the daytime.

Thaim had always wanted to come and was very pleased he could show off to Jerome by taking him to this increasingly famous spot. All the other guests—and there were not many, because this secret club only sat one very long table a day—were foreigners. Thaim was the only local. They were greeted with a complimentary glass of bubbly and shown to their seats.

As chance would have it, opposite them was another gay couple and the foursome ended up talking all evening, in between eating the delicious food and drinking the fabulous wine. This couple—Jerome never got their names—was a little bit unusual in that one of them was an American white guy and the other was Indian. And they had met while the American was on a long holiday in India.

It was clear early on what the power dynamic at play was, and it was disappointingly familiar. The white guy was older and made more—much more—money, and the brown guy was from a poorer background but was younger and better-looking. They were also clearly in love.

Watching them, and reflecting on this type of relationship, gave Jerome pause for thought. His and Thaim's situation could not be said to be the same, but he really struggled and was very conflicted with what he saw was his role. Could he be forever the younger, more attractive man in this scenario, being showered with gifts by older and/or more affluent lovers? He knew that he could not play this part forever, but he also knew he could make it last a long while and make the most of it. But on the other hand, he could also learn to be more independent and less reliant on others' whims. But it was scary. He wasn't very good at being independent.

Finally, he came to the conclusion that if he had to settle for being reliant on someone financially, it had better be for serious money, and in the meantime he was going to try to become a bit better at looking after himself.

When Jerome told Thaim his decision, his boyfriend was in tears. In hysterics. As soon as Jerome mentioned that Dahlia was leaving and that he had decided to go with her, Thaim was beside himself, crying, pleading with him to reconsider, repeatedly asking him why, what had he done, was he not enough?

Jerome really didn't know what to say. He thought that anything that came into his mind would only make things more difficult, more painful, harder to extricate himself from. And he couldn't have that. He really couldn't. For once in his life, he wanted things to end without drama, without torn clothing and shredded belongings, without screams and slammed doors, without threatening messages and places that he felt he could never go back to. For once, he wanted to be able to hold onto the memories of Thailand, of Koh Tanu and of Thaim in a good, pleasant and positive way.

He sat there, in Thaim's house, and waited until his boyfriend ranted and spilled all his tears. He remained calm and tried to answer only when he thought the questions coming at him were genuine, and not rhetorical ones. Slowly, gradually, Thaim regained control of himself.

They spent a few hours talking, again throwing into stark contrast the different expectations that various cultures had about relationships. Thaim had professed his love again and again. Jerome had only once—and it had been a big deal—and Thaim was already planning the rest of their lives together, while Jerome didn't even know what he was going to do from one week to the next. His own second visa was ending soon. Dahlia was leaving, so were most of the other people he had met on the island. The rainy season was fast approaching, and the universe appeared to be singing a song to him about leave-takings and new beginnings. He had to go.

They hugged, cried some more, kissed, and ended up in bed, which may have been a mistake, because in the early hours, when they were snuggled up together, Thaim had whispered to him. "I love this so much. I'm glad you're not leaving." At which Jerome stiffened and decided to keep quiet till the morning.

The next day they had to go through the whole thing once again, and Jerome had to make it very clear that whatever was going to happen between them in his last few days on the island—and things were going to happen—it did not mean he had changed his mind. So why not enjoy the last few days they had?

Thaim was on board with the idea, anything to lessen the pain of separation. But a little while later, Jerome caught him looking up flights and accommodation in Bali. This was going to be harder than he thought.

Dahlia seemed happy that Jerome was tagging along with her and Adrien. They had booked a two-room house in Bali for them all to share. They even had their own swimming pool—that was how cheap Bali was! So he was very excited; although, Dahlia had made him promise he would stick to her work schedule, or he would be out on his own. It wasn't ideal, but it was one of the best prospects he'd had in a while. He wasn't ready to put himself out there and fall back into his old ways.

Just as he was preparing to make his flight arrangements for Bali, Thaim asked him to spend his last few days in Thailand by going to Bangkok with him. A kind of last hurrah in their love affair. He would take Jerome to a fancy hotel, to rooftop bars and all of that stuff. Of course, Jerome jumped at the idea. He had only been to Bangkok for an hour at the airport, connecting flights, and he loved being treated to this kind of experience. So, he hurriedly took care of all remaining business on Tanu, packed his bags, and then he and Thaim were on a plane to Bangkok.

Thaim had booked a swanky hotel in the Sukhumvit area. Their suite was on the thirty-fifth floor, with a breath-taking view of the white, polluted skyline. A few floors above them, a rooftop infinity pool attracted a steady stream of Instagram-hungry visitors, some even brought their own props and change of wardrobes. Thaim and Jerome sat on the loungers watching the whole spectacle, photographing the photographers, and once there was a lull in the flow of selfie-takers, the two of them went into the pool, swam about, kissed and played. After a few minutes, they sheepishly looked at each other, and without saying a word, grabbed their phones and started doing exactly the same as everyone else before, pulling faces and poses.

Later, after a delicious and huge dinner, they went to a sex club—Thaim had never been to one but had friends who had sent him some recommendations—mostly just to watch, goggle and marvel at everything that was on offer. They let the atmosphere seep into them. In any case, Jerome was too full from dinner to think about getting down and dirty.

The next day they went shopping. Jerome had only a few things with him, mostly island-style clothing, and Thaim wanted to take him to a rooftop bar that night, but the dress code was quite strict, even for *farangs*. So, the two of them went to one of Bangkok's famous clothing malls—not one of the swanky, luxury designer-led ones, but one of those that did mass produced, decent quality, hot-of-the-moment clothing from nondescript brands. They did a quick update of both their wardrobes, of course all paid for by Thaim.

Showered, creamed, suited and booted—metaphorically speaking—they headed to the rooftop bar. They had a great time, drinking late into the night, ending up at a drag karaoke bar and stumbling back to their hotel, giggling and happy, as dawn was breaking. This was bad news for Jerome as he had to be at the airport by noon and he had heard about, and experienced, the sheer terror of Bangkok's traffic. With a heavy body and a slurred mind, he went to take a long, long shower, almost falling asleep under the rushing water. He managed to drag himself out, dry off, and then he started to put his things back in his bag, just randomly. Thaim came close to him then, kissing him, pawing at him and pulling off his towel.

"No, Thaim. I have to get ready."

"Oh, come on. Come on, baby. You are leaving, give me a good last memory."

They kissed passionately. Jerome could taste all the alcohol they had had on Thaim's tongue. When Thaim tried to get Jerome down onto the bed, Jerome shook himself free.

"I can't. It's late already. I can't miss the flight."

At this, Thaim lost it. He started screaming and pulling off the bed covers, throwing them all around him, like a toddler having a tantrum. Jerome watched him for a moment, then resumed his packing.

"How can you leave me? Why?" Thaim pleaded in between sobs.

Jerome knew he could not say anything more than what he had already said. Flashbacks to similar situations were insinuating into his mind now, so his alertness kicked up a notch, the fog in his head cleared and he sped up his preparations.

Thaim was rolling around with the bedding, a mix of cries and screams coming from his throat. Jerome got dressed, zipped up his bag. And just then, Thaim fell completely still, his eyes vacant.

Jerome looked at his lover. Was he having some sort of fit? He came closer, and Thaim recoiled a little. *Not a fit.* Jerome looked around the room for the last of his items, grabbed his little backpack, then patted various parts of his body. "Passport, phone, money."

Satisfied, he came close to Thaim again and kissed him on the head. "Thank you for everything, my love." And then, before he moved away, "I'm sorry,"

Jerome turned, grabbed his bag and walked out.

CHAPTER 55 - MARTIN

The day of the fight had finally arrived. Martin had woken up at 5:00 a.m. and, as instructed, went for a forty-five-minute run. Then he went back to sleep and woke again in the early afternoon to start carbo-loading.

He had a meal of steak and chips and also a full pizza, washed down with fruit shakes. Then a little bit more dozing before the prefight prep began.

He walked to the gym, where the trainers went through everything once again. His whole bag was packed for him and then they drove him to the stadium together with two other fighters from the same gym, who would be fighting before him. Since he was a *farang*, and having his debut fight, he would be going on last. *The headline fight. Jeez.*

He knew Rose was flying in that afternoon. They had discussed the logistics, and he knew she would have enough time to arrive on Koh Tanu, drop her bags off at the bungalow and then rush to the stadium, just in time for his fight. So, he hoped there were no delays. But Bamon had requisitioned his mobile in the morning, so he could not get any updates. The trainer wanted Martin to relax and not be distracted.

Martin kept on replaying in his mind one of the last messages Rose had sent him.

There is so much I want to share, so much I need to tell you.

He knew they had left things as friends, however he couldn't help but feel that things were moving in a distinctly different direction. Rose got him. Rose had looked him in his eyes as he told her about his addiction, and she hadn't recoiled. She had held his hand and told him that he had this, that he could get to grips with it. For the first time in a long time, he felt positive about the future. He couldn't remember the last time he had even remotely entertained the idea of a relationship, and here he was now, daydreaming about life with Rose. They could travel where they pleased. They could be honest and open with each other. They could have the best times, following summer around the world. *I also have so much to tell you.* But first, he needed to get this fight done and out of the way, and then he would have time for everything. And that meant...everything.

 I can't wait to see you.

That's what she had texted last night. And now here he was, at the stadium, almost completely naked bar these baggy, shiny Muay Thai shorts, surrounded by guys who were coating him in oil, Tiger Balm and God knows what else. The fumes of it were making his eyes water. *Yes, it's the fumes.*

As was tradition, Bamon, his head trainer, was wrapping Martin's hands with purposeful, slow and careful movements, in a ritualistic way. Martin let his mind drift while all those around him spoke softly to each other in Thai.

His muscles were being massaged with the creams, and they even spread a little bit inside his underwear. He flinched at this. He didn't want any of the fiery stuff anywhere near his privates, or it would be hell.

Then Bamon took him to the bathroom where Martin had to fit the protective cup to his groin. It was a fiddly, uncomfortable business, but it had to be done. Finally, Bamon applied sticky tape—yes, sticky tape!—to his wrapped hands, which now resembled those lightweight casts you put on limbs for sprains and similar accidents.

Back outside, Martin and the other fighters all got in a line on the side of the stage near the entrance, so that the audience, who were finally starting to come in, could admire them, their bodies, their entourages. The owner of his gym came by to have a word and shake his hand, then pictures were taken. But there was a lot of waiting around, and he felt a bit bereft without his phone.

He would sit down, and every few minutes one of the gym trainers would come and give him a quick massage, to keep him nimble and warmed up. Time dragged on.

Kids ran around excitedly, music was on endless loops, lights were flashing, people came and went, and Martin was feeling suddenly very tired. He so much wanted this to be over with.

Then an English-speaking voice came on the PA system and the atmosphere became feverish—the fights were about to start! The trainers swarmed around their charges, massaging, encouraging, slapping, strutting around. Then they were up and moving. They had to walk up to the stage and be presented, one by one, into the ring. The get-ups on show were impressive: superhero-style capes, headdresses, beautiful traditional woven armbands. The announcers, one in Thai, one in English, introduced the fighters one by one, and Martin was the very last one to be called out. When he was, a huge roar came up from one side of the stadium. He looked over and, even despite the strong lights shining in his face, he could see some TribeHutters excitedly waving their arms, clapping and even holding up some homemade banners, which he couldn't read. One of them was a poster of Martin's head photoshopped on what looked like Chuck Norris. He heard them chanting, "Mar-tin! Mar-tin!"

He went on stage, bowed and stood next to his opponent. He looked him over and suddenly his opponent seemed much taller than he remembered—they had met at the weigh-in a couple days prior. On that occasion, Martin had thought the guy could not possibly be in his weight category, being shorter and thinner than him, but then he saw someone fiddling with the scales and knew some adjustment was taking place. Today, his opponent seemed to be standing taller and broader. It worried him. *Wait, is it even the same guy?!* He had no time to check.

After the introductions, everyone came off the ring and went back to their staging posts, except the two littlest kids, who would be fighting first. They were so small! Martin tried to concentrate on the fights and not look at the time, or at the entrance of the stadium, to see if Rose would show up on time.

The cacophony of the *sarama*, the ringing and the music lulled Martin into a kind of trance.

Much later, hours later, he wasn't sure how many, he found himself on his feet, screaming, shouting and cheering on Yak, one of the other fighters from his gym. They had sparred a few times, but Yak was a lot smaller than Martin, and therefore also a lot faster, so Martin knew that Yak was going easy on him during practice.

But now, in the stadium, Yak was a blur of limbs. His slick skin reflected the stage lights, and droplets of sweat would arc up off the fighter's body every time he landed a blow. Martin had never seen such a fierce and balanced fight up close. He was enraptured. He screamed and aaaahhhed together with the crowd, surging, wincing and flopping with every nuance of the battle. Nothing else mattered. Until Yak kicked his opponent, got him off balance and finished him off with an elbow blow. As the fighter went down, the stadium and everyone around Martin erupted in cheers. People hugged and screamed. Some trainers rushed the ring and lifted Yak up high, his arms held aloft in victory.

Out of the craziness, Bamon approached with a face like death. His eyes locked onto Martin's, he grabbed his arm and started bringing him toward the ring. *Oh, shit! I forgot I'm here to fight! I'm up next...*

As the crowd took toilet and drink breaks, Martin and his entourage walked closer to the ring for some last-minute preparations. A voice inside Martin was screaming *No! I'm not ready! I was watching the other fight! It can't possibly be time yet! Who the fuck made me do this?!*

Bamon and another trainer were massaging Martin's body vigorously. And then, the voice in his head hit him like a hammer blow.

Where's Rose? Has she arrived? Shit, I stopped looking. Rose, are you here?

But now the lights were so strong, he really could not see anything; although, he was looking around the stands frantically. Bamon snapped, grabbed his chin and made Martin look him in the eye.

"Focus. Calm. Okay?" Bamon nodded, and after a few seconds Martin nodded, too.

Up the ring they went, and the *sarama* music started. Martin wasn't even aware of what he was doing during the time in which his opponent, now looking like a veritable giant, was going through the motions of the ceremonial dance.

Martin's field of vision reduced almost to a pinpoint. He could not see anything beyond the ring itself, and even within it he was struggling. He realized he was hyperventilating.

What the fuck?! What the fuck?! Whatthefuck?!

The music ended and Martin found himself in his corner, the blue one. Nuay was massaging his arms and Bamon took the mouth guard from his pocket, rinsed it and put it in Martin's mouth. It was ice water! The brain-freeze threatened to engulf the last of his consciousness, but he fought against it. Bamon was saying something. *Concentrate on what he's saying!*

Martin opened his eyes. Bamon grabbed his head and stared at him.

"You can do this. You are strong. You are good fighter. Huh?"

I don't want to do this. Why am I doing this? This guy is going to rip me to shreds. Rose. Where is Rose? I don't want to do this. I don't want her to see this.

"Yes," Martin heard himself say, nodding. He had never experienced such a disconnect between his brain and his body. Bamon seemed to sense this. He gave him a slap, not too hard but hard enough.

"Martin. Stop. Breathe." Bamon showed him a really deep breath. Martin did the same. And again. And again.

"Keep going," Bamon said, encouraging him. "You have trained. You know what to do. You strong!" he shouted the last word, and it seeped into Martin's body, emboldening him.

Bamon removed the little ceremonial headdress from Martin's head, then turned him around to face the opposite corner. The umpire was in between them. Bamon slapped him on the shoulder and Martin took a step forward.

The umpire came forward, he checked Martin's mouth guard, then his gloves, and finally wiped his face and chest with a filthy, stinking rag. As Martin tried not to gag from the smell, he watched the umpire do the same thing with his opponent, whose eyes had gone dark and dead, hooded.

Martin took another look around the stands. Where had the TribeHutters been? He could not remember. He squinted in the light.

Then, as if from very far away, the bell rang, and the crowd roared.

Almost automatically, his body took the correct stance, bouncing on the balls of his feet, his arms up, hands in front of his face and head. His opponent was doing the same.

They circled each other a bit, no one moving much. Then, fast as a snake, his opponent lashed out with a front kick. Martin stepped back but not quick enough, so the kick grazed his stomach. *Shit, this is really happening!*

His gut twisted painfully; he realized with a sinking feeling that this is what fear felt like. He could sense his mind sending panic signals throughout his body, and he fought back hard. *Breathe. Move. Focus.*

The other fighter feinted and jabbed, testing the water. He had seen that Martin was not a total fake fighter, so now he had to get his measure before attacking him for real.

Get your head in gear! The voice inside him shouted. He crouched a little more, his head down a little more, protecting the vital organs and the brain. Now Martin feinted and then jabbed—his punch landed! He was ecstatic! Couldn't believe it. But the joy was short-lived, because his opponent now answered him in kind. And so, the fight proper began.

When the bell rang for the end of the first round, Martin felt that the bell that had started the round was in a different lifetime. *What timeline are we in now?* He felt as if all he had ever been doing, since eternity, was hopping around this ring, eyes fixed on this Thai dude intent on hurting him. To suddenly stop was bewildering.

He walked to his corner while Bamon, Nuay and another trainer set up the tray and stool for him. He sat down hard and Nuay doused him with ice-cold water. He almost didn't feel it. He could not gasp enough oxygen into his lungs.

Bamon crouched down, took his mouth guard and fed him water.

"Good, you do good." He nodded. "Watch his left hook. Your right arm, higher." He made a gesture to show him how he should hold his right arm.

Martin nodded. He wanted to speak, to say something, but realized he had no breath in him at all.

His eyes searched the crowd. During the break, disco lights were shining on the audience, so he managed to get a glimpse here and there. He could now see where the TribeHutters had huddled, also judging by their crazy screaming every time he did something remotely positive on the ring. He still could not see Rose. *Get that out of your mind right now. You have to survive this.*

The bell rang for round two.

Nothing else existed. Only breathing, chaotic noise and dodging. Back, duck, skip back, hop sideways. His Thai opponent was fast and was not playing. The fear that Martin had felt initially now had a cold grip on his heart, but his body was still listening to the weeks and months of training. Just.

At times Martin even managed to be quick enough to land some knees or punches—he did not risk proper kicks, because he knew he wasn't fast enough with those—and once he even grazed the head of his rival with an elbow. All in all, this gave him some confidence. But he knew that between fear and stamina, he didn't have that much longer.

In the break between rounds two and three, Bamon was encouraging. "Good fight. Good. Keep going. He strong but you more strong." He smiled.

Martin knew that round three was the magic round. If he made it into round three, the trainers would get paid in full for his match, which was a huge deal to them. Their massaging was reaching a fever pitch. It was almost painful on Martin's sore muscles, but he knew he needed it. He looked around at the TribeHutters' corner, trying to see if Rose was there, and just as Nuay pulled him up on his feet, there she was!

"Rose!" he couldn't help but blurt out. She couldn't have heard him but nonetheless she looked in his direction and waved manically, a huge grin on her face. He felt his face try to make a smile, too, but then Nuay shoved the mouth guard in again and brought him back to earth with a bang. "Ready!" Nuay looked him in the eye.

Bamon slapped him on the shoulder. "Go!"

Okay, Martin, now focus. This is your chance. She is here. You can do this.

The bell rang.

Martin had renewed vigor and hopped around, avoiding all his opponent's attacks. The Thai man was getting tired, too. Martin managed to punch him in the gut, to a huge roar of the crowd. The man in the red pants counterattacked and landed a light kick to Martin's leg. He almost didn't feel it. *Should I be worried about that?* He shoved the thought away with another punch.

They hopped from foot to foot and turned round and round in the ring. Martin saw an opening, and in a flash his elbow started going up. This time he could hit him full-on. Just then, one of the strobe lights illuminated the crowd behind his opponent and it was where the TribeHutters were, where Rose was sitting. As if in a movie, time slowed to a crawl. The strobe light illuminated Rose like a stage spotlight. She was turned to her side. *Look at me, Rose! Look how I am going to knock this guy out!* Martin's elbow was making its arc toward the Thai man's exposed temple.

Why won't she look this way? Rose, look!

His eyes followed Rose's gaze and landed on the guy next to her. In slow motion, he felt he knew what was about to happen even as his own mind screamed, *No!*

Rose leaned in, and she and this random fucking dude kissed. *Kissing?! On the lips? What the f—*

There was a bright flash, a feeling of grinding bones, and then the world plunged into black.

CHAPTER 56 - DAHLIA

DMK airport had been refurbished not that long ago, but it was already showing signs of wear, thanks to the thousands and thousands of people who travelled through it on low-cost airlines.

Dahlia and Adrien had been on a stupid-early morning flight out of Panat Buri and were now at Bangkok's second airport to get their connection to Denpasar, Bali, and to wait for Jerome, who was supposed to join them. *Supposed to* because Dahlia had the sneaky, sinking feeling that Jerome had bolted. Or was going to bolt. Or was just going to miss the flight. And the sad thing was that any of those things would have just been ordinary, nothing new, nothing surprising. Even expected, by chicken-shit Jerome's standards. The worrying thing was, his visa expired today, so he had to leave Thailand no matter what. And if he didn't make their flight... Oh, she couldn't even bring herself to think about that. It was too much. She couldn't face, yet again, the painful process of starting over again with Jerome. It was definitely a habit with him, and she was just too willing to be his anchor, his safe harbor, in life. No, this time it would be different. *If he doesn't make it, that's it. I won't have him in my life anymore—not like this.*

She and Adrien were sitting in an airport Starbucks, imbibing caffeine to stay awake and using the Wi-Fi to catch up on work, since it was a weekday. Starbucks felt like such an alien luxury now, after months on the island. Its polished sameness, its sleek offering and familiar-sounding products were like an island of calm in the tide of humans sweeping through the airport. But it was also a super busy café, so the two of them had to share a small table, their laptops perched precariously, screens bumping into each other.

"Do you want another drink?" Adrien asked her, getting up and making the whole table, and therefore the laptops, wobble perilously.

Dahlia checked the time. "I guess so, we still have some time to kill. I just hope Jerome gets here on time." She shot a look toward the door of the café. She had sent him a text letting him know where they were.

"Same thing again?" Adrien pointed to her empty plastic container. The amount of plastic these places went through on a daily basis was staggering to her. She loved iced coffees but even if you sat in the café they would still give them to you in plastic containers.

"No. Can you get me a hot cappuccino this time, please? In a mug, you know?" Adrien nodded and walked to the counter.

She compulsively checked her email and phone, in case there was an update from Jerome, from a client, from anyone, really. She tried to concentrate on the data she was reading through, but between tiredness and worry, it was like wading through treacle.

She started watching the café entrance again, intently, and was startled when Adrien's arm appeared next to her head to put her coffee down on the limited space on the table. Automatically, she thanked him. Then she looked at the coffee.

"Oh, no. I said in a mug!" They had put it in a disposable cup, again.

"I know. I am sorry. They said they didn't have any."

Dalia huffed and shrugged. Today was not going well.

Adrien sat back down and started slurping his iced coffee. Dahlia desperately tried again to concentrate.

Her email pinged and she was startled. Was it Jerome? No, it was a client who was wondering if he could have five minutes of talk time with her. She hesitated. When clients said five minutes, which she didn't bill for, it almost always went on for much longer than five minutes. But this was a good client and, in fairness, she was achieving nothing at the moment. It may take her mind off Jerome's lateness.

She grabbed her headphones and phone, locked the laptop and got up. She knew Adrien would look after her laptop. She took a few steps out of the café and tried to find a spot where it was less busy and noisy. She then called the client over Skype. He was very happy to hear from her and made some small talk before addressing what he wanted to talk about.

CHAPTER 57 - ADRIEN

Adrien hated working out of cramped cafés. His gangly legs and elbows were forever bumping into tables, chairs, people. Normally he would be wearing his huge noise-cancelling headphones and trying to block out all distractions. But between having a flight to catch soon, having to keep an eye out for Jerome and also looking after Dahlia's things strewn all around him, he felt that the headphones were not a good idea.

The screeching chattering of travelers unnerved him immensely. He felt that a lot of people, when travelling, reverted to less evolved versions of themselves, doing dumb things, asking silly questions, shouting and wanting to do everything together with their companions, even when there was no reason or need to. In these situations, he turned into a right old misanthrope, and every little annoyance that added to this seemed to him the proverbial straw that broke the camel's back.

He kept taking deep breaths to avoid reacting to all these triggers. He focused intently on his laptop screen. He had been tweaking his app. He was almost happy with where he was with it and was now on the verge of getting friends to beta-test it. He had been feeling the excitement about the idea flooding back in him; he thought he had lost it. But now that he was in sight of the finish line—or approaching the finish line—all the tingles came back.

Just then, his mobile pinged, distracting him and making him swear under his breath. He checked the message. It was from Aaron, an old Vancouver friend he met on a previous job when they were fresh out of uni. Adrien was about to dismiss the notification—he could read the message later—when some of the words in the preview snagged his attention.

His gut suddenly tightened, and he opened the message with growing dread.

> Hey man, this just landed in my newsfeed. Is this you? I remember you telling me you were developing something like this. That's so cool! Gonna download it when I get home. Congrats, man!

Aaron had sent a link.

Increasingly frantic, Adrien opened the link and the floor dropped out from under him.

"Fuck. Fuck. Fucking shit," he muttered. A lady with a child at the table next to him shot him a disapproving look.

The link showed an article describing an app that had just been released without any prior press or warning. And the description sounded eerily similar to his own app. It was called "H-ears." *What a shitty name*, Adrien thought. But then he remembered he hadn't decided on a catchy name either.

Hands in his hair and with mounting panic, Adrien read to the end of the article, almost not taking it in. Only a few words and concepts pierced the veil of rising bile within him. "Fabulous idea", "industry approval", "innovative…" He slammed the phone down on the table. He rubbed his face, his glasses precariously perched on his hands.

This can't be happening. Fuck. I was too late. I was too late. I dithered. I tinkered. I hesitated. And now my idea is out there. A fully formed app, out in the world. I am done. I am totally done. Done and finished. Fuck. I was too late. I was too fucking late. What am I going to do now?

He sat down again, overcome with despair, his head in his hands. It was only the faint awareness that he was in a public place that stopped him from breaking down into an anxiety attack on the spot. He started hyperventilating a bit, head down, trying to control it.

He didn't know how much time had passed, or what was happening around him, when he felt a hand on his shoulder and Dahlia's rising voice.

"Adrien! Come on. We have to get to our gate. Jerome's still not here, but at least we should not miss the flight."

He looked up; he felt as if he was breaking water after having swam in the ocean depths. He took a breath.

"What?"

Dahlia was already unplugging her laptop and cables and placing everything in her hand luggage.

"We have to go. Our gate has been boarding for a while." She looked at him then, not understanding why he was so frozen, so slow. Then she huffed and shrugged and continued packing.

With limbs like lead, Adrien began to do the same.

The rest went by in a blur. He remembered glimpses of Dahlia looking behind them, worried, and at the same time urging him on. She looked back once again as they walked into the gate.

When they were in line to take their seats, he was aware that Dahlia turned around excitedly. Jerome had shown up at the last second and was boarding the plane.

When they had taken their seats, he put his headphones on, and retreated into himself; the heated conversation between the siblings sitting next to him was just another bit of white noise. He finally fell asleep and descended into the black depths.

CODA

CHAPTER 58 - ROSE

There was something about Kuala Lumpur that Rose loved. She usually did not enjoy very big, urban cities, but KL was easy. It wasn't *too* big and it was also quite cheap, so she could get Ubers everywhere without having to deal with learning about public transport. The food was absolutely delicious and varied, and you could find all the luxuries of the West at a fraction of the price. And it was the gateway for a lot of arts and crafts from around Southeast Asia, so she had her work cut out for her.

She was only staying for a week but had many friends who happened to be passing through or were staying for an extended period, so she had a full social calendar of café coworking days, dinners, cinema dates and also a trip to an escape room. So much fun! She missed her island life, but she knew she would be back soon, and a little break surrounded by modernity was good.

On day two of her stay, she had gone to meet some friends at a café for a chat and some work. She had walked from the blistering hot street into the freezing air-conditioned room, her breath short from the change in temperature, and saw her little group of friends a few tables in. And then her breath caught for real. Among them she clearly saw a face, a smile she knew very well, but one she had not expected to see. Not here, not now!

It was Andrew. American Adonis Andrew! She could not believe her eyes.

Turns out he had heard she was in Southeast Asia and had left fate in charge of having them bump into each other. He wasn't much for planning or staying in touch over social media—he wasn't even on any social media that she knew of—so she had no clue. She thought he was either in the US or in Oviedo, where they had met.

The day before, Andrew's mutual nomad friends had mentioned Rose, so he had tagged along, wanting to surprise her. She was speechless.

Andrew had always been her one-who-got-away. Nothing had ever happened between them, and while it was obvious to everyone that she was very much into him, Andrew's own view on the matter had been curiously murky. Eventually, after many months, they got separated by life and were taken in different directions. She had thought of him often in these last few months. Since he had been good friends with Frances, too, she would have liked to talk to him about whatever was going on with their mutual friend, but the couple of email messages she had sent him remained unanswered, so she had moved on. She was reminded of how, in many ways, he represented her typical romantic prospect—a guy who she thought was out of her league but over whom she obsessed anyway, who kept her close and yet not close enough, who would not give of himself. Still, despite being aware of this—and of the patterns that she kept on repeating—she had been enraptured by him, enamored, and she guarded the memory of these feelings like a long-lost treasure.

That day in KL was magical. They all had a good time at the café, but she was struck by the fact that Andrew's attention seemed focused on her alone, like a laser beam. She could remember the first few interactions very clearly, like watching a film, but after that, the rest of the day and the following days were all a big blur. He had not left her side. They spent so much time together that she forgot all about work, money, Martin and Frances for the entire time. That first evening, as they walked toward her apartment in the dark of the hot, tropical night, he had stopped to look at a street sculpture, and then turned to her to kiss her slowly, passionately, deliberately. They went back to her place and almost didn't go out again for two days—so much so that it became a joke among their mutual friends.

But then, the day of her departure was approaching—her flight back to Thailand, where she was due to stay for a couple more months. Where was Andrew going? What were his plans? She could not believe that, in all those hours and days they spent together they hadn't tackled this topic. But when she broached it, he made it seem all so simple and easy. He had no plans, he was letting the universe do its thing, so following where she was going seemed the clear thing to do. He booked the same flight as hers and delighted in her telling him what Koh Tanu was like, what he could expect about the coworking space, the people, the island. It thrilled her to be able to bring him back with her and show him her life on the island, and show him off to her friends, as well. What was Dahlia going to say? She had to pinch herself. Only a week prior she could not have imagined that this was the turn her life would take. American Adonis Andrew, in her arms, all for her, following her!

She had mentioned to Andrew her friend Martin, the German—she had conveniently neglected to tell him of their initial connection and drunken embarrassment—and had been talking about his Muay Thai fight with excitement. Andrew professed some interest in the sport, but he was more of an MMA guy; however, he was happy to go along with Rose. They flew from Kuala Lumpur to Panat Buri like two honeymooning lovebirds, never straying from the other's side, Rose's head leaning on Andrew's shoulder for a mid-flight nap.

When they arrived at the stadium, Martin's fight was almost about to begin. It was pure chaos, and the atmosphere didn't feel any better than the last time Rose had been to a fight. Maybe even worse, because this time she had a personal stake in the game. The cacophony of music and shouts, the disco lights and funny smells, all contributed to make her feel uneasy. Martin had also been strangely quiet on text, so she had no idea how he had been feeling going into the fight, and she was worried, not to mention that she herself had been a little distracted by the whole Andrew thing.

As soon as Rose and Andrew entered the stadium, they ran into some TribeHutters, so Rose introduced Andrew. Drinks were bought, conversations were had slightly away from the ring, having to shout in each other's ears to be heard. Every few seconds, Rose shot a look over to the ring to check on Martin. She was eager to take a seat and devote her attention to the match—or better still, to Martin's safety and wellbeing—but obstacles kept getting in their way. People stopped them for a chat, or another drink. Rose felt all warm inside every time a TribeHutter was introduced to Andrew and did an appreciative double take, looking at the way he held her hand, clearly a couple. Laura in particular looked Andrew up and down with barely disguised lust and gave Rose a surreptitious thumbs-up.

They finally managed to grab a seat next to other TribeHutters during the break between rounds two and three. Just as she looked up into the ring, Martin seemed to see her, and she waved and smiled. She wanted to give him the thumbs-up but thought he would find it crass.

The bell rang and round three started. The crowd surged. Martin looked so good, so professional up there. She was in awe. He had buffed up considerably. It was clear both fighters were winded but also committed and in the zone.

"Go Martin!" she screamed before she even realized what she was doing.

The TribeHutters started the chant again. "Mar-tin! Mar-tin!" and she joined in.

She heard Andrew join in with the chant, and then almost felt him smile beside her, so she turned toward him. He was looking at her and, as every time when they looked into each other's eyes, there was this magnetic power, pulling their lips together. It was inescapable. As their lips touched and then parted, the crowd gasped in surprise. She whipped her head around to look at the ring and saw Martin falling down. The crowd screamed, and Martin's rival started to strut around the stadium letting the crowd's pleasure wash over him.

Martin was down. He wasn't moving.

"Martin! What happened?" she shouted as she elbowed her way down the bleachers and toward the ring. The umpire was waving his arms, counting, over Martin's prone, still body. "Help him!"

His trainers surged into the ring to attend to him.

Rose felt her arm being pulled back, she turned and saw Andrew was holding her back.

"Let them work," he said with a frown.

The umpire grabbed the Thai fighter's hand and raised it up high. The crowd cheered and clapped, and the fighter ran and jumped up onto the ropes, hoisting himself up high to receive the crowd's praise. Then he got down and rushed to Martin's side, bowing, kneeling and doing the *ai* gesture, apologizing for having hurt him. Martin was still motionless. A man was holding a bottle under his nose. *Salts?* thought Rose. A medic was brought to the ring to examine Martin.

As the stadium quickly emptied of the general audience, the TribeHutters all stayed behind, crowding around the ring. Some cries of encouragement rose up to try to rouse Martin. Rose turned to Laura.

"Did you see what happened? I didn't see…"

Finally, after what seemed like an eternity, Martin's eyes fluttered open. The medic gestured to someone and a stretcher was summoned beside the ring. Martin's trainers hoisted him up. He looked very confused and disoriented as they led him and half carried him out of the ring and onto the stretcher, which was quickly lifted and taken out of the stadium.

"Where are they taking him?" she asked Andrew, as if he would know.

"Don't worry, we'll find out, OK?"

At around 1:00 a.m., Rose and Andrew were sitting on the patio of Laura's bungalow with a few other people, all milling around waiting for news of Martin, making idle talk, chugging beers. Laura's phone rang and she got up to answer it, which was funny. She always seemed to need to be standing when taking a phone call. Everyone quieted down to see what would transpire from the call.

After several "uh-huh's" and, "okay's" from Laura, she hung up and smiled.

"It's okay. He's okay. They said it is nothing to worry about, but they will keep him in the clinic tonight to be on the safe side. He'll be out tomorrow."

A cheer went up and people clinked bottles. Andrew hugged Rose's shoulder and squeezed. "See? It's going to be okay."

She smiled back.

They all went to bed pretty late. Once the tension about Martin's condition had loosened, they stayed up drinking and talking until the wee hours. There was a lot of interest in Andrew, who he was, when they met and so on and so forth, and Rose enjoyed being the center of attention for once.

Spending the night with Andrew in her own bungalow was weird and satisfying at the same time. In all her time on Koh Tanu she hadn't hooked up with anyone, had sex or even a fumble with anyone—let's forget about her drunken almost-snog with Martin—so to be able to do that now was hugely gratifying. Plus, sex with Andrew was pretty good. He was focused on her responses and her enjoyment, like any decent man should be. As they were falling asleep, she told him that in the morning she wanted to go and see Martin at the clinic, help him get home or whatever he needed. Andrew nodded sleepily and they fell asleep intertwined.

The next morning, or almost afternoon, they had a quick breakfast at a vegan café she knew—Andrew had been vegan for over five years—and then they took a tuk-tuk to the clinic where Martin was convalescing. When they arrived, there was a bit of confusion with the staff. It took a few minutes for them to realize what Rose was asking, and for them to convey the relevant information. Martin had already been discharged.

"Oh." Rose was confused. This worried her. Why was Martin getting around on his own when there were people ready to help him? Plus, she wanted to introduce Andrew to Martin. She knew they would get on. She was excited to share this momentous life development with her friend.

They took another tuk-tuk—actually the same one, the driver was just idling outside the clinic—and went to the TribeHut bungalows. Rose made straight for Martin's bungalow and knocked, but when she did so, the door opened by itself, unlocked.

Slowly, she pushed the door open, not wanting to intrude on Martin.

"Hey, Martin? Why didn't you wait for us? We came to get you—"

But the bungalow was empty. Not just of Martin, but of all his stuff, too. Gone were all the hanging boxing wraps, the gloves, the chaotic pile of clothes over the suitcase. All that was left was some discarded bits of papers and tissue.

"Apparently he left early this morning." Rose turned to see Laura on the patio. "Nobody knew. He didn't tell anyone. I just found out from the cleaning staff."

"What? Where has he gone? Has he moved, maybe?" Rose asked hopefully.

"He was paid up for another two weeks at least…" Laura shrugged.

Rose looked around some more. She noticed, on his bedside table, a cut-up Thai SIM card. How odd.

"All I know is that he got a taxi off the island. Someone said he's gone to Singapore."

Rose couldn't compute.

"That can't be." She pulled out her phone and opened WhatsApp. She tapped a quick message to Martin and sent it, only to realize that his profile now showed no picture, and that her message only had one single gray checkmark beside it. Had he…blocked her?

Frantic, she opened Facebook and searched for his profile. He wasn't very active on FB at all, but he kept a profile to help him with travel and to use Messenger. She searched, but FB returned no results. She did the same with Instagram. Nothing.

"What the—"

Next, she opened Messenger and scrolled to a previous message thread they had. Again, his profile picture had disappeared and the whole thing was grayed out.

As a last resort, she tried calling his European number, but all she got was a recorded message in Thai and English. "The number you have called could not be connected."

She turned to Andrew and felt like angry crying. "He left. He just…left?"

Laura shrugged. "Maybe it was the bump on the head?"

Andrew went to comfort Rose. "I don't think they would have let him leave the clinic if he wasn't okay, don't you think?"

Rose leaned into the hug. But deep down she felt, she knew that something had happened, she just didn't know what. "Why did he block me? It makes no sense."

Laura turned her phone toward Rose. "I don't think he's blocked you. It just looks like he is off all social media, everything."

What the fuck, Martin?

** THE END **

ACKNOWLEDGEMENTS

As in many fictional stories, the idea for this book came to me as a bolt out of the blue. Little did I know how much time and work would end up going into it before it took a half-decent shape.

And it never would have gotten there were it not for the support and help of some wonderful people. First of all Julia and the gang for being right there at the start, reading the first few pages and egging me on. After that, a disparate group of people offered help, feedback and support at various stages, so I would like to express my heartfelt thanks to Philippa, Jules, Paolo, Elena, Mark, Jessica, Paul, Shira, Sabina, Scotty, Jacqui, Maria, Gerald, Jonathan and others that I'm surely forgetting.

Huge thanks to Joel Bahr for his insightful and encouraging editing, and to the Reedsy community at large for being so full of talented and kind people. Many thanks to the various writing groups and cohorts I belong to, which I am unable to mention here.

I also want to thank my family and friends, for never ceasing to ask me how the writing was going, and for never punching me when my reply was always "It's going."

And finally, a big thank you to all the various digital nomad communities and spaces I have encountered around the world. They have provided not only the spark of inspiration, but usually a safe harbor in new and unknown places. Some of these spaces have become home, and some of these people have become family. As we like to say, I'll see you at some point, somewhere.

DIGITAL NOMAD ADVENTURES

WILL CONTINUE...

AT A NEW DESTINATION...

To stay in touch with Blake, find out about
upcoming books and receive exclusive content,
please visit www.blakesalazar.com

Printed in Great Britain
by Amazon

65461769R00210